SANDS
of Time

Also by Joseph Colwell

Canyon Breezes: Exploring Magical Places in Nature
Lichen Rock Press, 2015
Zephyr of Time: Meditations on Time and Nature
Lichen Rock Press, 2016
Ravens Nest: A Life, A Place—Stories and Reflections
Lichen Rock Press, 2018

SANDS
of Time

A Flight of Discovery and Search
for Meanings of Time

JOSEPH COLWELL

PAGE PUBLISHING, INC.
New York, NY

First originally published by Page Publishing, Inc. 2018

ISBN 978-1-64138-296-0 (Paperback)
ISBN 978-1-64138-297-7 (Digital)

Cover photo and author photo by Katherine Colwell

Printed in the United States of America

I met a traveler from an antique land
Who said: "Two vast and trunkless legs of stone
Stand in the desert. Near them, on the sand,
Half sunk, a shattered visage lies, whose frown
And wrinkled lip, and sneer of cold command,
Tell that its sculptor well those passions read."
"My name is Ozymandias, King of Kings"
Look on my works, ye Mighty, and despair!"
Nothing beside remains. Round the decay
Of that colossal wreck, boundless and bare,
The lone and level sands stretch far away.

—Percy Bysshe Shelley

There was never a king like Solomon, not since the world began.
Yet Solomon talked to a butterfly as a man would talk to a man.

—Rudyard Kipling

Backward, turn backward, O Time, in your flight,
Make me a child again, just for tonight.

—Elizabeth Akers Allen

Author's Invitation

THIS NOVEL SPRANG from one simple thought: What if I found something embedded in a sandstone cliff millions of years old that was made by an intelligent being? What would be the meaning and the implications of such a discovery?

I love the slickrock canyon country of southern Utah. I lived for four years in Bicknell, near the site of my imagined discovery. While I was working for the US Forest Service out of Teasdale, Boulder Mountain was my office. I spent countless hours and days exploring the magnificent canyon country around Boulder Mountain and Capitol Reef National Park. It is magical and the implications of that scenery on time and history are staggering.

So I took that germ of an idea and put it in my active imagination and came up with *Sands of Time*. It is of course pure fiction and any resemblance to any people is strictly coincidence. Any resemblance to places, such as Torrey, the National Park, or other locations, is real but may not be totally factual.

This was originally written in 2001–2002. I have not updated the dates to reflect the present and any changes in the intervening years. Thus, keep in mind that things like GPS, smartphones, or other technological advances were not in widespread use when Ev and Mida were doing their research and explorations. I finally decided to hurry up with publishing this story before a real Orion was actually discovered. Maybe it has been, but we don't know it. Think about that.

Sit back and enjoy a tale of discovery, adventure, confusion, and exploration. I enjoyed it. I hope you will as well.

Contents

ONE

✳

A Walk in the Desert

We shall not cease from exploration
And the end of all our exploring
Will be to arrive where we started
And know the place for the first time.

—*T. S. Eliot*

The finest workers in stone are
not copper or steel tools
But the gentle touches of air and water working
at their leisure with a liberal allowance of time.

—*Henry David Thoreau*

THE IDES OF May 1998 dawned a brilliant red as Ev crawled out of his tent, sleepily unaware his life was soon to change. The red spilled from the cloud-streaked eastern sky, meeting the rock cliffs that surrounded him, and onto the sand that oozed between his bare toes. He loved rocks and he loved springtime in the Utah slickrock desert, although he appeared a small presence in this expanse of space and time. Several years ago, he discovered this secluded corner of Boulder Mountain, where the slopes of the looming lava-capped plateau slid eastward into the maze of contorted canyons of Capitol Reef National Park. Few people drove in this area, for good reason. Roads were scarce. Even fewer people hiked here since they didn't know about it. The more famous rock cliffs and canyons of Capitol Reef gathered the crowds, if you could call them that. Even Capitol Reef was relatively undiscovered compared to Bryce and Zion a few miles to the west.

But where Ev camped wasn't even the National Park, something preserved for special reasons. It was part of the Dixie National Forest. Not your common Smokey Bear Forest of mountains and peaks, evergreen forests, and flowery meadows. This was desert canyon country. Smokey didn't need to worry about protecting this corner of his domain from forest fires since there was precious little here to burn. Ev realized that when he tried to build a campfire the previous night. He scrambled to pick up a few branches of juniper and pinyon. Each one probably lay on the sandy soil for decades waiting to decompose in this arid climate.

He threw a makeshift lunch into his pack, studied his topo map again, and decided on his course into the small but isolated canyons of this area. Not as remote as some parts of southern Utah, this was a tame type of remote. It was within sight of a scenic highway that cut across the side of Boulder Mountain, a few thousand feet above him. That was the normal access to this area. However, in a normal year, by the time springtime advanced the snowline up to the highway allowing for access down into the lower plateau, it was getting too hot and dry in this desert segment. The near-impenetrability of Capitol Reef to vehicles eliminated access from the east except for one isolated, rocky and little-known, former uranium prospecting road. So his little corner of the world this May morning belonged to Ev and no one else. Or so he thought. The pot growers used to occasionally wander in here in the summer, tending a few hidden gardens, but the federal law dogs eliminated them the past few years.

He shifted his pack on his back as he left his camp and headed southwest, away from the rising sun. Hiking about a mile down a side canyon, then into the main Sheets Draw, he turned up the draw to where it became a serious canyon. Sweat ran into his eyes as he clambered up onto a bench, then down into another larger canyon. He stopped to sit by a small mountain mahogany on the slope, its branch tips gnawed to stubs by hungry deer. As he wiped his forehead, he looked toward the sun, now climbing well above the rock wall of the Waterpocket Fold before him, and closed his eyes. He did a few deep breathing exercises, thinking of what this place looked like over the millennia. Then a canyon wren warbled its descending scale. Ev peered up on the cliffs all around him but could not see the elusive bird. He rarely did but loved to listen to them. They owned the canyons, these miniature lords of rock cliff and hanging clumps of grass high up on the walls. Their song evoked in him the feeling of magnificent loneliness and unbridled freedom. Ev puckered his lips and answered with his own imitation. He rarely heard a reply to his call but occasionally did get a chickadee to come see who was intruding on its domain.

"I guess," he thought to himself, "if a canyon wren thought he had anything to fear from another wren that chose to hang out on the valley floor rather than scramble about three hundred feet straight up a cliff wall, then he was too dumb to come challenge the intruder. Wren, this is my rock down here. You can have yours up there. I just wish I could come fly with you."

Ev found it normal to talk to wrens and chickadees as well as trees and rocks. He liked that they didn't answer but often wished they would. He was totally fascinated by the cliffs and slickrock. He was also enchanted by the animals that could live in this tough environment. Actually, it was more like envy.

Another canyon wren called him back to the present. "Reality," he thought. "Whatever that is. I guess it's time to go find a little." He took a step, slid in the gravelly sand, then started sidling down the slope. He was crossing the hardened, colorful mud of the Chinle Formation and started seeing bits of petrified wood.

"I need to go higher up the mountain," he thought, forcing himself to ignore the tempting pieces of hundred-million-year-old trees lying at his feet. So he headed up the canyon. The Wingate cliff loomed high above, gradually disappearing as it sank back into the earth as he traveled uphill. He plodded for about a mile, lost in thought. Little side canyons started appearing more regularly as the red cliffs shrank in height. He chose one that looked promising and turned north into its shaded recess.

"If there were no sun to gauge by, I wouldn't have a clue of what direction I was facing," he thought. He had zigzagged too many times. "No wonder this country is unexplored and roadless. Anyone who stumbled in here is probably still here, bones and dust." He was still too close to civilization to think he was the first white man to see this, but he knew he could count on two hands the number that ever stood here in this exact spot.

A sonic boom shattered his world as he ducked, then looked up. Two air force jets screamed over his head, coming from low over the mountain that loomed out of sight to his west. The thunder in the sky raced east and lessened as he heard a new sound. A clattering and crashing echoed off surrounding cliffs as rocks cascaded onto the canyon floor. The cliff was over forty feet high here, and the fall had come from near the top. He glanced at the bottom of the cliff where the rocks landed. Orange dust was now mushrooming up from the ground. A glint of light caught his eye. Another small rockfall had occurred near the bottom of the cliff. He waited for the dust to settle, then scurried over to the base of the cliff. Shivering as he approached, Ev felt like someone was watching him. He looked around. Nothing. No one could be within miles. He could not see where he had stood only two minutes before. The cliff wall made a sharp jag, which hid it from nearly every view. It even had a small overhang, which blocked views from above.

An uneasy feeling raised goose bumps as he scrambled the few feet up to the cliff face. He looked up at the cliff wall where the first rockfall had come from. It looked smooth and solid to him. He didn't worry about any more falling rocks. He then looked at what earlier caught his eye with the flash of light. He just stared. Lifting his arm hesitantly, he reached out his right hand. He slowly touched the cliff, then jerked back his hand like it had been slapped by something. His mouth moved slowly, no words coming out. Finally he croaked to himself, "It can't be. My god, it can't be." Backing up to the edge of the new pile of rocks, he then sat down and stared at it for nearly ten minutes.

Ev was looking at a piece of metal protruding from the cliff. It was freshly exposed, seeing sunlight for the first time in almost two hundred million years. That was the age of the sandstone called Wingate. The formation in this area was several hundred feet thick red sandstone deposited by howling winds and caressing desert breezes two hundred million years ago. And buried within it was a piece of metal. Not some metallic ore, not some concretion formed by a pool of water, not some strange piece of rock. Man-made, forged out of steel or aluminum or who knows what. The slight shading difference between the stained rock cliff with the freshly exposed surface where the rock had just split off a few minutes before told him it was not something someone pounded into the rock in the past one hundred years. This thing had been encased in solid sandstone. Windblown sandstone created in the middle of a Tertiary desert.

He slowly got up and walked back to the cliff. Goose bumps once again erupted on his arms as he shivered noticeably. Instinctively he looked around. He looked up at the cliff tops, looked up and down the canyon, and looked everywhere to see if there was anyone else watching. His own thoughts echoed in the remoteness that surrounded him. He was alone—utterly alone—yet someone was there. He ran his fingers over the metal. It felt smooth, cold, and surprisingly polished. There were no signs of rust or wear. He couldn't recognize what type metal it was. Pulling his rock pick out of his pack, he tapped at the surface. It didn't scratch. It wasn't aluminum. It looked as new as if it had just come from a factory. He tapped at the edges where it disappeared into the rock. A few more flakes of rock fell away, exposing more metal. He slowly worked all around the edges. The metal surface was starting to become rounded, disappearing deeper into the cliff. He was almost ready to quit when he gave one more hard tap, knocking off a piece of rock the size of a basketball. The shiny metal turned into a clear piece of glass or plastic. He rubbed the red dust off. It looked like the edge of a window.

He looked inside, but because of the bright sunlight, could see nothing but his own amazed expression. He tapped on it gently with his hammer. The glass rang like the metal surface. He thought of one of the *Star Trek* movies where they came back in time to Earth and wanted their forebears to make transparent aluminum, which Earthlings had not heard of yet. Maybe this was something like transparent aluminum.

The sense of overpowering excitement, awe, fear—he couldn't decide what the emotion was—finally got to him. He stumbled to the other side of the narrow canyon and sat up against the cliff wall, staring at the giant red wall. Mindlessly opening his pack, he pulled out lunch but could not eat.

Ev started talking to the cliff. "What a sight if these people could see me here. Some grubby sunburned character in boots, ripped cutoffs, and T-shirt advertising Ft. Lewis College, sitting against a rock in the middle of nowhere. Kinda like the princess waking up and seeing not a prince but a hunchbacked, cross-eyed stable boy. Not the high-tech "beam me up, Scotty" type of thing they might have expected. Or maybe they didn't expect anything.

"Here is the discovery to end all discoveries of the past two hundred million years and I happen to stumble on it because of two top guns drag racing over the desert. Do I just go up to the local ranger and say, 'Oh, by the way, you have a buried spaceship in one of your cliffs?' I'd love to see the environmental impact statement on that one!"

As in a trance, Ev finally ate a little of his lunch, calmly putting the wrappers and empty bottle back in his pack. He reached down and picked up a small chunk of sandstone that used to be part of the cliff. Carefully, almost reverently, Ev put it in his pack. Then he picked up a handful of red dust, walked over to the cliff, and smeared it as well as he could on the metal to dull the shine. Still in a daze, he started walking away. Stopping just before he went around the corner of the rock wall, he looked at it one more time, then headed back to his camp. It was three in the afternoon.

Ev was on a short vacation from his duties as instructor at Ft. Lewis College in Durango, just over the horizon where the sun now rose. Finals the week before brought the spring semester to a finish and the summer session was another couple weeks off. Ev looked forward to teaching a field seminar in June, but now he needed a break from campus and from scientific facts. Although he could rarely let his mind ease from analyzing data, he needed the fresh air and the rock wilderness to refresh his mind. He breathed in the desert air, thinking of his situation.

His home for the past few years was Durango, the booming new age utopia of Generation X. It was getting too crowded for him, but it beat most of the alternatives. He could not see himself in Missoula, Seattle, Berkeley, or even Flagstaff. Durango, with its small college, may have its faults, but it was close to paradise of about any type you wanted. High alpine peaks, remote desert canyons, ancient stone ruins, and deep forests. The Four Corners country, with Durango as its Mecca—this country had it all. This long weekend was therapy in this hidden Eden of slickrock Utah.

He knew this area well. It was mostly a Kayenta sandstone bench that was capped on its western end by Navajo Sandstone. The Wingate cliffs marked the eastern end, fading into the Chinle and Moenkopi Formations. At that point, the swell and upheaval of the Waterpocket Fold contorted everything into the wild ride that was now called Capitol Reef National Park. The Wingate was a very hard layer and bright reddish orange. Numerous little side canyons cut into its cliffs that wove an undulating line north to south along the fold. Those were the little paradises he had come to explore. Some had trickles of water seeping out of alcoves, some sheltered ancient Anasazi or Fremont rock structures, and some hid wonderful panels of rock art unseen by most modern eyes.

He had spent the past two days doing some mountain biking in the park and where he could get on the many old mining roads and cattle trails on the Dixie National Forest. Access was difficult at best. A few miners of a half century ago had actually found uranium, mostly in the Shinarump layer of sandstone, but there was nothing else here in the way of valuable minerals. Nowadays, there were more cows, elk, and deer than people within a hundred-mile radius. He didn't like the idea of biking cross-country since there was a lot of cryptogamic soil, soon to be renamed cryptobiotic. "Crypto" as he called it—that delicate crusty covering of soil by a combination of lichens, moss, and other assorted things that protected the fragile desert soil. Any disturbance of the crypto caused erosion and resulting bad things. So he tiptoed when he crossed it on foot.

Stopping to rest and attempt to take his mind off what he had seen, he leaned back and looked above him. The rock. That magnificent display of history, of art, of creativity. The rock mesmerized him. The cliffs and jumbled slabs and boulders lay like scattered toys thrown about by a two-year-old child. Often he amused himself by analyzing the era they were formed and exactly how, whether it be wind or ocean. "Too left-brained," he thought. "I have to just see it for what it tells us about our own history. This was a huge near-equatorial desert once, and I would have been in the middle of a Sahara, dead of heat and thirst. No dinosaur to come sniff my bones. Just the expanse of sky and the never-ending wind.

"Hell, that's even too analytical," he thought. His profession as a geology teacher often got in his way of just enjoying life. He tried to see through normal eyes, not his professional eyes. "The rocks are pretty. They are nature's art. They twist and swirl. Sculptures in sand and mud. A frozen kaleidoscope. Yeah, 'Now appearing, *The Sculptures of the Creator*, appearing for the ninety-four-billionth straight day at the Earth Gallery.' Not exactly sellout crowds, but then, good things take time to be appreciated." In a right-brained gesture, Ev ran his hand over the sandstone he was sitting on. It was sensuous: a silky yet grainy smoothness that covered an undulating curve. It reminded him of a certain lady in Durango. "Now that is more like it," he said as he smiled. Maybe too much, he chuckled to himself as he caressed the rock one last time.

Leaving his lady friend in bed, and in his mind, he returned to real life and stood up. As often happened when he thought of geologic time, he dreamed of getting in his time machine and going back and watching the scenery before him grow and disappear over time. He would be perched high above the earth, watching as seas appeared, then receded. Nearby mountain ranges grew, then eroded to flat plains. Rivers flowed into swamps, which then disappeared into sandy flats. Millions of years slid by as the wind and rain accompanied sunset and sunrise, never ending. Meanwhile, rock layer after layer slowly formed and receded underground, not to see sunlight again for eternities. Then, they were exposed in a flash, forming cliffs and plateaus and breathtaking vistas and expanses of rock.

Ev reached his camp at five o'clock. He did not remember any of the hike back to camp. Two hours of his life disappeared, erased by the mystery and total amazement of his discovery. "But I did gain two hundred million years, so what's an hour or two." He laughed to himself.

As he sat down in the shade of his small Toyota truck, he heard a distant canyon wren, then immediately fell asleep. He dreamed of ancient skies and falling stars, comets and northern lights in the November heavens. He awoke with a start when he heard a coyote singing to the evening sky. It was past seven o'clock, and the sun was low in the northwest. He scrambled to gather wood for a campfire. He didn't need it to cook, but he loved to become lost in the flickering glow of a good pinyon and juniper fire. It was an essential part of a desert experience.

He lit the little propane camp stove—so much for living off the land—and warmed a can of chili. Ev wasn't into fancy camp cooking. He ate to survive. He left the fancy stuff to the occasional meal he had when invited out to eat. There were three young ladies back in Durango who took turns giving him good home-cooked meals along with some female companionship. No one had yet really attracted him, but he was no hermit either. Ev would have been a good catch for many of the women he knew. He was handsome, smart and witty, and appealingly shy. Yet his aloofness sometimes got in the way. He couldn't seem to concentrate on anything but his passions of geology, bicycles, and rock climbing.

After eating his sparse supper, he put on his Paul Winter wolf howl tape and sat back and waited for the coyotes to continue their singing. He knew there were no wolves here, but he loved to play with the minds of the coyotes. They usually answered his wolf tapes. He thought their howls showed some sign of confusion and irritation. He always chuckled about that. He envisioned some coyote slinking into camp and devouring his tape player, then spitting it out while muttering something about damn humanoids.

Later, in silence around his fire, he continued to analyze what he found that afternoon. His gaze shifted from the flickering embers to the skies. Stars lit the sky like a billion fireflies. His discovery came from up there somewhere. He knew it. It came from out there but never returned. Did someone up there still wait for a return that would never happen?

"Someone. Listen to me. Some one person or being or space creature. Is that what happened? Did something come from some distant star and land here so long ago, they have long since turned to space dust? What else could it be? Maybe a Boeing airliner from a civilization that disappeared before the dinosaurs took over? No. That's not an alternative. There is no alternative."

He threw another branch on the fire. "Did they have fire, or were they so advanced they just used cosmic beams and x-rays? Maybe I am a descendant of them. Were they the first life on this planet? No, they couldn't be. Life started prior to two hundred million years ago." Ev's mind was racing. "Maybe they had been here for millions of years. The Wingate Formation is kind of iffy for age, but if I remember right, we think it covers something like two hundred thirty to one hundred ninety million years. Let's say my spaceship is about midway through the period. It's hard to comprehend that cliff took upward of forty million years to form. A million years for every few feet. I bet one howling sandstorm could have drifted the ship over in a day." His thoughts started going in several different directions.

Even though Ev dealt with geologic time every day, he still marveled when he thought about the time involved in these rocks. He could barely comprehend one million years, much less several hundred of those. Now he had to comprehend the idea of intelligent life all those years ago.

As his fire slowly faded to glowing embers, he crawled into his tent and snuggled into his down sleeping bag. "I need someone to share this discovery with, but who? Who will believe me? Who could I trust to show this to?"

He ruled out the government, who he believed was already hiding evidence of UFOs. Not any politician he knew about. Anyone in power would be too concerned with keeping that power. This discovery would cast a new light on the idea of power on this planet. Who would accept all of what this meant? The implications were immense for religion, for science, for evolution. He thought of someone like Carl Sagan or Isaac Asimov. He smiled as he thought of confiding this with Captain Kirk. Maybe, he thought, this was the ship of Kirk coming back to Earth after a long star voyage. Maybe it wasn't from space after all. Maybe it was from our own future.

He seriously considered whom he could confide in. What about people he worked with? A pretty conservative bunch who would immediately want to do fancy research and lose touch with the implications. What about an investigative reporter? They would probably want to write about it and sell it to a big movie studio. He could see the headlines in the super market tabloids: "My Mother Was a 200-Million-Year-Old Alien." No matter who he thought of, the government would get involved and would somehow hide it. After all, it was on government property. The news of this would change the world, creating unbelievable interest. It would probably turn into panic and mass hysteria, knowing our reaction to the unknown. He tossed and turned in his sleeping bag as he made a large mental list of possibilities.

As the fire turned to cold, silent ashes, he finally fell asleep, hardly turning over in his bag all night. He did not dream at all. The Milky Way covered the sky with its cloud of stars and galaxies. A distant owl announced its ownership of this night landscape. The red cliffs glowed in the faint moonlight. A world was asleep, awaiting the next dawn, as it had in this very spot for over four billion years. A mere two hundred million years was a wink of the eye. Time changed and time remained the same. The universe teemed with life and with emptiness. Questions were asked and questions went unanswered. A few intelligent beings asked questions that had no answers. A loneliness separated galaxies in this silent existence. One being, known as Everett Edward Collins here on a little planet called Earth by its inhabitants, started a frustrating search for answers. He didn't even know the right questions to ask. Maybe he did dream after all.

The next morning, Ev seemed to still be on automatic pilot as he started hiking. He didn't want to think of the discovery. He just wanted to soak up the rocks and enjoy the scenery. This should have been easy to do. All he had to do was walk, which he did, not paying attention to where he was. He walked through the Moenkopi Formation and found slabs and chunks of rippled rock. Petrified raindrops frozen in time freckled huge slabs of rock, as did the ripples from river flows etched forever in sandstone. Next was the kaleidoscope of colors of the Chinle, a powdery mud turned to crumbly rock. Chimneys in the massive Wingate cliffs opened the petrified sand dunes of an ancient Sahara Desert. Climbing higher still, he wandered on the open plateau of Kayenta, scattered with pinyon and juniper and Indian ricegrass. Miles from his starting point, he scrambled up a small cliff and came onto the edge of the white slickrock expanse of Navajo Sandstone, covered with chocolate drop sprinkles of basalt boulders from the top of Boulder Mountain thousands of feet above. He found rock art, hidden alcoves, ancient rock structures of a people long turned to dust, and an array of color and twisted, gnarled, beautiful forms of life adapted to this desert.

Ev picked one final knoll to climb and survey the view. It was lunchtime and he was hungry. His food supply was running low so his lunch was unappealing. Of course, it would be unappealing even if he had a food box full of cans and boxes. He opened a can of sardines, grimacing as he ripped the lid off and spilled the smelly liquid on his bare knee.

Ev closed his eyes and listened to the wind. It was ceaseless and hypnotic. He started asking himself questions again. It seemed so soothing, so harmless, so never ending. Did the creator of these cliffs sit here and listen to this same wind? What did he or she think about? Did he find awe and wonderment and inspiration from the same spectacle now in view? Red sand and red rock. Juniper, cactus, and ricegrass. It is wilderness as wild as the creator ever imagined. There is no sign of civilization. There are no sounds but the pinyon jays, chickadees, and canyon wrens. And of course, the wind.

The scene brought out the poet in Ev. Rock upon rock. Ancient desert and ancient ocean. Himalayan-sized mountains to the north disappeared grain by grain, depositing their sand in rivers, lakes, seas, and deserts. Entire mountain ranges appeared and disappeared. And the sun rose every day to the east and set in the evening to the west. It rained, the wind blew, and the rock was formed. Layer upon layer. Millions of years upon millions of years. Then the entire horizon rose slowly, ever so slowly. It rose hundreds, then thousands of feet. Then it warped, then it folded, then it was covered with lava. Then at last, it dissolved, grain by grain and was carried away.

"To the far away sea that is as far from me here as I am from knowing any answers to the whys, the hows, and the whens." Ev found himself talking out loud again.

"Dinosaurs evolved from fish and creatures that crawled out of the sea. They wandered the swamps and seas that were right here. They lived and they died. Some are still buried right below where I sit. Trees grew and flowers evolved. Little furry mammals scurried about. And a spaceship landed just over there and was abandoned. And not a single person in the entire history of the earth knows about it.

"Except me. I cannot even fathom the view and the history I see around me. Now I have to understand what this discovery means."

He jumped as he heard a car horn in the distance above him on the mountain. Yes, there was civilization close by. He couldn't see the highway, but it was up there, hidden by the pine and aspen further up where rock was hidden by soil and big growing things. Rain and snow fell up there and life flourished. That was a different world. He was down here now in the rock where life was different, more open, more exposed. Raw life that fought to live without rain. Or at least without as much. Enough fell to give a hint of what life could do if it had to. Just barely.

A blue-tailed lizard scurried by his left foot, kicking sand on his boot. He decided it was time to head back down, through the display of rock and color. He clambered down cliffs. He followed a dry wash, then followed a trickle of water someone had named Tantalus Creek on his map. He thought about the Greek king Tantalus, who was condemned to stand in Hades with feet in water that receded whenever he tried to drink. We got our word tantalize from this. This little creek was tantalizing as it offered rich life within a few feet of the water, yet the earth became dry and parched only feet away.

He finally came to the road he had driven on a few days previously. Very shortly, he was back at his camp, exhausted and dazed from the journey he had just taken. The exhaustion was from the physical journey. The daze was from his mental journey through time. He needed to go back to civilization and think about what to do. Yet he didn't want to leave this place either. His discovery was holding on to him like a magnet.

The little town of Torrey was not far away. A good meal in a restaurant tempted him, but he was too tired now to pack up and leave. And he didn't want to drive back here in the dark to his isolated camp. So he fired up his little propane stove and heated a gorp of rice and canned corn and canned chicken meat. He downed his last bottle of Sam Adams beer, knowing he would be up by 1:00 a.m. returning the beer to the sand.

At 1:00 a.m., he was still sitting by the glowing embers of his fire, unable to sleep. He was thinking about the implications of his discovery.

This discovery could turn every religion on earth on its head. What would the Irish bishop James Ussher think about his date of 4004 BC as the year the earth was created? The opponents of Darwin used that date, created by a meticulous recounting of all the "begats" of the Bible, to prove Darwin wrong in his radical theory. What would those radical fundamentalists think about Adam and Eve and Eden and those grizzled desert prophets who heard the voice of God? Maybe they heard the whine of a spaceship instead.

What would this do to evolution? Maybe the beings in that ship became Adam and Eve. Maybe they were our ancestors. Maybe they were just smart dinosaurs or big woolly mammoths with thumbs. Or maybe they just simply died and there are two-hundred-million-year-old bones in that tomb lying buried in the cliff. Or maybe all the UFOs people see today are the rescue ships just now getting here to look for the ship. Lots of maybes.

What does this do to quantum physics and the theories of time? Could these people travel faster than the speed of light? Are there other dimensions, other physics? Are we at the other end of a black hole? Are we a giant discontinuity where other rules and laws govern another universe hidden beyond our own? If there is in fact intelligent life out there, why haven't we seen it for two hundred million years, or have we and not known it?

The last ember of glowing pinyon wood went dark as Ev slowly stood up and crawled into his tent. He fell into a fitful sleep after thinking that it would actually be dangerous to tell anyone about his discovery. Not only would no one believe him, there would be dozens of interest groups terrified enough of this discovery to probably kill him to keep the information from getting out. It would literally change the world. People often feared change, but this wasn't change. It was the most revolutionary thing to happen in the history of the world. And he was the only one who knew. He just couldn't get that thought out of his mind. He dreamed, of all things, about building a house in a cliff somewhere and living out his days eating potato chips and drinking wine. Alone and forgotten with a secret he would carry to his grave. He was getting paranoid, he thought.

When he awoke the next morning, he was ready to leave and go home to his other world. There would be plenty of time to think about this trip and what to do. He knew he somehow had to get inside this thing, if it indeed was what he thought it was, to answer some of the questions that were overwhelming him. The scientist in him demanded he do this properly. It would not be as simple as digging out a buried car and prying open the door. It would take a lot of thought and preparation.

Before he left, he would pedal his bike down the road, work off a little energy, then come back and pack. Except maybe he should go back to the cliff and try and hide the exposed surface. That would be a smart thing to do. It might be too risky to just leave and do nothing. Some lost hiker could stumble on the cliff like he did. Then his secret would be exposed.

Like a schoolboy reciting his lines for a play, he repeated his plan to himself: Take a short bike ride, break camp, hike up to the cliff for one last look, and hide the exposed metal. Then he could leave and decide what to do later, back in the familiar surroundings of his office and his books.

He pedaled down the road with a forced and uneasy smile, staring at the red cliffs and cloudless blue sky. He had discovered something that had already changed his life. He didn't know he was about to discover something else that would change it even more.

TWO

❋

A Companion on the Road

What is life? It is the flash of
the firefly in the night.
It is the breath of the buffalo in the winter.
It is the little shadow which runs across
the grass and loses itself in the sunset.

—Crowfoot

Man struggles to find life outside himself,
unaware that the life he is seeking is within him.

—Kahlil Gibran

Ev PEDALED DOWN the dirt track of a road, dodging old cow pies and avoiding the deep ruts. The hours of thinking and guessing left him confused. As much as he wanted to enjoy this scenery, his mind kept reliving his discovery. Less than half a mile down the road, he came around a bend and saw a car parked in the road. He was surprised not so much at seeing a vehicle but at seeing a car. A white car with its hood up. A small green dome tent was set up under a juniper tree next to the car.

"Who in the world is stupid enough to drive a car up this road to get here?" he said out loud to himself as he coasted to a stop.

The road wasn't four-wheel drive, but it certainly required a vehicle with high clearance. He looked at the license plates.

"New Mexico. Someone from New Mexico should know better than to drive a car down here."

It was a Subaru, and it was four–wheel drive, but it looked strange to him. Then he realized it was raised to have a higher clearance. Well, still it was stupid, he thought, to drive a high rider to this desolate place. And now it was broken down miles from nowhere, with a several-hundred-dollar tow charge for someone to come get it. "Serves them right," he mumbled. He glanced in the car and around the tent but saw no one.

As his eyes searched the open forest above the road, he saw a person coming down the slope. Wearing a big floppy hat, sunglasses, an oversized sweatshirt, and baggy sweatpants, she tried to nonchalantly hide a nearly empty roll of toilet paper under her sweatshirt. Ev smiled as he thought of the uncompromising position he almost caught her in, literally. Then he realized she was somewhat unusual since the clothes had no wording of any kind, unusual in this day of advertising and messages on everything from hats to shoe laces. He felt guilty about his T-shirt that stated loudly in bright colors "Durango Colorado, 4 Season Wonderland."

As he watched her stride down the hill, he sensed his private hideaway being invaded by an unwelcome visitor. "A dumb flatlander who wears boring clothes," he said to himself. Or he thought he said to himself.

"Well, good morning to you, too. For your information, I am not a flatlander. I live in the hills outside Santa Fe, was born and raised in southern New Mexico in the Sacramento Mountains, and can probably outlast you climbing to the top of Boulder Mountain."

The voice was husky, confident, and seductive. She walked up to him, extended her hand, and said, "You may call me Mida, short for Alameda. I obviously am in need of help and you were sent to give it to me."

He extended his hand, losing his balance on his bicycle. He fell against her as his bike went down. Backing away and stuttering, he said, "I'm sorry, I didn't mean . . . My name is Ev, short for

Everett." Why he added the last part, he had no idea. He never called himself Everett. She had him rattled and he knew it. His confidence dissolved as quickly as Mancos Shale in rainwater.

"I accept your apology and I know that you would never call me dumb." She took off her sunglasses and smiled at him. Her teeth were perfect and her smile could melt ice. Dark eyes highlighted a face that combined Native American and Anglo features.

As she took off her hat, she shook her head. Her hair was jet-black, cut short and glistened in the morning sun. She was beautiful.

"What happened?" he stammered as he looked at her car, trying to regain his composure. "Road too rough for you?" He was pushing it. Why he was doing this was beyond him. He was reacting to her as if she had caught him with his pants down and not the other way around. This woman was in control and Ev was acting like a schoolboy.

"Sorry I spoiled your morning by being here, but I have driven this car here before. As a matter of fact, I have driven this car places where you would hesitate to ride your bicycle." Looking down at his bicycle still lying in the road, she smiled at him. "No, I did fine on the road, but it did challenge me in a few places. I'm not sure what happened." She looked at the car with a puzzled look. "It's not the fuel pump or filter since I am getting gas. The plugs look fine and the electrical system is okay. It was not vapor lock. It has to be something simple, but I can't seem to find it. It just stalled last night as I came over the rise and here I sit. I have a cell phone, but can't get any service out of here." She stood looking at him with her arms crossed and feet apart. She never lost eye contact, which made Ev even more nervous.

Her automotive knowledge impressed him, as did her overall confidence and poise in what had to be an awkward situation for an attractive girl. "You seem to know a lot about cars," he said rather sheepishly.

"Grow up with three brothers on the rez and you get a good chance to pick up a lot of knowledge about junk cars and why they don't run," she said. "Think you can help me?"

"Not really," he answered truthfully. He walked over and looked under the hood, but this was more habit than anything seriously diagnostic. The way this was starting out, he knew he'd better not try to impress this lady with anything he was not an expert on. "The best I can do is give you a ride into town. I wasn't planning on going in until either tonight or tomorrow. I guess I could change my plans."

"No, don't do that." She walked over to the car, reached under the hood, and fiddled with what he thought was the carburetor. Or fuel injector. He really didn't know the difference. "Tomorrow would be fine. I was coming up here to camp and am prepared to stay for a few days. I would be satisfied if you simply had someone come out to look at the car. I could give you my credit card number to give to them. That is, if there is a mechanic in this county."

"Sure," he replied. "I know of one in Torrey. There's also a garage in Bicknell. Things are pretty remote out here, so people get by without a lot of big city conveniences. Actually, what I can do right now is go back and get my truck. I'm only a half mile down the road. I'll tow you back to where I'm camped. Not that you are blocking traffic, but I am camped in a really nice little spot. I would appreciate some company. That is if you want any."

One change she made already was to convince Ev to stay the night rather than leaving camp early. And she didn't have to ask him. There was something special about this person, and he wanted to learn more about her.

"I appreciate the offer," she replied, "but I don't want to impose on you. I'll be fine right here."

"Nonsense. My spot is off the road and in a much nicer setting. I really would like your company. Unless you don't want to spend a little time with a boring biker."

"All right," she sighed. "Yes, I will be glad to share your little campground. We obviously have something in common if we are both down here camping in this wonderful spot. I seem to have interrupted your ride."

"No, not at all," blurted Ev.

"Well, why don't you go ahead and do what you were going to do and I will get things packed. I can occupy myself for however long you will be gone. Patience is one of my virtues. Besides, I don't seem to have many other options." She smiled at him, closed the hood of her car, and started to walk over to her tent.

"That's all right. I would probably have been gone several hours. I didn't really have definite plans anyway. I was just killing the morning. I will go back and get my truck." Ev picked up the bike, turned it around, and was off down the road before Mida could say anything.

Mida watched him ride off as she thought about this interesting encounter. She picked up good vibes from Ev, despite his obvious floundering with her. Ev showed a nervousness she sensed was not normally in his character. Something was bothering him. She sensed he had a secret and was out here trying to figure out how to deal with it.

She packed the tent and traded her sweatshirt for a sports bra and tank top. She quickly changed from her sweatpants to a pair of denim cutoffs. As she pulled on her hiking boots, she analyzed Ev. He was tall, pretty good-looking and had blond hair about as long as hers. She normally didn't scope out guys, but she wanted to notice all she could about this stranger who for some reason attracted her. She then sat down under a juniper tree and waited, motionless like the lizard sitting on a nearby rock.

Ev pedaled back to his camp, excited as a little kid ordering an ice cream cone. He was rescuing a beautiful girl, but he was letting her intimidate him. Why?

He quickly drove his Toyota back to her car, where she was waiting, leisurely stretched out on the ground. He got out and walked over to her. She now revealed a well-formed figure and muscular legs. She was dark skinned, so he couldn't tell what was tan and what was just her natural color. He liked what he saw.

"That was sure quick," she commented as she slowly got up and opened the car door. "You act like you are in a hurry for something."

"I just hate to have a damsel in distress," he said as he took a sweeping bow.

"Yeah, and now you take me back to your castle where you fight off the dragon? By the way, Rock Boy, do you rock or is it your truck that rocks?"

Forgetting that his personalized plate said simply "ROCKS," he looked puzzled for a second, then sighed and said, "Oh, I'm a geology teacher. That's why I'm out here now. I teach at Ft. Lewis College in Durango. I guess I just like rocks. Let's get you back to the castle and off this busy road." Ev changed the subject as he got in his truck, slamming the door. He turned the truck around, taking care not to get stuck in the sandy soil off the road. With vehicles tail to tail, he quickly hooked his tow strap onto the back of her car. "It will be easier to pull you backward rather than try and turn you around. All you need to do is steer."

"Yeah, easier for you. It better not be too far. I don't like to drive backward and I'm sure I don't like to steer backward while someone else drives me."

Ev picked up the slack with a jerk, a little more than he intended. He was back at his camp before he knew it. He pulled her up a little rise so she was facing downhill, then unhooked her and parked his truck next to his tent.

She got out and looked around. "This is a nice little spot," she said. "I drove right by the turnoff yesterday and didn't notice a thing. We are well hidden, not that there is much to hide from out here."

"What are you hiding from?" he asked suddenly. "I mean, how did you know about this desolate place?" He walked over to his campfire circle, now in the shade of a large white-berried juniper and sat on the ground. He motioned her to sit down.

"You get right to the point, don't you? Is that from talking to rocks?" Mida stared at him with unsmiling, piercing eyes. Ev couldn't figure her out. Was she joking or serious?

She finally showed a smirk on her lips and grinned. "Well, you are sharing your home with me, so I will tell you who I am."

She pulled a blanket out of her car, cleared a spot, and sat down across the fire circle from him. "I already told you, I was raised on the Mescalero Reservation in New Mexico. It's probably no surprise I am half-Apache. And half–Minnesota Norwegian. Quite a combination, huh, Rock Boy? I am just finishing up my doctoral thesis at the University of New Mexico in Albuquerque. I'm out here because I don't know what I want to do when I grow up. Maybe I will get an idea or two from the rocks." She smiled and looked at Ev for a comment but got only silence.

She explained that she was working part-time at the Museum of Indian Arts and Culture in Santa Fe. A Ford Foundation grant allowed her to get her doctorate. She had taken a few days off to do a little exploring, looking for some rock art connected to spiritual beliefs and healing traditions of the Fremont culture in this area. Her thesis mostly emphasized the Anasazi rock art of the southwest, so she wanted to get a little different cultural tradition.

"I live with a roommate in Santa Fe, although she is leaving next month to get married. My grant is almost over and now I am looking for a better paying job, although I do enjoy working at the museum. I will probably go back to the rez and help my mom for a while. There is still a lot for me to learn among my own people." Looking up at the Wingate cliff across the flat to their east, she signaled this was about all she was going to share. She didn't often open up like this to anyone, especially a male stranger. She felt comfortable talking to this person she really didn't know yet.

"Well, you have my attention. Apache and Norwegian is an interesting mix. And a beautiful one. Your own people sounds like you mean the Apache. What about the Norwegian side?"

"The Norwegian side of things wasn't the center of my life. I grew up on the rez. That's where my interest is. The gods and heroes have different names in Apache and Norwegian and the history is different, but a lot of the culture is similar. People are people. At least the cultures of five or six hundred years ago. Nowadays, cultures are so jumbled up, you can't make any sense of them. Go back a few hundred years, and you find a lot of similarities. I might do some connecting of the dots later. Not now."

Ev let the subject drop. He still wanted to find out a lot more about this person, but would do it slowly. "Would you like something to drink? I am afraid to offer you a beer." He got up and went to his cooler, pulling out a can of iced tea.

"No thanks. Water is the best thing to drink anytime." She pulled a bottle of water out of her pack and stretched out on the blanket, with those golden brown legs aiming at him. "Your turn to impress me, Rock Boy."

He knew he was staring at her legs but couldn't help it. He opened his iced tea and took a tentative sip. "Well, you are going to get to taste a rock or two if you don't quit calling me Rock Boy. In case you missed it, my name is Ev. I am a geologist who teaches geology. I do not go around raping the earth with mining companies. I love rocks and cliffs and mountains and canyons. I also love to teach young people about what is around them. You could say I'm an earthy kind of guy."

He waited for a comment but got only a frown as Mida looked up at the cloudless blue sky.

"Before I got my doctorate at Utah and began teaching in Durango, I worked as a seasonal naturalist at the Grand Canyon for a couple years and worked one summer with Outward Bound. I'm originally from Boulder. Maybe that's why I got into geology." He cleared his throat as he changed the subject.

Looking west and pointing toward the canyon walls near them, he said, "In my wandering around here the past few days, I ran across several rock panels that were very interesting. My permit to lead personalized rock scrambling expeditions expires tonight, but I would be glad to hire out for an afternoon of hiking to remote castles."

"Now that's an offer that would be hard to refuse. But it does depend on what your fee is," Mida replied. "Since my original plans are temporarily disrupted, let's have an early lunch and get going. I would be satisfied if you would just point me in the right direction, but a guided hike by a real Smokey Bear Ranger is a dream come true. Did you get to wear the uniform and real Smokey hat when you were a park ranger?" She raised her eyebrows and exposed that dimple as she grinned broadly.

Once again, Ev didn't know whether she was making fun of him or just being curious. "Sarcasm is absolutely verboten on my tours," he announced, frowning to emphasize his sarcasm. "I could leave you out here, you know. And yes, I still have my Park Service uniform complete with the hat. I should have brought it with me if it turns you on."

She laughed a rather evil laugh. "It takes more than a hat to turn me on, Rock Boy. And you needn't try to figure out what does. As for leaving me out here, you leave me on a cliff somewhere and I would beat you back to camp. Then you would know how the Arizona pilgrims of the past felt when they knew Geronimo and Cochise where stalking them. For the moment, you are stuck with me and I am stuck with you. Let's go look at rocks."

"I'm almost out of food, so I can't feed you." Ev shrugged as he looked at Mida.

"Well, don't expect to get any good gourmet leftovers from me, Everett. I don't like to cook, although I am fairly good when I do. I do a better job of nourishing my soul rather than my body, sorry to say." She got up and walked over to her car.

"Well, I'm not sorry to say that it looks like you have done pretty well with the body after all," he said with a grin.

"And not so bad yourself either," she mumbled to herself as she bent over to reach into the back seat of her car.

Ev and Mida spent the afternoon wandering across sandy washes and scrambling up rocky benches. He led her through millions of years of sandstorms and mudflats. Picking up a crystal-studded piece of black petrified wood, he explained the Chinle formations of colored mud, the same formation that hid the petrified logs further south in Arizona. He showed her Moenkopi ripple marks on thin slabs of red stone. These made great stepping-stones for patios and pathways, he said. Trespassing onto Mida's expertise, he explained why rock art generally appeared on red Wingate cliffs and not white Navajo cliffs. When Ev talked of rock art, she politely nodded, although she knew much more about rock art than he, even some of the geologic details.

As they walked, Ev slipped into his teaching mode. He explained geology as if talking to one of his classes. The Wingate formed nearly impassable cliff barriers that were familiar to slickrock country travelers. Roads did not often go down the Wingate and often a traveler would go for miles looking for a way through the Wingate. The Navajo sandstone was composed almost purely of white quartz grains from nearby mountains that wore down to nothing. The Navajo desert covered this part of the West, often showing signs of small lakes that dried up, leaving an occasional trace of limestone. The Navajo weathered more often into rounded domes and cliffs, such as the namesake for the national park to their east.

Pointing to the black streaks on a red cliff before them, he told of the chemistry of desert varnish and how it stained the cliffs with either black or red, depending on the chemicals the bacteria had to work with. Pounding on a small red boulder with his hammer, he explained the even more detailed chemistry of how the sand formed sandstone by way of pressure and water seeping down through it. He finally lost Mida's attention as he explained the early chemistry of the earth and why there were so many red sandstones. The oxygen content of Earth's early atmosphere differed from today and the irons in the early rocks sucked up this free oxygen, turning rocks into rust. Once the oxygen content stabilized, that allowed for life to form. That's also why insects were larger then than now since the higher oxygen content allowed bigger bugs since their breathing mechanism was very different from our own lungs. When he said "but thank goodness for lungs" and made the mistake of looking at her chest, she pushed him hard enough to knock him over.

Although Mida knew some of the geology already, she enjoyed listening to his lecture. He obviously had much passion for his profession. Whenever she tried to slip him up with a trick question, he fielded it perfectly.

Finally, stopping at the first rock art display they came to, Mida told Ev, "Now it's my turn, Rock Expert. You have caused my poor little head to swirl with all this information. Now I can never look at all this as just rocks again. How can I keep all this straight? And more importantly, why do I need to?"

"Why? Because you want to know all you can about everything. That much I have concluded about you already. It may affect your rock art and where you find it. Right?"

"You think you have me pegged. You're not even close. I can't remember half of what you just told me."

"Give me that ridiculous floppy hat and I will write on it like a crib sheet. Actually your hat is big enough for me to draw a schematic cross section that lists not only the name of the formation but its time period, its chemical makeup, and probably even glue on an actual sample of the rock to boot."

"I'll give you the boot." She laughed as she playfully kicked at him. "I said it's my turn."

"Okay, Doctor, teach me what you know."

"Not a doctor yet. Almost. You wrote a thesis. You know how much more work is involved."

Mida proceeded to explain the differences between pictographs (pictures drawn or painted onto the rock surface) and petroglyphs (pictures scratched or carved into the rock itself). "No one has really discovered any Rosetta Stone to interpret these symbols, but there are many different explanations of individual symbols."

Not to be outdone by Ev, she went into her own teaching mode, explaining that certain animals had significant meanings, such as the snake and the sheep. There were many outlines of hands and the more famous flute player, Kokopelli, as well as stylized humans with horns, masks, and other adornments. Many of these figures were probably gods or idols and the pictures may have been a form of worship or prayer. A person could tell the culture and time period by the style of the drawings. There were several major styles. The panel they were looking at was Fremont but contained mostly Anasazi figures. Mida said she came to this area to study the Fremont culture, which didn't occur east of Utah.

She stood in front of a panel that Ev discovered a couple days ago and started pointing. The figures stretched across ten feet of smooth rock. She explained that the bighorn sheep probably was one of the main sources of food for the Fremont, but it also had a spiritual significance. As the bison was a vital part of Plains Indian life, the sheep may have played a similar part to the Anasazi, Pueblo, and Fremont cultures of the southwest deserts. Their descendants, the Pueblo, Ute, Piute, and others, had stories and legends revolving around some of the animals portrayed in many panels. The snake wound across the bottom of the panel as the symbol of continuity and possibly wisdom. The snake shape and the tracks it leaves in the sand are symbolic, she explained.

"Seems like the snake has played a similar role in Western cultures as well. Just think back to good old Adam and Eve," Mida said. "The serpent symbolizes evil and mystery."

Ev added, "Didn't it also symbolize sexual potency? I mean, the shape . . ."

Mida ignored Ev's question. She was too wrapped up in lecturing him on what she knew. She spent literally hundreds of hours doing research on creation myths and symbols, such as they were looking at. She knew the Native American legends but had studied African and other cultures as well. Whenever she tried to explain this information, she met with polite interest, which usually was short-lived. She looked at Ev to see if his interest was still there. He seemed to be attentive but wasn't saying anything. He was still thinking about snakes.

Mida continued, "The placement of the drawings and juxtaposition have meaning as well. Notice the snake is at the bottom and the sheep stands high in the upper corner. The hand outline is woven throughout. This probably meant the person doing the drawing was traveling and offering help to the sheep and expecting help from the sheep in return. The snake provided the continuity with ancestors of the person. This was a sort of prayer, just like many religious people would offer today to their creator. Certain themes seem to stay the same as long as humans have walked the Earth."

"But this is all just conjecture. Is there really any way to know?"

"As much conjecture as the fact that wind deposited this sand and the sand came from a mountain range that no longer exists."

"But we can scientifically prove those things. Your paintings are from a pretty nonscientific thing—thoughts from the human mind."

"Yes, and that is what I love about all this," exclaimed Mida, her voice rising. "We are dealing with an evolving thought process of these people. They had a tough life. They struggled just like we do with trying to figure out who we are, where we came from. They needed assistance from a higher source, just like we do today. Or at least a lot of us.

"Their spirits played a big part of their lives," she continued. "Early humans couldn't control nature, so they tried to appease it and then they worshiped and idolized it. Their relationship with the gods was to use them to impose some type of moral values. They tried to order their existence and give some meaning to phenomenon they couldn't otherwise explain.

"As a first step in cultural evolution, people needed to define what was good and bad, right and wrong. They had to define ethical codes, what we call morality. This differed greatly between cultures. In some cultures, for example, infanticide was considered acceptable as a way of population control. Some cultures defined what was acceptable murder and what was unacceptable killing. There was no agreement on universal standards of morality.

"The early cultures, for example, of my ancestors, both the Norwegians and the Apache, struggled with this. Go far enough back and neither had written languages, so they left a record of these standards on rock. You don't find much rock art of early Norse people but you find a lot here from early aboriginals of this continent. What's the difference?"

She looked at Ev for an answer. He looked puzzled at her, then replied slowly, "Weather? It's dry here and wet in Scandinavia. Type of rocks. Sandstone versus granites? The amount of time since they drew on rocks. Five hundred years versus a couple thousand? You tell me."

"You are perceptive for a college professor."

"But am I right?"

"You figure that out. I don't supply all the answers. Rock art may very well depict what their moral values were and how they prayed to their spirits in the form of animals and totems, often through a holy person. Earlier cultures called them shamans or medicine men or women. Nowadays, we let just anyone go to a seminary and we call them preacher or father. Do they have the special power that the shamans had?"

She put her hand against a painted hand on the rock. Hers was quite a bit larger than the rock hand. "Quite often a single hand outline was the signature of a shaman that people could call upon even after his death. The aboriginal people had various gods, often for different purposes. Think about the person who owned this hand."

Ev brightened as he stood up. He put his hand over the pictograph. "How is that really any different from the worship today of Jesus, Mohammad, Buddha, or Jehovah? Can any one of these really claim to be the one and only? To a strong fundamentalist Bible-thumping Christian, it would be heresy to say Jesus isn't the one and only. But to a strong Koran-thumping Muslim, or a devout Hindu or Buddhist, how do you convince them of that? Each thinks they are right. Look at the wars fought over religious beliefs. It's all a matter of your history and upbringing. We used to have a lot of gods. Now we have selected one and elevated him to the single almighty superpower."

Mida laughed. "Cool down, Rock Boy. This is my expertise. I'm the one lecturing here."

Ev sat back down. Not having strong religious beliefs himself, he had not thought seriously of some of these concepts before. He tried to concentrate on Mida's lecture but kept thinking of the person who painted his or her own hand years ago. Then he thought about the metal in the rock and whether those beings became gods. Or did they have their own gods they worshiped? Although he still watched Mida as she talked and pointed at the rock panel, his attention focused on the cliff a few miles west of them and the metal spaceship, or whatever it was.

Mida was animated as she summarized years of study for her. The early cultures identified their moral laws and taboos, then went through an initiation or rite of passage proving that they understood them. Some rock art panels dealt with that.

"We still have these rites today," Mida explained. I went through a puberty ceremony called the Sunrise Ceremony. It is sacred to young Apache girls. The Sun Dance Ceremony is sacred to the men of the Plains tribes."

She pointed a finger at Ev, saying he probably did something as simple as drinking his first beer, or conquering his first love after his senior prom. Ev mentally recoiled with the truth in that statement. His prom night conquest, then her rejection of him a week later left an emotional scar that he still carried.

Maybe drawing on a rock was such a rite, or maybe it just recorded it. As Mida paced back and forth, she said to think of the literature today that describes different rites. Twain, Dickens, Tolkien, and even Ian Fleming with James Bond. Some rites occur early in youth, some later in life. It's that *aha* moment where you step up to the next level in life's challenges.

Mida finally paused to take a breath. She looked at Ev who was sitting there staring at her with rapt attention. His attention was not at her, though. He was lost in multiple thoughts. His prom night, the spaceship, snakes. His mind was wandering in many directions, none of them directed at Mida.

By now, Ev was not even hearing what she was saying.

She continued on. "Gods and goddesses seem to be a constant through history, just like the snake. Many of the people who drew pictures on rock came from a goddess society. Can you distinguish gender in the people depicted on the panel? I can't tell but I really want to know if these people worshiped goddesses or gods. Were they matrilineal or patrilineal?

"Don't get me started on that whole issue. When we were a matrilineal society, things went much better. When the men took over, things just went to hell in a handbasket. Actually the ideal is neither, but a partnership where both men and women were equal and both vital to survival."

She stopped. She knew she was talking to herself. Ev had a blank stare that indicated he was not here. Neither said a word for several seconds.

Mida sat down next to Ev and looked in his eyes. "What is troubling you, Ev? You are struggling with a big decision. You either discovered it out here or came out here to find some answers. You have come to a conclusion that still bothers you."

Her directness surprised him. "Yes, I came out here interested in the rock. That is my background and my interest. And now I have to put something else involving people into that equation. And I don't know what it all means. I just wish I could tell you more."

Suddenly, Ev stood up. Yes, he thought to himself. Maybe he just might tell her more. He needed to think this through. Just maybe, he mused to himself, she may learn more than she ever wanted to know.

To Mida, he simply said, "My brain hurts. Let's go back."

Ev and Mida sat by the campfire that evening while the stars abducted the darkness of the crystal sky of the southern Utah desert. Both were thinking about what the other said that afternoon. It was about people and about time.

The bottle of Hess Napa Valley Vineyards 86 Cabernet Sauvignon made their meal edible. Mida's boss at the museum gave it to her as a thank you for her work. She brought it with her for a celebration of her soon-to-be-awarded Doctorate of Philosophy in Anthropology.

As he sipped his cup of wine, Ev thought deeply about bringing Mida in on his discovery. He weighed the implications, the significance of sharing this with her. The past ten hours were incredible. He met someone with whom he could really talk to. Talk to about serious, weighty issues but with a fun, challenging excitement. He never met anyone like her. He definitely wanted to learn more about her. She would understand the significance of the discovery. He needed her take on the spiritual side of human nature. And what was more spiritual than the thought of all religions and gods being rendered moot by what he found.

Ev gazed up at Jupiter and Saturn, jousting with the Milky Way for attention. These new gods he may have discovered probably came from up there somewhere. He was still staring straight up when he heard Mida saying, ". . . take you with me. That is, if you are even here on this planet tonight. Mida to Ev, Mida to Ev. Come in please."

Ev was startled back to the present moment. He jerked and spilled his half-full cup of wine on his shoes. "What? I'm sorry, I guess I blanked out on you the last few seconds."

"The last few seconds?" She laughed as she tossed a stick onto the fire. "You have been up there circling Saturn since this afternoon. I was telling you about a meeting in Taos coming up next month on Traditions of Medicine Women of the Four Corners area. I thought you might be interested."

Ev passed right by her comment as he floated back up into the night sky. "Mida, what is your concept of heaven? I mean if you were to die in your sleep tonight, what would you see when you opened your eyes?"

"Is that bottle empty already? Or don't you hold your alcohol well? I hate to think what would happen if I gave you a little Peyote." Mida gave Ev a very puzzled look.

"No, I'm serious." Ev leaned closer to Mida. The fire threw a flickering yellow light on the juniper trees around them and cast a yellow tint on Mida's light brown face. Shadows danced off the trees and onto their faces.

"Well, first of all, I wouldn't be opening my eyes if I were dead. But I, in the form of my spirit, would be welcomed by my ancestors. I would suddenly be aware of my past lives. I guess you could say I would also be greeted by my soul and introduced to all my previous soul mates. This is my own version, which doesn't agree with traditional Apache beliefs—or Norwegian beliefs either since I'm not sure they believed anything other than instant gratification as they plundered northern Europe."

Ev stood up and walked on the other side of the campfire, chased by the smoke of a shifting breeze. He stood there with his hands in his pockets. "I was thinking about my version of heaven.

I always thought that when I died, I would take a celestial tour of Earth. Fly up into the sky and back in time, see the universe form in the Big Bang, watch the galaxies created and the Earth form out of stardust of supernova explosions. I would look down and see the barren rock of Earth and the first rains and the oceans fill with water. Witness the formation of all the rocks we see here. All over the world. The volcanoes filling the skies with clouds that formed rain. The early continents cracking and moving and overriding each other. I would see life begin in the seas, watch the fish crawl out of the oceans, hear the dinosaurs roar and bellow as they wandered the swamps and plains. The mammals take over and the glaciers form and . . . I guess that is the scientist in me. I've never really thought of spirits and souls and gods."

Mida lifted her cup of wine in a toast to Ev. "Well, here is wishing you a safe voyage sometime far into the future after a long and creative life." She took a drink and set her cup down.

"You are fascinated by time but I bet you can't keep time yourself. You are late for class a lot aren't you?" Mida smiled.

"You think you have me pegged just like I thought I had you pegged this afternoon. Yes, yes, and no. Let's agree that I don't really know you and you don't know me."

"That's fine. Yesterday I didn't know you existed and vice versa. There is plenty of time to get to know each other."

"Oh, that was clever," said Ev. "You are interested in time as well. You have to be with your culture and your studies of history."

"Yeah. In my Apache tradition, the shamans, the medicine spirits, have abilities we cannot even imagine. I think they do move in time. Their spirits move in time."

"What do you think about the origin of the first civilizations?" asked Ev, quickly changing the subject.

"Well, gee, where do I start on a simple question like that?" mocked Mida. "Wanna narrow that one down a little?"

"I mean, what spark created that curiosity or whatever that led the early people to form cultures, languages, society, civilization? Animals don't worry about those things you mentioned earlier, about the tribal stuff and the rites of passage and our mortality.

What separated humans from the nonhumans? And when did it happen?"

Mida took a deep breath as she poured another cup of wine. "Well, first of all, I don't believe we are civilized. Advanced technology, sure. But there is more to success and progress than the type of gadgets we make to use energy. We are great at knowing things, at knowledge and facts. But polite and respectful behavior? An understanding of how we fit in with all other forms of life? No.

"All forms of life have some type of culture. Herd animals certainly have something that acts like a group consciousness. Ever watch a flock of birds as they wheel and turn in unison? Perfection that is guided how? There is intelligence out there that is not limited to humans.

"To become civilized," she continued, "at least the way I define it, we need a transformation of a person's very being. A wisdom tradition. Something that adds meaning to our comprehension of facts and stuff. Something that goes back to the gods and goddesses and how they created life and what they expected that life to do.

"What caused the spark of intelligence that took us from the stone age to where we are now? About the sixth century BC, powerful figures like Plato, Buddha, Lao Tzu, and Confucius, as well as the early Jewish prophets, all tried to explain our origins and our meanings. Did you ever think about why all that occurred about the same time, separated by half a world?" Mida furrowed her forehead as she plunged on, not letting Ev even think about her question. She knew he was so lost in his thoughts, he probably wasn't really listening. "After that, science took over by explaining our origins as well as our destiny in scientific terms. I think we lost something after that.

"Technology has taken us backward from our spiritual development. My ancestors had a better connection with nature than most of the contemporary Western traditions. Yours did too, but you have to go further back, before science took over."

Ev stirred. He looked at Mida to stop her while he formulated his thoughts. Finally he spoke.

"Don't knock science. It has done a lot. And I don't think your Apache ancestors lived a perfect life either. Does the bloodthirsty warfare of many aboriginal tribes demonstrate civilization as you wish to define it?"

"I didn't say it was perfect. And no, they didn't epitomize civilization. As I define it. We haven't reached perfection yet and that is my point. No one has achieved perfection. We have to look to the spirits and goddesses for that."

Ev thought about her last sentence. Maybe he found evidence of that perfect being that came to Earth a long time ago. Maybe that was the first and only civilization on earth. He looked at Mida, who was still talking.

"Sometimes I think we are two separate species—*Homo technologicus* and *Homo naturalus*. We are advancing in science at the price of our ability to live in and with nature. Is that a sign of civilization? My interest in history is not to learn facts. I want to go back and figure out what led us to make the decisions we have made. What made us into what and who we are."

Mida looked up in the eastern sky. "Do you realize how many cultures and individuals seriously think that we evolved from a civilization from out there?" She pointed by a nod of her head.

"Some traditions seriously think it was from the star cluster Pleiades. Why do they zero in on that group of stars? Why not Andromeda or the Big Dipper or Cygnus and the Northern Cross?" She pointed in the northern sky to the summer triangle, just showing above the horizon. "See the triangle? Famous stars. I learned them by different names, but you call them Vega, Altair, and Deneb. Deneb is in the tail of the swan and is flying one way while Altair is in the head of the eagle and is flying the opposite way. Why didn't we come from one of those big birds? That would give a new meaning to birdbrain, wouldn't it?" She smiled and looked at Ev but he once again seemed lost in the stars.

"Is such a thing beyond possibility? I won't make fun of anyone who thinks that. I also don't make fun of those who believe we were created from the earth. We sprang up from a cave or hot spring or other sacred place. Maybe we inherently know our ancestors did in fact come up out of the sea and turn gills into lungs."

Ev leaned closer to Mida and said softly, "What do you think? Earlier today, you said you have spiritual powers, like a shaman or medicine man. Do you have some insight into this?"

"I have some powers, but a lot of people do. You do. You may not realize it. And it's medicine woman as well as medicine man. Most people put no thought or energy into it. It is a sense that most people ignore. Just like someone who has their leg in a cast for months. They lose the ability to use those muscles. Use it or lose it. And we are losing it. What do I believe? I don't know. While in this body, on this earth, at this time, I don't know and doubt if I ever will. But I am looking for some hints from our ancestors. They are pretty tight-lipped about all that."

Ev pondered the idea that he had these powers but didn't know it. He let the silence build as he and Mida stared at the flames of the campfire. An occasional pop sent sparks flying from a large piece of pinyon. Finally, Ev blurted out, "Could there have been some type of advanced intelligent life millions of years ago?" He seemed to be asking himself as much as Mida. "There certainly has been time, geologically speaking, for things to happen. It doesn't require untold millions of years for life to advance from dinosaurs to humans. It really doesn't."

"No, and I'm sorry to say, my spiritual awareness doesn't quite go back that far. I have been in touch with some of my ancestors a few generations back, spiritually so to speak, but a few hundred years, not a few million. I like to think I am open-minded and anything is possible. I have enough other things I am curious about and I guess that doesn't rank high on my list of priorities. You raise interesting points that I doubt if you or I will ever be able to know. At least in this life."

Ev just stared at the fire for another minute. "I'm intrigued by quantum physics, although I'm damned if I really understand it."

"Who does understand it? And what brought that up?" replied Mida with a scowl. She was concerned where Ev was leading, if anywhere. Something serious was troubling Ev and he was meandering through a long maze to get to some answer. She was on a witness stand being grilled and his shooting star questions were starting to worry her. She felt like she had been speaking to herself, in front of an audience that was in another world.

"Well, time is supposedly a dimension, just like up and down and sideways. Could you understand the third dimension if you lived in a two-dimensional world? Of course not. Then how can we understand the fourth dimension called time when we haven't been able to master it or move in it?"

We are back to time again, thought Mida. "We do move in it. That's what I'm trying to say. Some of us move better than others. Your problem is you have a tremendous left brain. You don't focus on the spiritual side that time lives in. I tend to be more right-brained. I may see the dimension of time better, or at least differently than you do. I am thinking of the human side of all you are talking about. Yes, I would love to go back in time like you, but I would be looking more into the thoughts, the beliefs of not only people but of all life-forms. Understanding the science would be nice, but I would be trying to tap into the energy created by the dinosaurs, the palm trees, the furry little mammals trying to keep from being eaten by *T. rex*. How did the early people form cultures, languages, religions? Remember, we covered this already."

"Gods, goddesses, patriarchs, matriarchs," mimicked Ev.

"More relevant to us than Wingate sandstone, Colorado uplift, Uncompahgre, and Ancestral Rockies," shot back Mida.

"No, not more relevant. Just as relevant because the landscape where we chose to wander determined who we were and how we formed cultures. Compare the Piute struggling in the harsh desert of Nevada with the Columbia River tribes living in the resource rich luxury of the Pacific Northwest. Richness and wealth hinges on the natural resources of the place you live."

"Okay, they are both important. It is the partnership model I was talking about this afternoon. Male, female; physics, metaphysics; left brain, right brain; yin and yang. Just like a marriage takes the best and worst of each of the participants. Nothing is all one way or another. It is the joining of the best and worst, the balancing, the melding. All this goes into creating the life force, the spiritual power that is what defines our own heavens and hells."

Ev started to speak but hesitated. Mida tensed up. She stared at him as he stretched his legs and put his hands on his knees. She immediately knew he had made the decision that had been tormenting him.

"Okay, Spirit Woman, you want union of two divergent beings? I have just the offer for you. But you will have to wait until tomorrow. After a good night's sleep, you will accompany me to a discovery I made two days ago. This discovery will turn your beliefs and spirit powers on their heads. You will never be the same after that. Guaranteed."

Ev emptied the last of the wine into his cup and set the bottle down in the sand near the edge of the fire.

"Well, you sure left me clear-minded. I will sleep well, knowing that you think you will change my life tomorrow. You can't tell me now?"

"I am going to take you on a two hour hike. And I will show you something I found. And it is something that you cannot even guess now and will have a hard time comprehending tomorrow. Sleep tight."

Without even waiting for Mida to respond, Ev got up, grabbed Mida's hand, and shook it. He then lifted it to his lips and gave it a light kiss. "Good night, Alameda," he said as he drained the last of his wine and then disappeared into the darkness.

Mida looked into the flickering fire, then looked up at the bright light called Jupiter. She thought to herself, "I have no idea what just happened, but I do believe him. My life has just changed." She lifted her metal cup and drank the last sip of wine.

Mida—May 15, 1998

The strangest thing happened. Early afternoon, two Air Force jets buzzed me. They roared out of the west, skimming cliff tops, right over me, then did a climb straight up to clear the cliffs of the Waterpocket. Scared the hell out of me, then they were gone. Right after they passed, all the birds quit singing, no noise from anything except my heart still thumping. Then goose bumps covered my arms and legs. I had a crawly sensation over all my skin. Something happened, and I don't know what it was, but it affected me in a way I've not seen before. Different than my vision quest and different from White Eagle's peyote rituals. I had to sit down and recover for a while. Of course, the car was still high-centered in this rock jumble they call a road. I couldn't get it off, but an angel passed by later (a Park Service employee on her day off) and got me clear. I was so shaken, I camped the first level spot I came to.

Took a nap, and when I awoke, I remembered Mom telling me about the day John Kennedy was killed. She had a vision that scared her. She says it changed her life. She became much more involved in trying to change things. She knew all the good things happening had disappeared. Look what happened. Vietnam, the race riots, the trouble on the rez. But I spent the evening not thinking about the rez or even Mom or Dad. I couldn't get out of my mind the Norwegian side of things. My ancestors not in Minnesota but in northern Europe. I hardly ever think of that side of the family, but it was very clear in my mind. I saw the stone houses, the fjords, the howling winds off the sea. It's as if I was seeing the world through their eyes. How else could I envision something I've never seen before? Was one of their spirits visiting me?

Whatever happens, I think I date it from today. Things have changed. What? What?

Mida—May 17, 1998

Talk about premonitions! Yes, something changed. I thought having the car die on me yesterday was the big event. It was the means to something else. I met Ev. He didn't come riding on a white horse, but pedaling a bicycle of all things. Like a couple days ago with the Park Service angel. What is it with bicycles out here?

Tonight was one of the strangest nights ever. That's after an afternoon that I thought was strange, but nothing compared to this. Couple of glasses of wine and a campfire discussion that has me reeling. Can't sleep but can't write coherent thoughts either. Ev is a hunk of a geology professor from Durango. He is weirded out big time. Something is bothering him (maybe the jets spooked him too). He had this strange discussion that was leading in circles and loop-de-loops. I think he had me on trial for something and I think maybe I passed. Good or bad? Have to wait and see. It was not a come-on and I don't believe it was romantic. If he intended it to be romantic, this guy has a lot to learn about what turns a girl on! That's why I feel safe with him, but more importantly(!), I feel he and I are destined to be together. What is happening to me?

Went for a walk this afternoon and the talk from both of us was strictly academic. You think a guy meets a girl out in the middle of nowhere and it's all a prelude to a bed quest. Not from Ev. This guy is like a little boy. He is cute, intelligent, shy, even goofy, but he is as solid as this rock out here. I call him Rock Boy, which I think he hates. So I will keep calling him that! Keeps him frazzled. He keeps staring at my legs and my boobs, thinking I don't notice, yet he has made nothing resembling a pass at me. Why? Maybe he is gay? No, don't think so. This has been one of the strangest days in my life and I can't get down my thoughts. I sit here and stare at the paper, thinking of what has this guy doofussed up. I know tomorrow will change everything. I know he decided to include me in his big discovery but won't give me a clue what that is. In a way, it scares me, but I also think it is more important than either of us can imagine.

THREE

Two Makes a Conspiracy

*Sit down before fact like a little child and be
prepared to give up every preconceived notion,
follow humbly to wherever and
whatever Abyss nature leads,
or you shall learn nothing.*

—*T. H. Huxley*

Perplexity is the beginning of knowledge.

—*Kahlil Gibran*

Ev sat by the cold black ashes of the campfire, watching the
eastern sky brighten from a faint blue glow to a golden sunrise.
After a restless night, he couldn't go back to sleep, so he got up and
watched the stars fade to daylight. As soon as he finished his sparse
breakfast, he rifled through Mida's cooler and food box for the
makings of a lunch. He was out of food himself since he expected
to be on his way home by now. Mida's food supply was simple, but
at least it existed. This minor bit of theft didn't bother him. He had
already mentally melded their partnership, so he rationalized they
might as well start sharing more than knowledge. Besides, he was
hungry.

Listening to the oncoming flock of pinyon jays chattering in their morning commute, Ev heard a stirring in Mida's tent that seemed to take forever to produce anything. Finally, as the last straggling jay flapped overhead, there was a slow methodical zipping sound, first of a sleeping bag, then eventually of the tent flap. Mida stuck her head out and looked around. Her hair was sticking in all directions, like a cartoon character who stuck her finger in a light socket. He still found her very attractive, but he could not hold back a laugh as he stared at her. She threw a slipper at him as she emerged from the tent.

"What are you looking at?" she rasped. "And what are you laughing at?" She tried to get her tongue working properly but seemed to be having trouble.

"I was sitting here, wondering if Mida is not short for Alameda but instead was a nickname your brothers gave you. Is it actually short for some long-winded Apache word that means 'she who snores like a wild boar'? You sure kept me awake snoring."

"Thank you very much for such a thoughtful comment. And good morning to you too." She was wearing the familiar plain baggy sweatshirt and sweatpants. She unfolded from the tent like a butterfly coming out of a cocoon, barefoot and unsmiling. "I heard you going through my food box. I hope you found something to your liking."

"I was hungry and I figure I earned it listening to you overnight." Ev was not sure how she would take his teasing, but he plunged ahead anyway. He always felt more adventuresome in the morning.

"Listen," Mida cautioned with a stare that frightened Ev, "that is a secret between you and me. Besides my brothers, there are very few men who have slept close enough to me to know my little secret. I do not respond well to wine, a trait common to both sides of my family. And I am sure a gentleman like you will never find any occasion in the future to ever again comment in any way, shape, or form on this little secret. Isn't that right, Everett?"

He didn't like the way she pronounced the word *Everett*, especially with her teeth clenched. He also noticed a total lack of any sense of humor from her.

"All right," he said as he backed off, figuratively and physically. "I hope you slept well and are ready to share my secret."

"Well, now that I am your partner in crime, do you mind letting me in on just what this earth shaking secret is? But hold that thought, I have to go behind a tree first. This isn't the movies and I have to answer a call."

Ev watched her as she shuffled off toward a large boulder. She turned to look at him staring at her. She picked up a small rock and tossed it at him. It fell far short of Ev. "I don't need an audience if you don't mind," she growled at him.

"And you throw like a girl," he shot back as he got up and walked toward her tent. He picked up the slipper she had thrown at him earlier and laid it by the door of her tent. He also took his comb from his back pocket and laid it on the slipper. He was pressing his luck.

It was nearly nine o'clock by the time Mida was dressed and ready to hike. She spent the time pressing Ev for details on what his secret was but he would only repeat that he was taking her for a little hike. She picked away at a poppy-seed muffin like a bird testing seeds at a feeder. She made a concoction of orange juice and cranberry juice to drink, a combination he found absolutely revolting. Finally, after throwing a few packages of peanuts and dried fruit in her pack, she announced she was ready.

"Will you at least tell me where we are headed?" she queried him. "Do I need to take my camera or anything else?"

Ev raised his eyebrows. A camera was something he hadn't even thought about in the shock and surprise of his discovery. He usually took lots of pictures for his classes but not on this trip. "What kind of camera do you have?" he asked hesitatingly.

"Just an old Pentax," she replied. "What does that matter?"

"I'm not sure I want pictures that someone else has to develop."

"What is this, a dead body or something criminal?" Mida asked as she leaned over to tighten her bootlaces.

"No, I just haven't thought all this through. That's why I need you to help me. I simply found something that I don't want to describe to you until you see it. Just trust me. Let's walk for a couple hours and then you will see what it's all about."

"A couple hours? I thought this was a little hike."

"Two hours, one way. That is if we walk fast with no looking for rock art. Please. I can't describe it and I don't want to try right now. It won't hurt you or scare you or anything like that." He wasn't sure about the "scare you" part of that last sentence. It scared him. "Let's not take the camera yet," he added as an afterthought.

"Yet? That means we will be going back?"

"Yeah. I'm sure of that." Ev started walking.

As Mida followed him down the hill, she looked back at the camp. She felt a sudden and sharp sense that someone was watching. She often saw things other people didn't. As she surveyed the camp, she saw nothing unusual. 'Yet,' she thought to herself.

Ev easily retraced his steps of a few days ago. In many areas, he could follow his old footprints when they crossed dirt or sand. He needed to be more careful about leaving tracks, he thought. He would follow a rockier route on the way back. Even though people rarely came to this area, he didn't want to make an obvious trail. He expected to be making several more trips to this remote little canyon.

After half an hour, Mida wanted to sit down and rest. She still had a slight headache from the wine. She sighed as she took a drink of water. "Even if you won't tell me what it is you are taking me halfway around the world to see, can you at least tell me how you found it? Did you know it was here?"

"I just stumbled on it by accident. I was exploring. Just wandering, looking for whatever serendipity I could find." Pointing to a small drainage to their right, he said, "Just up that little draw is a panel of rock art. We can go up there later. Not much different than the one we saw yesterday."

"Is your discovery a serendipity?" she asked as he stood up and gave her a look that told her it was time to move again.

"You will be the judge of that. I wouldn't use that word, though."

They continued on in silence. Mida thought about what he had discovered. She kept coming back to the idea he found a mummy or skeleton. Maybe a Spanish conquistador with a bag of gold or treasure map. She envisioned the large metal helmet and remains of a silver-decorated saddle.

Or maybe it was a cliff dwelling perfectly intact. No, there wouldn't be one all by itself in this setting. And surely, you couldn't hide something like that from the air. There had to be air traffic over this area even as remote as it seemed. And compared to some parts of Utah, it wasn't all that remote. The highway was not very many miles away and much of this area could be seen from the road.

Mida asked Ev again if it was an artifact. He said she would have to wait and see. Giving up in silent exasperation, she started humming a song that her father had written. She could never remember the words correctly, so she was satisfied with humming. Ev wouldn't respond satisfactorily to any of her questions, so she quit talking to him.

It was late morning when they finally came down a cleft in the canyon wall and rounded a curve in the Wingate cliff. Ev half-expected to see a solid cliff with no metal protruding. This was so weird, he thought. Maybe he had dreamed or hallucinated the whole thing. He told Mida to stand still for a minute, then he edged forward to where he could see the cliff base. Sure enough, the silver object was there, a little dulled by his red dirt but obvious as a pigeon on a statue.

"Okay," he said as he stood in front of Mida. "I want to recreate for you how I discovered it."

"Aren't you getting a little melodramatic? Just show it to me."

"Let me do this my way. I was standing right here. I want you to close your eyes and walk over to me."

Mida closed her eyes after a quick frown at Ev and held them tightly shut. She then shuffled the ten feet to stand by him. He turned her so she was facing the cliff. He felt her muscles tense in anticipation.

"It was about this time of day and I was standing here. I heard a couple jets fly over very low as they created a sonic boom. Scared the hell out of me."

"I remember that. Couple days ago. They scared me too. I was on the road in the Park. They flew right over my head."

Ev continued, "As I watched them scream away from here, I heard a rockfall from the cliff right in front of you. When I looked up at the cliff, I saw rocks falling down. Then near where they landed, I noticed another small rockfall near the bottom of the cliff. Now I want you to open your eyes. This is what I saw."

Mida opened her eyes without saying anything. She scanned the scene in front of her. It looked much like what she had been seeing all day. Then she spotted the object. She didn't say anything. She just stared, frowned, twisted her face, and puckered her lips. She looked at Ev with a questioning expression. He waited for her to say something, but silence was all he heard. She continued to stare at the cliff, obviously trying to figure out what she was seeing.

"I had a strange feeling when I heard the sonic boom. Now I know why. Can I go up and get a closer look?" she asked. It made Ev think of a little girl asking her father if she could go up to the cage and see the lion or tiger close up.

"Let's go," he calmly replied. He was still awed by it but was more frightened of it now than when he first saw it. He remembered the initial impact it had on him. Now he felt a kind of pride of ownership, yet he wondered if she would understand all the implications. Was she the person to share this secret with after all? Had he misjudged her?

She eagerly clambered up to the object. Cautiously touching it as if it were a child's magical toy, she slowly ran her hand over the metal. She even put her face up against it, coming away with a tint of red on her cheeks. Still not saying anything, she walked to the nearest boulder and sat down on it. Then she stared at the cliff. She closed her eyes, still not saying a word. Ev anxiously waited for her to say something more, but he did not want to speak first.

Finally, she opened her eyes, stood up, and said something in Apache.

Waiting for an interpretation, which didn't come, Ev finally asked, "What was that you just said?"

"Just an Apache prayer. 'O Great Spirit, whose voice I hear in the winds and whose breath gives life to all the world, hear me! I am small and weak, I need your strength and wisdom. Let me learn the lessons you have hidden in every leaf and rock.'"

"Saying a prayer was the last thing I thought of," mumbled Ev. "Did you make that up?"

"No, I try and read a different prayer each morning. I'm not religious but I do consider myself very spiritual. I thank the Great Spirit for everything good that happens and ask guidance in most things I don't understand. Well, whatever I believe," Mida carefully thought as she spoke, "has now been turned upside down."

Suddenly her voice and composure changed as she turned around to face Ev. "How could you have kept this to yourself the past few days? How could you have been so calm and not told me about this?" She was almost yelling. "You were toying with me. What did you expect me to do? Do you know what this means? Does anyone else know? Oh my gosh, there are so many questions." Her arms were flailing as if she were trying to fly.

"You wanna say another prayer? Maybe one to calm down? Let's just sit down and talk about this."

"Let me do one thing first," she asked as she reached over and touched Ev on the shoulder. "I want to go up to it by myself and see what I can feel. Without your energy field close by. I almost sensed something when I put my head against it a while ago. I can see and feel the energy around some people and some things. I can't explain the science of it, but it is real. Give me a few minutes by myself."

"Maybe I will go sit in the shade and make up a prayer of my own," said Ev. Not a bad idea, he thought. He might actually be looking at what turned out to be a god. He sat down on the sand, leaning up against a sandstone boulder and started looking through his pack. He was hungry.

Mida leaned with her face against the metal. She caressed the metal again, then the glass. She tried to look inside, but most of the time, she had her eyes closed. Part of the time, she hummed what sounded like a chant.

After five minutes, Mida came over to Ev and sat down next to him. "I sensed something in there. An intelligence. Is this thing as old as the rock surrounding it?"

"Yeah, it's sandstone. The rock is old. The entire Wingate formation is thought to be from about 195 million to 230 million years old. Where the ship is, is probably about 200 million years old plus or minus a few million." Ev felt goose bumps as he realized he had just said this out loud to another person for the first time.

"And you said the Wingate was wind deposited. This was an ancient dry desert for millions of years? You think it took millions of years to bury this thing? What do we call this thing?"

Her last question caught him a little off guard. "Well, I have been thinking of it as a ship. A spaceship. What else can you call it? We could give it a name, like Maude or Phil."

"Oh, get real. Phil the spaceship." Mida rolled her eyes.

"Well, call it what you want. And no, I imagine it was covered in a very short time. Even though it took millions of years to create the cliff as we see it, and remember, about half of the cliff is still buried where we are right here. It was like the Sahara is today. The winds shifted back and forth and the sand slowly built up. It is hard to fathom something like that, especially the time involved. It could have been buried in one day by a strong storm. Then uncovered hundreds of years later. Then buried again and back and forth for millions of years. There is no way to know."

Ev started tapping at a boulder next to him with his rock pick. "These time scales are hard to imagine for us. It's like trying to imagine coming back to the Sahara Desert in a few million years and finding it a tropical rainforest with occasional outcrops of sandstone, which today are moving sand dunes in the middle of a desert the size of the United States.

"You need to understand the geology of this to get the full perspective," he continued. "This whole area of the Colorado Plateau has been up and down, so to speak, for literally millions, maybe billions of years. From the Paleozoic through the Tertiary, even almost up to the modern times, this area was under oceans, part of estuaries, covered by meandering streams and swamps, then was uplifted just a little so it was desert, covered by sands. Up and down, under and above." He realized suddenly that he was standing up waving his rock pick around in the air. He sheepishly sat back down.

"During a lot of that time, this very spot was pretty close to the equator. Continental drift has moved us quite a bit north over time.

"Some of these formations are hard to date since they don't have fossils. The Wingate is one. We can't be exact about its age. But it covered a vast amount of time. The bottom line is this was part of a vast sea of sand that stretched across Utah and into Colorado and south into Arizona for a very long time. It's like the Gulf of Mexico being deep water now, but then uplifting to form a dry desert, then a swampy area, and on it goes."

"Everett, dear," Mida said slowly, "you are lecturing again. This isn't the time for another lecture on geology."

"Well, excuse me. You need to know this stuff to understand what happened here. I know this and I teach it and it still staggers me. It is nothing short of a miracle on a grand scale. At one time, or maybe more than one, we had a huge mountain range, on a scale of the Himalayas, rise up from a level plain, then erode down to nothing, then rise up again. People talk of putting their feet on solid earth. Well, this here earth is as unsolid as a piece of ice on a stove top. Things are constantly changing and moving. We don't see it because it is so slow. Our entire lifetime is like one frame of a motion picture. One part in billions and billions. It shows us nothing of what was before and what will come after, but it's all we have." He was lecturing still. He set the pick down and folded his hands in his lap and just smiled at Mida.

Mida thought for a minute, then replied, "Well, the rocks may be a miracle, but what we are seeing is a miracle in its own league. First of all, what is it? And where did it come from? How did it get here? Most importantly, who was in it and what happened to them?"

Ev waited for her to catch her breath, then added, "I hope those are all rhetorical questions. I certainly don't have any answers."

Mida continued as if she hadn't even heard Ev. "If they were here, right here where we sit, then where else were they and what did they do while they were here? Are they still in there? Maybe it was unmanned. Maybe it is recent and burrowed into the rock when it landed."

"No, it didn't burrow into the rock." Ev sounded exasperated. "It could be a probe, like we sent to Mars. But you said you sensed something."

"I did sense an intelligence. I can't tell if it was in there now or just made the thing. There can't be anything still alive in there, but then again, maybe there is some form of suspended animation where they just put themselves into a deep hibernation for a few million years, awaiting the day sunlight activates a wake up response."

"Oh, great!" Ev almost shouted as he jerked upright. "I uncovered that window three days ago and sunlight has entered the thing. What do you sense and how strong is it?"

"Well, I didn't see any googly eyes or antennas staring at me through the window, so we are okay for now anyway. I'd like to come back at night to look inside the window. I couldn't see a thing in there with all this sunlight."

"Neither could I," answered Ev. "Now I'm not sure I want to look very closely."

They sat there, mesmerized by the object in the cliff. Mida broke the silence, talking to herself more than Ev. "I want to review some of the aboriginal myths and stories. Most cultures had creation myths, just like the Christians had Adam and Eve."

She looked up at Ev. "Remember yesterday I mentioned that some people have their ancestors coming from outside the earth, like the Pleiades. Some have them coming from within the earth. We are looking at a scenario that could accommodate both ideas. Think about that. Crawling out of a buried spaceship that came from outer space."

"But two hundred million years is a long time to have been wandering around waiting to create intelligent civilizations."

"Look outside the envelope, rock head. Don't limit your thinking. We have just discovered something that voids everything we've ever learned. Maybe it has voided science and its laws as we know them. There are no longer any rules. Let your imagination go to the stars."

"Don't think I haven't thought of a million different scenarios the past few days. This has been twisting my mind into knots. I'm glad you stumbled along so I had someone to share this with."

"Now this makes sense why you have been acting so weird yesterday and last night. I was really starting to wonder about your sanity. Besides, maybe I didn't stumble along. Maybe I am one of them!" She jumped toward Ev with her arms extended. When Ev didn't react, she sat back down. "Well, you have had a few days to think about it. I need a few days myself. There really is no hurry. After all, she has been here for two hundred million years. Can there be any leeway on that time?"

"A few million years, but what's a million here and there? The only way I know to date it for sure is to go back in time, but I haven't seen very many textbooks on how to do that. Wouldn't do any good anyway since I doubt they have a calendar posted on the wall."

"Surely there are tests like carbon dating or something like that that scientists use to date things like this."

"Well," Ev drawled, "first of all, there really aren't things like this. You might call this unique. Sure, there are several tests. Carbon dating wouldn't work here. It's too old and you need something that was alive. This may have been alive, but not like we are used to. We need a piece of it, then we need someone we could trust to use their expensive laboratory tools to date it. We don't just sneak in a piece of metal that is two hundred million years old and not have some scientist raise his eyebrows just a little."

"Okay." Mida took charge. "You want to know what this is, how it got here, what it's made of, where it came from. I want to know what they were like, what they believed, and how they influenced life on earth, especially people. You are the scientist here and you need to think of a plan of action. I guess for now we need to keep this secret, but surely we have to bring in someone else. Agreed?"

"I took that vow to myself a few days ago and now here you are. For now, yes, I agree. And don't forget—you know about research and plans of action. Do you think you get a PhD by passing some little multiple-choice test?

"I have thought about what would happen if the authorities found this. The authorities. I sound like some mobster or outlaw saying that. But I don't think we can trust a person in any position of power. There are so many vested interests in politics, religion, science that would be ousted from their little power kingdoms if knowledge of this got out."

Mida gritted her teeth as she thought about Ev's last reply. "I think you are a little paranoid. But maybe not. Think how many people honestly believe that aliens frequent Roswell. Or that our government is hiding spaceships in southern Nevada. Site something or other. What would be the public reaction if Jacques Cousteau found this huge whirlpool in the Bermuda Triangle? With a magnetic or electronic force that broke his instruments. How many discoveries have been hidden from us? Remember the ending of that movie about the lost ark? The ark was crated up and lost in the huge cavern of a warehouse. Hiding the discovery of ours could be about as significant as hiding the Ark of the Covenant."

"First," Ev said slowly, "I think you watch too many movies. Second, you are just as paranoid as me, you know that?"

Mida looked at the cliff, then back at Ev. "So how do we keep this a secret, yet answer the questions we want answered?"

"Well, first of all, we need to erase our tracks as we go back," Ev said as he looked down at the clear tracks they made in the red soil. "We need to take different routes when we come back. We need to decide on how often we come back and where we park and how we get here. Repetitions of any kind draw attention. Then we need to camouflage this red flag so it can't be seen by innocent eyes.

Most important for me now, I need to go home and think about a million thoughts on what to do next."

"Why do we need to keep coming back? What can we do? You plan to poke a hole in it and crawl in?"

"I don't know. You got any ideas?"

"You've had a chance to think. I haven't. I guess I want to study up on the different creation myths to see if any of them give us any kind of clue on origins of life. Similarities in stories can tell us something. So many cultures have flood stories, there has to be something they are based on. Melting of glaciers in the last ice age for instance raised sea levels and there is your source of floodwaters. I don't know how that will help, but I can't think of anything else right now."

"Well, you need to keep in mind this thing is embedded in rock two hundred million years old. When did humans or human-like creatures start reasoning? Two million years at the most? I don't think there is a match there. How does a two-million-year-old remember something two hundred million years old?" Ev raised his eyebrows and looked seriously at Mida.

Mida looked at Ev with that same questioning look she gave before. Neither said a word for several seconds. "I don't need to leave yet so I want to get more into my own intuitions. I can spend more time here getting a better feel for just what I do sense when I touch this thing."

Ev stood up and walked over to the cliff. "Well, I really do have to go home. I suggest we try and chip away a little more rock today. Then I'd like to come back tonight with a flashlight and look in the window. You said you wanted to do that, too."

"I planned a few days in this area. I need to do what I originally intended before you changed my life and showed me this thing. But I will come back once or twice before I leave." Mida looked at her watch, thinking about dates and what she had scheduled.

"Let's pile up some rocks in front of this so it is hidden in case someone happens to walk by here. Normally Wingate cliffs do not have much rubble at the bottom. We are lucky since there is enough talus and rubble against this cliff that it wouldn't seem out of place. Can you do that yourself?"

"The idea doesn't appeal to me, but I think if we start a pile and take it up to the metal, then I can add a few more on top to hide the thing before I leave."

"That sounds like a good start of a plan for now." Ev picked up his hammer a few minutes before and started tapping at the edge of the rock. "Let's uncover a little more of that window so we can get a better look tonight. But I'm not in a big hurry to let in a whole lot of sunlight just in case there is a light alarm sitting on a table next to a sleeping alien."

Mida looked at Ev, then punched him on the arm.

"What the hell did you do that for? That hurt," grumbled Ev as he glared at Mida.

"You are going to leave me alone here tomorrow. You come rescue me, knowing about this all the time. Then you don't tell me a thing about this, testing me and evaluating me. Then you tease me with a big secret and tell me you are going to change my life. Now you have changed my life, and you just up and walk out and leave me. You sure are a real sensitive guy for someone else's feelings."

"Well, what else do you expect me to do, sunshine? You want to come home with me so I don't leave you out here. I should have been back today. I'll probably have the police out looking for me if I don't show up back at work. I can go back to the house I am staying in and tell the owner, 'Oh, by the way, I found a puppy dog, but since you don't allow dogs, I brought back a girl instead.' I think you'd enjoy being with me more than being alone out here."

"Don't be so sure about that." Mida glared at him as she stood up and started walking in circles. "Just what do you expect me to do? Go back to the rez? Can you just go back to Durango and pretend this didn't happen? You think I am going to come up and move in with you? Do you? Really?"

"Well, we might as well move in with each other. I cannot walk away from this and you cannot either. And I get a feeling this isn't going to be over anytime soon. You want to move to Torrey and sell rocks to tourists?"

"Boy, I've heard some pretty lame come-ons from guys. This takes the cake."

Ev fingered his rock pick, moving it to his left hand. "I may have only known you for a day, but I am a pretty good judge of character. Especially when that character is trapped in the wilderness. I thought a long time before I invited you in on this."

"Oh, you had a real long time all right. What, almost six hours? And most of that time you were talking like some crazed desert prophet sitting around a campfire talking in riddles."

"You are hooked and you know it. You are also too proud to admit you are loving this. You wouldn't have even come to camp with just any old guy. You judged me just as much as I judged you. You deny that?" With that, he swung his pick in the air and strutted over to the cliff and began to chip the rock at the edge of the window. He was very careful to not hit the metal or the glass.

Mida tossed her head back and looked at the cliff top. She stood there with her hands first on her hips, then with her arms crossed. Her life had indeed changed and she didn't know for the worse or the better. Who was this guy who had come into her life like a sledgehammer? Had she fallen for him? She, who had been so aloof to most guys, wasn't even sure what love was. She had been too busy getting her career on track, whatever that career was. She loved her father, only to be abandoned by him by death before she was even a teenager. After that, she withdrew from her carefree tomboy existence to become silent, serious, and studious.

She walked in a circle, then sat down and started looking through her pack. She pulled out a bag of dried apricots and started nibbling away, more from nervousness rather than hunger.

As Ev hammered away at the rock, he realized he was taking out his frustration at the hard red sandstone. He didn't know what was happening. He found someone to share his discovery with. That's what he wanted. But was she the right person? Did he have anything in common with her?

Ev was never comfortable with most girls. He would rather read a good book or go hiking than go to a party or social gathering. He never allowed himself to get serious or even very close to a girl after his high school steady dumped him. He occasionally dated in Durango, but he wouldn't let himself get serious about anyone. Now Mida comes along, and after only a couple days, he was thinking differently about her than anyone since high school. Could they really be meant for each other? She seemed to think all this was meant to be.

Ev made a little progress with uncovering the window, but the shape of the object was curving deeper into the rock. He was afraid to hit the rock very hard, but the rock that needed to come off was getting thicker. He needed a chisel. The rock on the other side of the opening was thinner, so he started tapping on that side. It wouldn't gain him anything other than make the whole thing more obvious. Suddenly, as a small flake of rock fell off, he noticed a marking on the metal. It was dark colored and looked like writing.

"Hey, look at this!" he called to Mida, who was still sitting absentmindedly watching him. Her mind was sorting through many questions. She jumped, coming back to consciousness. "What?" she asked.

"Come over here. I found something."

She jumped up, spilling her bag of apricots. She hurried over, seeing what he was looking at.

She looked at the lettering. "If it says USS *Enterprise*, I'm leaving."

"It can't be English," he said as he chipped off another small piece of rock. A full two letters came into view. They weren't very large, maybe three inches high at the most. They reminded him of Greek letters.

"Well, they named their vessels just like we do," Mida mused. "Look at that. 'Phil' in a language two hundred million years old. Look closely at the letters. They don't look painted on. They look like they are a part of the metal."

"Might not be a name. Could say something like 'radioactive, stay away' or 'stand back, waste dump.'"

Mida started laughing. "Or 'government property, one-thousand-dollar fine for tampering.'"

Both put their faces almost against the metal, touching each other. Ev diverted his eyes to Mida's. Mida stared into his eyes. They backed off; Mida reached over and grabbed Ev by the hand causing him to drop the hammer. She slowly put her arms around him and leaned her face up against his. She gave him a tentative kiss, then accepted a not-so-tentative embrace from him.

"Damn," she said as she suddenly backed away. Tears started to well in her brown eyes.

"Oh, now what?" cried Ev. "Women. You come on to me and then I react like any red-blooded man. What do you want?"

"Oh, you goofball. Don't you see what is happening? Here we are with the biggest discovery of all time, with a million secrets waiting to be answered, and we can't get past the basic animal instincts of being human. I don't want to complicate this. We have to stay focused. Don't you see? This is exactly what I am interested in. The emotional, the spiritual side of life. You are interested in the science side of things. The two have to go hand in hand. The yin and yang. The Tao. The partnership."

"You complicated it. You grabbed me. You kissed me. And now you blame me?"

"No, I don't blame you. It just happened. That is what I don't understand. I didn't ask for it. You didn't do anything to cause it. It just happened. Don't you wonder why? What caused it? Fate? Chemistry? What is it?"

"You expect me to know?" questioned Ev as he sat down on the sandy ground. "You just accept some things. Just because you are a doctor of philosophy, you don't have to philosophize everything. We are nothing but animals with big brains and opposable thumbs. Hidden deep in those brains are electrical impulses that pull human lips and other body parts together like big fleshy magnets. What the hell do I know?"

Mida laughed and cried at the same time as she fell down on him. She pinned him to the ground as he fell limp.

"I'm not doing anything and I am being attacked," he stoically sputtered as she rolled onto him laughing. They just lay there laughing and holding each other, finally rolling over and lying on their backs looking at the sky.

FOUR

A Night under the Cliff

Not until we are lost do we begin
to understand ourselves.

—Henry David Thoreau

"Would you tell me please which
way I ought to go from here?"
"That depends a good deal on where
you want to go to," said the cat.
"I don't much care where," said Alice.
"Then it doesn't matter which
way you go" said the cat.

—Lewis Carroll

Ev AND MIDA started almost immediately on their return to the cliff after their long hike back to base camp. They hardly spoke on either trip. Exhausted, arriving at the cliff as the last photons of sunlight bounced weakly off the highest clouds, they sat down amid their silence. Ev didn't start his customary evening campfire, nor did Mida unroll her sleeping bag. Neither had brought a real backpack, but they managed to tie their sleeping bags to their daypacks. They each carried a flashlight with extra batteries.

Ev seemed to be sitting awkwardly next to a stranger. He didn't dare go over to her and put his arm around her. This afternoon was just a breakdown of her iron stoicism. Too bad he thought. He felt a very strong attraction to her. But she still remained an enigma. Actually, he realized, he had only known this woman for less than forty-eight hours. The past few days distorted time for him. If he had not come on this trip, he would have spent another weekend biking around Durango or renting a video, or even spending the night with Elaine. Time really was relative. So were space and people as well.

As they stared hypnotically at the darkening star-painted sky, they both saw a shooting star streak straight from the Big Dipper to Gemini.

Ev exclaimed. "Wow. That must be a sign, huh?"

Mida slowly said, "Yes, it is." She thought indeed it was a sign and it told her many things. The Chinese held the Big Dipper significant. It collected chi from all other stars since it rotated throughout the year, collecting energy from all directions of the universe in its cup. A shooting star from the Dipper meant something special. The direction as it came out of the Dipper meant how the energy would affect the viewer. She smiled since the direction was toward them.

"It is time to go see what we can see," Mida said. She kept her thoughts about the Big Dipper to herself.

They both got up hesitantly and walked over to the cliff. They edged up to the window. Mida grabbed Ev's hand. "Let us share our strength. We join together the best of both worlds. Science and spirit. Man and woman. Into the unknown." With that, she reached over and kissed him again, then pointed her flashlight into the window and turned on the switch. Ev did the same, not saying a word.

The window was tinted and did not allow much light to shine through. What they could see was huge, or so it seemed. There was a wall about 10 feet on the other side of the room. The floor had a red tint to it. They could make out a black stripe down the middle that was about a foot wide. At the edge of their vision, there was a table or counter in the middle of the room, but they really couldn't tell.

There may have been an end to the wall, like a doorway, but they just couldn't get the light to penetrate that far. The wall was smooth with no switches, cabinets, alcoves, or anything else on it. They spent only a few minutes staring, like two kids sneaking a look through the crack in a circus tent. Mida pulled a sketch pad out of her pack and tried to draw, describing in words every detail they agreed on. She asked Ev to shine his light on her drawing pad, which he did.

"Let's turn off the light and see if there is any reaction from in there," said Ev, thinking of Mida's earlier comment about some form of light activated response. They switched the lights off.

"Look at that. What does it mean?" Mida said as she saw a faint glow from the ceiling.

Ev had a hard time seeing it. "Are you sure it isn't just afterglow in your eye? Remember when you look at a bright light like a window, then close your eyes? You see an image on your retina. A good physics experiment. Same thing with different colors."

"No," Mida said. "I am seeing a definite glow. It has changed from yellow to red. Now it is fading away to blue. Can't you see it?"

"I'm not sure. I think maybe, but it might be my own eyes. Wait, you are right. I don't see it when I look up at the sky," he said as he craned his neck upward.

"Oh, Ev, I sense something powerful in there. Or that was in there. I can't tell, but there is or was an energy there that I have never felt before. I can't describe it, but I feel something that scares me. Not in a fear type of scare, but as in something more powerful than we can imagine."

"Well, duh! Yeah! Do you think some dinosaur whipped this thing together in the middle of a desert? Yes, something powerful built this and put it here. Only not powerful enough to take it home. Or maybe left it here for some reason. For us to discover?"

"We need to give this a name. This is becoming very personal with me and I can't just call it a ship or our discovery. Phil won't do either."

"Since you are the right-brained creative intellect here, I will leave that up to you, but I will exercise veto power. It has to be a name I can pronounce and not one of those Apache tongue twisters. I guess it needs to be some code word so we can discuss it without worrying about anyone hearing us."

"Let's call this Orion. I always liked that name and Orion is my favorite constellation. Our people called him the Great Spirit Hunter, although I won't even try to pronounce the name in our language for you."

"Okay. As long as you refer to it as Orion and not its Apache name." Ev looked at the western horizon as the Gemini twins were disappearing below the trees. The sky Orion he was familiar with would not be visible again until later in the fall.

"I know. Orion has many mysteries. Here is one more."

Ev accidentally flipped on his flashlight switch, causing Mida to jump as the light shone in her eyes.

"Sorry about that. Are we done window peeping? I don't think we can see any more than we have."

"Ev, you didn't swing the light toward the window just now, did you?"

"No, I was facing away from the cliff. Why?"

"I thought I saw a light come from the window right before you blinded me."

"No way. Maybe it reflected off you or something."

Mida edged away from Ev and the cliff. She rubbed her eyes, then looked behind her. "I saw something in the window."

Ev turned around and looked back at the window. It was black. Or maybe blue-black. He was tired and his eyes were starting to burn from sun and wind exposure. But it did seem to him that he saw a flicker of dark blue. It reminded him of electricity. As he stared at the window, he didn't see it any more.

"No," Ev drawled. "I think your eyes are playing tricks on you. I know mine are getting hard to keep open."

"Yeah, I am tired. Mentally and physically. Okay. I am done for now. I will come back tomorrow and spend some time by myself here. Then I will rock it up. As long as you help build up the rocks before you abandon me in the morning."

"Abandon you? You would still be stranded on the road if I hadn't come along."

"And my life would be normal, without this thing haunting me."

"Okay. I will take you back to your car and hit you on the head, and you won't remember a thing. You won't remember this, you won't remember me."

Mida reached over and touched his arm. "Ev, just drop it."

"Listen, I have to leave tomorrow. I'd prefer to stay here. With you. I've only been here a few days, but for some reason, I can't imagine being anywhere else. If I go back to my regular work, this will seem like a dream. And it will seem empty without you." He wondered if she would read anything into his last statement.

"I agree. You, me, and Orion. What a story. Only it doesn't end tomorrow. It just takes a breather. Then what?"

"I guess we try and continue our real lives if we can." Ev walked back over to the cliff and held his hand on the window. It felt warm, warmer than it should after being out of the sun for a couple hours. He started to comment on it, but only said, "This has to sink in. I have to do a lot of thinking. And a lot of research. I just wish I could go to the greatest minds in the world and explain this to them. But we can't, can we?"

"You've thought more about this than me," she replied. "That's your call. I may consult some souls but not what you would call living. I saw and heard some things that I'm sure you didn't. Couldn't. And that's no reflection on you. I think something or someone may try to communicate with me. It sounds crazy, so bear with me on this."

"Concerning this, no one is crazy in anything they do. This whole thing is crazy and all rules are off. You do what you have to and I do what I have to. We just keep it to ourselves. Damn, I wish I could just open a door and go in there right now. Then again, I would be too scared to set foot in there."

"Well, Everett." Mida smiled as she grabbed his hand and led him over to their camp. She was ready to change the subject. "Let's talk. We are bound together now so let's find out who each other is."

Ev suddenly shivered as she said that. Did she mean what he thought she did? No, of course not, he realized. She was right. They did need to talk. They needed to know who was the conspirator with them in this mystery of all mysteries. Their long walk in silence this afternoon meant nothing. Ev decided she wasn't this iron-willed stoic after all. Sometimes silence is necessary. Not now. They spent much of the rest of the night talking.

Ev carefully built a small fire. He scraped a small depression in the sand. He knew how to hike and camp without leaving a trace. He was an Outward Bound instructor and could easily live off the land if he had to. Most of the time, he didn't have to, nor did he want to.

He got their minds off Orion as he explained to Mida about building a fire for heat or for cooking or for just watching. Different wood burns with different qualities, he told her. She sensed another lecture coming on. He said you can smell a juniper or pinyon wood fire a long way off but aspen wood burns without much scent.

Mida said she thought all campfires were the same. She usually built hers small. Her ancestors were experts about survival skills, but that was one thing not passed on to her very well. She camped and hiked a lot as well as Ev but couldn't explain why she did some things and not others.

Mida unrolled her sleeping bag and laid it next to Ev. She lay down on top of it. The night was cool but the breeze was from the east, which meant it was warmer than it would be otherwise for mid-May. "Am I safe lying this close to the fire? I know I am safe lying this close to you. You are still scared of me, aren't you?" She laughed, more like a giggle.

"Yes, you are safe, and no, I am not scared of you. I know your bark is much worse than your bite. You think you are pretty tough and independent but you haven't fooled me. You may be the expert on psychology and sociology and people but I am pretty perceptive myself. I observe a lot of things. Being a geologist, you learn to be patient. Rocks don't talk, but if you give them time, they tell you a lot of things. People aren't that much different."

Ev poked at his fire with a stick. "I've worked a lot with troubled kids. Some of our programs were within shouting distance of right here. That's why I know a lot about this area. These were tough but troubled kids. A trip conducted the right way in a place like this can build confidence in a kid who didn't have any. That's why so many of them played tough. They learned to talk big and brave to survive in their troubled environments. They had to since they lacked the self-esteem and confidence to make it on that. But you have to be careful in dealing with it. Success can turn a kid around but failure can make things worse. I saw a little failure but I was part of success that built my confidence as well as that of the kids.

"This is marvelous therapy. Helping with all that, I learned a lot of practical psychology, not just the theoretical babble. I also know how far you can take people. Some farther than others. I know how to survive in a place like this. I also know a lot about people. So you may think I am just a shy, quiet loner who wants to avoid people. Well, sister, I can take care of myself. I just don't brag about it. And I think you want someone to take care of you but you are too proud to admit it. You may have learned a lot about people through textbooks and on the rez. But you and I know the rez isn't like the rest of the world."

Mida lay there for several minutes staring at the sky. Gemini had disappeared in the west and Aquarius was rising in the east. It was well past midnight. She thought deeply about what Ev just said. She was mad, but she also knew he was right. Ev pegged her pretty well. She rarely opened up to anyone. She did intimidate people. She was different in many ways and she covered herself with a shield that protected her from many dangers.

As they watched the flickering campfire, she thought back to her childhood. The campfire awoke memories of camping with her father and mother in the White Mountains of Arizona. Her father would tell stories about his ancestors and their wanderings in Northern Europe. Her father and mother would then get in arguments about who had better survival skills. Although he tried to defend the Scandinavians, he admired the Apache for their understanding of nature. Mida was confused about the difference of these cultures; all she knew was the Apache way of life since that is where they lived. She wondered what she would have been like if she had grown up in Minnesota with lakes and endless forests. She visited her grandparents near Bemidji only once. She remembered very little of them or their farm. After her father was killed, she shut out that part of her heritage.

She was hurt by her father's death. It happened right before her Sunrise Ceremony. This traditional coming-of-age ceremony for girls was very important for Mida since she was only half-Apache. She wanted to impress her father but also her Apache friends. Without her father to watch, she went through the motions of the ceremony, but it lost a lot of meaning for her.

His death left her bitter and she withdrew and rebelled for several years. Her mother and brothers conferred with the elders how to bring her back to life, but their advice was very traditional. They said that Mida had the strength and courage to return to this life, but it was up to her. The spirit people would carry her back when she had used up her hatred and mistrust. It happened suddenly when she turned sixteen. She went on a vision quest on the summer solstice and never explained to anyone what happened. She came back a new person. She was confident, assured, and assertive and set out immediately on a course to get scholarships, go to college, and help people in general, her people in particular. But deep down inside, she was still lonely and frightened that she might not live up to expectations of her. Most of those expectations were her own. She felt guilty that she focused on the Apache culture and not the European/American culture of her father.

As Mida and Ev sat by the fire, Ev watched her out of the corner of his eye. After a period of silence, he looked at her and asked what she was thinking. She decided what she could share with Ev and slowly began to explain to him some of her history. She said that she had powers that most people did not have but had not tried to develop these spiritual powers. Her mother encouraged her in the tradition of her people, but Mida fought it. Only later in college did she accept her gift, but still felt pulled in too many ways to stay in the traditional path.

Ev asked what kind of powers she was talking about. She said she could read people and had an uncanny ability to know what they needed to be healed, both physically and spiritually. She heard things others did not. She saw light and vibrations in people and things. She was gradually developing that power, but she knew she needed to be careful and go slowly. This was how she knew that Ev had something bothering him.

Mida related to Ev that her father, a musician with a college degree in history, was an activist in the antiwar movement of the 1960s. He met her mother while they were at a peace march in Washington in 1967. Her mother was disturbed by the way her people were being drafted and dying in Vietnam, yet they couldn't come home to the type of life they were fighting for. Her grandfather had done the same thing a generation before, during World War II. So Mida's mother felt she had to do something for her people. The antiwar movement pulled her in like a magnet. She fell in love with Mida's father, married him, then brought him back to the reservation. They did fine there for several years, escaping the mainstream hippie movement and living in their own private commune on the reservation. He formed a band and traveled over much of the southwest. He incorporated native music into his band, but they soon found it hard to stay near the reservation and make a living. A tragic hunting accident in 1981 left her mother widowed and Mida a bitter young girl, lost between two cultures.

She looked at Ev as the firelight flickered on his face. She said, "I am proud and have every right to be. I don't need anyone to take care of me, but when I find someone who is thoughtful and considerate, then I will share more of myself. People are in too much of a hurry to see the life they are leading. You said you are patient. I think you are. And I think you are waiting to find someone you can share a lot with also. Maybe we were meant to be. Remember yesterday I said you were sent to rescue me with my car breakdown. I believe you were. But I can outlast you in patience. And when you prove your worthiness to me, you will learn more than you want. But until then, Rock Boy, you dance carefully with me. Now I want to know more about you. I don't dance with strangers."

"I won't tell you anything if you keep calling me Rock Boy."

Mida smiled at him.

It was Ev's turn to think silently for a while. He unrolled his sleeping bag and laid it next to Mida's. He put a few more sticks on the fire and then lay down. He rifled through his pack, finding an apple to eat. He offered it to Mida but she shook her head no. Instead of staring at the sky, he stared at the cliff. He was earthbound, not cosmic, tonight. "I think we are both stubborn, so heaven help the mule that gets in our way, Spirit Woman. And by the way, you have dimples when you smile that are driving me crazy."

"My father used to call me Dimples," Mida hesitated as she looked at the fire. "But he used a Norwegian phrase that I can never remember. A Viking Apache princess with dimples. I got the words *dimples* and *dumplings* mixed up, so I was always telling people in Norwegian that I had cute dumplings. I was only five then. He laughed so hard when I said that . . ." Her voice broke and she stopped talking.

Ev tried to change the subject quickly. "I was born in Iowa, but we moved to Boulder when I was only two years old. My dad taught physics at the university and my mom was a nurse. The first thing I ever remember was wading in Boulder Creek. We had a cabin up Left Hand Canyon and went there nearly every weekend. That's how I got interested in geology. There were lots of old mines and mine shafts all over the place. I was an only child and Mom and Dad and I spent a lot of time together. We went camping and skiing and lots of outdoorsy type things. I went to CU and got a degree in geology as well as a teaching certificate. Then I went to Golden and got my master's. I wanted to travel, but I just couldn't leave Colorado. I guess I'm in love with the Rockies. There is so much to see and learn right here at our feet. Most people don't pay any attention to what is right in front of them. That's why I wanted to teach. My dad was so good at opening my eyes. Every discussion with him taught me something."

"I thought you had a PhD."

"Yeah, University of Utah, but that's bragging too much for a first date." Ev paused. "Dad died three years ago of a brain tumor. It happened so fast, we didn't know what happened. Mom remarried a few months ago."

Mida noticed that Ev trailed off into silence. She thought how interesting that they had both lost their father, whom they loved dearly. Her mother had never remarried. She sensed that Ev was not happy that his did. This was not uncommon. She wondered if he would get over it and embrace his mother's happiness. It was part of the healing process. Maybe that's why it took Mida several years to get over her father's death. Maybe her mother should have remarried.

But then, no one could have replaced her father and she would probably have been resentful and even more withdrawn. Funny how life plays out, she thought.

Mida found herself continually glancing over at the cliff looking at the window. She looked for a glow or light from within, but all she saw was a reflection of their campfire.

They both knew they would get very little sleep if any that night. They were enjoying just sitting or lying there, watching the stars rotate through the sky, sharing their likes, dislikes, favorites, and other mundane but important things. They talked a little about Orion and what may have happened, but they were more interested in learning about each other. They had a lot in common, yet they differed in a lot of things. Mida, who had spent a lot of energy studying the male and female role in culture, realized that she and Ev fit the models almost perfectly. Ev was scientific, left-brained, detail oriented, not as patient as he claimed, and physical. Mida was intuitive, right-brained, big picture oriented, and patient. She immediately thought of yin and yang. They complemented each other's strengths and balanced the weaknesses. She thought of the partnership model of society rather than the traditional matriarchal and patriarchal models. They were the perfect partners.

Mida woke with a start. An owl was hooting nearby. She didn't know she had fallen asleep, but she was lying up against Ev on his sleeping bag. Ev was awake. He softly said, "Did you hear an owl call your name?"

"How long was I asleep?" asked Mida. Ev didn't answer. "Yes, I did hear an owl. The owl is very special. In the right setting, an owl speaking to you is a good sign. It is my ancestors telling me that I am traveling the right road. They are sending me on my way and I can go with confidence. I think it may also mean that you can leave here in confidence today and we will both be okay. Ev, it's all going to work out right. I know it." She smiled a gentle smile, with a soft emphasis of her dimples. "But we really do need to get going and build up that rock wall."

"In a little while. I am just enjoying the painting of our morning sky. Look at the colors. I watched it from a faint glow, slowly increasing in brightness. Now it is fluorescent orange and changing by the minute. How many people have ever seen such a sight as this? And with such nice company. What were you dreaming?" What he didn't tell Mida was that he spent more time watching her as she lay there asleep. He smiled as he thought about her.

"I don't remember a thing. I was out like a light."

"And no—" Ev stopped abruptly, biting off the word snoring. He quickly looked at Mida, silently apologizing for what he didn't say.

Mida looked into Ev's eyes with a glare which turned into a smirk. She thought for a minute, then very slowly said, "You were very lucky just now. You are allowed one mistake and you had that yesterday. You are down to zero. If you value certain things important to you, I suggest you try and dream what an Apache can do to a sleeping man. And I don't mean anything romantic."

They sat and watched the light increase until the first ray of sunlight broke over the red cliffs to their east. The sun slowly rose as the shadows crept up and over and down the cliffs and draws. Soon the birds increased their songs until it seemed a full symphony. Ev smiled when he heard his first canyon wren.

"You may feel a special message from the owl. When I hear the canyon wren, I feel the world cannot treat me or anyone else wrong. He is saying that life is good."

"She is beautiful, isn't she?" Mida said, smiling at him with a smirk.

"You are amazing," said Ev. "You have this feminine thing down pat. You never crack. To me, I call things he. You almost always respond with she. That has to take some concentration. Very few people do it."

"A matter of priorities," said Mida. "And a mind-set. Your world is male dominated. Mine is female dominated. From my creator on down. My creator is a goddess, yours is a god. I'm swimming upstream, but that's okay with me. We can spend another few nights on that subject."

They ate the few things they brought for breakfast, then packed up to leave. Ev very gently erased all evidence of a fire. He even restored the whole area to where it showed no signs of anyone having been there. Mida watched with interest, even though she had seen her brothers do similar things. Such detail, she thought.

Ev walked over to the cliff, then started piling rocks. Some were already there from the rockfall. He was very careful and selective at which rocks he chose and how he placed them. Mida helped with the smaller rocks. Soon they had a four foot high pile that looked natural. It came to the base of the exposed Orion. He picked a few dozen smaller rocks that would cover the metal and laid them near the pile. He showed Mida how to stack these when she was finished with her work. He even showed her how to throw sand and dirt on the whole thing to make it look like it had been there a long time.

When they were ready to leave, Mida looked at the cliff wall as it undulated like a snake for several hundred feet in the side canyon. "Is anything exposed anywhere else?" she asked as an afterthought.

Ev gave Mida a puzzled expression. "I didn't look. I never even thought about it."

He quickly looked along the cliff wall. "Obviously nothing here on the cliff face. I didn't think to go up on top and look around. That would be the only place there could be anything. Unless this thing is the size of a small town."

"We need to go up there," she nodded to the top of the cliff, "and look around before we leave. This thing could be several city blocks long, couldn't it? Remember the mother ship in that movie about Devils Tower in Wyoming? It was monstrous. Hundreds of feet tall and wide. This thing here couldn't be that big or it would be exposed somewhere else. Then I'm sure someone would have discovered it by now. We need to look anyway."

"I wouldn't exactly take a movie depiction as a standard for spaceships. Or ET. But you are right. We should look around to make sure," Ev replied. "You know, the thing could be huge and we are only seeing the edge.

"You double check the rest of the cliff along here and I will find an easy way up top," Ev said as he started walking back the way they came. Mida looked at him as he walked away from her, then she headed over to the cliff. She walked slowly, crossed to the other side of the narrow canyon, and walked back, past the exposed metal. After circling back to her starting point, she muttered to herself, "Nothing here."

About the time she finished, she heard a noise above her. She looked up and saw Ev peering over the edge. "Find anything?" he yelled.

"Nothing at all. What about you?"

"You better come up here. Go back the way we came and you will see an easy way up just a couple hundred yards down the wash." He was waving his rock pick as he talked. She knew that meant he was excited about something once again. She put on her pack and walked quickly down the wash.

Ev sat cross-legged on the ground by the edge of the cliff when she walked up panting a few minutes later. "What did you find?" Mida asked expectantly.

Ev got up and walked a few yards inland from the cliff edge. He got down on his knees and pulled away a rock at the base of a small bushy juniper tree. "Look at this."

Mida kneeled down next to him and gasped as she saw the shiny metal rod protruding from the ground at the edge of the small tree trunk. The rod was about two inches in diameter and rose out of the ground about six inches. The tree trunk was grown up against it, effectively hiding it. "How in the world did you even find it?" Mida asked in bewilderment.

"Pure unadulterated luck," he replied as he grinned at her. "I saw a green lizard running along the ground and threw a rock at it. I missed of course and I heard a clink when the rock hit the pipe. I never would have seen it otherwise."

"Why were you throwing rocks at a poor little lizard?" Mida scowled in disappointment at him.

"You tell me. I've never done that before in my life. Something wanted me to find that pipe. I looked around and I didn't see anything else. This looks like some type of antenna or something that stuck above everything else."

He started to dig at the base of the pipe. It looked like the same type of metal exposed on the cliff below. It was perfectly smooth and the top was rounded without any seams or other marks. He was able to dig down about two inches before he started hitting the tree roots. The soil was thin, and he hit solid rock about an inch deeper when he tried to dig a few feet away from the pipe.

"Looks like we won't get very far right now." Mida sighed as she felt the exposed pipe. "One more clue that leads to a dead end. Let's go back."

After filling the holes they dug, they started their long hike back. Since they were on the plateau above the canyon they came in on, they took a different route back to camp. Neither spoke as they walked quickly on the flat ground. Ev looked back toward their discovery. He noticed several crows circling overhead. He could swear he heard them call to him. He thought they said 'hurry back.'

As they neared camp, Mida stopped to look at a large piece of petrified wood. "Ev, isn't this pretty? Would you carry this back to camp for me?

Ev stooped down to turn it over. "Use your special powers to levitate it back. That must weigh fifty pounds. I'll get it later. It's a beauty and worth coming back for."

"We find beauty in this," Mida said, running her fingers over the rock. "But I am imagining what it meant for the people who tried to live here a few hundred years ago."

"Or maybe two hundred million years ago," added Ev.

"The scenery is fantastic for us and not for a minute do I take it for granted," Mida said. "Every step takes my breath away and I continually thank my creator for allowing me to see this. But I can't get past the sacredness this must have held for the people who lived here. They had no such thing as the National Park. Or private land. It was all the same to them. No idea of a vacation to enjoy it. There were no weekends or holidays. They carried their world with them. They noticed the rocks, the birds, the very air they breathed. They had to notice."

"But this rock was just another rock," said Ev. "It was different, but all rocks were different from each other. They didn't know this was wood or that the red rocks were sand once upon a time. Why should it matter?"

Mida turned the rock back over and positioned it exactly as it was. "I think it did matter. Their life depended on it. They were part of their environment. They may not have known the science, but they knew the difference. Could we survive as well as they did? I bet you and I together don't see half of what any one of them saw in this one rock."

"I'm not so sure about that. I think both of us are pretty perceptive," Ev said out loud to himself. Then, to Mida, he asked, "What would they have thought if they had discovered what we did?"

"It would really have been quite easy for them," Mida stated matter-of-factly. "They would have taken it as a sign from their creator. They had never seen metal so it meant nothing to them, other than the curiosity of a new kind of rock. They would probably have looked around for smaller pieces in other rocks they could carry with them for some kind of protection or totem. Their only thought would be how it could help them live from day to day. Was it a good sign or bad sign? It might depend on what else was around when they saw it, such as a crow or a rabbit. They made a lot of associations that we would call superstitious or just plain silly. That may be, but it was as important to them as the scientific meaning is to you. That is what intrigues me. Can we ever know the answers to these things?"

"Just maybe we found a Rosetta stone and are on a mission to read it," answered Ev as he took a drink of water. He poured a few drops on the rock and watched as the glistening water made the ancient grains of wood sparkle. "Maybe that it is as simple as wetting a stone to make it come to life. We could be holding the answer in our hand just like this. Not knowing it, we are just throwing away a golden opportunity."

They continued on the short distance back to their camp. As they topped a small rise within view of their vehicles, Ev stopped as he saw another vehicle parked by theirs. "We've got company," he said as he grabbed Mida who was a few steps behind him.

"Not to worry. We have done nothing wrong. We haven't broken any laws by camping there have we?"

"Not that I know of. But I don't like the idea of anyone else even knowing we are here. They haven't seen us yet. Let's drop the sleeping bags behind this rock so that part of it doesn't look suspicious." They undid the bags as they knelt behind a red boulder. Then they stood up and briskly walked down the last few hundred yards to the camp. Mida quickly started babbling something about rattlesnakes and their role in keeping down mice. The conversation was so absurd that Ev couldn't help but burst out laughing. Mida grinned and said, "That's exactly what I was after. You didn't think I had a sense of humor, did you?"

Her ploy worked as the person turned around to look at who was sauntering out of the wasteland toward this camp. He acted surprised and a little embarrassed. They noticed as they got closer that he wore the familiar green of the Forest Service. His truck was white, not the usual green Ev was used to. At least it didn't have the big law enforcement logo.

The ranger introduced himself as he explained he noticed tracks leading off from the road and just drove over to see what was happening. They exchanged small talk, finding out that his name was Wally and he was from the local office in Loa. He was scouting out the road for an upcoming bicycle race. This caught Ev's attention. The race was next weekend and went from the highway to here and on through the Park. Wally was looking for a water stop and checkpoint where they could have a vehicle parked. Ev suggested the top of the rise a few hundred yards to the east. From there, it would be all downhill to the end. He explained that since he was a biker and raced a lot, that made sense to him. Wally liked the idea and said he would probably do that. He wasn't a biker and didn't know some of these minor details.

He didn't ask what Ev and Mida were doing out here. Ev thought that he seemed young and not that familiar with the area. Mida pointed out some interesting things to see further north, the opposite direction of Orion. When Mida commented that she had car trouble and Ev was going to tow her back to town, Wally shyly asked if he could help. He liked to tinker with cars and had rebuilt several engines. He said he worked his way through college by helping at the local Honda/Subaru dealership. It was more as a gopher and not a mechanic, but he learned a lot from the real mechanics. Mida thought this was too good to be true but just replied, "Sure, have a look."

She told him the symptoms and what she had already checked. He looked under the hood and started asking her questions she had never even thought to consider. He tapped and poked and pounded, but the car still wouldn't start. He thought it was a computer problem. He offered to radio in for a tow truck, but Ev said he was going to tow her into Torrey himself.

Wally said, "Wait a minute. I can't reach out of here with my cell phone, but let me drive up the road a mile where I know I can get out and I will call a mechanic I know in Richfield. He might have an idea."

Once again, Mida said, "Sure, go ahead." She liked Wally but was getting tired of him being here. She wanted to be alone, or at least alone with Ev. She surprised herself at how possessive she was.

Wally drove away as Ev and Mida just stared at him. They laughed at how they tried to divert his attention from this spot. While Wally was gone, they agreed they needed to get across to Wally that they might be here more in the future. That way, they had an ally with the local agency who would not be concerned if he saw them here often. They came up with a story of their writing a book about how the geology affected the Fremont culture. They were hiking around here doing research. Sounded good to them, they thought. Wally seemed pleasant and simple enough he should buy it.

When Wally returned a half hour later, he was grinning. "I think I know what it is. Simple vibrations. I think a wire pulled loose down here." He crawled under the truck, not worrying about getting his clean green uniform dirty. He asked Ev to hand him a screwdriver and a wrench. Ev complied quickly. "How about a flashlight?" asked Wally. Ev again complied quickly as he opened his pack and took out the flashlight that was most recently used to see two hundred million years into the past. Ev thought 'if Wally only knew where that light had been.'

"Yep," Wally muttered confidently. He scooted out from under the car, handed the tools to Ev, and said, "Try it now."

Mida got in and turned the key. The car started right up.

Wally stood up, dusting himself off. "Kinda rough bringing a car like this in here. Even if it is four-wheel drive, they aren't built to take this kind of road. Which way did you come in, from Highway 12 or from the Park?"

"The Park," answered Mida, not in the mood for a lecture about driving a car in on the road.

"You might want to go out the other way. The snow is all off the road. Actually, they just graded the road, first time in five years, and the crossing of Tantalus Creek is really good. I understand that most of the time, you don't even want to come down that grade in four-wheel drive. Not nearly as rocky as the other way. You just vibrated loose a wire. Let's just leave it at that. Too complicated to tell you and too hard to show you. Modern technology is great when it works."

Mida just looked at him in mock astonishment. She was sure her mouth was open. She looked at Ev as he started laughing at her. Ev shook hands with Wally and thanked him. He then related why they were here and they would probably be coming back fairly often.

"Don't want to have you see us here all the time and think we are out here growing pot or stealing artifacts or something like that."

"Don't worry about that. We almost never get out here anymore. Don't even have money to buy gas for our trucks, much less get out of the office very often. I doubt if I will even get out here anymore this year after next weekend. Range folks come down here on horseback about once a year, but they stick to the road. Too rough even for cows."

"How about helicopters or something like that?" Ev pressed Wally for more information.

"You kidding? Takes money for that. Fire people are the only ones to fly and not much down here that burns. You could hide a nudist colony down here and no one would know. You're not into that, are you?" Wally laughed as he slid into the driver's seat of his truck.

Ev almost said, "Now that's not a bad idea," but he was stopped by Mida's glare as she read his mind. Ev ended up by meekly mumbling that certain parts of his body might get seriously damaged if they got sunburned.

Mida thanked Wally again and wished him well on his big bike race. Wally drove off down the road into the Park. Mida and Ev watched him until he disappeared in a cloud of red dust.

"I think we have luck on our side," Ev finally spoke as they started settling into camp.

"I don't really believe in luck. I do believe that we are doing the right thing and the spirits are watching over us. I know things are going to fall our way. But I know you and you will swear that we are just plain lucky. Go get our bags and I will make us some lunch."

Ev sauntered back up the hill and returned in a few minutes with the two sleeping bags. Mida made quick work of slapping a piece of sandwich meat between bread. She didn't bother with anything else. Just meat and bread. She opened a bag of chips and set all in front of Ev. He laughed when he realized that was lunch. "Did you have to thumb through a recipe book for this?

You really are a gourmet, aren't you?" he mumbled as he devoured the sandwich.

"I didn't spend eight years in college so I would have to cook as well as have a prestigious job. I will hire the domestic help, not do double duty myself."

"Let me know when you start taking applications. I might apply."

"You can't cook any better than me. You told me so."

"I might learn if the pay is right."

With that, he threw his sleeping bag in his truck, then walked over to his tent and quickly took it down and packed it away. Within five minutes, he had everything in his truck and was silently removing all traces that he was ever there. When he was finished, he came over to Mida and sat next to her. He looked at her like a puppy dog expecting to be petted.

"What will you do without me?" Mida laughed as she stroked his head.

"The same thing you will do without me. Think of me all the time. You will need something to remind you of me. This is the best I can do right now," he said as he handed her one of his business cards. "Afraid it doesn't have my picture on it, but I can draw it on real quick." He grabbed the card back from her and went over to his truck and came back with a pencil. He scribbled a stick figure on the back.

"What a remarkable likeness." she said. "I don't need anything more detailed. Sorry, but I don't have a card right now. And there is no way I can draw as well as you can. Maybe you can draw a portrait of me real quick."

"Well, you better give me something since I don't have a clue how to get in touch with you once I drive away from here."

"Get me something to write on unless you want me to autograph your butt. That might be hard to do with a pencil."

Ev got up grumbling and went to his truck again. He returned with a piece of paper and a pen. "You probably should put your address and phone number on this, but when you are done, I'm ready for the body art."

"Yeah, I'm sure you are, Rock Boy. Not now. Maybe next time. I'm sure I couldn't survive the next few weeks if I got to touch those buns of steel, then have to leave them."

Ev suddenly reached over and hugged her tightly. She returned the hug, along with a long kiss. They remained in the tight embrace for several seconds. She whispered in his ear, "I'm gonna miss you, Everett."

"Me too," he whispered as he got up and walked over to his truck. "I gotta go now. You gonna be okay here?"

"Yeah, even if the car acts up again, I know where to go to get my cell phone to work. I just need to be by myself and think. Plus, there are a few things I came here to do and I still want to do them." She followed him to his truck and shut the door after he slid into the driver's seat. "You drive carefully and I will call you as soon as I get back to Santa Fe."

"Why don't you call when you leave? Make sure your phone does work up there on the hill. I should be home by sundown."

"I won't call tonight, but I will give it a try when I leave. Don't know if that will be tomorrow or the next day."

He held out his hand as he started to drive away. She gently touched it and then dropped back as he pulled away. She stood staring as he hit the main road and followed it out of sight. She heard a honk in the distance as he topped the hill and went down the rocky path back to civilization.

"Rock Boy," she whispered as she held back tears. "What have you done to my life? I had it so planned and now you have left it a shambles. What do I do now?"

May 19

Missed yesterday. In more ways than one. Yesterday really doesn't exist. Where do I begin? Superlatives abound the last few days. The jets the other day really did start a new life for me. They released the energies of something supernatural to be sure, super galactic probably. If not the face, then I at least saw the chariot of God. Someday I can look back on the past few days and be amazed, laugh, cry, shudder, but it will be the beginning of everything. OK, here's what happened . . .

Ev left and boy did he leave me. I can't ever remember feeling this way. Is this the way Mom felt about Daddy? Rock Boy did OK for having his brain tied in knots—I knew something was bothering him—and now he tied mine in knots. How can you fall in love with someone after being together only two days? Is it love? I wouldn't know. But I do know my life changed. Although this is so unbelievable, somehow it feels right. There is something reassuring and familiar about it. I remember how I felt right when I first met Sarah, and found out her mother's maiden name was Peterson, from Thief River Falls, Minnesota—a distant relation to Daddy. I don't understand this discovery, but I know it was meant to happen to me, and evidently Ev as well. When I first looked inside this thing, I felt a pain first in my eyes, then it went through my teeth (yes, my teeth hurt!), then it traveled all the way down to my toes. I could feel it moving. Then settled in my chest. It was a tingling, like right before something turns numb. Right now, I am numb. And reeling. I feel like I am in some teen romance movie. Remain calm, Alameda!

FIVE

✳

Reordering Lives

Living is a form of not being sure,
not knowing what next or how.
The moment you know how,
you begin to die a little.

—Agnes de Mille

Although the myriad things are
many, their order is one.

—Chuang Tzu

AFTER WATCHING Ev drive off, Mida went back to her tent and stretched out on her unrolled sleeping bag. Opening the tent flaps, she lay in the cool breeze. For the first time in many years, she felt unsure, vulnerable, and frightened. She didn't understand why she was feeling the way she did. Her life, which she had struggled so hard to plan and organize, was now turned upside down. Always putting a barrier between her and others, especially men, she now had fallen for a guy she hardly even knew. She had controlled others; she was always in charge. Now she wasn't. She should be happy, satisfied that she found a man she felt comfortable with. Why wasn't she thrilled?

She wanted to just lie there and cry, but she couldn't let down her guard. She was Mida, her father's little Apache princess. The world was dancing the way she wanted, and up until now, with her in charge. Trying to regain her composure, she starting chanting one of the songs her mother taught her. But she quickly choked up and couldn't continue. She stared out of the tent at the blue sky and the red cliffs. Suddenly she broke down and buried her face on her pillow and cried like she hadn't since her father died.

Ev topped the hill that separated the National Forest from the National Park. Lying on the horn in a farewell to Mida, he started down the rocky road into the Park. Mida would continue on with her life and would make this a successful working vacation. He wished he had the power that she seemed to have to focus on whatever she wanted and not be bothered by peripheral issues, such as two-hundred-million-year-old mysteries. He reached into his glove box and picked out a tape. A rollicking collection of Mason Williams quickly got his blood pumping. He turned the volume up high and tapped his foot as he bounced down the road. Looking at the rock outcrops and looming cliffs up ahead, he focused on the explosion of color and texture, matching it to the music. He was able to put his excitement of his discovery behind him, at least for the moment.

When he reached the Visitor Center, he stopped to buy their best topographic map and talk to the ranger about the road access he just used. They locked the gate during the winter at the end of the graveled road at Capitol Wash. He knew that snow closed the road from the Boulder Mountain highway, usually by November. Orion was effectively closed off from any vehicle access for nearly half the year.

He switched from Mason Williams to Mannheim Steamroller as he left the Park and headed through the geologic fantasy world of the Mancos Shale badlands. Most people saw this stretch of real estate as something to get through as quickly as possible. Ev saw it as a lesson in how geology effects man's ability to eke out a living. This Mancos Shale desert was the Black Hole of Calcutta in economic opportunities. A few people lived along the highway near Caineville, but very few. He always wanted to stop and talk to these pioneers and find out more about the type of person who would try and survive on this land. If he wanted isolation from the crowds of civilization, he would certainly pick somewhere else. Although he loved rocks, he also liked to see a few green plants supplementing the rocks. Battleship gray ruled out here—miles of dry and desolate rock and mud deposits of a once vast ocean. Unforgiving. And quite humbling. Battleship shapes also loomed on the horizon as he passed Factory Butte and the other mesas and rock behemoths that reminded him of ships floating on a remote and desolate gray sea.

As he neared Hanksville, he kept repeating the adjective *desolate*. This had to be the most desolate town in America. Anyone desperate enough to live in this god-forsaken-hole-in-the-wall needed help, so he always gave them some business, even if it was only getting a few gallons of gas. He wondered why anyone would live here. They must be escaping something. Or else they were so pathetic and dirt poor, they couldn't move somewhere else. Who could enjoy this? He wouldn't mind the remoteness of an old mining town high in the Colorado Rockies, even with the nine-month-long winters. But this windblown, lifeless expanse of nothing? But then, why did some farmer in Pennsylvania a hundred and fifty years ago leave that lush place to follow a pair of lumbering oxen across a thousand miles of prairie to find some looked for paradise in a distant Oregon? Each person carried a cart load of his own baggage, with experiences and dreams unknown to any but himself. The grass was always greener . . .

He shrugged as he entered the outskirts of Hanksville at midafternoon. Five seconds later, he was in uptown, then downtown. He always felt that every politician in Washington, every corporate CEO, every Broadway producer, and every rich celebrity in America should be honored with spending a full day in downtown Hanksville, Utah. Throw in uptown Hanksville as well as the outskirts. Let them walk the highway, since walking the streets would only get you a better view of the mobile homes, the junked cars and the goats and horses that outnumbered people. See the gritty existence these pilgrims lived. Try to get a customer into the rock shop, the motel, the gas station, or the restaurant nestled in the bowels of a sandstone cliff. Feel the blast of the wind covering you with blowing red and gray sand off the surrounding desert. Taste the summer heat and the winter cold as you listened in vain to hear any familiar sound of civilization that you were used to. Any sound other than the endless wind blowing off the desert, the sound of a lonely dog barking, or a footloose chicken clucking as she wandered down the road. Watch the loneliness and absence of crowds as you compared the daily struggle of life in DC or New York or LA. This wilderness out here in downtown Hanksville was much easier to cope with than the crowds and the noise and the congestion in the downtown or uptown of these other places. Whenever Ev ended up in these metropolises, which was as seldom as he could, he thought only of how quickly he could get back to a rocky desolate place like southern Utah. Just different kinds of wilderness, he mused.

He stopped at the rock shop and talked gems with the crusty cowboy owner. He bought a four-dollar agate dug up somewhere in the San Rafael Swell an hour north of Hanksville. He exchanged stories about how to find the best agates and how they were formed. He chuckled to himself as he envisioned Mida calling this guy Rock Boy. He stopped at the gas station to fill his thirsty Toyota, then pulled into the Cave Restaurant. That wasn't its name, but it's all he ever called it. He ordered the special and relaxed, waiting for the lone waitress to serve him. She sauntered over, chewing gum, hair a dirty blond and still sandblown. He was the only customer. What did she do for fun when she got off work? Maybe she was the daughter of the cowboy rock hound. Not much promise for her life if she stayed here. But then, was there really much promise anywhere else? He wished he could talk to Mida about this philosophic subject. Young people in small towns always wanted to leave their lonely boring place for the adventure of the big cities. Did they ever really find happiness? You carry it with you was what Mida would probably say. He joked with the waitress about how busy she was, left a big tip, and smiled as he walked out, fingering his new agate.

After Mida exhausted her tears, she wiped her eyes and looked around to see if anyone witnessed her bout of weakness. She held onto the tent flap and slowly stepped out into the bright sunlight. A canyon wren warbled a lonely song in an adjacent canyon. Now Mida thought of Ev and almost started to cry again. She kept blinking and trying to organize herself, but all she could think of was Orion and Ev and her father and the fact she had cried like a baby. She got out her map and started planning her afternoon. She had come here for a purpose and she always did what she planned. That was who she was. All she could see on the map were lines. They had no meaning to her.

Mida hiked back to the pictograph panel Ev told her about on the way to Orion. She didn't want to go to Orion yet, so this would get her back into her research. She took a different route and came to the cliff from above. She walked several hundred yards along the cliff top before finding a way down to the bottom. Even then, she had to jump about six feet to get to the bottom. It was a good thing she knew an alternate way back, she realized, as she hit the sandy wash and rolled. She would never get back up the way she came. It hit her as she stood up that this was a pretty stupid thing to do. She could have broken a leg or sprained an ankle with that jump. Ev, somewhere in the middle of the Utah desert, would not be able to come help her. She had been hopping off rocks for years, most of the time by herself miles from any help. Why was she worrying about this now?

She walked over to the panel and sat in front of it, looking at it closely. Taking several pictures, she pulled out her sketch pad and started drawing. Most of the symbols were familiar to her, but there was one she found interesting. She had seen many hands outlined with paint. There was one on this panel with only three fingers plus the thumb. What had happened to the right ring finger? Was the person born without it, or did he lose it in some accident? Or cut it off in a rage of grief? Or was this some practical joker who purposely splattered paint with the finger held back by someone else? As with a lot of questions with rock art like this, she would never know. Nor would anyone else.

Just as she finished her sketch, a pair of ravens flew overhead complaining loudly to the world. They soared in a wide circle, then disappeared behind the cliff. Two seconds later, an eagle soared into view, with the ravens following close behind, dive-bombing him. Laughing, she said, "Hang in there, big guy." She watched the aerial circus until all three eventually disappeared over the horizon back toward her camp. Her culture and that of many other tribes found deep spiritual meaning in animals. Eagles meant power and prestige. Ravens were not tricksters like their friend coyote, but they signified knowledge and creation. She knew that seeing these birds meant something, but she was not able to focus on what it was.

A honking and a screech of tires on the highway several miles above her brought her back to the present. "This place is getting too crowded for me," she said, getting up and putting away her pad and pencil.

Mida headed back down the draw toward camp but veered away from the main route to Orion. She scrambled back up the cliff the first chance she found, but banged up her knee, climbing up the last ledge. The blood trickled down her leg, staining the sandstone with a couple drops. "My sacrifice to the goddess of Wingate. Protect me, great one. I shed my life force for you." It was only a little darker red than the color of the rock. For some reason, it made her think of Ev.

Ev headed south out of Hanksville on Utah Highway 95, a 120-mile stretch of exquisite loneliness. The desolation of the gray Mancos Shale brightened visibly into the more colorful, but just as desolate sandstone. Ev brightened with it. Desolate was not the word for this place. That had a negative feeling. This wilderness was remote and isolated but not in a negative way. Yeah, exquisite loneliness was a good description. Some country singer should sing about this desert of exquisite loneliness. The waitress back at the restaurant could lament how she lost her cowboy lover in its expanse of green and white and red. Don't forget the blue of the sky. *Does she even realize the beauty of this place?* he wondered.

The road dropped down into the valley of the big river. First, he crossed the Dirty Devil, saluting it as he always did. He loved the Dirty Devil. It was the Fremont back when it cut through Capitol Reef, but when it combined with the Muddy just outside Hanksville, it became the Dirty Devil. Not by any plan or purpose. It's just that John Wesley Powell saw its mouth when he floated by on the Colorado and named it the Dirty Devil for obvious reasons. He didn't know it was the same river someone else had already named for that intrepid explorer Fremont. So some clever map maker stitched the two rivers together at Hanksville and made it look like a plausible name change. Ev's salute was for Powell, whose insightful observations on western living were ignored by everyone. If our ancestors had listened to him, life in this water-hungry west would have been much different and much more realistic. But his salute was not for Powell's visions but for his accident of symbolically turning the overblown windbag Fremont into the dirty devil he really was. Such wonderful ironies of life passed by most people. But not Ev.

After his salute, he crossed the Colorado on one of only three bridges in the entire state of Utah that crossed this mighty river. There were actually only three more bridges that crossed it in Arizona from Page to Las Vegas. This was a river that didn't want to be seen. Or crossed. It shouldn't be, Ev thought. Just like a sultry, beautiful movie star valuing her privacy, being seen only on her terms by an admiring public, the Colorado valued her privacy in this wilderness of rock sculpture. She wound through a wonderland carved into sandstones of red and white and orange. She created this temple that really should only be viewed from a rubber raft or, as Major Powell dared, a wooden dory. How many drivers who crossed here, or even in Moab or Page, stopped to look down on the flowing water of this great river and say a silent thank you for what it had carved over the millennia? Very few.

Ev glanced behind him, then ahead. There were no other cars. He stopped in the middle of the bridge and looked down at the river that was turning into a lake before his very eyes. Lake Powell. What a travesty, he thought, that this powerful river, now tamed behind that monstrous dam, was now named after John Wesley Powell, the man who discovered the wildness of the river. Ev didn't say any fancy prayer like in Mida's book, but he did say a thank you. And an apology for what man had done in the past one hundred years. What would the inhabitants of Orion think about how we had screwed things up in such a short time? Or were they so advanced that they had long ago destroyed nature and tamed it to their uses?

After a few silent moments with his eyes closed, Ev heard a vehicle coming down the hill behind him, so he continued on across the bridge. The road climbed out of the river valley and onto that marvelous stretch following alongside White Canyon. He put on the David Lanz tape called *Desert Vision*. This tape was meant to be played while driving this stretch of slickrock desert. This scenery should not be viewed without listening to this music. The two were absolutely meant for each other. Ev was flying like an eagle soaring over the canyons as the selection called "Eagles Path" played. He rewound it and played it again and again. Ev and the desert were one.

This was the highway that inspired Edward Abbey to write *The Monkey Wrench Gang*. Ev understood the passion Abbey had for this desert. Ev loved this road and was glad it was built, but it had to be heartbreaking for someone who loved this trackless canyon country before the highway existed. Just like one would feel about Glen Canyon before the dam. Ev was born too late to see either in their pristine glory, so he could only guess the loss. He knew it was immense. Could the intelligence in his hidden discovery understand this loss? They probably had a much greater loss. No matter where he looked, he still thought of that cliff that now belonged in secrecy to him and Mida.

There were no clouds in this brilliant blue sky. There was no pollution. There was no traffic. There was no sign of civilization other than the road he was on. No fences, no power poles, no houses. Nothing but scenery that defined Ev's concept of a prehistoric earth. Ev tried not to think about the Wingate Sandstone but he could only focus on Mida and Orion. He imagined flying like an eagle over this magnificence of God's creation. The eagle turned into Orion. He didn't want this moment to end.

He turned south on Utah 261 toward Mexican Hat. Then a zag toward Bluff and a zig to Aneth. He counted the number of different highways he took to get from Capitol Reef to Durango. It was eight or nine. There was no easy way from point A to B in this country. He crossed the state line into Colorado as the sun sank low in the west. This was home now. Mesa Verde lay hidden to his right as he sped past Towaoc and the ugly casino that kept the Ute Mountain Utes going. Tourists, he sighed. Tourism not only kept the reservation going, it kept Cortez as well as Durango booming. He thought of the canyons between him and Mesa Verde. Part of the reservation, they cradled more ruins and cliff dwellings than the Park did. But virtually no one ever got in there. He usually spent a weekend a year in that jumble of canyons with one of his classes. He had to have a couple guides from the reservation, but that was fine with him. That trip, along with a weeklong field trip into the San Juan's near Silverton, then over to Moab and back down through Mexican Hat, kept his spring Introduction to Geology class full every year. He made his students work, but they loved it. So did he. He had the best job in the world, he thought, as he came down the hill into Durango. He parked in his driveway and sat there for a full five minutes before going inside and collapsing on his sofa.

Mida got back to her tent about the time Ev crossed into Colorado. She didn't even think of him. She thought only of gathering a few sticks for her campfire. Getting in her car, which started right up, she drove up the road to a denser patch of pinyon, where she filled the trunk with branches and sticks. Then, back in camp, she changed into those baggy plain sweatpants and shirt and started a fire. There was still sunlight, but she wanted to just sit and watch the fire as the sun faded behind Boulder Mountain. She picked up her journal, a simple wire-bound lined notepad, and spent an hour writing her thoughts. A distant owl greeted the darkening sky as Mida finished her writing and sat silently, hypnotized by the flickering fire. She would sleep well tonight and if she wanted to snore, then no one on earth would hear her. Laughing, she threw another branch onto the fire. "Good night, Rock Boy. And good night to you too, Father." She looked up to the sky at a jet contrail glowing purple orange from a sun long below her horizon.

Mida awoke refreshed the next morning as the eastern sky was turning a crimson orange. Reddish clouds would lead the way as she headed for Orion. Taking a direct route this time, she didn't worry about leaving tracks. They could be erased when she returned later in the day. With the heat of the summer approaching, she didn't feel it was critical to hide her steps from viewing eyes. There would not be many viewing eyes down here. Or at least, human eyes.

She got to the cliff as clouds started drifting in from the southwest. Usually this time of year was dry, but occasionally a storm would come in from the southwest, previewing later monsoons that would hit in July and August. The wind picked up a little, but any storm activity would probably be several hours away. At least that's what she planned. She usually had a pretty good feeling for major changes in the weather. It was her Apache intuition.

Cautiously stepping up to Orion, she gently caressed the metal. She peered in the window again but saw nothing except her own reflection. After she rested her face against the window, she stood there for the better part of an hour. This was her attempt to connect with the energy that she felt inside the structure. She silently said a few prayers but mostly just tried to keep her mind totally clear. It was a form of meditation, but it was also a way to tap into her intuitive senses.

With closed eyes and her face pressed against the metal, she felt energy pulse through her as she experienced a vision. A stream gurgled soothingly as it fell over rocks. A voice whispered quietly. She couldn't make out any words, but the voice was soothing. Someone was walking through a meadow. It looked like her father, but his back was to her. The vision brightened to a white light, then faded to darkness.

Mida knew someone called her. Hoping it was her father, she prepared herself. She walked back to her pack, reached into it, and pulled out a white deerskin dress she often carried with her. She also pulled out a piece of deer antler from the buck her father killed as his last act on earth. It was a secret; no one knew she had it. Her father never had a chance to carve it, but she carried it as a sacred memento reminding her of his unfinished work. She also was an unfinished work of him. This was what pushed her in her determination to succeed.

She hadn't felt this loneliness since that terrible day in 1981 when her mother told her that her father had been killed. It was a cloudy and cold November day. She was planning to take the coming of age Sunrise Ceremony the next summer. Her father told her he would furnish the deerskins for the ceremony. Her mother and aunt would help her make her dress out of three skins. A fourth would be used for decoration, for her to lie on in her special tent.

Her father did not like to hunt, but he usually got several deer on the reservation each year for venison. He shot the first three deer for her dress and was out with her uncle Samuel to get the last. They had been out all day in the rain, tracking a large buck. Her father wanted a good rack of antlers to carve for her dancing cane for the ceremony. He got off a good shot at the buck across a small canyon. The buck didn't fall but was stumbling along the hillside dragging a front leg. Both Samuel and her father ran down the hill and started crossing the small creek bed to get another shot. Her father made it across and had a clear shot at the deer. He fired and the deer fell in its tracks.

Samuel was carefully stepping across the stream to help when he slipped on a slick boulder. He lost his balance and accidentally pulled the trigger as he fell. The bullet hit her father in the leg, severing an artery. They tried to stop the bleeding but couldn't do it. He bled to death on the hillside. It took until midnight for the rescue crew to get him to the road. Samuel went back the next day and got the deer. He skinned it and tanned the hide, which

Mida used the next year, along with her beautiful white deerskin dress with fringe and tassels. By the time of the ceremony, she had produced all the tears her body was capable of. She didn't cry at all as she spent the three days dancing and going through the ritual that her father never saw.

Mida slipped out of the cutoffs and shirt she was wearing and put on the deerskin dress. Over the years, she had done some major modifications in order to be able to still wear it. It was very short, but she added longer fringe as well as a strip on the sides. She wore it only on special occasions by herself when she wanted to connect spiritually with herself and with her spirit protectors, including her father. This was such an occasion.

After she was in full costume, she took out a bundle of dried grass and lit it, waving the smoke around to purify the air around her. She pulled out a small tube of yellow powder and rubbed it on her forehead. It was pollen and was important in rituals in her life. She then started dancing in place, chanting a Hopi prayer. She was borrowing from several traditions. A true wise person, she believed, recognized the value of connecting with others, including borrowing their beliefs and rituals. She was a half-breed, and this had always set her apart from her mother's people. She considered herself Apache, but a modern one who kept and altered traditions as she saw fit. Any true spiritual being in the twentieth century and beyond had to recognize the universality and timelessness of all peoples, she believed. This did not sit well with some of the elders in her tribe.

When she finished dancing and chanting, she sat down on her other clothes, protecting the white deerskin from getting red dust on it. She sat cross-legged and rocked back and forth for several minutes. Then she got up, took off her dress, and lay on the ground, facing east, bare to the world. She was normally very shy about exposing her body to anyone, but in this setting, she knew she was visible only to the spirits, who didn't care that she was as naked and pure as when she entered the world. This was a way of setting aside all pretensions and claiming humbleness before her creator. When she was done, she got up, dusted herself off, and dressed in her T-shirt and denim shorts and hiking boots. She carefully put away her dress and artifacts.

It was well after noon by the time she finished her rituals. She walked over to the cliff and started piling the rocks the way Ev instructed her. When she was satisfied the metal was completely hidden, she picked up several handfuls of red dirt and threw them all over the rocks. They looked like they had been there a long time. She backed away, erasing her footprints with a juniper branch. As she started to walk away, a clap of thunder broke over Boulder Mountain to the west. She had not even noticed the sky for several hours. It was black and ominous looking. The wind suddenly whirled a cloud of dust around Mida, surrounding her with red.

"If it rains, I get drenched. Not too many other choices," she said out loud to herself. It was a two-hour walk back to camp. Her only thought was stay out of narrow canyons in case of flash floods. She tried to remember how she left camp and could distinctly remember leaving the tent window open, but at least the flap was closed. She couldn't remember about the car window, but she usually closed it and locked the car.

Leaving the side canyon, she started to carefully erase her footprints, but the wind was doing a good job of sandblasting everything. She actually started jogging when she got to the main canyon. She didn't like to jog, but in this case, she made an exception. Rain started to come down gently, then harder. A loud clap of thunder shook the canyon. She looked for some shelter or rock overhang. There was a slight alcove about two hundred yards in front of her on her left, partly hidden by a scraggly juniper. She made it to the cliff and slumped behind the tree and under the rock. This was not a safe place to be, but it certainly was not the highest point around. If only Ev were here to ask about that. She knew he would know the answer about lightning and trees and cliffs. Luckily, the rain was from the southwest and her little alcove faced east. She wasn't getting rained on but feared her sleeping bag in the tent was getting soaked. She sat down against the cliff and watched and listened to the storm spend its fury.

Suddenly, a cluster of lightning flashes lit up the sky in quick succession. The thunder, which came almost immediately after the flashes, echoed ominously on all sides of her. The echoes bounced from canyon to canyon and back again. She thought one strike was almost above Orion. She was right but didn't know it. She also didn't know that right at that time, the overhead glow she saw in the ship the night before became alive. The interior of Orion glowed bright blue, then faded to a greenish yellow. The light flickered and seemed to move throughout the craft. Unseen by any eyes, it danced for several minutes before dying down and finally ended with a pop and total darkness once again.

Small rivulets and cascades of water poured off some of the cliffs as the rain started its journey downhill on the bare rock. The trickle and fall of running water could barely be heard among the splashing of the raindrops. Mida closed her eyes after the echoing thunder died down. The fury of wind and rain continued while Mida again saw visions. She saw a flash of lightning hit the cliff around Orion. The rock exploded, going up in the air and not falling to earth. The entire spaceship rose out of the cliff into the darkening sky. She saw dinosaurs and palm trees where the cliff used to be. Waves of water crashed against a barren sandy shore. Sea gulls flew in formation in all directions. A crimson sunrise and golden sunset were replaced by a triple rainbow. Orion glowed a brilliant blue with light emanating from it in dancing pastel colors, then disappeared in a lightning filled sky.

She opened her eyes. A raven landed in the tree above her and squawked at the blue sky. She looked up and saw the black cloud disappearing over the cliffs to the east. A beautiful complete rainbow touched the bright red cliffs of Capitol Reef. A trickle of water came down the main canyon and a few small waterfalls splashed down side draws but it didn't appear to have been a heavy rain for very long. What did her vision mean about Orion? What was the significance?

She watched the raven as it looked around, cocking its head. When she spoke softly to it, asking it how it was doing, it jumped off the limb and squawked vigorously, circling up over the cliff. It continued to scold her and announce to the world its indignation at being surprised like that. She laughed as it disappeared to the west. To her, the raven was a bringer of life and creation. This was significant to her. She was being recreated and would be a bringer of life herself.

The sun was brilliant now in this lightning-cleansed air. She breathed deeply and looked around her. Her eyesight seemed enhanced as she noticed a clarity and sharpness to every tree and rock. The air almost vibrated with purity. She continued back to camp, not worrying about the footprints she was leaving in the damp soil.

She rounded the last rise and got her first glimpse of the camp. The tent was upended but everything else looked all right. She noticed the open tent window was facing up. She winced. Her sleeping bag and clothes would be drenched. At least the car window was closed. Sunlight glinted off the windshield as the sun approached Boulder Mountain.

She ran to the tent and tipped it upright. The winds had ripped the pegs out of the sandy soil. The weight inside kept it from rolling halfway to Colorado. Carefully unzipping the door, she looked inside. Her sleeping bag was dry, but her clothes bag was drenched. Water puddled on the floor when she tipped the tent upright; water had collected on the wall when it was upended. She took everything out of the tent and draped wet things on the car doors and tree branches. There was still almost an hour of sunlight left, so hopefully things might dry a little, she thought. "Not too bad, considering," she muttered as she reset the tent. She seriously thought about leaving right then, but decided to look around a little more the next morning for more rock art. She would definitely leave the next afternoon. She would be eating juniper berries and cactus fruit if she stayed any longer. She couldn't rifle anyone else's food box like Ev did hers.

She debated with herself all the rest of the night about which route to take home. Durango was only a few miles out of the way from the route she planned to take. "Maybe I could meet Ev in Farmington. No, I don't want to appear anxious to see him. It will only have been a day since he left. We don't have that much to talk about. But he will want to know if I hid Orion. Then again, I could tell him that on the phone. Oh, damn. I'll see what he says when I call him. What if he isn't home? Then I will drive on through."

She read until the light was totally gone, then tried to read by firelight, but decided Abe Lincoln must have had awful eyes if this is the way he read. She was restless all evening, getting up and wandering around, then sitting back down, then getting up again to look at stars. She tried to write a little more in her journal but couldn't keep focused. Finally, she crawled into her dry bag and tried to sleep. She went right to sleep but was awake a half hour later. She tossed and turned all night, waking and catnapping. She didn't dream but couldn't help thinking what her vision meant. If it was in fact a vision.

Mida was up before the sun the next morning, quickly packed her daypack, and headed off into the canyons. This highly focused woman aimlessly wandered, looking for likely spots for rock art or anything else interesting. She did find a couple spots, but nothing new for her research. Or at least anything she was able to think about long enough to form any opinion on. She sketched what she found and wrote a few notes but was just going through the motions. About noon, she wandered back into camp. It was time to leave. She packed up all her gear and drove the few yards to the main dirt road. Stopping her car, she went back and erased her tire tracks and imitated Ev in obliterating all traces of a camp. She felt proud that she was able to fully restore the campsite, probably as well as Ev could have done. She never thought about doing this in the past. There was never any need and besides, most spots she camped were pretty well established as obvious campsites.

She turned left instead of right, the way Ev went. She wanted to see what the other road was like. There was plenty of time to call Ev later and she already knew what the road through the Park was like. As she crossed Tantalus Creek, she noted with pleasant surprise the good quality of the road. It was a little sandy and steep, but she made it okay. As soon as she climbed up out of the bottom, the road became hard packed and almost rock paved. It was basically level until she passed the turnoff to Bowns Reservoir. Then a short climb up to the highway and she was back in civilization. She turned right onto Highway 12 and was soon in Torrey. She thought Torrey seemed a nice quiet little hamlet. She wouldn't mind living in a place like this someday. Not exactly the amenities of Santa Fe or Albuquerque, but it might be nice to rough it away from such things as Walmarts and Olive Garden restaurants. Well, maybe, for a short time. But then a person has to work, so there is the tradeoff. She always had the option to go back to the rez, she concluded. That was home, safe, and comfortable, and her mother and friends were still there.

She gassed up at one of the new gas stations in this growing tourist mecca, stopped at the local restaurant, had a passable Navajo taco, then turned east and, once she reached the Park Visitor Center, retraced Ev's route as far as Hanksville. As she passed the Battleship Buttes, she realized she had not called Ev as she promised. She pulled off the road just outside Hanksville and looked through her planner for his phone number, but hesitated to call him. She really didn't know what to say. Thinking of him was like thinking of some dream. She had never even heard of him the last time she went through this little town and that was only a few days ago. He had changed her life and she had fallen for this guy even though he was basically a stranger to her. Now she was supposed to call him, but she didn't know what to say. Would she stop by and see him if he asked?

She punched in his number and waited while the phone rang. After four rings, an answering machine picked up. She felt relieved, yet disappointed. She slowly said, "Hey, Rock Boy, this is Spirit Woman, and I just wanted to check in." Then Ev came on the line. Breathing heavily, he told her he just got home and heard the phone ringing as he was unlocking the door. He asked her to wait a few seconds for him to catch his breath.

"You mean you're not breathing heavy because it's me? I thought you were in shape and a healthy hunk of a manly specimen, Rock Boy. Can't you run a few feet to answer the phone without getting out of breath?"

"For your information, my answering machine is upstairs and I can't answer the downstairs phone once the machine has picked up. Running upstairs, I slipped and fell, dropping a bag of groceries. Then I stepped on a can of spaghetti and sprained my ankle. You don't need to know what landed on the jumbo-sized jar of peanut butter. Does all that make you feel better?"

"Do you want me to call 911 for you?" wisecracked Mida as she stifled a laugh at the thought of what he just described.

"No, but you can certainly give me a little sympathy. I almost lost my manhood just now because of you. I expected you to call last night. Where are you?"

"I'm in Hanksville on my way home. I forgot to call when I left."

"Are you alone?" Ev asked hesitantly.

"What do you mean am I alone? Of course I am alone. Why wouldn't I be? Did you think I kidnapped some alien from Orion? What kind of dumb question is that?" Mida transferred the phone to her other hand while brushing away a fly buzzing her ear.

"I passed a bicyclist on the way out the road and figured he may have stopped and camped with you. He had packs on his bike and looked like he was ready to rough it for a week. Didn't you see him?" Ev felt silly as he finished giving what he realized was a lame answer.

"No. He didn't come into camp and I didn't go out the way you did. I drove up to the highway and into Torrey. I didn't notice any bicycle tracks. And what are you, my mother? I sure wouldn't bring him home with me if I did see him. And what's it to you if I did? You sound jealous."

"Well, I was worried about you." Ev started rubbing his ankle as he sat down by the phone. "You seemed a little shaky when I left."

"Well, I was tired, and by the way, you did dump a nice huge burden on me, you know?" She wanted to change the subject quickly on this one.

"Did you get Orion covered up okay?" Ev asked anxiously as he wanted to change the subject also.

"Yes. You will have a hard time finding Orion yourself. And for your information, I got caught in a downpour yesterday as I started coming back to camp. A storm blew by and I was trapped out there dodging lightning and torrents of water."

"Well, you obviously made it back okay. Any problems?"

"Other than my tent blowing over and me almost getting my sleeping bag drenched and other than me fearing for my life of being hit by lightning, no, I had no problems." Mida hesitated about telling him about her visions. That type thing should be told in person, if at all, she thought.

"I'm glad you made it. I just hope the thunder didn't vibrate anything loose on our rock pile or on the cliff itself. I don't suppose you went back and checked those?"

"No, it's safe to say I had other things on my mind. I did hike around and find a few more pictographs, but nothing of importance. Now I'm on my way back to try and resume my life, finish my thesis, and find a new roommate. How are you doing?" Mida was trying to finish the conversation and avoid Ev asking her to stop by Durango.

"Other than my little accident here, I guess okay. I'm trying to get ready for the field camp session coming up in a few weeks. I'm having a hard time concentrating, though. I've already been to the library three times looking for books or articles on time travel. I rented a movie last night on time travel. The Jane Seymour one . . ." Ev thought of Mida when he thought of Jane Seymour. He could see himself going back in time and finding Mida, then being jerked forward to never see her again. Then he thought of him going back to Orion's time, finding a beautiful young alien and falling in love with her, being jerked back to find Mida waiting for him. This was all getting pretty silly, he thought.

"You faded out mumbling something. I couldn't understand the last thing you said." Mida looked puzzled as she sensed Ev being distracted. Mida watched as a cattle truck sped by on the highway. She stepped back just in case anything flew out the side.

"Nothing. I'm just having a hard time getting back into a routine, that's all. How long will it take you to get home?"

"Oh, it's still about six or seven hours from here. I think I might stop at a friend's place on the Jicarilla near Cuba. She and I have visited a lot of sites in the Grand Gulch area south of here."

"Grand Gulch is one of my favorite areas." Ev stopped there as if the conversation was over.

Mida was a little surprised. Relieved yet disappointed. *I think we are both pretty tired*, she thought. She said, "Yeah, neat country in there. Well, hey, I gotta get going. I'll drop you an e-mail probably tomorrow or the next day after I get home. You go put your groceries away and a nice hot bath would do you good."

"Thanks for calling. Drive carefully and take care of yourself."

"You too. Bye." She hung up and wondered if the last few days were just a dream. She wished she could go soak in a nice secluded hot spring somewhere, but she didn't know of any close by. She got in the car and headed down into Hanksville. She thought of the Anasazi and Pueblo and any others who may have lived back in these canyons once upon a time. They would not have comprehended speeding down some hard surfaced, smooth path like this at seventy miles per hour.

Ev stood by his phone wondering why he was acting like a teenager again. Mida was able to rattle him and he didn't know why. He thought earlier about asking her to stop by and see him but he totally forget to mention it. Maybe he didn't want to for some subconscious reason. Ev leaned over to rub his ankle again and stopped to look at his groceries scattered over the rug. "Why the hell did I carry the bag up the stairs anyway?" he said to himself. His kitchen was downstairs. Why didn't he set the bag down before running up the stairs? "That woman has me turned inside out," he muttered as he started picking up frozen dinners and canned stews.

May 20

If this wasn't a sacred place before, it is now. As I lay there this afternoon, I had what the Old Testament prophets would have written down as a vision, a talk with God. Then, my version of a burning bush came in the form of lightning hitting the cliff over my head. Only instead of the voice of God, I talked to a raven. Unless God is a raven. Ussen comes in all forms as the elders always told me. My vision also included Daddy. I saw him. I know it had to be a dream, but I was awake. I really did talk to him. He was talking to me. His lips moved but I couldn't hear any sound. I have had visions before, but this was different. I felt like I was either seeing the past or previewing the future. Or both. Or neither. I need to talk to Bluebell. She is the only one I know who I can really share this with. But I can't really tell her the details of this place. She probably knows without me saying anything . . .

I put on Daddy's dress and lay before my ancestors and asked their blessing and their help. I need it. I talked to Raven and I know that she gave me a rebirth. This is the new Mida. What a day. Whatever my plans were, that I spent my life developing, have changed. A new partner, a new mission. I know who the partner is. I am not quite sure what the new mission is. The spirits will guide me. I think they will be found inside Orion . . .

I will somehow have to help Ev because I don't think he will experience what I have already and will experience more of. He will think I am totally weird if I tell him all this. How to deal with that. He is still scared of me. That's the way I want to keep it. I did show some weakness yesterday, though. Shape up, Mida. I am in charge. But what is next?

SIX

A Return to Normal

Take your life in your own hands
and what happens?
A terrible thing: no one to blame.

—*Erica Jong*

From the seed grows a root, then a sprout;
from the sprout the seedling leaves;
from the leaves, the stem . . .
We cannot say that the seed causes the
growth, nor that the soil does.
We can say the potentialities for
growth lie within the seed,
in mysterious life forces, which, when
properly fostered, take on certain forms.

—*M. C. Richards*

MIDA SPENT THE evening and following day with her friend Bluebell on the Jicarilla Reservation in northern New Mexico, southeast of Durango. Bluebell was a traditional medicine woman who had mentored Mida for several seasons on herbal healing and spirituality. They spent their time together comparing herbal remedies and medicinal plants. Mida questioned her about sacred sites and what specifically made them sacred. She explained she had stumbled on a site that contained evidence of ancient ones. There were strong forces in the area, more powerful than she had ever sensed anywhere else, but wondered what would make it sacred versus just a collection of spirits. Or was there a difference? Bluebell knew something significant had changed Mida, but didn't say anything. She would not press for information another person was not ready to give yet.

She could tell, however, that Mida had changed. She knew Mida had faced a force more powerful than Bluebell could even imagine. The older shaman mentioned to Mida that she seemed to have a blue aura around her. She wanted to confer with another mentor of hers before she counseled Mida, but she sensed a power beyond her abilities. This scared Bluebell.

After a long day of sharing stories, Mida invited Bluebell to stay with her in Santa Fe at the upcoming conference. Bluebell gave Mida a blessing as she left. She also gave Mida a silver and turquoise hummingbird pendant. Mida didn't remember telling Bluebell that the hummingbird was her personal totem, symbolizing healing and endurance.

Mida pulled into her driveway in Santa Fe as the sun sank into a bank of purple and pink clouds. She walked into her adobe duplex to find her roommate standing before the hall mirror in tears. Pre-wedding jitters had thrown Sarah into a crisis. "I don't know if Rob loves me. I think he is seeing another woman."

"I've had enough tears and personal crises of my own the past few days," Mida told Sarah as she set down her pack and empty food box. She went over to the doubtful bride, still in her nurse's whites, and hugged her. "Whatever it is, it isn't worth contorting that pretty face. Think a happy thought and tell me what it is."

"Oh, Mida, what do I do?" Sarah sighed as she wiped her eyes. She tearfully told Mida of her discovery that her fiancé, Rob, had taken his attractive legal secretary to New York for a conference.

"Don't you trust him?" Mida looked into Sarah's eyes.

"I thought I did. Now I don't know. He has dated a lot. I know that."

"You don't know that anything happened, do you? You are making a big assumption, aren't you?" Mida frowned at her as if she was scolding a young child. "And did either of you promise to be faithful? Remember this is the nineties. Just because you are true blue, well, you know. Something about breaking old habits." Mida smiled and reached to wipe Sarah's eye.

"What will I do without you?" Sarah sighed as she blew her nose.

"About as well as I'm going to do without you, but you will have someone who will more than take my place. I might even . . . ," she let slip before she realized what she said. She was usually very cautious about sharing such secrets, even with Sarah. But she was as close to Sarah as a sister. Sarah knew Mida better than anyone. She saw more than most people who only saw the reserved, stoic side of Mida. Mida clinched her teeth and held back a grin as she took off her floppy hat.

"Mida!" squealed Sarah as she jumped over to hug her. "Tell me what wonderful person you found out there in the wilderness. Sit down right now and tell me. Everything."

"I can't tell you everything," she hesitated, then smiled again and said, "but all right, I will tell you all you need to know. It looks like you need to focus on your own relationship." Mida plopped herself on the couch and proceeded to tell about Ev and her adventures. She never mentioned anything about Orion but just the facts about Ev had Sarah grinning and forgetting all about her jitters.

After a few minutes of swapping stories about men and what makes them tick (which usually amounted to one thing), Mida looked at her watch and said, "Speaking of Ev, I should call him to let him know I got here. Last I talked to him, he was suffering because of me." She laughed as she explained the grocery bag accident to Sarah. "But no listening in. You may go in the kitchen and prepare me a nice meal since I haven't eaten well for several days."

"I really worry about you once I leave. You can't boil water by yourself. What are you going to do about eating real food?" Sarah loved to cook and had done nearly all the cooking for the past two years they had been roommates.

"Listen." Mida frowned. "I have survived quite well for the twenty-eight years before I met you. And for your information, I can cook. I did a lot of cooking when I was little and you know that. I just have other things I prefer to do. Besides, how can I cook when you hog the kitchen like you do?"

Mida rubbed her eyes, then looked up at Sarah. "I'm not really sure what I will do after you leave. I keep thinking about going back to the rez. Then again, I may end up spending more time—" Mida caught herself thinking of Durango. She was sharing too much right now, even with Sarah. She smiled, but beneath the smile was a shudder of apprehension. Things were moving just too fast, she realized. This was not like her to be acting like a schoolgirl when it came to a man.

Sarah patted Mida on her butt, then disappeared into the kitchen, turning on the radio as Mida picked up the phone and punched in a Durango phone number. Ev answered after the first ring this time. There wasn't much new to discuss since it had only been yesterday since she called him from Hanksville. He had spent the day at the library and on the internet finding information on time travel and UFOs. He laughed as he told her he prepared a list of over one hundred books and magazine articles on time travel and cosmology. Some of these were novels but many were scholarly works on the physics and scientific impossibility of time travel. He even purchased two videos of movies with a theme of time travel and already mailed these to Mida. She warned him he had better not start mailing her the one hundred books.

She mentioned her visit with Bluebell. What she learned from this holy woman could help her with her upcoming search for spirituality relating to the Orion epic as she termed it. She did not tell Ev that she almost told Bluebell about Orion. As she was thinking this, she also realized Bluebell might already know. Mida was getting confused on who already knew what without being told. She wondered what Ev knew about her own thoughts.

She asked if Ev was going to come visit her for the conference. He said his field seminar started a couple days after that and he had to stay home and get ready for it. The course lasted three weeks. He didn't see how he could break loose before that. She whined something about losing her roommate right before the conference and how lonely she was going to be. Ev was surprised by her forwardness on that issue. He didn't say anything, partly for fear of being jumped on, even over the phone, but also for his respect for Mida, who seemed to be at an uncharacteristic weak moment. Ev was sure that Mida was opening up to him like she did with no one else. What was causing each of them to act totally out of character?

He did say that Mida could come up for a few days and help him prepare for his seminar. That thought appealed to her, but she said she wanted to spend as much time with Sarah as possible. Her best friend was getting married, leaving town after the wedding, which was two days before the conference, and she may never see her again. The bride was moving to San Francisco right after the Taos wedding. Ev commented he was sure they would see each other again. Best friends often took precedence over husbands, after the honeymoon of course.

Mida was surprised when Sarah came into the dark living room and said, "I hate to break up this lovely little high school romance, but your dinner is ready, princess." She reached over and took the phone from Mida's hand and whispered in her sexiest voice, "Hi, this is Sarah, the keeper and feeder of Mida. I have slaved at her request to prepare her a lovely meal since she says you ate all her food and she has gone without a decent meal for days. I am going to steal her now. Say goodbye Ev. Nice talking to you." She handed the phone back to Mida, smiled, and quickly slinked back into the kitchen, turning the radio volume up as she walked by it.

Mida laughed as she said she'd better go now. They said goodbyes and she hung up the phone. She was shocked when she looked at the clock and realized she had talked for thirty minutes. It had only seemed like a few.

Mida went into the kitchen and feasted on Sarah's chicken casserole. The two then sat in the dark talking until 1:00 a.m. Mida fell asleep lying on top of her bed, fully clothed.

After he hung up the phone, Ev walked out the door and drove down to the local pizza and beer hangout near the college. It was deserted now that spring classes were out and summer classes not yet begun. He sat by himself as he slowly ate a whole pizza. As he nursed his third glass of dark beer, he tried to think about Mida, but the vision of the red cliff kept coming to mind. He then went to his office and sat down to read a physics book on black holes, quantum mechanics, and time travel. He fell asleep somewhere in chapter 4.

Because of the upcoming field seminar, Ev had to pace himself on what he could read anytime soon. His main goal was to scope out the work he had in front of him and to organize it somehow. It was hard not to get sidetracked and start reading in earnest. When he stopped by his office the next day to catch up, his secretary made him aware of all the minor details of the seminar that were unraveling at this late date. Such as the recent blown engine of one of the twelve-person vans that was a mainstay of the transportation. And the call from a BLM contact who told him about a big rockslide that obliterated a critical piece of road accessing part of the San Rafael Swell field site. And the last-minute cancellation due to illness of the professor who was scheduled to instruct San Juan pyroclastics and volcanism.

Minor details, thought Ev. "If I can deal with two-hundred-million-year-old starships, then I can handle little problems in this current time. I sure wish Mida were here to help me." He quickly sent Mida an e-mail that simply said, "Help me. I am trapped in a time warp. Send food. No money, just food and comfort. Heavy on the comfort." Ev was thinking about Mida more often.

Mida spent the next day working on odds and ends on campus in Albuquerque. She met with her doctoral adviser and agreed on what she hoped were final corrections and modifications to her thesis. Her goal was to have it done by September. She scheduled a meeting with her committee before fall classes started. Then, glad to leave campus just before a thunderstorm rolled over town, she drove back to Santa Fe to her office at the museum. There were several urgent phone messages from her contact at the Ford Foundation. Her proposal for creating an intertribal spirituality traveling display was causing some problems in DC. The display was to become part of the permanent American Indian section of the Smithsonian after its tour in six cities. According to her contact at the foundation, it seemed the Smithsonian standards were a little demanding. Since Mida's standards were very high as well, she knew this was a clash of style and display and nothing more serious.

Mida groaned when she hung up the phone after talking for forty-five minutes with New York. "That display is more than a full-time job, my thesis is a full-time job, my part-time job here at the museum is a full-time job, and now I can't concentrate on any of these because of Rock Boy and his stupid spaceship. Life can't get any more complicated."

It did twenty minutes later when Sarah called and said she just got a call from the reservation clinic. Mida's mother had suffered a mild heart attack and was in the hospital in Alamogordo. She was doing fine and had begged the clinic not to bother Mida, but they thought Mida should know. Actually heart attack was not the word they used, but it amounted to that, although it didn't appear dangerous. Sarah was apologetic when she told Mida, knowing that Mida's life was complicated enough right now. Besides, she knew Denzee Peterson and loved her like her own mother. Mida said she would be right home, and asked if Sarah would like to accompany her on a quick trip to Alamogordo. Sarah said it sounded like Denzee would probably be home before they could even get down there. She would go with Mida as long as they could be back within two days. Sarah was having her own last-minute crises with details of the wedding plans.

Mida quickly checked her backlog of e-mail before she went home. The latest message was from "Rockhead." She erupted laughing. She either hadn't known or didn't remember what Ev's e-mail address was and found it to be just the relief she needed.

She laughed as she read it and quickly sent a reply. "No food. Crisis central here, so no relief. Please, let's just go crawl in Orion and go back to a simpler time. Zoom down here in your time machine and pick me up. Life is crazy. Gotta go on emergency trip to rez. Mom in hospital. OK but interrupts already hectic life. Go eat a dinoburger and quit whining. Love, Mida."

Mida quickly organized her desk, still in a total clutter from being gone for a week, then left a message for her boss telling about her mom and the fact she would be gone for a couple more days. She drove home and packed a few clothes, groaning over the size of the wash she would have when she did get back from this latest trip. Sarah was ready to go and even had food packed for the trip. Mida called the hospital to find out if her mom was still there. The nurse told her they would keep Mrs. Peterson overnight, even though she was throwing a fit, saying she felt fine and didn't need to be there any longer. Mida told her she and a friend were coming down and they would be there in about four hours. The nurse told Mida that visiting hours would nearly be over by the time they got there, so be sure to ask for Nurse Thompson when they arrived.

The nurse continued very businesslike. "I will make sure not to give her a sleeping pill until after you get here. Mrs. Peterson is fully awake to put it mildly and may never get to sleep unless I knock her out. She needs the rest, so I will let you say hi, then I will make sure she gets a good night's sleep. I'll do the same for you if you need it. Then you can take her home tomorrow morning if things look okay. If you need a place to stay, we have a hospitality house next to the hospital. I will save a room for you."

Mida thanked the nurse profusely, then almost dropped the phone into its cradle. She looked at Sarah, then burst into tears. Sarah just hugged her, rocking back and forth, saying nothing. Finally Sarah said they needed to get started. She would take her car; it was a brand-new Lexus, a wedding gift from Rob.

Their trip was quick and uneventful. Once past Albuquerque, Mida ate the fried chicken and potato salad, then traded places with Sarah so she could eat. They were in Alamogordo before dark. Denzee was happy to see both Mida and Sarah, but was embarrassed by her situation. Mida told her about her trip to Utah but did not mention Ev or any other details. She didn't want to throw this new twist into her mom's life at this point. She would ease into it later. Denzee asked Sarah all about her wedding and gave her a few Apache tips about married life. Denzee was a liberated woman and had very modern ideas, some of which weren't all that modern from an Apache standpoint. However, there were still some traditional Apache beliefs, such as belief in witches, which Mida could never quite understand. Very inconsistent she thought to herself.

Mida's brother had been at the hospital earlier to see his mother but already went back to Las Cruces, where he managed an auto parts store. Another brother called earlier, but Denzee talked him out of coming from Arizona. The third brother was in the army in Greenland and hadn't been contacted yet. So, with everything under control, Mida and Sarah settled into the cozy room at the hospitality house. They talked for a few minutes, but were fast asleep before the evening news was over on TV. The special "Bluebell's Apache blend" herbal tea that Mida prepared for both of them did a much better job than a pill in putting them into a restful sleep.

The next morning, Denzee got the all clear from the doctor, with only a mild list of potential life changes she needed to make. The problem was more genetic than life style, but she still needed to do a few things differently. Mida chided her on the exercise part. She had been on her mom's case for years about doing more exercise. Denzee was starting to plump up after being quite trim and petite all her life.

Mida and Sarah spent the rest of the day waiting on Denzee hand and foot, continually ignoring the constant string of objections. They did a thorough cleaning of the house, including cleaning gutters, pulling weeds, and finding years of dust accumulation in out of the way places that no one had seen in decades. It made Mida feel good and made her mom grateful but still embarrassed. It also took Sarah's mind off her worries. Mida even drove into Las Cruces to talk to her brother and buy an exercise bike for her mom. Denzee started to complain when Mida brought the bike into the living room and whimpered something about not using it, but Mida hushed her and told her she would be back in two weeks when her conference was over to make sure she was riding it daily.

Sarah cooked a dinner that made Denzee nod in approval. She said that even Geronimo would think that was cooked by one of his wives. Sarah commented that San Francisco was probably not ready for Apache cuisine, but maybe she would open Geronimo's Diner on Nob Hill. They all laughed as they settled into the comfortable living room for a quiet evening of playing mah-jongg Apache style.

Mida and Sarah left midmorning the next day after a tearful goodbye. Denzee wished Sarah well, apologizing for not being able to attend the wedding. She gave her a wrapped present for the wedding. She giggled as she advised her not to open it during the reception but to wait until she and her new husband were alone. Sarah blushed and Mida scolded her mother in a mock sense of embarrassment. Denzee smiled as she watched the fancy new car drive down the gravel road.

Denzee had done all right with her children she thought, including this informally adopted one. She wasn't sure about her own career, which had started so nontraditionally over thirty years earlier as she marched in demonstrations and traveled the country in the revolutionary protests of the sixties. Her education in journalism was not very well used, she thought, as she reflected on what might have been. If she had taken that job with the Indian News Service, if her young husband hadn't been killed—if, if, if. Too late now, she thought as she shook her head. Her job as stringer for the Albuquerque paper, plus a job with the Alamogordo paper had produced a satisfactory living. Her culture emphasized the future, not the past, she had to keep reminding herself. As she turned to walk back into the house, a chill went through her as she envisioned herself sitting at the base of a red sandstone cliff. A sign said, "Redrock Cultural Center." As she was talking to reporters next to the sign, the vision faded as quickly as it came. It gave her something to think about for days afterward. Mida might understand it, she thought.

Mida and Sarah spent as much time together as they could. Mida was able to concentrate on her work, both at the university and at the museum. She worked out problems to everyone's satisfaction and life returned to a normal hum. Sarah resolved her jitters and slowly erased her presence from the apartment. Mida clenched her teeth every day when she came home wondering what wonderful little trinket or kitchen utensil was now in a moving carton ready for a new life in the big city. She shared Sarah's excitement but also shared many hugs and tears. Mida wrote Ev nearly every day, usually answering a worried note from him about his latest crisis and phoned him a couple times as well. Orion had faded into some magical dream as her mom's life, Sarah's life, and Ev all took over her thoughts.

The magical day of Sarah's wedding arrived. The ceremony was outdoors just outside of Taos. The groom was stately and dignified; the bride was enchanting and beautiful. The ceremony was low key and informally humble. Mida noticed several details that seemed to her quite Apache or at least aboriginal in their spirituality and their ritual. Despite her reputation for being above the fray, Mida was quietly in tears the entire ceremony. She was losing her best friend, although she knew it was a wonderful graduation for all involved. She wished several times before and after the ceremony that Ev could be there. She knew that she was in his thoughts. Or at least she had better be in his thoughts.

Actually, during the ceremony, Mida was not in Ev's thoughts. On that early summer afternoon, Ev was in a panic, lying under his truck in the middle of the Utah desert. He was on a hurried trip, frantically searching for a campsite and study area to replace the one they now couldn't drive to. In his search for new roads and nonroads, he high-centered his truck on a sandstone boulder on a trail miles from anywhere. In his disgust of kicking and flailing tools around, he had somehow punctured a tire and was changing the tire as well as hoping he had not bent a tie rod. He did not think of Mida once.

Ev did not have a very peaceful interlude in this time between classes. He did not do any research related to Orion. Nor did he spend time thinking of much of anything but the seminar. Things were unraveling at the seams. The class was full, actually too full for his comfort. It was a lesson on Murphy's law. More things were going wrong than there were things that could go wrong.

Besides the seminar problems, Ev seemed to be somebody's voodoo doll. He lost his Visa card and learned someone used it to make purchases in his name. He got that straightened out and was getting a replacement card. It hadn't arrived yet and he kept forgetting to carry his checkbook. He was embarrassed more than once as he discovered at the cash register that he didn't have money or even a check. He wondered if there was some curse brought on by Orion. He got little sympathy from Mida whenever he would call her or e-mail her. She even asked him once if he remembered anything he learned in fourth grade. She said he was too young to be an absentminded tousle-haired professor. Ev was not even going to tell Mida about the library book he forgot he had (probably because it fell behind the truck seat and was not found until he pulled out the tire iron for changing his punctured tire). The book on parallel universes was torn and almost overdue. He had to get his life back on track, he thought, as he stalked away from an ATM, having forgotten his code number.

His seminar opened on a Monday morning to the rhythm of pouring rain. That was unusual for June in Durango. After a morning of previews and preparations, the group left for Utah. Luckily, Ev's last-minute selection of a new field site was graced by a rocky road and not a muddy one. His luck held. The Utah slickrock opened its long held secrets to inquisitive minds. His students were eager to learn and he was eager to get his mind off all other things that had plagued him for almost three weeks.

The rest of the seminar went as smooth as the water-worn sandstone cliffs they studied. The finale, a trip into the high country near Silverton, capped almost two weeks of scrambling, picking, scraping, and discussing. Other than that first day of rain, the seminar was dry and warm and without the almost traditional early summer snowstorm in the San Juan highlands. After the last two days in the classroom back on campus, Ev added a last-minute addendum to the required paper. He usually asked each student to list a dozen questions about what they had seen and how they could answer their own questions through research. This was standard every year. His new twist, which caused a few raised eyebrows, asked them to outline how they would present this to an alien civilization that landed a starship while they were doing their research. Using that starship to time travel was an accepted way to do the research, but they had to explain how they would do the time travel. He knew this had nothing to do with geology, but he was desperately looking for ideas. When the department head learned about this question, he smiled as he asked Ev what he had been smoking and did he plan to go forward or backward in time.

He went three weeks without talking to Mida. He guessed she spent a productive weekend at her medicine woman conference. He looked forward to hearing all about that. He also knew she went to visit her mother immediately after the conference. And he knew even though she thought she was as tough as granite, she was lonely and probably going through a minor life crisis. And he knew it didn't do her any good when he thought about her every night as he gazed at the stars as he left a dying campfire, pausing before going into his tent. At least he assumed it didn't do her any good. He didn't yet understand that it did do her a lot of good. She was able to utilize her powers and the power of good thoughts between two people. He had a lot to learn about Mida and about things he never imagined.

A phone call to Mida as soon as the seminar was over got only her recording. The new recording was Sarah's voice, with a final message for any and all callers. She was poignantly saying goodbye and wishing a good life to everyone. Ev never met Sarah but knew a big part left Mida's life, no matter how much she and Sarah kept in touch in the future. He thought about calling Mrs. Peterson but didn't feel comfortable doing that. For all he knew, Mida hadn't told her mother about him yet. He didn't know when Mida would get back from the reservation, so he just left a message that said, "Call me. Orion beckons."

He needed a day or two to tie up loose ends from the seminar, but other than that, he was done for the summer. Fall classes didn't start until the end of August, and he planned to spend the rest of the summer doing research on Orion, hopefully in the company of Mida. He was anxiously awaiting her call.

Monday evening, as he came in his front door, he had a strange feeling about Mida. He envisioned her driving into Santa Fe and pulling into her driveway. He didn't even know what her apartment looked like, but he sensed her coming home to a lonely place. He sat down by his phone, almost expecting it to ring. It did. It was Mida. She just got home from visiting her mother.

"Mida, I had this strangest feeling that you would call. I just sat down here and watched the phone. This is weird."

"Everett, it is not weird. It is great. I was thinking of you very strongly for the past twenty minutes. I was trying an experiment. Bluebell and I spent a lot of time together during the conference. Remember it? Well, she has tremendous psychic powers. She uses them in her healing. She is mentoring me in my skills. Well, I just used them. Kinda spooky, huh?" she squeaked as she picked up a heart-shaped pillow from the sofa and started running her fingers along its edge.

"Yeah, *spooky* is the right word," muttered Ev as he started to doodle on a pad of paper by the phone. He noticed he was doodling hearts and arrows.

"Well, we can talk about that later," said Mida as she quickly changed the subject. "How did your seminar go? It's all over now?"

Ev gave a quick overview of the three weeks and how things turned out great. He was relieved to be done and ready to put his full attention on Orion. He asked about her and how her mom was and if she had heard from Sarah. It was turning into uncomfortable small talk. The telepathy thing bothered him. He wondered if she could read his thoughts.

Before he could ask her about them getting together, she interrupted him and said quickly, "By the way, do you have room for a visitor? It's kind of lonely here and I'm as caught up with my work as I will ever get, and I would love a guided tour of Durango.

Do I need to talk to your appointments secretary or can you handle that yourself?"

"Oh man, you can read my mind, can't you?" sighed Ev as he switched the phone into his other hand. His doodling had turned into lightning bolts and exclamation marks.

"No, not yet, but if I could, would I be blushing right now, Rock Boy? There are some things one doesn't want to find out too much detail on. At least not yet. And by the way, the answers are yes, no, yes, yes, and what if someone saw us?"

Ev was somewhat startled by this seemingly sudden change in Mida's personality. He liked it, especially for what it promised to him. He had gained the confidence of this very independent and aloof person. But he also sensed a very serious responsibility on his part to live up to some high standards. He was no longer feeling intimidated by her.

"How long will it take you to get here, Lozen, warrior princess? Do you come by yourself, or with your tribe of raiders?"

"I plan on about four hours, but I don't really want to drive any more today. I already drove almost four hours coming up from the rez and need to rest up a little and do some laundry tonight. But I will be there around noon tomorrow or earlier if I can get out of here sooner. I don't have anyone to cook me a fancy breakfast and treat me to stimulating conversation anymore."

"Well, don't expect me to cook anything fancy for you but I will definitely stimulate you. With conversation I mean," he quickly added, realizing the double meaning of what he said. Ev brightened as he thought of seeing Mida again. "You need instructions on how to get to my place." She was coming through Chama and Pagosa, which made it easier to find his not all that findable place. After a little more chitchat, they said goodbye. Both sat and stared vacantly at the phone after they hung up. Ev was mumbling "Spooky" while Mida was grinning as she said out loud "It really worked!"

The next morning, Ev went to his office before six o'clock and finished several things he was working on with the seminar and its follow up. It was difficult to concentrate. He wanted to get home early and clean the apartment. Needless to say, it had gone weeks, if not months, without proper cleaning. As he rushed in the door and grabbed the vacuum cleaner, he thought once again that he really needed to hire a cleaning lady. He worked so feverishly in cleaning the bathroom, he literally worked up a sweat. He thought of taking a quick shower but was afraid Mida would knock on his door while he was in the shower.

He flopped down on the sofa right at the stroke of noon, wondering where Mida was. He awoke ten minutes later as he heard a horn honk. He looked out the window and saw the familiar white Subaru. Her car looked as dirty as he felt. Mida got out and saw him looking out the window. She was wearing her floppy hat and white sweat pants, but instead of a white sweatshirt, she was wearing a surprisingly revealing halter top. She hollered something about curb service but he just opened the door and said, "My you look stunning." They both burst out laughing. She walked up the steps and he came out and hugged her. She gave him a long and quite encouraging kiss as they slowly walked in the door.

They went up the small flight of stairs of the split-level house. Mida asked if this was the infamous grocery bag stairs. Ev laughed and said yes. The house belonged to a professor and his wife who were out of the country for a year sabbatical. They would be back the end of August, so he had to find a new place to live before then. Mida glanced around and commented that it was very nice but looked like he had lived here for years. Ev grimaced and said he spent the last two hours cleaning it. She apologized and said she didn't mean dirt; she meant it was cluttered with rock things and other items that could only belong to Ev.

Ev just muttered that it is easy to accumulate stuff. "I was starting to get worried about you. But I do give you credit. You said you would be here by noon and you were pretty close. I thought you were a lady of honor."

"I am very honorable. Didn't you get my message?"

Ev looked quickly at the phone. "You know I didn't even look at my phone messages. I was rushing so fast this morning, I got home and had to do a few chores and forgot to look." He started to hit the Play button when Mida put her hand on his and said, "No, not a phone message. I was sending you a mental message."

"Oh, not that woo-woo stuff again. No, I didn't get it. I was so busy."

She quickly interrupted, "I sent it right at noon as I was coming into town."

"Oh," Ev stuttered. "I sat down on the couch right at noon and I think I fell asleep."

"Well, how can I send you a message when you are sleeping?"

"You probably send them to me all the time when you are sleeping. Don't you dream of me every night?" kidded Ev as he sat down on the couch.

"In your own dreams, Rock Boy." Mida whispered as she plopped almost on his lap. "Don't you have lunch made for me?"

"Later," Ev grinned. "Just let me look at you for a while first. I'd almost forgot how pretty you are. Even in those silly sweatpants. But that top is rather enticing. You sure you want to be seen in public in that?" He snuggled up against her on the sofa.

"It was a long hot drive and I don't have air conditioning. Then again, maybe I don't plan on being seen in public. We need to get reacquainted first before I want my tour." She looked him in the eye and grinned, showing her perfect teeth and Norwegian dimples.

They talked about Sarah's wedding and his seminar and Mrs. Peterson and the rez, then both went into the kitchen and scrounged through the refrigerator and cupboards for a makeshift lunch. Mida expressed mock horror at the depleted state of food in the house. Ev apologized but recovered quickly when he emphasized he had been out of town for three weeks and had been working long hours at the office since he got home. He knew Mida would be coming, so he wanted her to help him shop. She accepted his story but still said it was pretty lame. She said the kitchen probably looked like this all the time. Ev grinned and said nothing.

After finishing a quick lunch, they went out to her car and got her suitcase and a couple large boxes. She explained one box was her thesis and another box was a gift from her mother to Ev.

"Oh, so she knows about me, then?" asked Ev as he raised his eyebrows with a grin and frown all in one expression.

"She knows as much about you as I do, which really isn't very much. I intend to remedy that in the next few days or weeks. Which will it take?" she asked as she put her arm around him.

"Get to know me? Oh lord, let's change that to years. How can you know me when no one else on this planet does," he commented as he struggled through the door with the heavy boxes. "No wonder you grabbed the suitcase before I could. I hope your clothes don't weigh as much as these boxes." He dropped them on the kitchen floor.

"Listen," said Ev, "I didn't have a chance to take a shower this morning after I slaved and sweated to get this place clean for you. Let me go in and shave and shower before we take our big tour of Durango or whatever you want to do. I don't want to embarrass you by looking like I just spent three weeks in the wilderness. Just get comfortable here, and I will only be a few minutes. I don't really have anything special planned for you."

"Except go buy groceries," they both said, laughing at the same time.

Ev finished shaving and stepped into the shower. It felt good just letting the hot water hit his back. He was thinking a massage would be nice when he thought he heard the door to the bathroom open. The wind must have blown it open, he thought. He was about ready to yell at Mida to come shut the door when suddenly the curtains to the shower opened, and Mida stepped into the tub with Ev. He dropped the soap in surprise and just stood with hot water pouring over his back, staring at this beautiful body standing there with water splashing over her. Mida put her arms around him and said, "Hope you don't mind. When I said I wanted to get to know you, I meant it."

The next few minutes were forever etched in Ev's memory. He would never think of a shower the same again. They both disappeared from conscious thought, only to reappear again later as they noticed the hot water was no longer hot. It had turned warm, then cool.

They eased out of the shower and dried each other off, then she led him to the bedroom. They spent the rest of the afternoon getting to know each other even better. Neither Ev nor Mida was inexperienced in such things, but they both learned things neither knew they didn't know.

Finally Mida turned to Ev and whispered in his ear, "Apache women know how to treat their men. But they expect a lot in return." She got up, dressed, and disappeared into the kitchen. Ev could hear her clinking dishes and rattling papers as he just lay there. He was stunned by the past couple hours and was reliving it in his mind.

Finally Mida stuck her head in the door and said, "You gonna just lay there the rest of your life or are you going to show me the biggest and best grocery store in Durango? We both need energy after all that and you don't exactly have enough calories in this house to feed a bird. How do you survive?" She went over to him and pulled the covers off the bed. Ev quickly covered up, embarrassed by his sudden exposure, but he quickly pulled clean clothes out of drawers as Mida stood and laughed.

"At least you do have a few clean clothes, better than we can say about your food situation." She laughed.

"You are getting a kick out of this, aren't you?" asked Ev as he realized he had put his socks on wrong side out. "No wonder our government was scared of Geronimo and Cochise if they attacked half as quickly and fiercely as you did."

"You don't worry about what Geronimo could do. You better worry what the spirit of Lozen, warrior princess, can do. She was my heroine but most men she attacked didn't survive very long." Mida laughed as she walked out leaving Ev standing there still in shock.

They made a quick tour of Durango, which this time of year was filled with tourists. He showed her the train station, where the afternoon train was just returning from Silverton. They drove through campus, which didn't take long. He pointed out the science building where his office was, then he headed to the new City Market, where they spent a long time cruising the aisles. Mida took charge of the shopping. He was impressed by her choice of real food, not the cans and boxes he usually just tossed in the cart as he absentmindedly did his routine shopping.

"I thought you couldn't cook," Ev commented as they got to the checkout line.

"What made you think that?" asked Mida as she pointed to her purse asking with a look if Ev was able to pay.

"I got my new credit card and I finally learned to keep a few bills in my wallet," he replied as he pulled it out of his shorts pocket. "Well, first, you said you couldn't cook. Then, I got a very long letter from Sarah a couple days ago," Ev replied as he took out his new credit card. Mida perked up but with a surprised look on her face.

"She was writing from Seward, Alaska, where their honeymoon cruise ship docked for a few days. She was very nice and wanted me to take good care of you. She shared a few secrets, which will remain secret, about how to give you what you deserve. She obviously loved you very much by what she said and told me that I had better take care of you by the highest standards, to use her term. She had found her prince charming and was starting a new life and wanted the same for you." Ev had been very impressed by the letter but wouldn't admit to getting choked up when he first read it. He looked at Mida and noticed tears welling up in her eyes. This conversation was getting too serious, he realized as he swiped the card through the machine. "Anyway, she said you couldn't cook very well or at least you never did cook much and something about I needed to feed you well." Ev pushed the cart out the door and looked for his truck. He always forgot where he parked it.

Mida just wiped her eyes and growled, "Well, how could I cook when she hogged the kitchen? She is a gourmet cook and lives to prepare food fit for royalty. She knows I can cook and quite well. Sometimes I think she wanted to be my mother and was jealous of the real one. Oh, I miss her," she sighed as she obviously remembered exactly where he parked. "Let's go see what I can whip up."

They went back to the house and Ev put groceries away as Mida fixed dinner. They spent the rest of the evening talking about

Orion and what each learned the past month. They had a huge task researching what each of them wanted to know.

Finally, about ten o'clock, Ev realized he had been yawning constantly as Mida tried to explain her traveling exhibit that was going to end up in the Smithsonian. He put his hand on her hand and said, "I don't mean to be rude, but I just can't stay awake. It is definitely not your stimulating conversation, but I am just plain worn-out. I think the past month is catching up to me. There is a spare bedroom down the hall with clean sheets if that is what—"

She interrupted him. "Why dirty up extra sheets? Your bed was big enough this afternoon unless you are still embarrassed. I am okay with that, and I think Sarah would approve if you are concerned."

Ev started to say something, but Mida just put her hand on his mouth. She led him into the bedroom. He didn't complain. A few minutes later, he was already in bed, almost asleep, when she slipped into bed beside him, wearing nothing but her golden tan skin. She didn't snore that night.

June 25

It is strange how your life can suddenly change. One day things are plodding along according to schedule. Then something changes and life takes a road you don't even see coming. I know I shocked Ev, but I saw what I wanted. He was it. I am in control of him but we are both under the control of Orion. I keep thinking I don't need anyone else, but I have always needed someone. First it was Daddy. Then Mom became my support. White Eagle turned my life around on the rez and was responsible for pointing me in the direction I took at college. Sarah was my life support the last couple years. Now Ev has taken over from her. I guess I do need people but only on my terms. Ev and I are destined for something but what? What is Orion all about? Is Orion the end result or is it a distraction for something else? Wow, so many unknowns. Right now is a vacation of sorts and we are acting like it. The calm before the storm? I'm so close to being done with Q, but I can't walk away yet. Ev keeps talking about his research, but what can either of us do to study up on Orion? There is really nothing either of us can do. It's there, calling us, and all we can do is go to it. It controls us. Maybe it is researching us. Good luck figuring either of us out! One minute I think I have Ev figured out, then he surprises me with some new twist. He is one complicated dude!

SEVEN

—✳—

Looking for Answers

We must welcome the future, remembering
that soon it will be the past,
And we must respect the past,
remembering that once it was all
That was humanly possible.

—George Santayana

We cannot escape fear. We can only
transform it into a companion
that accompanies us on all our
exciting adventures . . .
Take a risk a day—one small or bold stroke that
will make you feel great once you have done it.

—Susan Jeffers

MIDA AND EV spent two weeks on a lovers' vacation. They celebrated the Fourth of July hiking the trails and tundra of the alpine wonderland west of Lake City. A summer thunderstorm provided them with real fireworks as they huddled under a clump of small trees just below timberline waiting for intense lightning and hail to pass to the east. They rode the Durango-Silverton railroad, the first time for both. They explored nearby Mesa Verde, then spent several more days with a close friend of Mida exploring the back canyons of the Tribal Park of the adjacent Ute Mountain Reservation. Mida showed Ev some hidden rock art she discussed extensively in her thesis. It was composed literally of entire cliff faces.

In her first e-mail to the real newlywed in San Francisco, Mida told Sarah she felt like a newlywed herself. Sarah immediately picked up the phone and called as soon as she read the message. Ev was in the kitchen washing dishes but could hear Sarah on the phone as she was obviously rejoicing about Mida's situation, acting like a teenager over a new steady. Ev tried not to listen but did hear Mida say, "I can't say that, Ev is standing right here." She then took the phone into the bedroom and shut the door. Ev just shook his head and muttered, "A boy yearns to be a man as soon as he can, but a girl always wants to stay a girl. Women, you figure them out." He was talking to the refrigerator since he knew it was safer than saying that to Mida.

Ev and Mida planned a trip to Utah as soon as the July heat wave eased. They needed to visit Orion, but neither really knew what they could do there. First, Mida had to go to Santa Fe and officially quit her job. She knew she was finished anyway since her grant money was gone and the museum did not have an opening, regardless of how much the director wanted to keep Mida. She needed to move out of her apartment since there was no reason to stay in Santa Fe. After September 10, she would not need to return to Albuquerque. That was the date scheduled for her meeting with the doctoral committee. She briefly considered going back to the reservation but she didn't want to be away from Ev. They both came to the obvious conclusion that she would stay with him in Durango. But Ev was having thoughts about quitting teaching and spending full-time with his Orion research, although he didn't mention this to Mida. He had to visit Orion first and figure out what he wanted to do. More importantly, he needed to decide what he would even be able to do. There was no precedent for research into something like Orion. Life was at a crossroads for both and they knew it. They were stalling making the big decisions and they knew that, too. They were having fun and being carefree before that opportunity ran out.

After the short drive to Santa Fe from Durango, they prepared for a brief stay at Mida's apartment, giving the landlord a couple weeks notice. They sorted which of Mida's few possessions would go to the rez and which would go back to Durango with them. Mida gave Ev a tour of the Santa Fe area, including a two-day hike into Bandelier National Monument, where she had done some of her early research several years before. She also took him to visit several friends at some of the nearby pueblos. Ev was learning a lot of Native American culture and history. He needed it if he was ever going to fully understand Mida and some of her traits. She was surprised at his lack of knowledge of this cultural aspect of the southwest.

He was uneasy about going to visit her mom. He didn't want to admit it, but he felt strange about going to a home on the rez. Even calling it the *rez* instead of the *reservation* was awkward for him. He felt it was degrading, but this was common terminology for Mida and evidently for residents of the rez. Ev was comfortable with Mida and she told him it was no different there. There was one exception, though, she said. He would be the minority, and if he was having problems over that, then he had better "get over it." She said it nicely, knowing the feeling herself, but she gave him an extra hard poke in the ribs every time she said it. Ev practiced saying a special greeting in Apache and Mida made sure he made all the right gestures and protocol of Apache traditions. She wanted to impress her mother as much as Ev did.

They finally loaded the pickup and made the drive south on I-25 to Socorro, then east to Carrizozo. By the time they got to Ruidoso, Ev was feeling queasy in his stomach. When they turned off the divided highway near Mescalero, Ev felt like he was back in grade school trying to learn a big piece for the Christmas play. He was nervous almost to the point of being sick and was starting to complain. Finally, Mida made him pull over to the side of the road and said to him, "Listen, Geronimo never lived here. He died at Ft. Sill, Oklahoma. Cochise never saw this place, he died in

Arizona. You know our history. We are just like you except we look different. You look different to us. And yes, it is my mother. She knows we are sleeping together and she doesn't care. You want to know how the Apache traditionally got married? We just had a little ceremony and moved in together. We divorced just as easy. If the man came home one day and all his things were laid outside, then you were divorced, my friend. And if you wanted to end it, you just said you were going hunting and you left and simply didn't come back. No big deal, no stigma, no guilt. You are seeing my mom. After this, we go see your mom. You want a ceremony, we can go visit the tribal holy man. Or the priest. Most here are in the Reformed Church and pray to Jesus and Mary. We don't scalp and we won't circumcise you. Get over it." With that, she reached over and really poked him, only not in his ribs.

Ev doubled over, as much as was possible sitting behind the wheel. "Damn, that hurt. You know that hurts. What the hell are you trying to do to me?"

Mida laughed and said, "We have ways of relieving your kind of fright. We take your mind off the stupid thoughts you are having by giving you a new type of fright. You are acting like a child and I brought a man to meet my mom. Act like one. Now drive. We are almost there."

Ev noticed that his stomachache was gone, and he did feel better despite that fading ache down below. He looked at Mida and wondered what kind of shamanic thing she had done to him besides give him a symbolic castration. It worked. Finally, Ev started chuckling along with Mida. "Spooky," he thought again, not for the last time.

Mida pounded the horn as Ev parked in her mother's driveway. He told her to stop, but she was a little girl again as she jumped out of the truck and ran up and hugged her mom. Ev shyly got out and walked up and said in fluent Apache that he was honored to meet her. He started to shake her hand, but she grabbed him and hugged him, kissing him on the cheeks. She then told him he was never to call her Mrs. Peterson again. Her name was Denzee. He could call her Mom if he wished, she said with a grin. Mida said something in Apache, and both she and her mom burst out laughing. Ev asked her what she said. Mida just said that she told her mom what Ev was called, thus the name on his license plate. Ev mumbled something about getting his plate changed.

They spent nearly a week with her mother. Ev hit it off very well, even being able to talk about places familiar to this former hippie. Denzee had spent some time in Boulder in the sixties and knew a lot of places where Ev used to go as a kid. Ev and Mida visited a lot of places on the rez where Mida spent her childhood and even hiked to near the place where Mida had her life changing vision quest. Mida didn't want to go to the exact spot again. Ev shuddered when he thought about Mida being there alone for three days.

The three spent the evenings sitting on the front porch, watching sunsets, and playing mah-jongg. Ev could see where Mida got her sense of independence and self-assured attitude. Denzee was certainly no provincial reservation Indian. He tried to figure out how he could say this to Mida without offending her or her people. He gave up and said nothing. He also noticed in her mother a strong undercurrent of impishness and mischief that he was aware of in the daughter. He complained more than once about being taken advantage of by these two women. They just made comments to each other in Apache and giggled.

By the time they were to return to Santa Fe to finish moving out of the apartment, Ev didn't want to leave. Mida jumped behind the wheel after saying goodbye while Ev gave her mother a big hug. He thought the air was being squeezed out of him and she almost wouldn't let go. She said something in Apache, then explained to Ev that she said a prayer for safekeeping for both Ev and Mida. Ev thanked her in Apache, then hopped in the truck as Mida was already backing out of the driveway.

Mida was very talkative the whole way back to Santa Fe. The trip seemed to energize her. Ev felt pretty good about things himself. When Mida asked when she was going to get to meet Ev's mom, he started to change the subject, but Mida kept after him. He finally said he hadn't written or spoken to his mom in over six months. Ev didn't feel comfortable about visiting his stepfather. Mida gave him a lecture on that and asked if he wanted her to pull over and she would cure him of this stupid hang-up. Ev groaned and promised they would call his mom when they got back to Durango. She lived in Colorado Springs but spent a lot of time traveling.

They pulled into Santa Fe just as the sun was going down. As they opened the door to Mida's apartment, she made Ev go in first. She only explained it as some superstition, but Ev noticed she was unusually quiet for the rest of the night. The place seemed to be sterile since there was very little of Mida left in it. They spent the next day packing the rest of her things, then they cleaned the place top to bottom. Mida went next door, turned in her key to the landlord, and said her goodbyes. Ev stayed in the background, knowing that this was very difficult for Mida. He respectfully kept quiet all the way to Pagosa Springs before she finally broke her silence. They got into Durango after dark and unloaded the pickup. They just piled the boxes of Mida's stuff in a spare bedroom since they knew they would be moving it again in a few weeks. Then they both collapsed in bed.

July 16

Seems like I visited the rez for the first time. I brought Ev, the first time I ever brought a man home with me. Mom liked him but I really felt strange. Made me think about the rez and what it means to me. Even though I have lived away for years now, I guess this has still been home. Of course, it always will be. Ev was really nervous coming here, which made me nervous as well. I guess I was nervous whether he would like it or still like me. Why am I reverting to a teenager?

I thought about what it means to be from the rez. So many here are only comfortable while here among their own kind. Isn't that wrong? Their own kind? Why have we labeled people so? This is my kind, yet it really isn't. My kind is also half a continent away. My kind is also up in Albq, wandering around campus and on other campuses. My kind is those who don't accept what we were born into. I want more and deserve more. Why must we huddle with those we think are our kind and put all others into another box with a label?

I have been thinking more about this lately. Orion has touched me in a big way and made me realize that our kind is all of us here on Earth. How many others can have that perspective? Weird! There is another totally different kind out there—or at least there was. Think back only 150 years ago and it was so different. How about 1,500 or even 15,000 years ago? Things are so temporary, so transcendent. We try and learn all there is to know, but all we succeed in is seeing such a brief snapshot.

I have put all my effort into figuring out what my ancestors, or at least some of my ancestors, believed in. But it is so fleeting. It is what they may have thought about or worshiped for a few years, but what was it based on. How did it evolve and change? If I could go back 150,000 years, what would I see? Would we still huddle around with our friends, labeling all others as outsiders? We probably always have done this. And I suppose we always will. Maybe we need to. All the creatures do this. Look at a flock of birds when a newcomer arrives. They peck at it, chase it off, even kill it. Wolves do the same. Ants probably do too. Is it part of a basic survival instinct that cannot be changed?

If Ev and I ever meet the inhabitants of Orion, will they peck at us and treat us as if we crashed their rez? Maybe I hope for too much.

Ev impressed Mom. I ended up being more nervous than him, but he will never know it. He is making a real effort to learn some words and phrases. That meant more to Mom than anything. She thought I was turning into an old maid, with no interest in men—no interest in uninteresting men and what men have I met lately that were interested in anything more than my body. Ev was, but he made a very strong effort in pretending not to be. I think my brain overwhelmed his animal lust, but when the lust arrived, it overpowered all intellect. I think I surprised him. I surprised myself, too. Maybe that is basic animal instinct as well. Try as we may to gain a higher intellectual plane, two naked bodies set us back into the primeval times. So be it. (Don't hear me complaining!)

The weather in Durango was still hot and tourists seemed to be swarming everywhere. Both Ev and Mida found this a good excuse to lie around the house and plan their future. After constant prodding by Mida, Ev finally called his mom, but got an answering machine. He left a message, saying he wanted to talk to her. He said he was sorry he hadn't written in quite a while and wanted to know if he could come visit her one of these days. He was glad he got the machine, but Mida was relieved he had called at all.

They talked about what they needed to research in the library and what they needed to check out at Orion. They each had different goals. Ev focused on the science, the theory of time travel, of interstellar space travel, of alien civilizations. Mida talked of what these travelers would have been like, their society, their gods, their mastery of physical and spiritual powers, and how they manifest their energy.

Ev insisted on a detailed scientific plan of action for their trip to Boulder Mountain but became irritated and frustrated when Mida went into seclusion to chant various prayers or songs or whatever they were. Grumbling to himself, Ev jotted down his list of activities, without any significant contribution from Mida. They bought the most powerful flashlights they could and even got a pair of night-vision goggles. Ev borrowed a special infrared sensing device from one of his friends in the physics department. They also bought several blank videotapes and borrowed his landlord's video camera which Ev discovered several months earlier in a hallway cabinet. They packed their new tan-colored tents since they didn't want to be visible in their old blue tents when camped by the red cliffs. When Mida said Ev was getting anal about secrecy, he declared she would do the grocery shopping since he didn't want anything anal involved with food. When she said that would give her a chance to show off her camp cooking skills, he said that was fine. He didn't want to spend time cooking, and he was surprised with the quality of the cooking she had done the past few weeks. Maybe Sarah was wrong and Mida was a good cook after all. Compared to Ev's cooking skills, that wouldn't be hard to do.

They pulled out of Durango at 5:00 a.m. after an hour of arguing over how to pack things in the truck. They wanted to get there early since it had been extremely hot, and they didn't want to be driving in the heat of the day. They had given up on waiting for the heat wave to break. As they drove the desert highway north of the Grand Gulch area, both pointed out their favorite spots in this archaeological wilderness paradise.

When they passed a road construction sign, Ev made an offhand comment about Edward Abbey. They then spent the next hour arguing over Abbey's novel *The Monkey Wrench Gang*. Mida wouldn't believe this was the highway that inspired the book and the original environmental terrorism. Mida saw Abbey as a drunken anarchist. She expressed her dismay when Ev said he looked on Abbey as a cult hero. Ev didn't like anyone bad mouthing Abbey, so he quickly changed the subject.

As they approached Lake Powell, Ev described in vivid detail what the canyon looked like before the dam. Mida asked how he knew so much about its original state. Ev explained one of his geology professors in college had spent weeks in the canyon before the dam was constructed and had cases of photos and slides. Although Ev never floated the river through the canyon, he felt he knew it intimately. They both agreed they wouldn't mind seeing Glen Canyon Dam blown up; they spent the next half hour plotting how they would do it. Dam or no dam, the canyon would not return to any pristine scenic glory until well after their lifetimes.

As he usually did, he stopped on the bridge at Hite crossing of the Colorado and performed his strange ritual. Getting out of the truck, he walked to the edge of the road, saluted the river, said his silent prayer and apology, and tossed a small granite stone from Trail Ridge Road into the green river-lake. He carried a small bag of these rocks for just such an occasion. He watched the small stone fall silently, then disappear in the center of a growing ring of circles. He didn't even hear the small plunk. The wind carried a pair of complaining ravens over the bridge right at that time, drowning out the far away plop of the stone. When Mida told him to get out of the road, he looked up to see a pickup truck coming onto the bridge. He jumped into the truck and headed on across the bridge. He laughed, thinking the other vehicle probably thought he was taking a leak off the bridge.

Mida didn't ask about his ritual since she knew she would end up just shaking her head at his strange explanation. Ev explained it to her anyway as her quizzical look invited comment. This small piece of rock would normally have spent millennia traveling from the high peaks of Colorado to the Gulf of California. It was impossible to make such a journey any longer due to the myriad of dams on the imprisoned river. Although it still would not get past Glen Canyon Dam, much less Hoover Dam and the others, this was his small way of helping keep the geologic tradition going. That small piece of granite would have been a grain of sand by the time it got this far, so Ev was confusing the river gods by placing this piece of gravel this far downstream. It would also confuse future geologists who happened upon a piece of granite embedded into the sandstone conglomerate that was once a riverbed in the far distant past.

Mida jumped on the opening and said maybe that's what happened with Orion. Some star traveler from the two hundred millionth millennia before us had dropped a pebble, namely their spaceship, into the sandy desert on their way to get a decent hamburger in the next county. Ev frowned at her and told her to get her math right. It would not have been the two hundred millionth millennia, but the twenty-thousandth millennia. Mida had to get out a pencil and paper and spend two minutes calculating that both were wrong. It would have been the two hundred thousandth millennia, but who was counting then anyway?

"You may be on to something, though," pondered Ev as he whipped past a thirty-foot travel trailer being towed by a BeeGeeVee, his name for the behemoth gas-guzzling vehicle. "He must be getting all of about one m.p.g.," he grumped as he looked disgustedly at the Hawaiian-shirted driver as he passed. "At least we don't have to worry about camping next to him."

He continued with his previous thought. "Maybe they left Orion as a message. What else could they leave that would survive millions of years of Earth's movement and rock building and tearing down. Or maybe it was like our lunar lander that is still sitting up on the moon. It was the expendable part of their journey here."

Mida joined in. "Or it is like a cocoon or nest egg for their offspring. That goes with my theory that sunlight will bring them to life again. Or an influx of fresh air."

Ev winced. "I wish you would stop bringing up that theory. It scares the hell out of me that we will be looking in there or go in eventually and be grabbed by some googly-eyed creature."

"Oh, get real," said Mida as she reached into the back of the cab and pulled up her daypack. She started scrounging for something to eat. "What life-form could possibly last for two hundred million years?"

Ev brightened considerably by Mida's actions. "What you got to eat?" He crossed the center lane as he swerved. He was intent on looking at the food bag. "Do you think the googly creature will like Fritos? Save some for him."

Mida hit him with a bag of pistachios. She told him to pay attention to his driving. She then had to shell them for Ev as he held out his hand begging for some. Ev passed through Hanksville without stopping, although he did comment that his Rock Café had a cute waitress. Mida halted her ritual of shelling a pistachio, then tossing the shell out the window while they went through town. She resumed at the west edge of town as Ev started begging again.

"Drink," was all Ev said as they got a few miles west of town.

Mida looked at him like a he was some googly-eyed creature himself. "Think you could maybe talk like a PhD. since you are one? Complete sentences along with a little courtesy might be appreciated as well. You must be a real joy to travel with cross-country. Don't ask me to drive with you across Kansas. How come you were so well behaved driving down to the rez?"

"You didn't know me then. Now you do and I don't need to be on good behavior. Drink?"

"Oh god. You are like a little kid." She pulled a can of generic pop out of the cooler behind the seat and handed it to him.

Ev opened the can and immediately spilled some all over his face and lap as it erupted in fizz. "What'd you do, shake it first?" he complained as he started coughing and choking.

"I don't know how you got a PhD. without passing first grade eating," scoffed Mida in disgust. "You can be a real slob sometimes. What kind of example do you set in your seminar?"

"Well, sorreeee," he choked. "I guess I didn't feel I needed to impress you now that you adore and worship me."

Mida just stared at him a few seconds before saying, "Let's revisit that asinine statement after we stop and set up camp. Then you can see how much I worship you in a separate tent about one hundred yards from yours." Mida put away the bag of pistachios and turned to look out the window on her side, with her back to Ev.

"Okay, I am sorry," enunciated Ev slowly. "I guess this dry air got to my brain and dried out my cerebrum. I humbly apologize. Don't turn into Lozen."

Mida laughed when she turned around and saw Ev puckering his lips like a monkey. "What am I going to do with you?" she moaned as she sat back upright. She kissed her fingers and touched them to Ev's puckered lips. He tried to bite them but she quickly poked him in the ribs. "Just drive goofy boy. I'm getting tired. And it's cerebellum, not cerebrum."

They pulled into the Visitor Center at Capitol Reef National Park just before noon. The temperature was already over ninety-five. Inside, Ev studied the large three-dimensional map of the Park, which included the lower reaches of Boulder Mountain where Orion was hidden. Mida noticed a few errors, one of them rather significant, in one of the displays on rock art and early cultures of the area and pointed this out to one of the rangers. The young ranger acted appreciative but diplomatically (rather poorly) and patronizingly (rather arrogantly) said an expert who should know better had done the research (implying it therefore must be correct), but she would bring it to her attention. Mida walked away seething, but knowing that she really didn't expect any different.

"I should have told her expert to stop by the Smithsonian in a year or two and look at my exhibit if she wants to know the truth," muttered Mida as she slammed the door of the pickup.

Ev was mentally off on some distant planet as he ignored her mutterings. He drove down to the picnic area, in the shade of a giant cottonwood so they could eat their lunch. He was studying his maps when Mida slammed the food box down on the table and asked if he would like to join her on this planet. He looked up and innocently said, "What's the matter? You sure seem upset. Were they out of toilet paper or something critical like that?"

Mida lifted a cooler out of the back of the pickup and slammed it down on the table. "Put a uniform on someone and they think they know everything. Did she think I was some yokel off the nearest turnip truck? I know more about rock art than all her experts combined."

Ev folded his map, looked quizzically at Mida and said, "I guess I must have missed something. Fold your feathers back into place and just calm down. I don't even want to know what happened, but it is not worth whatever you are doing to your blood pressure. Just put it into a balloon and let it go."

"Oh, put yourself into a balloon," Mida huffed as she pulled sandwiches out of the cooler. She knew Ev was right. After all, she was the one who usually told him to put a bad thought or frustration into a pink balloon and watch it sail away over the horizon. She was mad and deserved to be mad and so there. She would like to put the parkie into a balloon along with her erroneous display. She tossed sandwiches and cookies on the table and sat down to eat. They ate in silence, Ev still wondering what set her off like this. He had never seen her as angry as she was. Maybe she was just venting off months of built up frustration.

There were still apricots on the trees in the orchard near the picnic area, so after finishing their lunch, they picked a large bag full. Ev was teetering on a ladder when he felt a plop on his back. He looked down and Mida was innocently turning away. She was eating as many apricots as she was picking. He noticed another apricot go flying by his head. As he looked down, Mida was picking up one lying on the ground and heaved it at him again. This one hit his leg. Before he could get down off the ladder, Mida had chucked half a dozen more, hitting him twice in the back.

As he jumped off the last rung of the ladder, he reached on the ground, picked up one choice juicy apricot, and grabbed Mida, squeezing the apricot in her right ear. He was glad they weren't charged for the ones Mida threw at him, but he would gladly have paid for the one he managed to stuff in her ear. Mida hollered uncle about this time and they took their bag to the card table set up as a checkout stand. No one was checking the fruit, but there was an honor system with a scale and locked cash box with a slot for self-payment. Ev added a few cents for spent apricot weaponry when he stuffed a dollar into the box. Mida complained that she didn't want to stop in the Visitor Center again to clean up, so they went into the campground restroom to wash out her ear. Ev had to wash apricot puree off his face.

When Mida finally wound down, they discussed their next step. They decided to drive up on Boulder Mountain and camp below the highway, as close to Orion as they could drive. It looked like the Oak Creek road might take them fairly close, but they had no idea of the status of the road. The map showed it continuing on east, but it might be closed or impassable. The Forest Service had been doing a few road closures and they may have closed this one somewhere along its length.

The sleepy community of Torrey was humming with tourist traffic as they approached the new highway intersection with its new motels and gas stations. Ev almost ran off the road again as he was gawking west while turning south onto the Boulder Mountain highway toward Escalante. Mida's yell got his attention. When they leveled off after their climb up the mountain, Ev pulled off on every turnoff so he could try and spot the cliffs where Orion might be. He couldn't quite get his bearings. He almost drove past the Oak Creek road before quickly turning left. As Mida was complaining once again about his driving, he started bouncing down the rocky road off the mountain. A little over two miles from the highway, Ev had to stop and put the truck into four-wheel drive. The road had been rocky, but when it leveled off on the flats, it became sandy. He wasn't sure exactly where Orion was, but he had a pretty good idea. After a while, he pulled off the wheel tracks that constituted the road and drove into a grove of large yellow-bark ponderosa pine.

"This is it?" puzzled Mida as Ev stopped the truck. "Do you even know where you are?"

"We are right here right now and if you have a better idea, then I'm open to suggestions, Miss Norwegian Dimple Princess." Ev got out and said, "Where do you want the tents?"

"We aren't going to try and get any closer?" asked Mida as she got out, rubbing her ear. She was still picking bits of apricot peel out of her hair.

"Not right now unless you know the exact route to take. I don't know where to go and I don't look forward to winding around and doubling back with a forty-pound pack on my back. Let's explore first, then we can pack in closer. Tomorrow." He started scraping the twigs and years-old cow pies from underneath a large pine tree. "Looks like a honeymoon camp spot to me!"

They quickly set up camp and gathered branches and limbs for a campfire. Ev took his binoculars and scoped out the view from their camp. He couldn't see the highway and was sure no one from up there could see down here. He hadn't seen any fresh tire tracks or other evidence of anyone being there recently. From the looks of the road, a few hunters were about all that ever came this way. By the time they were set up, Ev suggested they hike around and find the best way to reach Orion.

He climbed a rise near the camp and got a better bearing of where he was. This area gave a totally different feel than the slickrock canyon where Orion was embedded. This was the edge of a pine forest, with actual soil and flowers and other foresty things. At the top of the rise was a rock outcrop surrounded by a ring of oakbrush scattered among a few small pine trees. There, he noticed a pile of chips and projectile fragments lying on the ground. Evidently, someone else a long time ago thought this a good spot to sit and work and probably just look around, too. He carefully looked through the pile of chips. He put a few in his pocket as a future gift to a river or other Ev depository. As he scrambled down the slope and fought his way through a thick patch of oakbrush, he scared up a turkey. It flew down past where Mida was sitting, losing a tail feather as it soared over her head. The feather floated down and landed near her feet.

"Well, if that isn't a sign," exclaimed Mida as Ev came jogging to her. "I think the direction he was flying is the direction we need to go. Trust me on that one. Someone spoke to me through the bird."

"You're on, sweetness, since that is the direction I think Orion is located, by my more scientific observations. I think I saw the cliff, but cliffs down here all start to look the same after a while." Ev put his binoculars in his daypack, hitched it up on his back and started walking down the sandy track. As Mida stared at him, he hollered back at her, "Aren't you coming?"

"Yeah, Rock Boy. Thanks for the invitation," she muttered to herself as she grabbed her pack and hurried after him.

They walked down the track for about a mile where it started becoming more entrenched in rising cliffs on both sides. Oak Creek was fairly wide here, although the cliffs soon towered over one hundred feet into the blindingly blue sky. There were numerous side canyons carving small enclaves and alcoves on both sides of the main canyon. They soon had a hard time telling there was even a track they were following. Whatever soil was present further up had been replaced by sand. Cactus and other sparse desert growth slowly replaced the sage brush and oakbrush.

Suddenly Ev stopped. He looked up one side canyon and said, "You know, this looks familiar. Let's walk up this a ways."

Mida closed her eyes for a few seconds and then opened them and laughed. "Yeah, Rock Boy, this should look familiar. Right down this draw is where I hid during that thunderstorm that tried to drown me. Orion is just over there." She pointed straight ahead. The cliff curved away from them and as they rounded it, they saw their rock pile.

"I'll be damned," cursed Ev as he took off his cap and ran his hand through his hair. "And to think of the long hike we took to get here from the other direction. This is so much easier."

"It's strange that neither of us could tell this was a main canyon with a so-called major road down it." She laughed as she said that.

"Well, maybe major road is a little bit of an overstatement, but isn't it a major road on the map?"

"Yes," Ev said as he pulled out his map. "Not that there are a lot of roads in this country, but it is one of the few that come down here. Obviously not a lot of people care to explore this part of the world. But the canyon is wide enough here that neither of us actually came all the way down to the creek. There is almost a second channel on this north side that doesn't carry water. It really does look like this is the canyon bottom, but the actual low point where Oak Creek flows is back over there. It is kind of tricky from this angle. I think we were justified."

Mida laughed. "You just don't want to be wrong. You're the expert here. I'm not, at least on the rocks and canyons part of this endeavor. I think I will file this one for later use if need be."

Ev just ran his fingers through his hair again and started to say something but just puckered his lips.

Mida quickly said, "Well, while we are here, I want to go over and say hi to Orion. Just a peek. Want to join me?"

"You go ahead. I think I will scramble up on top and look around up there some more. I am thinking we may want to camp up by the periscope."

"You mean I will have to carry my heavy pack up there? What's wrong with down here by the water."

"I don't know. I just want to look around. We can decide tomorrow." With that, he hiked down the canyon and disappeared around the bend before she could say anything more.

Mida walked reverently over to the rock pile and slowly took off the top few rocks. There was the shine of the metal hiding patiently behind the rocks. She smiled and reached up, touching the smooth surface. She stood there for several minutes with eyes closed, occasionally moving her lips. She felt like she had come home. A sensation overcame her that she had never felt before. It seemed to fill her like a light. Then it left. As she opened her eyes, she looked up and saw a golden eagle soaring overhead. It disappeared over the cliff, suddenly replaced by Ev as he poked his head over the edge and said something to her. She looked up at him and said quickly, "Let's go back. Now."

They got back to camp as the sun was hugging the top of Boulder Mountain. It wasn't that late, but from their angle, they lost an hour of sun before it even thought about disappearing over the far western horizon. Ev hauled the food boxes and coolers out of the truck as Mida set up the propane camp stove. While she was fixing supper, Ev wandered around looking for more projectile points.

He came back with two small perfect bird points. He waved them in Mida's face as he sat down and watched her finish dinner. "Recognize any of these?" he asked.

"Yeah, my great-great-granduncle Naiche shot this one at a bird brain Ute. Probably hit him in the butt. Did you see any butt bones nearby?" she laughed as she told Ev to sit down and eat. His turkey stew was ready.

After eating and going down to the creek to wash their dishes, Ev built a small campfire. The cool air flowed down from the distant summit of Boulder Mountain. They huddled next to the fire, much more intimately than the previous evenings only a few short weeks ago. They both commented how things had certainly changed since their last visit to this hidden paradise. Then, breaking the romantic mood, Mida said they had better enjoy this since the weather would change. "We are going to get wet tomorrow," she said matter-of-factly. "I hope you brought a good raincoat."

"Did your prescient turkey tell you this, too?" asked Ev as he stood up and picked up another stick to throw on the fire. "I didn't see a newspaper today and we didn't even have the radio on."

"I hate to keep reminding you of this, but I know things. Besides, this is July and we are in the monsoon season. It's been hot and I feel a change in the pressure. Plus there are subtle things like the noise of the crickets, the way the birds are hopping around, the way the twigs snap. You white boys need to become more observant." Mida stood up and stuck her finger in Ev's ear. "And whether my finger goes easily into your ear or whether it gets stuck," she laughed as he grabbed her and kissed her.

"Tomorrow is a big day," Ev said. He reached into the apricot bag and pulled out a handful to eat as he disappeared in the dark past the tent. Mida sat back down by the fire, intently gazing into the flames as she watched them slowly die to embers.

Early the next morning, they packed their gear in the backpacks and cleaned up the evidence of their camp. Ev wanted to see how far he could drive but he didn't intend to leave the truck so close to Orion. He would drive as far as he could, unload the stuff, then drive back up to near where they had camped.

They were able to drive as far as they had walked the day before. This was a nice discovery since it meant if they had to, they could drive right up to the base of Orion. Ev dropped off Mida and the gear, then drove back up the track. Before he left, he told Mida to erase her footprints leading to Orion. He would walk back by a different route. When he drove about a mile, he was glad he had Mida cover her tracks. A couple riders on horseback were coming his way. As he pulled off and parked, the two came over to him. They were both in uniform; one was Forest Service and the other Utah Division of Wildlife. They introduced themselves and said they were riding around down here looking for trespass cattle. They asked what Ev was doing. He said he was just exploring and would probably park here and just wander around in some canyons. They laughed and warned him not to get lost. They asked if he had seen any cattle. If he saw any, just let the office in Teasdale know when he got back to civilization. He asked where they would be going since it seemed difficult to get a horse through these canyons. They said they were going to circle south for a few miles and then head back west to the highway. Ev silently hoped that they would turn south before they got to where Mida was.

Ev mentioned that he had met Wally down in this area a couple months ago. The ranger laughed and said that that was probably the only time Wally had ever been down here. He reiterated that they seldom got down here, so Ev had better not get lost. He might stay down here until hunting season, then he motioned to his companion, George, the game warden, who would have to bring him out. George muttered that if you could lose a dozen head of cattle down here, you sure could lose a few hunters. They exchanged a few more pleasantries, then rode east down another track. Ev made a visible effort of putting on his daypack, then unfolding a map which he pretended to study. He noticed by the time they disappeared from view, they were veering right heading cross country.

Ev headed north and climbed up the top of the canyon above Orion. He wanted to see if this route would be drivable in case he needed to drive to the periscope. He enjoyed his walk and was pleased to discover that the plateau headed straight east, with no major canyons or gullies between his route and Orion.

He walked for about fifteen minutes before he looked up and noticed the cloud bank creeping north and east. A breeze started to rustle the oak leaves. This would not be your typical July afternoon thunderstorm, he thought. He picked up his pace and was soon standing at the edge of the cliff looking down at Mida. She was sitting where they had camped back in May near the base of the Orion cliff. She was singing but he couldn't recognize any words. He sat down and watched her for a few minutes. She was beautiful in the orange light. It contrasted with her black hair. Then he realized she was meditating and singing one of her Apache chants. Or he assumed. It sure didn't sound Norwegian to him. When she seemed to come to an end, he stood up and hollered at her. She smiled and said that he sure did come by a different route.

He was sitting beside her just a few minutes later. "I think it would be better to pitch our tents up on top. We just dodged a bullet," he said as he told her about his encounter with the two riders. "I don't want to take any chances with anyone coming over here or seeing us. I would like to pitch our tents over the periscope and do some digging up there. The tents will be a perfect camouflage. We can drive right to that spot as well as here, but I think up there may be a little safer to hide." He didn't even wait for Mida to answer when he hefted his backpack and put it on. "Thank you for bringing this over. Did you get your tracks erased?"

She said yes, she did, and asked if he brought all his rock hammers in this pack. It weighed a ton. He owed her for that one.

He replied rather sheepishly that he had in fact put several small picks and trowels in the pack. He had intended to do a bunch of digging but forgot to mention it to her. She said she was certainly glad that there were no secrets between them. He said it was a last-minute thing. Besides, if women could change their minds all the time, a man, struggling to achieve parity with the opposite sex could certainly change his mind once in a while. She smiled and said if that was the price of getting a mind, then it was all right to change it.

They pitched their tents on opposite sides of the periscope. Ev apologized as he cut down the small tree that hid the pipe. He needed to dig and have room to excavate. He would be able to hide the pipe by piling rocks and the tree would have to be sacrificed. Mida said it understood and was glad to have helped hide the pipe up until now.

By the time the clouds obliterated the sun and the cool wind started swirling dust and sand, Ev and Mida had a clever working space set up over the pipe. They spread an extra piece of plastic tarp between the tents as a roof. Ev cut the tree in half and propped each half between the tents to serve as makeshift walls. Cleverly enclosed, the space was ready for excavation. But Ev and Mida spent the rest of the afternoon in his tent as rain and wind confirmed Mida's prophecy. Ev took down the tarp roof after the wind whipped one end of it loose. No need to be out there, thought Ev, as he and Mida settled into a spirited game of mah-jongg. The afternoon passed in blustery solitude. Soon, the two disappeared under their sleeping bags, oblivious to wind and rain.

EIGHT

Into the Rock

*A creature without a memory
cannot discover the past.
One without expectation cannot
conceive a future.*

—*George Santayana*

*In rivers the water that you touch
is the last of what has passed
And the first of that which comes.
So with time present.*

—*Leonardo da Vinci*

B Y LATE AFTERNOON the winds died down, but a light drizzle continued. A soft gray blur hid the canyons, turning everything into ghostly haze. The temperature had cooled over twenty degrees. It was downright cold and miserable, grumbled Ev. But he was anxious to dig, so he put the plastic back up as a roof and set up the cooking stove in his little excavation room for heat. He retrieved a trowel and pick from his pack and started to dig around the pipe. Mida stayed in the tent writing in her journal. He had never looked at one of her entries but imagined it was a mixture of thoughts, opinions, and ideas. She could be unpredictable in what she thought and said. Sometimes he felt intellectually inadequate compared to her, though this was not a problem he had with anyone else. She was a powerful force whose talents were not yet recognized. Not yet. As he picked rocks and sand from the slowly deepening hole, he envisioned her standing tall above him, in long flowing robes, moving the dirt by willpower alone.

As Ev hit the roots of the small tree, he was impressed how extensive the root system was in this sandy soil. The pipe went straight down, embraced by the twining roots, disappearing into what appeared to be solid rock. The bedrock of the cliff was close to the surface, but it was fractured by action of tree roots, soil moisture, and chemical weathering. This was the raw material of the earth itself—rock being turned into soil. As he slowly and methodically picked away, he found the rock fractured into pieces that he could easily pick out of his widening hole and pile next to it. Soon, his pit went from tent floor to tent floor. He wished he had put the tents another couple feet further apart. By the time Mida came in to steal his camp stove to cook dinner, he was down almost three feet.

"What do I do if you used all the propane to heat the sky and left me none to cook with?" asked Mida as she stared in amazement at his hole in the ground. "And are you going to dig all the way down to the base of the cliff?"

"I have absolutely no idea what I am doing," he answered weakly as he wiped his forehead with his red stained shirtsleeve, leaving a reddish smudge the color of the dirt around him. "I want to find something here or rule it out. I can't imagine a pipe fifty feet long being on this thing. It would not be very functional going through millions of light-years of empty space. It can't be very far to the main body. Imagine a Boeing 747 or the Space Shuttle *Endeavor*. What we see down below on the cliff indicates a big vehicle. We really aren't that far away from it here if you take away all the rock. Could be a door or window close to us here. And imagine how much easier it would be to access it unseen here than to go in the side of the cliff down below."

"Okay. You know what you are doing," Mida said as she stared at him. Muttering to herself, she added, "whether you do or not."

Leaning over to pat him on his head, she whispered, "I'm going to cook something before it gets any colder out here. Come on in when you get tired." She looked at her hand, then wiped it on her pants. "Can't get much dirtier. You might want to stroll down to the creek and wash yourself off before you come in and try and snuggle me. I really don't care if you want to eat with all that dirt, just stay away from me." She took the stove and crawled into the tent.

Ev stared into the hole and touched the pipe. It didn't seem to change any at all in the nearly four feet now exposed. He just couldn't imagine it being much longer. He scraped out all the loose dirt and sand he could. The rest, as deep as he decided to go, would be pick and hammer work.

He eased out of his make-shift room and walked west until he found a route down the cliff. He ran over to the creek, washed his face and arms off, shivering in the sudden coldness of the water. It was muddy from the rain, so he wasn't sure if he had achieved anything or not. He went back up the way he came down, not worrying about any footprints with this rain. He opened the tent flap and smiled at Mida. She had laid out a neat dinner, with plates and silverware spread on the tent floor.

"Reservation for two. Name is Orion," announced Ev as he put out his hands, like a little boy showing them to his mother.

"Yes, come in clean, little man. You pass inspection. I don't need to see the rest of you. Like I expect anything else would be clean. Your table is waiting. Will you be dining alone?" asked Mida as she reached up and grabbed his hand. She gently pulled him down to the floor. "Don't step on the food, please. Our menu is short tonight, so you have no choice. You may begin."

Ev wolfed down his food, impressed by the way Mida had made a mixture of rice, vegetables, and canned meat taste so good. And he couldn't believe it when she produced a good imitation of apricot cobbler. Actually, it was more than an imitation. It was the real thing.

"If you don't mind, please eat your apricots and try not to decorate body parts with them," she said as she scooped some out of the pot for him.

"How in the world did you make this? We didn't bring a fully complete kitchen with us," stated Ev in amazement as he made quick work of the cobbler, including seconds and thirds.

"When are you going to learn to whom you are speaking?" Mida said as Ev suppressed a belch, not very successfully. "I come prepared for anything. And you were hungry enough that a mud pie would have tasted good to you. You never know when you will run into a wild raspberry or serviceberry patch, or even an apricot orchard. We had an apricot tree in our back yard as a kid and I learned to cook apricots in about a dozen different ways."

"I'll bet you that for every way you can cook them, I can find a way to eat them," Ev said as he licked his spoon clean.

After they finished eating and sat back to enjoy the peace and quiet, Mida said he should go down to the creek and wash dishes before it got dark. She said she would go with him. When they opened the door of the tent, they were surprised to see they were completely in a cloud. Fog turned their world into a hazy, eerie, mystical place. They carefully went down the cliff by Ev's new route and slowly made their way to the creek. Mida was dismayed by the muddy water but said it would work. She said her motto was we lived too cleanly and antiseptically anyway, so a little dirt made our immune system stronger. Ev laughed when he said he must have a strong immune system the way he ate before Mida showed up. By the time they started back to the camp, the fog was lifting, only to show a darkness replacing a sun, somewhere above the clouds, that was sinking into the west. They made their way back to their tents and each went into their own tent, to spend the evening reading. They decided against trying to see in the window of Orion that night. They would try tomorrow night.

Morning greeted the sunrise with a crystal clear but cold sky. Mida said she wanted to go below and uncover the window to Orion. She felt something was waiting for her. She dreamed about the inside of the ship and the beings that had lived in there. Ev winced when she said that and told her she was getting spooky again.

Birds broke the silence with a cacophonous uncoordinated concert as the sun quickly warmed the air. Steam rose off the wet rocks in curling, grasping tendrils. Ev walked around the general camp area to inspect it more thoroughly. When he discovered the pipe a few weeks ago, he stopped exploring any further. Now he wanted to make sure there was nothing else exposed. He found a wonderful expanse of crypto soil about three hundred feet from the tents. It was nested in-between two ancient gnarled juniper trees. There were several large slabs of Kayenta sandstone that formed a walkway across the black fuzzy soil. He got down on his hands and knees and marveled at the artistry of the picture. The ground was three-dimensional and alive. Miniature tufts of black and brown fuzz stood up from the sculpted surface like towers in a city. Lichens on the red rock painted the scene with orange and green splotches. A blue-tailed lizard scampered across the rocks while Ev was kneeling face to the ground. He smiled as he heard a canyon wren warbling somewhere down below him, hidden as usual in the labyrinth of canyon walls.

He went back to the periscope and got his hammer, a chisel, and a small pick. He sat on the ground and started pecking away at the rock. He was pleased that it broke easily. It was still close enough to the surface to have started its slow process of eroding into soil. He quickly deepened his hole by another six inches. With one quick tap of the hammer, he loosened a piece of rock that made him gasp. The pipe turned black and changed texture. It almost looked like a hard plastic. It was rounded and started flaring out horizontally. He wanted to yell at Mida, but he kept tapping at the edges, hoping to expose more before he interrupted what she was doing. He had to carefully break up the rock at the bottom of the hole since it was now only a thin layer covering another metal surface. He soon had the bottom of the hole rock-free, with only metal of the ship exposed. He would have to move the tents in order to expose any more surface. Standing up and dusting himself off, he called to Mida to come see this.

While Ev had been chipping away rock, Mida was carefully removing the top layers of rocks from their make shift wall at the base of the cliff. Half the window now reflected the blue image of the sky and orange glow of surrounding rocks. Leaning on top of the pile, she stared into the window. Nothing had changed from the last time she looked in. She put her face up against the window and closed her eyes. Humming one of her father's songs, she felt a quick pain behind her eyes. She tried to pull away, but it felt as if something was holding her up against the window. An electrical buzzing filled her head. Or was it coming from inside the ship?

A blue light overpowered her, even though she kept her eyes shut. She opened them quickly and could feel, more than see, that same blue light inside the ship. She jumped back off the rocks and fell to the ground. The pain had gone away but she rubbed her eyes instinctively. She looked up at the window but saw nothing. Slowly, hesitantly, she got up and eased back up, very cautiously putting her face against the window. All was quiet and as dark as before.

She stifled a small scream as she put her hand up to the window, immediately jerking it back. The window was so hot, her hand immediately started to blister from the burn. She felt the metal right next to the window but it was cool. Running her hand all around the metal, it all felt the same. Her finger slowly hovered over the glass, then touched it lightly. It was now cool, just like the metal. The blister faded away as did the pain. Staring at the window, Mida lowered herself to the ground and sat down. She started to feel light-headed and dizzy as she heard Ev say something from behind her. She fell over unconscious.

At first Ev thought she was playing around with him. Then he saw that her lips were turning blue and she had a blue tinge to her face. Falling to his knees, he sat her up. She was breathing, but not normally. Her pulse was racing. She said "Daddy," then she just moaned. Ev's heart started racing as he tried to figure out what was wrong with her. By rubbing her hands and face, he got her color to return and her breathing became more rhythmic. He moved her to a sunny spot and sat her upright. He sat next to her and rubbed her hands some more, talking to her. There were no visible signs of anything that happened to her.

He laid her back down on the ground and walked over to the window to see if he could see anything there. He put his face up against the window and looked in. Seeing nothing, he felt a tingling in his face as he jerked it back. He felt, or heard a very faint vibration. His first thought was an electrical current. He backed away from the cliff and went back to where Mida was lying. He sat next to her and waited. Ev was scared. He stared at the cliff and watched it as he heard a pair of ravens fly overhead. He heard another canyon wren but he didn't smile this time. After a few minutes, he went over and piled rocks back up, covering the window and the exposed metal. He walked back to Mida and sat down again. All he could do was cradle her in his arms and rock back and forth. After a while, he laid her back down and lay down next to her.

He woke up as Mida was singing to him. He jerked upright, looking at her with his mouth open.

"You look like you have seen a ghost," was all she said as she rubbed her eyes. "You think you can come down here and grab me for a quick roll in the sand?"

"Don't joke around. I thought you were dead. Or about to die. What the hell happened to you? You were out like a light."

"Rock Boy, I just met someone made of light. They touched me. And spoke to me. Damned if I know what they said, though. It was the weirdest sensation. Not unpleasant. Scary. Yeah, spooky as you say." Mida looked directly into Ev's eyes and just stared. She started feeling her body from fingers to toes. She looked at her right hand, then quickly put it in her pocket.

"Well, whatever happened, you scared the goobers out of me," Ev said as he stood up. "Tell me exactly what happened."

"Later. Gotta make sure I'm okay first." She got up and walked around to make sure all her parts still worked. "I want to go up and see your big discovery. I want to see what that black pipe is. I will help move the tents so we can get to the window."

Ev looked at her in disbelief. He took off his cap and smoothed his hair back. He took off his sunglasses and reached out and held her hands. "Mida, I didn't say anything about my discovery to you. How do you know? What do you think I discovered?"

"I saw it," she said calmly. She proceeded to describe exactly what Ev had uncovered. She said she knew there was a window directly under her tent that he hadn't uncovered yet. Ev accused her of watching him. She said, no, she had been down here since before he started working.

"Holy mother of Geronimo," Ev said as he looked up at the cloudless blue sky. "You are scaring the hell out of me. What has happened?" He rubbed his arms as goose bumps became visible.

"Let's go up to the tents. I'm really hungry. And thirsty. I bit my tongue and I need to get something to drink." She looked at Ev. His wild-eyed look frightened her. "Come on and we can talk it through. I'm not possessed by anyone or anything. I don't think I can turn my head all the way around." She turned her head from side to side. "See? It stops here.

"I'm the same old Mida and you are the same old Ev. I just experienced something and I'm not sure what it is." She grabbed Ev by the hand and pulled him behind her as she started walking toward their path to the cliff top.

They got to the tents in a few minutes, where Mida rushed to look into the hole. She smiled as she looked at Ev and said, "It looks just like what I saw in my vision. I am impressed. If you keep digging to the right," she motioned to her tent, "you will uncover another window much like we have down below. And you want to hear something that will really spook you out?" She looked at Ev to see his expression. "There is a door next to the window."

"Oh man, I don't want to even ask you," groaned Ev as he plopped down on the ground in front of the tent. "You better start from zero and tell me everything and what it has done to you."

Mida sat in the shade of the tent and took off her boots. She rifled through her overnight kit and found something she put on her tongue. She looked up at the sky as a flock of pinyon jays flew over in formation, chattering and scolding as they disappeared over the distant trees. She took a deep breath and closed her eyes. Then she began slowly.

"I felt an energy in the ship. I tried to connect with it. Something weird happened, sort of like someone or something entering my body. Or at least my mind. It was a tingling, almost a vibrating sensation. But I wasn't frightened. It wasn't a threatening thing. Maybe it was how Moses felt when his bush caught fire. Humbling. Yeah, it was very humbling."

As Mida relived her experience, she relaxed more. She started talking faster. "Everything was blue. Then I talked to some people. Or they talked to me. Time stopped. I have no idea how long the whole thing took. Then you were there." She looked at Ev waiting for a comment.

"What do you mean you talked to people? Who? What did they say? And who were they?" Ev leaned toward Mida and looked at her intently. He waited.

"I think it was while I was out. I must have passed out because one second I was touching the metal, the next I was lying on the ground with you asleep next to me."

"Well, don't expect me to answer that one for you. I have no idea. I was busy scraping sand. It couldn't be very long because you weren't down here for much more than an hour." Ev waited for Mida to answer his earlier question. "Well?"

Mida began slowly as she searched the sky for something. "I saw things very clearly. I saw the hole you were digging. As I was standing looking in the hole, I saw people in the ship." She hesitated. Her eyes continued to search, then settled on Ev.

"You better sit tight. I talked with my dad. Actually, I talked to him but he never said a word to me. He played his guitar and the song was the most beautiful tune I've ever heard. And I talked to an old man with wild white hair. He had a German accent. I remember one thing he said to me—'Let go ov all preconceifed notions.'" Mida's poor German accent made Ev laugh.

"He said, 'Imagination is more important than knowledge. You haf been chosen for a mission that vill change the vorld.' He reached out to touch me. His eyes were deep. I've never seen anything like it. The wisdom and kindness in those eyes. He said, 'I envy you, child, for you vill learn things I spent a lifetime seeking answers to.'"

"Einstein?" asked Ev hesitatingly. Mida only shrugged.

"We will move to Torrey. You will quit your job. Or at least get a different job. Things got kind of fuzzy." She trailed off, then chuckled when she said that Ev would be talking to animals and they would talk back to him. Mida was now talking to herself, not even looking at Ev.

"Oh, now we are into fortune-telling? Wanna give me some stock market tips? And who wins the World Series?"

Mida took a breath as Ev just stared at her. "You better close your mouth before flies start breeding in it."

Ev reached over and put his hand on Mida's forehead. "One of us has just gone off the deep end and I don't know which one it is, you or me. If what you are saying is true, then it's you. If it isn't true, then it is still you. I'm sitting here with a crazy person."

Mida burst out laughing as she reached over and kissed Ev. "Poor Rock Boy, you need more attention than I do. You would not have made a good prophet back in the desert of Palestine three thousand years ago. It is very simple. You have witnessed a miracle that is not really a miracle. It is just a revelation of what we all are. I was given a glimpse of reality. We are both going to enter this new world, but I don't know when. Get used to it. I just got there first with a preview of coming attractions."

"I can't . . . but I . . . it's just I . . . I mean you . . ." Ev could not complete a thought as he stammered like someone struck dumb.

Mida started laughing again, which just made Ev mad as well as incoherent. She fell onto Ev and started rolling him over on the ground. Finally he broke his silence and started laughing.

Ev stood up and wiped his eyes. "It is you," he said as he walked in a big circle. "You have gone entirely crazy and you are going to pull me in there with you. I have thought of quitting my job. I must have mentioned it to you." Mida shook her head no.

Ev said quietly, "When my dad was a little boy, he met Albert Einstein at a youth science conference at Stanford. Einstein told a group of the students something Dad always remembered. I read the same quote somewhere in a book once. It was 'imagination is more important than knowledge.' You probably read the same quote."

Mida, still chuckling to herself, stood up, shaking her head no, and walked into the tent. "I think I need to lie down and rest. Without you if you don't mind. Then we need to dig a little more, after we move the tent. We need to get this window uncovered and see what our door to the future looks like. Or the past, as if the future and past are separate things. Maybe I will have more insights, Rock Boy. Your life is in my hands now."

Ev sat by himself and watched the shadows crawl along nearby cliffs as the sun slowly made its way toward Boulder Mountain, then past the huge pine-and-fir-covered hulk. Ev thought about the flower meadows and lakes on the Top. Since Mida had never been up there, he thought about taking an additional day to drive up there. This slickrock country was starting to unnerve him. He needed the comfort of the high mountains.

He wished he had brought his mountain bike, but Mida did not own one and she was not used to bike riding. He made a mental note to buy her a decent bike when they got back. Ev thought about how the view from the Rim over this vast expanse of desert would fit with Mida's newfound philosophy of space and time.

Mida lay quiet in the tent. She thought about whether she would be able to communicate with her father or whether that appearance was just her imagination. When she considered she had never paid any attention to Einstein, she thought it had to be real. Why else would he have appeared and spoke to her the way he did. She knew her psychic powers had suddenly been heightened. Knowing this fact was proof of her powers. She just knew. There was a confidence she had never felt before.

After an hour, Mida got up and left the tent. Ev was sitting against a rock, fast asleep. She sat down next to him and put her head on his shoulder. He opened his eyes and jerked back.

"Don't look at me like that. I may have powers I never imagined, but I don't have a clue how to use them. Don't have a clue. Don't know how to find out other than you go do it. Answer your question?" Mida looked at Ev and gave him her serious look that always confused him. It reminded him of either a Viking ready to raid or an Apache ready to attack.

"It scares me to think of being zapped like you were. You already had spooky powers that I don't have. I might just keel over dead if the blue light came into my brain. Now I'm not sure I want to try and go into this thing," Ev calmly said. This attitude surprised Mida since until now, he had talked of nothing else than getting inside.

"Well, you want to travel in time. I think I just did," Mida said as she reached over and held Ev's face in her hands. She looked deeply into his eyes. "And I think I found out something about time that changes your dreams of time travel."

"That's what scares me," said Ev as he gently moved her hands from his face and held them in his hands. "You may leave me behind. I'm the one with an interest in physics. Remember, my dad was a physicist. When I was in college, we would discuss and argue theories. I'm the one who has dreamed of time travel. And here you are the one who does it. I would like for you to use your powers and think us both back in time right here and now, but that raises a silly question."

Mida smiled at him and said, "First of all, I'm not sure I would really call it time travel. But what may that question be?"

Ev laughed, "Sitting here right now, how would we know if we went back ten years or ten thousand years? This view would be the same either way. The only way we would know anything changed would be to look up on the Top and see a glacier cascading off, bringing those big round black boulders bouncing down here. Maybe we would see a dire wolf or cave bear or saber-toothed tiger sitting over there licking himself." Ev frowned as he pondered his dilemma.

"I have no idea how to use this power. I need time." She got up. "What I do propose is that we go back over there"—she pointed to the tents with a sidelong glance—"and dig. I want to prove there really is a window and a door. Don't you want to know that?"

"I guess you are right," Ev said as he got up and dusted himself off. The thought of finding the door and window as Mida predicted gave Ev a shiver. He was not so sure he really wanted to know. As they started to walk, he commented, "But it is a logical guess. Maybe I was thinking the same thing."

"It was no guess. It was no conjecture. It was no dream. It was real. As real as you are right now."

"Yeah, I was worried about that," Ev said as he looked up at the mountain one more time. He really needed to go up there.

They went over and unpinned both tents and moved them about eight feet farther apart. Ev asked Mida if this was far enough and she nodded yes. They secured the tents and Ev climbed into the hole and continued to dig, with Mida removing the rock. The rock and dirt pile next to the hole was getting large.

It took Ev only a few minutes to chip away enough rock to expose the edge of a window. It looked just like the one at the bottom of the cliff. Ev had to be very careful with his hammering since he only had about three inches of rock before he reached the glass or whatever that material was. The window was the same size as the one down below. This one had a large crack cutting diagonally across the window. It obviously had been there before and was not created by Ev. There was a red stain embedded within the material along the crack. The surface of the window was crusted with a silicate that scraped off with a little effort. It reminded Ev of what happens when wood is petrified, with silicates replacing carbonates. Ev realized this window was different from the lower one in that this one could have had standing water on it. He wondered whether the inside air had been contaminated or was being contaminated now that the protective rock was removed. Mida intently watched Ev as he progressed with the rockwork. As soon as they saw the crack, Mida cautioned Ev not to let the blue light squeeze through to get him. Ev saw no humor in that.

Ev continued chipping the rock away beyond the window but did not come to any door. He looked at Mida and asked if she was sure it was there. He was getting to the edge of the hole and was almost ready to start undermining the tent. Mida said she was sure it was there but wasn't sure of its location in relation to the window. It was close to the window but maybe it was below or above it and not next to it. Ev grumbled about enlarging the entire hole, which meant removing a few feet of overburden as he called it. It was easier now that Mida was there to help throw it out of the hole, but it still was a lot of work.

He finally uncovered a small crack in the surface of the metal. As he removed rock, the line turned ninety degrees. He knew this was the door opening, but the crack was so tight he couldn't even slip a piece of paper into it. It was a door with precision fitting. As the crack disappeared beyond the edge of the excavation, he decided it was time to quit for the day. Getting the door uncovered was going to create a huge hole and Ev was getting tired. Mida disappeared behind the tent to start supper.

Ev went down to the creek to wash off and was gone only a few minutes before he returned quietly. He tiptoed up behind Mida who was humming to herself, intent on her cooking and embraced her. She must not have heard him coming since she let out a scream that would have awakened Geronimo himself. She turned around and hit him with a wooden ladle, splattering him with spaghetti sauce. As soon as she did that, she put her hand to her mouth to suppress a giggle. She told him he had better go back down to the creek to wash the sauce off. He suggested she lick it off, which provoked another splat with the ladle. He went back down to the creek and was gone a half hour. When he returned, she had dinner ready. He commented that all they needed was a good bottle of Zinfandel, but he needed a good night's sleep. Mida reached for the wooden spoon, but Ev disappeared into the tent. He poked his head out sheepishly a few seconds later and demanded a truce.

After supper, Ev sat staring at Mida with his quizzical look that always made her giggle. She knew something bothered him, maybe seriously or just maybe in that impish way that still surprised her. He started to say something, then stopped. Now she thought he looked like a monkey and that did cause her to giggle.

"Ev, what in the world is going through that brain of yours? Just spit it out."

"Well, you are doing it again. You have that 'I know something you don't' look. I don't know how to take it."

"I'm sure there are a lot of things I know that you don't, sweetie. Unfortunately, there are probably a couple things you know that I don't either. So where does that leave us? Can't I just have that look and it not cause a congressional investigation?"

"This blue light thing bugs me because you are seeing or hearing or feeling things I can't. What does that mean?"

"No doubt in my mind that it means you are probably more at peace with life than I am. I don't know what it all means. You are the scientist. Maybe it's some subatomic particle thing, like quarks or bosonic morons gone berserk and following me around like a lost puppy dog."

"Quark my ass. You may be the bosomy meson acting like a puppy dog. There is no scientific explanation for this. You are in touch with something out there that for whatever reason has chosen to ignore me and make contact with you."

Mida tossed her head back and ran her hands through her hair. That little gesture always made Ev crazy. She looked at him and stepped back. "You may not be aware, but I can tell by your energy field that your level of energy fell down below your waist just now."

"Oh god," Ev moaned. "How the hell can I live with someone who can read my mind? What chance do I have?"

"I didn't used to have this power." Mida grimaced. "Actually it would have come in handy on a few dates I can remember."

Ev interrupted, "Somehow I don't think you needed to see their energy field to know they were undressing you in their mind."

"I know you weren't undressing me that first time we met." Mida smiled as she thought back to their first meeting on the road and him on the bicycle.

"You intimidated me and you knew it at the time. I was trying to be polite. Contrary to your impression of me, I don't automatically want to hop in the sack with every female I meet."

"What, just every other one. Or every third one?"

"Get serious. I can't see the energy cloud that you talk about. I don't see blue lights. I don't feel woo-woo. Either you are going crazy or I am."

"It's all energy!" Mida said in exasperation. "Life is energy! You and Mr. Einstein will have to explain what that really means. But this energy is out there and is talking to me. I apologize that it likes me and hasn't learned your good qualities yet. Maybe it's female and she knows your thoughts before you have them. Maybe it's an Apache energy and knows your ancestors didn't like him. You explain to me why it is happening." She waved her arms in frustration.

They spent the evening sitting by the small campfire discussing their future options. They talked about Ev's job and whether he really intended to quit. He said he had given it some thought, but was committed for the fall term. He could give notice and be done by Christmas. Mida asked how he could support himself. Ev countered with the question of how Mida intended to support herself. She shrugged and raised her eyebrows as she said that was a good question. She could write a book, expanding and simplifying her thesis, but that was not a sure bet for a big paycheck. She had been so intent on her degree that she had not started sending out resumes. Her line of work would be limited, especially if she wanted to stay in this immediate area. She smiled at him and asked if he could support them both.

"I wasn't going to tell you this, but I am moderately wealthy," Ev said shyly. Mida could tell this was a subject that he was not comfortable with by the way he eased into it. "My father left me quite a bit of money in a trust. When I was growing up, I never did consider us rich, but he was a college professor all his life and teaching at a place like Boulder does have its rewards. When Mom sold the house a year ago, she put half into the trust that Dad set up several years ago for me. I don't know if you realize how much houses are worth in Boulder, but when you buy a big house in a nice neighborhood in 1963 and sell nowadays, you are sitting on a pretty pot of money. It's not quite like owning a house on the rez." He expected a reaction to that last statement, but Mida just nodded and agreed.

Mida looked at him and cautioned a question, "Am I out of line asking how much? I mean it is none of my business, but . . ."

Ev looked at the fire for several seconds before answering. "Well, I haven't checked for nearly a year, but the house itself added nearly five hundred thousand dollars to the account. Dad had a lot of shares of little-known companies like IBM and Coca-Cola that he bought before he even got married. I think his parents left him a pile of money. For his wedding present, they bought him a small house in what is now known as Silicon Valley. He was a graduate student at Stanford at the time and my grandfather was a lawyer in San Francisco. I never had any idea of what he was worth, but let us say I am a millionaire." Ev threw a few sticks onto the fire.

He waited for Mida to say something, but she didn't even blink. He continued, "I have a philosophical problem with rich people. Especially people who don't make their own money. There are a lot of trust funders in Durango and around the big ski areas like Telluride and Aspen. These are people our age who are rich from no work of their own. That's why I haven't paid much attention to my trust. I want to pay my own way. I always figured I might use it later to travel or buy a mountain somewhere when I retired. But I can get into it any time I want. Does that answer your question?"

Mida lowered her eyes and watched the fire throw shadows over Ev and the nearby trees. An owl in the distance broke the silence. "What can I say?" she finally answered. "I didn't know. I'm not a gold digger. I never had money nor did my parents. We always worked, but there are not a lot of rich people on the rez. I have had some type of job ever since I was fourteen, but I think my bank account has maybe five hundred dollars in it. I don't even have a savings account. I had grants and scholarships, but those simply allowed me to get where I am today. I am a stranger when it comes to money."

Mida didn't tell Ev that this new fact about him made her suddenly feel very uncomfortable. She did feel like a gold digger and would now be self-conscious about even being with a person with this much money. She knew that was silly since it didn't change Ev—he had been rich all along and wasn't going to change his personality now that he had told her about it.

Neither said anything for several minutes. Ev finally stood up and poked the fire with his rock pick. "I wouldn't touch my fund unless for a special reason. I think Orion counts as a special reason. And you have no reason to feel guilty. You have come into my life and you are not about to ever leave it again. We are a pair now. Me. You. Together." He leaned down and put his arms around Mida. She answered with a hug and long kiss. Tears welled in her eyes.

She quickly stood up and changed the subject as she sniffed and wiped her eyes with the sleeves of her sweatshirt. "Well, let's sleep on this subject. We need to talk more before making any decisions. I don't know about you, but my tent was lonely last night and that owl scared me. How about singing me to sleep?"

Ev laughed as he walked with Mida to the tent. "Boy, do you have the wrong person. You have heard me sing. I think that blue light did erase part of your memory."

Mida smiled as Ev touched her dimples. "It's not what you sing or how you sing it. It's your rhythm, Rock Boy."

Ev and Mida awoke to a beautiful sunrise. Birds were singing and not a breeze stirred in their wilderness. They walked out of the tent and both just sat down on the red sandy soil and absorbed the scenery. This was a moment to remember forever. They scanned from horizon to horizon and saw nothing but the blue of the sky, the red of the rocks and soil, the green of the scattered trees and distant mountains, and the white puffs of a few drifting small clouds. They saw or heard no evidence of mankind other than themselves and their camp. Ev again thought that they could very well be anywhere in time. Mida was trying to figure out what the blue light had done to her perceptions and senses. Both were there in the present as well as the past. They were thinking also of the future. Neither could tell which was which.

They both decided that tonight might be the last night camped here, so they needed to finish the hole and find out what the door looked like. They would wait before filling in the hole so they could use their fancy flashlights later that evening. They had lain awake the night before debating how and when to try and enter the ship. Ev worried about contaminating the air inside. He didn't want to just open the door or window and walk in. They needed to somehow do some testing of the air and other things such as magnetic fields, electrical forces, and whatever else a physicist or engineer could think of. This needed research.

A chickadee chattering in a pinyon nearby brought them both back to the present moment. They leisurely ate a light breakfast and got to work expanding the hole. Hopefully for the last time, thought Ev. Mida was slowed down in her rock handling by a blister on her finger. This was not from touching the window, but from scraping her finger on rocks she was removing from the hole. She wrapped it in a bandage, which lasted about five minutes before being worn off. After a half dozen bandages, she gave up on it and let it cover itself with dried blood. Ev soon had blisters of his own as he chipped and picked away the equivalent of a pickup load of rock. By midmorning, the door was exposed. It was not a full-sized door, but more of a rectangular hatch, about two feet by four feet. He thought this size odd, but then he had no idea what type of creature used it. There was no way to open the hatch from the outside. It was totally smooth, with no door handle or handholds or anything visible to open it. There was some dark-colored marking on it, but it didn't look like the lettering on the ship at the bottom of the cliff. The marking made no sense to either him or Mida, who was the expert on symbols and picture language.

By the time the sun was nearly overhead, Ev climbed out of the hole, shook hands with Mida, and said, "Well, I think we have finished phase 1." Looking down at their exposed treasure, he shook his head and said, "Now what?"

Mida laughed and said, "I guess we fill it in. We could succeed very well in the army."

Ev frowned and said, "I hate to say this, but you are right. We fill it in very carefully but not yet. How about if you use your fine artistic skills and draw it. I will measure it for dimensions. We will fill it before we leave tomorrow. So what do we do the rest of the day?"

Both of them stood and stared into the hole. The sun was at an angle that allowed them to see into this window much better than the lower window. As they were staring down, both gasped at the same time. They noticed a glint of light from inside. Mida was the first to jump down and put her face up against the window. Ev commented that he was not about to do that after yesterday.

Mida pulled her face back quickly after making a strange noise. She looked up at Ev and blinked. "You ninny. What a scaredy-cat. It's only a reflection of the sun off a shiny surface. I can see my face. It's either a mirror or something polished like a mirror. Come down here and look. I don't feel or see any blue lights this time."

Ev crawled down in the hole and slowly put his face next to Mida, who was looking into the window again. The window was darkly tinted like the other, but they could barely make out what looked like an instrument panel and a couple objects that could be chairs. There was not much room inside this part of the ship. The room reminded Ev of a cockpit of an airplane. It was only a few feet across and didn't appear to be much larger than their hole. They both stared into the room for several minutes when Ev jumped back and said, "I know what it is!"

Mida stared at him like a puppy dog waiting for a pat on the head. After a few seconds, she blurted out, "Well, Sherlock, do you care to share your knowledge, or are you waiting for me to guess what is in your mind?"

"I'm thinking," he slowly said after waiting another ten seconds.

"You can't think. You already said you knew what it was. You don't need to think about it. Why did you say you knew what it was?" She hit him on the shoulder with her hat.

"I don't want to sound like a fool," he said as he rubbed his shoulder. He had been working without a shirt and was showing a bright red sunburn.

"Now that is a stupid statement," she sputtered. Mida was getting mad. "You are already looking like a fool. Tell me what the hell you were thinking or I'm coming after you with your hammer!"

"It is a cockpit of a shuttle vehicle." Ev blurted it out quickly as he dodged as if expecting to be hit again. "It is not the main ship but a small shuttle that attaches to the mother ship. It is used to get around once you get to where you are going with the bigger ship."

"Wouldn't such a thing be stored inside, though?" Mida looked at him with a very confused look on her face. She started picking away dried blood from her finger, but stopped quickly as she grimaced in pain.

"Just leave it alone," said Ev as he grabbed her finger and kissed it. "Don't you have some magic potion that you and Bluebell invented?"

"I'll put something on it later. Do you really think that's what this is?" she said, looking down at their feet. "So this may not be the way into the main ship after all?"

Ev frowned at her as he replied, "You know as well as I do. You think I was here two hundred million years ago when they parked this? Or crashed it."

Mida sat down in the hole and curled her legs up against her chest. She puckered her lips. "This is just too big for the two of us to deal with by ourselves. You realize that don't you. We have to bring someone else into this."

"I've known that since last May. I just don't know who. You're right. We are there." He sat down next to her and put his hands on the door and ran them back and forth across the metal. It was warm from the sunlight.

The pair of tan-colored tents sat inconspicuous on top of the red sandstone cliff in the isolated expanse of canyons and rock in the huge landlocked desert. Mida closed her eyes and watched the scene disappear as she soared high in the sky, Earth gradually getting smaller and smaller until she could see it no more.

A breeze stirred as a small whirlwind moved across the mesa top, scattering red dust and sand. Ev watched the whirlwind get closer as it moved red sand across the unending desert, red and featureless. The wind, a timeless agent, shifted sands one way today, then back again tomorrow. Grain after grain piled in huge dunes, building a huge rock hundreds of miles across that one day would erode down to meandering cliffs and canyons.

Ev and Mida sat in their newly created hole, huddled like two scared children guarding a fire-breathing dragon. They looked at each other, not saying a word.

July 22, 1998

It was not a dream. I have to keep telling myself that. The other day probably was a vision. This wasn't. I didn't tell Ev this, but I actually went into the ship. It was another world. I've heard Ev talk about his physics and such things as parallel universes, wormholes, such stuff that I never cared about. I know I went in there, maybe a wormhole. I not only heard these people, I felt them. I was floating. I felt like my brain was outside my body. There is no way to put all this in words. One of the strangest things was the noise. It was like a rumbling, a wind blowing, a sensation of moving, yet I don't think I was. Old Lizard Tail back on the rez told me once of his trips where he felt like he was flying. That was probably the peyote or the other things he smoked or drank or whatever he did. This was not like that. The old man, if it was Einstein, he touched me and whispered my name. He called me Mida, then chuckled. Then he handed me a couple strands of long white hair. He said that was proof. He said he was big on proofs, then laughed again. These strands of hair are what I put in the journal. I don't have any tape but will remember to tape them onto this page when I get back. For Mr. Scientist Ev, that should be proof. My hair may be that white by the time this is over, but for now, let him tell me where else I would have gotten them. He will probably say a white buffalo that I met in a dream.

This is beginning to get old, but I will say once again: my life changed. I have to think, "Why me?" but would it happen if someone else were in my place? Would it have happened to Ev if he were here alone?

I hate to say it, but I want to enter this thing with Ev right now, but I know we have to wait. I think it doesn't matter if we contaminate anything, but I also realize it should be done right. This power is friendly and is trying to tell me that. I know it.

NINE

Transitions

To See a World in a Grain of Sand
And a Heaven in a Wild Flower,
Hold Infinity in the palm of your hand
And Eternity in an hour.

—*William Blake*

First say to yourself what you would be;
And then do what you would have to do.

—*Epictetus*

Ev AND MIDA stood hand in hand on the east rim of the flat plateau of Boulder Mountain. Locals called it Boulder Top. At eleven-thousand-foot elevation, it was enough to cause both to breathe a little harder as they hiked through trees and rocks to get to the edge. They stared at what seemed like half of Utah, from Green River to Moab to the Arizona line. The Henry Mountains, just south of the isolated hamlet of Hanksville, rose defiantly in the distance beyond the swell of Capitol Reef. Ignoring for the moment, if it was indeed possible, the expanse of view before them, they both were intently focused looking for their campsite of the last few days, down below in the maze of canyons and plateaus. They had left one tent pitched next to their excavation, but could not see it from their cliff-top perch. Not with their naked eyes or with their binoculars. If it was in fact visible from here, it was certainly so inconspicuous in this scenic expanse that it might as well be invisible. Oak Creek peeked between canyon walls as it wound eastward to disappear in the Waterpocket Fold. They spotted the edge of Tantalus Flat where they camped several weeks earlier. But they could not find their tan tent next to a small pile of rocks. They both breathed a sigh of relief. Earlier, on their drive along the Boulder Mountain highway on their long way around the mountain to the Top, they could not spot it either.

The view before and below her hypnotized Mida. She was on top of the world. Actually, she felt as if she were in another world, so different than that mystical world she entered with Orion. Boulder Top was a subalpine wonderland of its own, completely opposite of the canyon wonderland below. This tabletop of a mountain was an island in the desert. Being almost flat and spread out for miles in all directions, there was nothing to offer any perspective of height or distance. Spruce forests enfolded wildflower meadows dotted with lakes and ponds in an endless quilt of color. Ev had been on the Top several times before but now he was disoriented trying to find their tent overlooking Oak Creek Reservoir. The headwaters of the creek that brushed the edge of the Orion cliff, the reservoir sat like a jewel at the base of the basalt cliffs far below them.

Earlier that morning they broke camp, leaving one tent set up to help them identify the site from the Top. They drove up to the highway and circled to the west side of Boulder Mountain. There were no roads onto the top from the east or north side and only one decent road onto the Top from the west. And calling it decent was a stretch of the imagination. Mida was fascinated by the changes in scenery they went through on the journey from Orion to the Top. The east side of Boulder Mountain was a forest of pine, aspen, and spruce, with grasslands and meadows interspersed among the sandstone outcrops. The Aquarius Plateau, on the west side of Boulder Mountain, was named for the numerous lakes and potholes. It was an expanse of sagebrush, mixing with stands of aspen and spruce. As Ev drove along this rolling plateau, he enjoyed racing small groups of antelope. He would round a curve and come on a group of five or six, half of which would start running to keep up with him as he hit thirty-five and forty miles per hour. He had trouble maintaining his speed on the winding, washboard gravel road. The antelope did fine bounding past sagebrush and flying over prairie dog holes.

After Ev turned on to the main road to the top and started the long climb, Mida thought back to the day before. She struggled with her experiences and their meaning. When they had finished digging at Orion, they mentally collapsed at the meanings of what they found. She felt like she was transported into space, possibly to where the ship came from. Ev felt as if he was transported back in time, possibly to when the ship arrived. Both were transfixed for what seemed like days, but it was only an hour, according to Mida's watch. When they both returned to the present, at almost the exact same time, they spent the rest of the day trying to figure out what occurred. Mida said it was the blue light energy; Ev thought it was just a daydream. Exhausted physically from digging and mentally from the impact of what they were digging, they decided they needed a break from Orion. Ev convinced Mida that a quick trip up to Boulder Top would be just the right remedy.

As Ev topped the last rise that took them suddenly onto the Top, he made Mida jump as he started honking the horn. Mida's intensifying headache was not helped by the blaring noise. Before she could ask him to not go into one of his lectures, he started his explanation of the history of the Top. This high elevation plateau was here because of fire and ice. The fire was the molten lava that oozed out of several places millions of years ago and formed a hard protective cap covering the softer sandstones beneath. As the sandstone not covered by the lava eroded away, it left this capped plateau. Then came the glaciers of the last ice ages. Ev said the ice that covered Boulder Top to unknown depths was not your typical mountain glacier, but a continental glacier like the one that covered her father's homeland of Minnesota. It plucked off pieces of the basalt cliffs as it cascaded off the rim, carrying with it those black boulders that now dotted the east side of Boulder Mountain all the way down to where they were camped on Oak Creek. Because of the elevation of Boulder Top, there was plenty of moisture up here, which resulted in the flower-dotted meadows and the lush spruce forests, all mixed with countless lakes, potholes and swampy depressions. Mida nodded occasionally as Ev droned on with his geology lecture, but the nods were more from trying to stay awake than from any comprehension of his science facts.

As they wound through the monotonous but colorful meadows, Mida thought back to the previous night. They spent it looking into the new window of Baby Orion, her name for the newest discovery. Ev pulled out the night-vision goggles and they both peered into the window. They couldn't see much more than what they had seen in the daylight. They tried out the flashlight and got a fairly good look around. The crack in the glass had allowed water to seep in slowly for millions of years. There was a deposit on the wall below the window. It reminded Ev of a stalagmite in a cave. He was disappointed there was not a stalactite on the window itself. The small vehicle, if that's what it was, was sitting on its side, unlike the larger ship below. They could see a window on the other side just like the one they were looking in. And there was another door, the same size as the one at their feet. The door was not closed all the way. They could see there was an opening about two feet wide. They couldn't see what was on the other side, but it was not solid rock. Ev concluded the shuttle was up against the opening to the mother ship or maybe even part way inside. They couldn't make out anything else on the far side except empty space.

They then tried out the infrared sensing device Ev borrowed from the physics department. This would detect infrared radiation, or heat. He doubted this would show anything, but he was surprised when it indicated a faint glow from an object on the shuttle's control panel. There was also a faint glow coming from behind the opening of the other door. Both were very dim but did indicate something different from the surroundings. Mida asked if the object in Baby Orion could have been heated by the sunlight coming in the window while they were working on the hole. Ev agreed that was the likely answer, not wanting to think that anything else could be producing heat for two hundred million years. He wondered if there could possibly be some type of battery that would still be producing power. He didn't think even plutonium or uranium radiation from nuclear energy would last that long.

Now on Boulder Top, Mida stared vacantly at Ev as he stopped the truck on the edge of a meadow to emphasize a point. He was talking about the thin soil and how glaciation had affected it up here. He pointed to tire tracks going across a grassy opening and the fact that grass was thicker in the tracks, where the soil had been slightly compacted by the tires. Mida mumbled something in mock understanding and interest, amazed that Ev could be pontificating for so long without realizing he lost her attention miles earlier.

The previous night, when they shone the regular flashlight on the object that glowed under infrared, it looked like a crystal about six inches long and an inch in diameter. It seemed to be clear, but it was hard to tell in the tinted light. As Ev moved the light around the small room, Mida gasped as she glimpsed a notebook half-hidden underneath the console—a spiral-bound lined paper notebook, which looked like something she could buy at any supermarket. She bit her lower lip as she stared into the darkness. Ev didn't seem to notice it or her reaction. Looking more carefully, she recognized the notebook as the same one she was using now as her journal. Not the same type of notebook, but the exact one. On its cover was written her name, along with the date she started it. Ev continued to look for a few minutes longer, but Mida stood up on shaky knees. She told Ev she had seen about all there was to see and she was really tired.

She went back to her tent. Tripping as she entered, she fell on top of her sleeping bag. Reaching to the floor, she picked up her journal that she had used for the past six months. Cradling it in her arms, she tried to make sense of what she had just seen. She got very little sleep the rest of the night, while Ev snored in his tent. She said very little the next morning as they packed up everything but the one tent and hiked back to the truck.

Mida stood on the rim of Boulder Top staring down. She was so close to the edge Ev walked up next to her and very carefully pulled her back. As he commented that she seemed "off in the ozone," she looked at him as if awakening from a dream and laughed. She said she had not been with him for over an hour. Ev looked at her with a puzzled expression, then whined about her missing his great lecture. When he asked if she knew where she was right now, she slowly shook her head. Not only did she not know where she was, she didn't remember walking almost a mile through the forest to get there. But she did marvel at the view. She also marveled to herself at the secret hidden in the rocks somewhere down there. A secret very gently covered again after their hour-long effort to fill in the hole with the dirt and sand taken out only a day before. They left a pile of rocks next to the tent. They would have to go back down there to get the tent, but she didn't want to return to the ship, at least not this trip.

She and Ev previously agreed to have no secrets from each other, but she couldn't bring herself to tell him about the notebook. How could she make sense of it? Would an advanced civilization that could travel to distant stars use a lined paper spiral notebook? Her journal was here, cradled in her very own hands the entire trip up to the Top. It was more than a diary. It contained drawings and maps to secret rock art sites. It contained her philosophies, her dreams, and even her recent changes of life due to meeting Ev. She used it extensively in her doctoral research and she planned to use it as the basis of a book. Ev knew she kept the journal, but he never asked her about it. He tried keeping a journal several years ago, but didn't have the discipline to keep it current. He admired and envied Mida for having the patience to do what she was doing.

Ev commented again that Mida seemed to be rather quiet. She smiled at him and said she was just tired. They walked the mile back to the truck, which was parked at the edge of a meadow. They set up their one tent under a grove of spruce trees and Ev wandered around collecting firewood, which was a much easier task here than down below. It was already getting cold as they settled by the campfire to toast marshmallows. They had stopped at the market in Bicknell and Ev bought makings for s'mores. They argued over whether saltine crackers or graham crackers made the best s'more.

Mida let Ev win the argument since she still didn't have her full attention or interest on anything but her notebook. They now ate s'mores a la graham cracker under the starlit skies of Boulder Top. Mida stared up at the twinkling dots of distant starlight as Ev stared down at the flickering flames of firelight.

Finally, Mida looked down at the fire, then at Ev. She reached over and held his hand. "You remember that night by the fire down below when we first met? You were acting really goofy and I thought you had too much wine. You said you would change my life and I thought you wanted to marry me."

Ev just nodded. He thought for a few seconds, then replied as he stretched out his legs away from the fire, "Sure seems like a million years ago. Or more correctly, two hundred million."

"Ev, I'm confused like never before. Maybe even scared. More than when my dad died. More than when I went on my big vision quest. Even more than when I first saw Orion. As far as I'm concerned we are married. Remember how I told you traditional Apaches did it? We just move our things in together and maybe the holy man spreads pollen on my forehead for fertility. Well, I moved in with you, only no one smeared pollen on me. I didn't want the fertility part of it yet. That move changed my life and for the better." She paused and looked at him until his eyes moved up from looking at the flames to looking in her eyes. She slowly said, "But other things have now changed my life."

Ev blurted out as he jumped up, spilling crackers all over the ground, "Oh my god, are you pregnant?"

Mida looked up at him and burst out laughing. "You are being goofy again, you big rock head. That would also change my life, but it wouldn't scare me like that. We might make very good parents, but no, that's not it. I didn't tell you before because I didn't understand it. But it is eating away at me and I have to tell you."

Ev slowly sat back down next to Mida. He had a very perplexed look on his face and started to say something but just stared at Mida.

Mida continued, "Remember when we were looking in the window of Baby Orion last night? I saw something on the floor. It was the notepad I carry around with me and write my journal in. I know it is the very one sitting in my pack right now."

"How could that be?" Ev said very slowly. "That ship has been sealed for millions of years. You must be mistaken. I'm sure it was something that looked like it. I mean, your notepad isn't unique. There were probably things that looked just like it—"

Mida interrupted him. "I know it. Ever since two days ago when I had my encounter"—she reached over and held Ev by his arms—"I have a strange sensation. There are some things I just know. I knew about the window and the door. I knew we were going to stop at that market in Bicknell and I knew we were going to have the discussion about crackers. I knew the name of that reservoir below us was Oak Creek Reservoir and I had never seen it on a map and you had not mentioned a thing to me about it. Something happened to give me some strange power of perception or knowing the future or whatever. I don't understand it and it scares me." Tears welled in her eyes.

Ev put his arms around her and just held her for a couple minutes. Finally, he said weakly, "I don't know what to say. I guess I would be scared too, but it's something that most people would give anything to have. I guess you have to get used to it. You are the one person in this world who can handle it. You are a strong person. Determined. Strange already. Maybe I should say special instead of strange, so this just makes you more so."

Ev thought about all the times Mida had demonstrated special powers. The time she contacted him mentally about her coming up to visit him the first time in Durango. The time at her mother's house in New Mexico when she insisted on making extra food for dinner right before her brother unexpectedly showed up with several friends.

"Yeah, but think what this now means." Mida pulled loose from Ev. "My notebook, which I carry around with me now and yesterday and last week, it is in a spaceship that has been sitting there millions of years. I was in it once. I'm from outer space."

Ev just looked at her, stifling a laugh which he knew would be inappropriate, and quietly said, "I think you are jumping to conclusions. Do you actually remember being on it or is it just because your book is there? There could be other explanations. It has to just look like it." Ev was starting to get scared now.

"No, but what other explanation could there be? Something sucked my brain out of my body and I'm not me anymore? My brain is now in there and it re-created my journal?" Mida wiped the tears from her cheeks with her sweatshirt sleeve as she let out a big sigh.

"I think some kind of weird time warp or something happened," Ev said as he walked around the other side of the fire and put on a large chunk of spruce limb. "We've both been having strange daydreams or visions. I had weird feelings about time. You mentioned something about traveling out in space. If that really is your book, I bet it somehow got in there in the last two days and hasn't been sitting there two hundred million years. Boy, talk about time travel! That is the ultimate!"

"We have to get in there," Mida said, stepping back as the breeze shifted and blew smoke in her face. "And we have to get help from someone."

"I know. We already agreed on this." He looked into the fire, then at Mida. "Okay, we leave tomorrow. We go down and get the tent and head back to Durango. I will go talk to the dean and tell him I will be quitting. I still think you should finish your dissertation and get that done."

"Why bother?" Mida asked in obvious frustration. She hadn't even heard his comment about quitting.

"You have gotten this far. There is no turning back now. Finish it," he said, with a glare at her and a no nonsense tone of voice. "We don't know what is going to happen. Maybe nothing will. Maybe the ship will be gone tomorrow and it's all over. Maybe somebody else will discover it and Tom Brokaw and Walter Cronkite will both be there tomorrow doing live coverage of it. You get your doctorate in a few weeks. End of discussion."

Mida sniffed as she tried to laugh. "Where have you been? Walter Cronkite hasn't been on the air for years. Sometimes I think you are wafting out there lost in time more than me."

"I know Walter isn't doing that anymore. I was making a point. It would be important enough to bring him back out of retirement. 'And that's the way it is here in the twentieth century.' Geez. No sense of humor. Did they suck that out of you?"

"If I go write in my journal now, will that show up in the book that is in Baby?" Mida asked as if she were back in time twenty-five years, asking her mother if she could have a scoop of ice cream.

"If a tree falls in the forest, will it make a sound if no one is there? There is only one way to find out. Go write. Then come to bed. That's where I am going. We need to leave early tomorrow." Ev walked off into the darkness. Mida went to the tent to get her journal. She sat by the fire and looked at the pad of paper for several minutes. She thought about her words and where those words had been. She then wrote five pages worth of thoughts. Ev was fast asleep when she crawled into her sleeping bag next to his.

She did not close her eyes, for fear of dreaming about blue lights and who knows what. She tried not to think about her notebook. She tried not to think about this person lying next to her who told her the night before he was a millionaire. She did think about the way she moved in with Ev without really being invited and the way she had gradually become used to spending Ev's money. She tossed and turned as the breeze rustled the spruce trees guarding their tent. She thought about this magical forest up here on this sky plateau. Trees and flowers and lakes that probably could have been what things have looked like for thousands if not millions of years. Who could tell if they went back in time as Ev wondered? What would be different other than the toys and machines that they were used to? She slept fitfully, dreaming of silly things like circus tents and railroad locomotives and drive-in movies. She awoke in the middle of the night listening, but heard only the breeze. It was always the same, just louder or softer as it carried time from past to present and beyond.

July 24, 1998

And when I looked in the window, I saw my journal lying there. The journal I am writing in right now was in this thing embedded for two hundred million years. These words are there and have been all this time. It freaked me out and it has bothered me ever since then. I have tried to figure it out and there is no logical answer. So I have been thinking of illogical answers. Plenty of those. I am some kind of alien. Mom would love that. I am crazy and simply hallucinating. Ev would have told me before now if that were true. I have lived this life once before and it's just déjà vu. All over again. That brings up this feeling that has been growing for months. I do have some supernatural powers. Why? I have been touched somehow or I am part of some cosmic drama that is repeating act 3. Ever since the blue light episode, I have been fairly normal from a human physical standpoint. It's the mental stuff. I see things, hear things, feel things, know things.

I told Ev and he tried in his sensible left-brained manner to explain the journal. He said it wasn't mine but just looked like it. It was mine without a doubt. I could tell by the writing on the outside, but more importantly, I knew. Even Ev agrees that "when Mida feels it, you believe her."

Why did this happen to me and not him. Why did I come along that day and Ev rescued me? It was all meant to be. Which comes right down to the big question I have been working on for years. Did my ancestors have some powers all along? Power to communicate with the dead, with other animals or beings? Did they have some connection with the Great Spirit, and what exactly was this spirit? Most people, at least in this country, nowadays believe in God with a capital G and that he runs everything with some preordained destiny. My people believed in an all-powerful force that could control things as well. Was there really any difference in the two?

But now, how does the blue light power change this? Is this blue light God? Seems pretty strange that God would have been trapped in a buried tomb of some kind for all that time. Not much of a god if he or she couldn't get out. But maybe this thing is home and the blue light comes out at night and does its miracles. All too simple and easy. No, this just means there is other intelligence out there and it hasn't found god yet either. So there is no god, and we have spent the course of our existence ever since we fell out of the trees or even crawled out of the water inventing something to take the place of the responsibility we all have—control of our own lives. Isn't that a unique idea! We are in charge and we have to accept that responsibility. We can't shift that burden to something called god. Then we just go off and play and kill and create havoc and just say, "Hey, God can come in now and fix it. I'm off the hook."

Well, if there is no god, some other being sure has some potent powers to somehow get this journal back two hundred million years. Was I there with it? Why don't I remember it? Maybe I do and that is the supernatural powers I am getting. I suppose it is taxing anyone's memory to retain it for two hundred million years. Maybe Ev is wrong about the time. Could it have burrowed into the rock, or maybe melted down to it? The blue power is me (the old me) trying to contact me (now). Have I been alive somehow for all that time? Or maybe I am god. Goddess Mida, queen of earth. Or we are all god. The collective unconscious of Freud or Jung or whoever coined the term. Cool.

They pulled into Durango, tired and cranky, at sunset the next day. Reluctantly, knowing Ev was right about this, Mida went into seclusion to work on finishing her thesis and preparing for her dissertation. Ev noticed a change in her. She seemed much more distant. He assumed it was the pressure of the thesis combined with her worry over her new powers. Neither of them discussed it and Mida made no mention of any premonitions if in fact she even had any.

Ev spent a couple days cleaning the house since he would be moving out in a few weeks. He quickly found a new place to live. It was an old house a few miles out of town. The owners usually rented to college students but had such a bad experience with the last bunch to live there, they jumped at the chance to rent to a responsible couple. They were impressed with both Ev's and Mida's credentials. Ev signed a one-year lease, although he knew he would not be living there a year from then. He figured the seclusion and privacy were worth losing a few months' rent.

Ev tried to help Mida by reading her thesis, but she seemed cool to many of his suggestions. He reduced himself to simple grammatical editing. She did appreciate that. Once they were moved into the old house, Ev felt a sigh of relief. He enjoyed house-sitting in his friend's house but felt nervous the whole time being surrounded by someone else's life. He now spent his spare time riding his bicycle on all the roads and trails within five miles. The pine forest, logged decades ago, was full of old logging roads and skid trails.

Mida made a quick trip to Albuquerque in mid-August to make sure everything was ready for her big day in September. She then drove down to Mescalero to spend a couple days with her mom. She took Ev's truck and loaded it with a lot of her things. Her mother knew Mida was leaving for good since she took nearly everything she had stored there. Both Mida and Denzee cried as they said their goodbyes.

Ev talked to the dean of his department and explained that he wanted to leave after the fall term due to personal reasons. He said he came across an opportunity to do some very significant research that had to be done now and couldn't wait. He wouldn't elaborate, even with prodding from the dean, but said it was an opportunity of a lifetime. He would have asked for a sabbatical but knew he didn't have his time in yet for this privilege. The dean understood and told him he could leave anytime, although it would put them in a bind for fall term. Ev said he could stay for the term in order to give them time to find a replacement. The dean appreciated that and said they would plan on Ev being there until the end of the year. Then he would give Ev a one-year leave of absence in case the situation changed. He thought highly of Ev and said he would like him to come back when his research was done and published. Ev guessed that the dean knew Ev would never come back. Ev knew himself he was finished teaching.

Ev spent some time preparing for his fall classes, but spent most of his time preparing for his research. His mind soon started to swim in black holes and quantum mechanics, gravitational fields, and field equations. He even started an e-mail correspondence with a couple of his father's colleagues and former students at Boulder.

Mida continued to fuss over her thesis, which seemed to stay at arm's length from being ready. No matter what she changed, something else seemed to cause trouble. It was hard keeping her subject matter separate from her recent experiences. She kept bringing up creation myths and psychic powers that really had no place in her academic research. Although she kept in touch with Sarah, she was frustrated by the fact she really couldn't confide in her. She wanted to tell Sarah everything but knew it was too risky. Besides, who else would believe her incredible story? Mida tried to avoid Ev, not really because of her thesis, but mainly because she knew she was becoming really cranky and short-tempered. She would stay in her room on the computer for hours on end, breaking only to eat and go for short walks in the forests and hayfields near the house. She loved the birds and the deer that hung around the house. It reminded her of the rez. She occasionally rode the new mountain bike that Ev bought for her but rode mostly by herself. She always found an excuse not to go with Ev whenever he suggested a longer ride.

Ev was understanding of Mida and kept his distance. He knew what he had gone through his last months before his own dissertation and allowed Mida this difficult phase of her life. She was a perfectionist and was pushing herself too hard, but he learned quickly to give her room to be herself. He tried again to contact his mother, but found out she was on a trip to South Africa and India for several weeks and would not return until October.

Ev was thrown into a panic three days before classes began when another professor underwent emergency surgery and Ev was given his geography class to teach until the professor returned. He went into seclusion in his office boning up on the lesson plans and notes for geography.

September 1, 1998

Ev and I got into a big argument this evening. I think it came to a draw. I said that higher education is not all it is cracked up to be. Especially graduate level degrees. A graduate degree, especially a doctorate, is a form of intellectual welfare. You spent an inordinate amount of time studying some esoteric irrelevant bit of who cares type of knowledge. Ninety percent of the time, no one will ever read it or even care about it except other doctoral students, who then use it for reference in their irrelevant research.

Of course, all this offended Ev, who thought I was justifying not continuing with my doctorate. I played him. Of course, I will get that piece of paper, although I am convinced now it really will mean nothing, other than the discipline I put into the research, organization, and final product. I guess that actually was part of his argument. It is all about the ability to research, pull obscure, meaningless tidbits of information together into some meaningful form. So what if it does not affect the world order or amount to anything deemed useful by society. Most of society wouldn't know meaningful data or insightful conclusions if they bit them on the ass, according to Ev. I don't really disagree on that one.

Ev already told me his doctorate got his passport stamped. He is not playing the game of publish or perish. In a place like Ft. Lewis, it is not that big a deal. If he taught in Ft. Collins, Golden, or even Albq, he would obviously be humping his butt publishing some trivia about the fluvial sedimentation of Triassic red-bed volcanic burps. Whatever turns you on. You get a grant from some government agency, study your ears off for several years, or more likely get some pandering grad student to research for you, to meet his obligation for a master's degree, then come to some clever conclusion, and wham, send it to the Journal of Geologic Erotica, which is only read by other doctors of philosophy in geology.

But then, I chose to do this and I have to play the game, like it or not. How much has Orion twisted my attitude? Two years ago, I was excited to be making a difference. I knew that prehistoric societies were very advanced in their ability to think outside the box of everyday living. They were asking pretty powerful questions—many of them spiritually oriented. Their lives were spiritually oriented. So they weren't creating literary masterpieces, developing powerful technologies, building steel skyscrapers. They were stretching their minds trying to figure out questions we are still asking. We are getting no better answers than they did. They didn't give up, but we have gotten sidetracked. What do we ask questions about now? Irrelevant trivial crap! But the damn thing is, we don't really know what they learned.

So I thought I could add to our knowledge of them. Maybe I did. Maybe no one cares. And now, with this two-hundred-million-year-old albatross hanging around my neck, I'm not sure how much I care. I should, but somehow I know I won't complete what I started.

I will hunker down and write this damn thing and I will do a good job. But my perspective has shifted slightly. Relevance somehow takes on a new meaning. I supposed Ev would do research on the pyroclastic properties of extraterrestrial contact with Triassic sandstone. I would do research on the spiritual exclamations of contact with intergalactic wavelengths. We all somehow miss the very simple things we call the big picture.

Mida's big day came with her sitting in a third floor conference room at the University of New Mexico campus in Albuquerque. Since Ev had two classes to teach that day, he could not be with her, but he sent her on her way with a bouquet of red roses, for which she chastised him for spending so much money. She had her thesis printed a couple weeks before and was reviewing it with her committee. She impressed everyone with her thoroughness and originality. Her worries and frustrations were for nothing, as Ev repeatedly told her. The session was mostly a formality, although she successfully challenged a couple professors in some of their theories. When she walked out of the room, she felt as if a load the size of Orion had been lifted. She stopped at the Chocolate Factory on the way out of town and bought Ev and herself an assortment of chocolates that set her back over seventy-five dollars, which was, to her old way of thinking, a small fortune. She found a hunk of chocolate shaped like a bicycle that she wrapped with a big purple bow as a thank you present for Ev for being so understanding of her the past months.

Ev celebrated the next night by taking her to Durango's fanciest restaurant. He ordered a bottle of French Colombard and toasted "her doctorship" as he announced to the crowd her achievement. The small assembly at the restaurant applauded as she took a bow and sat down to poke Ev in the ribs for embarrassing her. Ev's hunch that red and not white wine was the cause of her snoring paid off; she slept the night through without waking him once.

They managed to make one quick trip to Boulder Mountain at the end of September, mainly to see the fall colors. Since Mida didn't want to visit Orion by herself, and Ev couldn't take the time off to spend more than a day away from his office, they spent what time they had getting to know more about Wayne County. They didn't even drive down to Orion but stayed at a bed and breakfast in Torrey. The house was one of the oldest in the county and was made of local sandstone blocks. The owners were a third generation local family who also had a large ranch just outside town. They said they were thinking of putting the ranch up for sale but really hated to see it developed. Torrey had started growing a few years before and was losing the small ranching town flavor it had for all its history. Tourism was the future, said the owners, who winced as they said it.

Wayne County was a remote, rural, almost isolated part of Utah. In the past fifteen or twenty years, better highways opened up the county, which was now being discovered by the outside world. This discovery was a double-edged sword since it exposed this very Mormon, very conservative and independent enclave to outside beliefs. It also exposed it to Californians and other urban refugees, who found it a quaint and desirable place to move to. Land prices were escalating.

They visited a real estate agent in Torrey to find out about houses. Several good places were for sale, but Ev kept insisting they were not interested in buying. They did find a couple old houses for rent, but nothing to match the setting they had in Durango. There was a very good market for undeveloped property—that is, if you liked sand and rocks, with possibly a little sagebrush thrown in as a bonus. They came away from Torrey laughing about the remoteness and different way of life in Wayne County, Utah.

Marybeth, Ev's mom, got home in October from her travels abroad and found several messages from Ev waiting for her. She was enjoying her new life since her remarriage but had been disappointed that Ev had not seemed to share in her happiness. She continually prayed for a reconciliation. She was hoping it would come when Ev said he was coming over to visit her for a long weekend. Ev didn't tell her about Mida, so she was surprised when Mida stood by Ev at her doorstep one Thursday night in October. She fell in love with Mida from that first meeting. Mida liked her as well, surprised at the contrast from what she had envisioned from Ev's coolness. Marybeth was a warm, friendly person who genuinely cared for her only son. She had prematurely white hair, though she showed few signs of aging. She was trim and almost petite, yet she had that subtle air of good taste, good upbringing, and a sophistication that Mida enjoyed.

Ev's stepfather, Boyd, was still difficult for Ev to accept, although Mida found him to be likable, like an eccentric uncle. He was balding, with a mane of gray hair that curled over his ears, an expanding middle, a permanent and convincing smile, and an infectious laugh. Mida came to the conclusion there was nothing wrong with the man other than the fact he married Ev's mom. The heir to a Texas oil fortune, he was wealthy, which grated on Ev since he wanted to think whoever married Marybeth did it for her money. Mida was annoyed with Ev over this but knew these things were often difficult for no logical reason. Ev had to work this one out himself. Boyd went out of his way to be nice to Ev without being patronizing or too eager to please his stepson. Mida felt that Marybeth and Boyd made a wonderful couple.

Boyd got into a three-hour conversation with Mida about her thesis. He encouraged her to write a book, adding in her newfound interest in creation myths. When Mida told him about her traveling exhibit, he wanted to know where it was right then. He was ready to hop on a plane to see it. He asked if she needed any funding to help the exhibit. When Mida explained it was already funded by a Ford Foundation grant, Boyd seemed disappointed, although he was obviously impressed at the same time. She joked that she could use an advance on her nonexistent book. Boyd picked up his checkbook and asked how much she needed. Mida thought he was joking but realized he was serious. She had to decline but couldn't stop thanking him for his generosity. Boyd did comment to Mida, out of earshot of Ev, that he wanted to do something for Ev but knew that Ev was not very receptive to him. He said his money was burning a hole in his pocket and he had already given his own daughter a trust "more than she needed," according to his description. He wanted a legacy and was eager to help people start new businesses. Especially in poorer communities.

They stayed until Sunday noon at Boyd and Marybeth's stone-and-brick house on the outskirts of Colorado Springs. Mida invited the two for a visit to Durango at Thanksgiving. As soon as Boyd answered quickly that they would love to come, Mida starting visualizing a scheme. Her discussion with Boyd had put some ideas in her head. She managed to put an idea or two in Boyd's head as well, although she only opened the package of cheese and didn't even put any in the mousetrap. That was the way Boyd described her whispered thoughts to him as he kissed her on the cheek before they left for Durango the next day. Since Ev did not tell his mother about his plans of quitting teaching, Mida was thinking of ways to break the news. She would wait until Thanksgiving and then work her magic.

On the drive back to Durango, Mida sensed that Ev was still hesitant about his relationship with his mom and stepfather. She vowed to herself to correct that but in due time. Thanksgiving would be the perfect opportunity, she thought again. When she got back to the old farmhouse, she called her mom and asked if she could make it up to Durango for Thanksgiving. When Denzee declined since she didn't want to drive that far, Mida sent her an airplane ticket from Alamogordo to Durango. Knowing her mother's shyness around strangers, an old Apache trait, she did not tell her that Ev's family would also be there.

The autumn days passed in near perfect bliss for Mida. She was now Dr. Peterson, although not officially until the winter commencement. Ev enjoyed his teaching, knowing it probably would be the last he ever did, at least in this capacity. The weather was perfect, as it usually was in Durango in October and early November. Days were warm, sunny, and clear. Nights were cool, with the skies like sparkling crystal. One night, while they were sitting outside before going in to bed, they saw a brief flickering of the northern lights. Mida knew it was a sign, someone sending her a message. What the message was, though, she didn't know.

Mida spent time writing prolifically in her journal and plotting on how to get Ev together with his mom and stepfather. She also had plans for her mother but had a hard time trying to fit those in with the rest of her ideas. Unknown to Ev, she made several calls to the real estate agent in Torrey. Also unknown to him was a quick trip she made to Torrey via a small chartered plane. It also carried another passenger. Boyd had chartered the plane out of Colorado Springs and picked up Mida one Tuesday morning. She was back by late afternoon and home before Ev returned from one of his long days in the classroom.

The first big storm of the winter hit Durango in mid-November. Ev and Mida had to hole up in their country house as two feet of snow brought everything to a standstill for a couple days. Mida spent hours versing Ev in Apache and other native traditions. She found him an impatient learner, but he did enjoy her storytelling. He loved the stories about the creation of people and how they first settled the world. What he didn't know was she had made most of these up, using what she had learned from her studies.

She made the stories up, but she often wondered how they came to her so easily.

Was she making them up, or was she recalling something from some far away past she had connections to? She lay awake for many hours thinking about these questions.

Whenever Ev tried to talk about what they were going to do after the fall term was over, Mida changed the subject. She told him she wanted him to put his energy into teaching and his constant reading on physics and space-time. She said there was plenty of time during the long winter months to plan on what they would do next. They did discuss bringing in a physicist or engineer to help them with the technical aspects of getting into the ship. They agreed on qualifications and criteria, but Mida did the research. Ev had no choice but to trust her lengthy phone calls and e-mails. He was amazed at her investigative ability. She found leads and connections to a wide variety of people. Of course, none of these people knew a thing about what they were being considered for. Most didn't know they were being considered for anything. Her lead-in was always that she was writing a book and wanted background expertise. She narrowed her search list down to two names.

Since her ploy was the need for research for a novel, Mida took the first two weeks in November to write a story line for a science fiction novel about time travel. She used the setting of southern Utah and a grizzled old uranium prospector in the 1950s who finds a space shuttle buried in sandstone that is millions of years old. She is going to have him break the window and take his mule inside the ship, where they travel back in time. But she needs to know a few technical details. Since he is radioactive from his work, she doesn't want him to contaminate the space shuttle. It turns out the shuttle is from our future, caught in a time warp and taken to the far distant past. Her story had all kinds of improbable twists and turns, but she made an impressive list of scientific questions furnished her by Ev. She still thought time travel to be a mental journey while Ev still had not lost his dream of physically going back in time.

She mailed her story synopsis to her two leading aerospace engineers for their responses and settled back to her Thanksgiving Day planning. She felt exhausted from her secretive scheming the past month and her creative storytelling. Still in touch with Sarah, she sensed trouble with her marriage. Sarah said she was trying to arrange a trip to Telluride skiing in February or March and wanted to stay a week with Mida. Mida decided that at that time she would tell all her secrets to Sarah but extract a blood pledge of secrecy. She had to talk to someone other than Ev about what she was going through.

Ev finished his classes on the Tuesday afternoon of Thanksgiving week. He got home to find Mida in a total panic. All the guests were arriving the next day: his mom and stepfather as well as Mida's mom. The weather was good for driving. Most of the snow had melted after a week of fifty-degree weather. But

Mida was not worried at all about that. She was frantic that the kitchen range had gone on the blink in the middle of her making cookies. They had a big Thanksgiving Day feast planned, with all kinds of good impressions to make, and Mida did not have a kitchen stove in which to cook. She had not been able to contact the landlord who was out of town for the holiday. Ev told her to just calm down. He would call the repairman and if they couldn't get it fixed tomorrow, they would just buy a new stove and worry about the landlord later. When Ev joked that she should be able to cook a turkey over an outside campfire like her ancestors did, she threw the two potholders at him. No sense of humor he mumbled, not for the last time.

By noon the next day, they had a brand-new kitchen stove, Ev's parents had arrived, and Mida met her mother at the airport after a flawless flight. The clan gathered around the kitchen table as they prepared to learn all about each other. Half the participants had some surprise for the others, but few knew what the others were to spring on them. But that was to wait until the next day. They spent the evening trying out the new range on two cakes and the tardy pumpkin cookies, Mida's mother teaching Ev's mother how to play mah-jongg, and Mida entertaining everyone with a new story about how coyote trickster taught brother bear to climb trees.

TEN

Mida's Plot

Of all our possessions, wisdom alone is immortal.

—Isocrates

*Whatever you cannot understand,
you cannot possess.*

—Johann Wolfgang von Goethe

THANKSGIVING DAY ARRIVED to meet a clear blue eastern sky being overrun by a wall of western clouds. By noon, a late fall thunderstorm blew over the Four Corners dumping bucket loads of rain, which by early afternoon turned to snow blown by a wild northwesterly wind. All in the old farmhouse were happy to be sitting inside around the woodstove, not having to travel anywhere for a couple days.

Boyd fell in love with Denzee, enthralled by not only her quiet dignity but by stories of her escapades during her youth in the 1960s. While his college days were spent drinking beer and playing football at the University of Texas, he found her antiwar marches and activities all across the country fascinating. She was surprised by Boyd's reaction, including tears in his eyes, when she told of her great-great-grandfather dying while imprisoned at Ft. Marion in

Florida. When she recognized his sympathy for her ancestors, she played on his emotions.

"My ancestors were what was left of the Chiricahua band of Apache, or Tinde as we called ourselves. They came from the Chiricahua Mountains of southern Arizona. Doesn't really matter to me where they came from. The thing to remember is they were used to the freedom and wildness of the southern Arizona and northern Mexican desert. They were a tough people who lived in an unforgiving land and became the most feared and hated of nearly all the American Indians. Geronimo took over leadership of the band when Cochise died. There were really only a few dozen who did the notorious raiding and eluding of the army. I laugh every time I think of the reputation these few people got. They simply refused to give in like most other tribes. They finally gave up after years of eluding the settlers and the US Army, after being on what was then the equivalent of the FBI's top ten most wanted list.

"A friend of mine is the grandson of one of our old chiefs. He made a statement in a speech twenty years ago that I still remember. He said, 'Freedom as defined by the whites is hard for the Indian to give expression to. He knows only freedom when the buffalo roamed the plains, when the rivers ran clean, and when the grass was green and abundant.'" She spit out a phrase in Apache as she squinted her eyes in a wildness that made Boyd blink.

Denzee had mixed feelings about her ancestry. She struggled between the modern feminism that attracted her daughter and the tradition of her people where women played a much different role. Even though most anthropologists said the Apache had a patriarchal society, it was very superficial. Women had a lot of power in making decisions. Most Apache had a strong fear of witchcraft, which often made relations with non-Apache very cautious. Women felt they could live without the men, but the men could not live without the women. Most women were very spiritual and spent a lot of time praying for nearly everything. Whenever Denzee thought of the rich tradition of her people, coupled with the reputation her ancestors had as bloodthirsty savages who terrorized the southwest a century ago, she got very angry. Especially when she thought of why she was from Mescalero and the story behind that. Denzee normally would not be comfortable speaking this openly to a man she had just met. A rich white man at that. But for some reason, Boyd seemed safe to open up to.

Boyd remarked as he tried to ease the tension he felt growing. "I remember playing Geronimo and the soldiers when I was a kid growing up in west Texas. Among the settlers and early pioneers of that part of the country, Geronimo was the equivalent then of Genghis Khan or Attila the Hun. Or maybe a Saddam Hussein of today. He had the whole southwest spooked only a generation or two before I came along. You mean he didn't have an army of thousands of painted warriors?" He smiled when he said that.

Normally Denzee was soft spoken. Her voice was starting to sing as she spoke words with a passion. "Geronimo was more of a holy man than a warrior. Same as Sitting Bull of the Lakota. However, he lost his wife and children to a raid by Mexican soldiers when he was young, and that changed him. You might say he was a war holy man. He channeled his hatred and revenge into killing. He was followed by a small band of his people, yet he was not a popular leader. He followed his god and tried to protect his heritage. You've heard all that before."

Boyd laughed a nervous laugh. "Of course, it's all political. Might makes right and all that garbage. Those in power, however they got there, call the shots. Our history is full of misbegotten, misplaced, and misused power. I guess it is right as long as you have the might. Few of us do." Boyd wasn't sure where this discussion was going.

Denzee continued as Mida sat down next to her mother and prepared to hear the history she had heard many times before. Geronimo and his band just got tired. General Crook promised them they would be reunited with their families within two years. So this angry and revengeful band of seventeen men, fourteen women, and six children that had the attention and hatred of the entire United States, including its army, surrendered to Crook in a place called Skeleton Canyon, Arizona, in September 1886. They and many others who had already settled on reservations were sent to inhumane conditions in Florida and Alabama. Almost five hundred people were forced to camp in one acre of space. There was no concern for sanitation. Certainly no concern that these people were removed from their natural medicines. No concern that Anglo visitors were allowed to mingle with the prisoners like they were circus animals. No concern that these visitors brought diseases that killed the Apaches like flies. The children were removed from their parents and sent to a white school in Pennsylvania where many died from disease.

Mida slowly placed her hand on her mother's arm since she knew what was coming next. She had heard this review many times before, but knew her mother still could not come to grips with history.

Denzee continued the sad history. Almost thirty years later, 275 Chiricahua finally gained their freedom out of 520 who were imprisoned. The rest died, broken and humiliated, removed from everything they loved. This was the reward of trying to maintain their freedom in their own homeland. The Apache didn't give in like most tribes and settle on a reservation. Denzee's ancestors were imprisoned for almost thirty years and they were one of the few tribes who ended up with nothing. Sure, they were now on the Mescalero Reservation. But they weren't Mescalero.

"We are Chiricahua," she said proudly. With that, she gestured with both hands, then clutched her chest. She was becoming very animated and emotional. "Now there is no such thing as Chiricahua. When Geronimo surrendered to General Crook, he said, 'We are all children of one God.' (We call our God 'Ussen.') 'Ussen is listening to me. The sun, the darkness, the winds are all listening to what we now say . . . Once I moved about like the wind. Now I surrender to you and that is all.'"

When she said the word *wind*, she made it sound like *whend*, and she waved her arms and looked outside as the howling blizzard bent the treetops and whipped them back and forth. When she said "That is all," she dropped her hands and fell back into the chair, pursed her lips, and shut her eyes. She did not see the glare Mida gave her. Mida knew she was playing to Boyd's emotions.

It worked. Boyd pulled out his handkerchief to wipe his eyes. Attracted by Denzee's waving arms, careful enunciation, and abrupt hand movements, Ev, who had been talking with his mother on the sofa, shifted his attention to listen to the end of Denzee's story.

Ev bent over to Mida and whispered, "Now I know where you got your storytelling skills. She is good. Very good."

Mida took over the conversation, letting her mother rest from her emotional story. "Verbal skills, especially telling stories, was central to our history. We didn't have a written language, so we passed on our culture and our history through our stories. My ancestors would sit around a winter night's campfire and tell stories. That is how we learned why things are as they are. How we say things is also as important as what we say. When we tell our myths and legends, they are real to us, they are alive. This is part of who we are and what we believe. We learned the character of our land, how to honor and sustain it. We learned respect for our elders. We learned about our culture.

"That is missing today in our society. How do our young kids now learn about our culture? From movies about violence and killing? From video games, where they turn into zombies? My culture and tradition is not dead. It is just in hibernation, awaiting the day we can return to the lives we lived for millennia. The quality of life that our ancestors lived was beautiful. It was about loving and sharing. I'm not sure we can say the same about this country today. People say America is young and still developing, a role model. That's not right. My country of the Chiricahua is old, well developed before Columbus ever saw the ocean. America is a model for how to destroy people and cultures."

Mida looked at Boyd squarely in the eyes and said, "You mentioned last month about patience. You admire patience in people, especially business entrepreneurs. You learn our history, you realize what patience is. Our people had patience. We had no meaning of time the way you do. You look at us now, those of us who struggle to maintain our traditions, our history, those of us who have not given up and have not given in to despair, alcohol, living off the dole, you will learn what patience is. Ussen put us here for a reason and that is to teach the world about patience. In our culture, we are taught to think of the future, not the past. We think of good, not bad. We know our history, but we do not dwell on it. Our history has been good because it created a strong, spiritual people."

Mida thought of telling Boyd about the Sunrise Ceremony but kept quiet. The ceremony was important to Mida since she was not full-blooded Apache. It meant more to her, she realized, as she was trying to prove herself, especially since her non-Apache father had died. The ceremony meant a hope for youth, for abundance in the woman's life, and for good health. She was dismayed that very few young girls took the ceremony nowadays.

"Those true to our beliefs walk the good road. We know the good road. Even if there are only one or two of us left who are pure, that is enough to start anew."

Mida sat back in her chair and looked at her mom. Then she looked at Ev and gave him a look with raised eyebrows that said "And that is all."

As Mida took a breath, she realized what she had just said. She was talking about patience and look at what she was dealing with on Orion. She was thinking about two hundred million years' worth of patience. She said Ussen put her and her people here to demonstrate patience. Her patience or lack of it was now tearing her apart, anxious to learn what was inside Orion. She couldn't even tell her mother about this struggle with herself. How would her mother handle it?

Boyd looked at Marybeth, then at Ev. The three of them sat there not knowing what to say after this short outburst and history lesson given by two very skilled storytellers. Marybeth thought of these two women who lived a completely different life than her. She thought of her middle class upbringing and her total lack of any contact with people of color until she went to college. Boyd thought of the culture he was raised in, where blacks and Indians were definitely second-class citizens. But he was proud that in his businesses, he made special efforts to hire and promote minorities. He tried his whole life to treat them like anyone else. He wanted to be treated by them as an equal, but still found a barrier. His wealth prevented that, no matter what else he did.

After a few moments of awkward silence, Ev finally got up off the sofa, put his hand on his mother's arm, and said, "Well, this is Thanksgiving, and I'm sure we all have something to be thankful for. I am thankful we are all here and we are family. We come from many different roads and places, but we all go forward together from here. Today, we will think of the future and not the past."

Boyd stood up, still looking at Denzee. It was not condescending; it was not surprise, but pure and simple admiration. He looked at Ev and said, "You don't have any bourbon in the house. I already checked. So I guess I will take a beer if you have that." He slapped Ev on the shoulder and walked with him into the kitchen.

He whispered to Ev, "I liked the fire in Mida's eyes the minute I saw her. Now I know where she got it. Denzee is quite a woman. You are a lucky man, Ev. A lucky man. To have two women as strong and powerful as these two. You will have an interesting life with these two women." Almost as an afterthought, he added, "Of course, your mom is just as special. I want to thank you for letting me share part of her life."

Denzee still sat with her eyes closed. Mida leaned over to her and whispered some Apache words. She opened her eyes and looked at her daughter. She smiled and winked at Mida. Mida poked her in the ribs and laughed as she looked at Marybeth and said, "Let's go see if one of these domestic turkeys tastes anything like our wild turkeys at home. And, Mom, you haven't lost the touch at all. I've always said you should be an actress."

The three women stood up, then pushed the men out of the kitchen and started the final work of getting the food ready to eat. Ev and Boyd complained about not being wanted. They took their beers and stood by the woodstove, watching the snow outside bending the tree branches. The wind had died down and the only sound was the crackling of the fire and the clinking of dishes in the other room.

Ev set down his beer and told Boyd to sit on the couch with him. He took a breath and reached down to retie his shoelace. "You know, Boyd, I didn't like you at first. Only it wasn't you. It was a person who tried to replace my dad. I wasn't fair to you and I was only thinking of myself. You have added life and happiness that was taken away from my mother. I must have thought she and I should mourn forever. I won't apologize because it is a natural thing to happen. It just took me longer to get over it."

Boyd started to speak, but Ev held up his hand and shook his head no. Ev continued, "This isn't easy for me. We were a close family. But Mida just said something about thinking only good and thinking of the future, not the past. I think the past was just blown away with the wind." He gestured as he emphasized *whend.* Both Ev and Boyd laughed when he said that word.

"I hope you understand I can't call you Dad. But Boyd, it's good to have you in our family." He reached over to shake Boyd's hand. Boyd's eyes teared up again as he grabbed Ev's hand and pulled him to his chest for a bear hug. Neither was aware of the choked breath from Marybeth as she came to the kitchen door to ask a question but saw her son and new husband in an embrace she had been afraid she would never see. She bit her lip as she held back a cry. Mida walked over to her and hugged her, not saying a word.

Mida waited a minute, then burst into the living room and said in a loud voice, "Listen, an old Apache tradition comes alive here today. When we eat turkey, we eat wild turkey, not drink it. We reach down and touch Mother Earth, then look up at the sky and say a prayer. Since you cannot see the sky from in here, we all have to go outside, stand in a circle, and say thank you to the Great Provider." Denzee started to say something about this being a totally made up story but just nodded in agreement instead.

After they put on their coats, they walked out and stood in the front yard. As Mida reached down to touch the ground, she felt a plop of snow hit her in the neck. Thinking Ev had thrown a snowball, she grabbed a handful of snow and threw it in Ev's face. Boyd said that wasn't fair since the snow had fallen from a low hanging branch of the big pine tree overhead. Marybeth then picked up a handful of snow and dumped it on Boyd's balding head. Denzee started laughing so hard, she slipped and fell. Four snowballs landed on her as she tried to get up. Marybeth had to push Boyd out of the way as they raced to the door to escape the snowy circus. They all stood by the woodstove as they brushed snow off heads and from underneath collars. Finally, Boyd said they didn't get to speak their thanks, but Marybeth said it was pretty obvious what they were all thankful for. With that, they sat down for a feast from two different cultures.

After supper, Boyd pushed back his chair and asked everyone to adjourn to the living room with him. Mida gave him a look out of the corner of her eye and followed behind the others. When everyone was seated, he said he had an announcement. "I have a secret I want to share with you. And I want to thank Mida for being a very good and very quiet accomplice." Ev looked at Mida with an expression of surprise that made Mida stifle a laugh.

Boyd continued, "Since I retired from the oil and energy business, which, by the way, made me a lot of money but not a lot of pride of doing something worthwhile, I have felt like I am not quite finished with my life's work. I have been trying to figure out what I want my legacy to be. Ev and Mida have given me some ideas and Mida finally convinced me of what I could do. She never said a word, but she convinced me by who she is. I've kidded her about when she's going to marry Ev, and she says they are already married, although not by white man's custom. She told me about Apache tradition and I warn Ev to be careful if he ever comes home and finds his clothes lying in a pile outside the front door." Ev laughed as he remembered Mida's description of the old customs. Marybeth gave Boyd a look with a question in her eyes.

Boyd stood by Marybeth as he continued, "I know that Ev and Mida have a special fondness for the area around Capitol Reef National Park. I saw it for the first time the other day, and it is indeed beautiful country. I would like to announce that I am in the process of buying a thousand-acre ranch outside Torrey." Marybeth started to say something in surprise, but Boyd continued on. "It really isn't worth anything as a livestock ranch and there is only one old run-down house on it and half of the property is rock cliffs. But that is its beauty. I am buying it in the name of a trust I am forming called the Orion Trust." Ev looked quickly at Mida but said nothing.

"I don't know why Mida suggested that name, but she insisted on it rather than my original creative name of the Doctors Trust or the Ev and Mida Collins Trust." He put his hand on Marybeth's shoulder as she smiled at him. "Mida told me that Ev has applied for a year leave of absence so he can do research about the geology of that area, with the idea of writing a book. Mida is interested in writing children's books about geology and her native creation myths. I think that is a wonderful idea, and this sandstone retreat will be a perfect spot for that."

Marybeth finally succeeded in interrupting with a question to Ev, "You never told me you were quitting teaching! Are you sure this is what you want to do? It's so risky."

Boyd patted her shoulder again as he continued, "Now, sweetcakes, let me continue. These two people are very smart and what an opportunity this will give them. I know Ev likes to bicycle and we all know he likes rocks. Mida and I inspected this property just a few days ago. It is perfect for biking. There are places to build trails and there are canyons and rock cliffs and hoodoos. Is that the right term, Ev? That's what Mida called them." Boyd looked at Ev, who just nodded. Ev was still too surprised to say anything. He was trying to decide whether he was mad at Mida or just shocked.

"I envision this place, which will need a lot of fixing up, as a retreat, cultural center, educational center, bicycling haven, spa for rich Californians and Texans—"

He stopped as Marybeth laughed and said, "Boy, you got it there. We know a bunch of people who are just looking for ways to spend money. But, Boyd, why didn't you check with me?"

"Honeycakes, it's my money, not yours I'm spending," he let out a bellow of a laugh. "And I expect that Ev and Mida will live there as soon as they are done here, which Mida tells me will be in a month or two."

Ev looked again at Mida and finally said something, "You knew about this? You snuck around and did this? When did you drive over to Torrey?"

Mida just smiled and said, "Honeybuns, like the man says, it is his money. I don't have any and I don't spend yours without you knowing it. At least not very much." She laughed as she looked at her mother. "And I didn't drive over. Boyd flew over and picked me up and we flew on over to Torrey. The Realtor was waiting for us on the property. Can you believe there is a dirt runway on the property?" She almost squealed with delight and astonishment when she said the word runway.

Boyd walked over to Denzee and stood by her. "And you have a place there too, Denzee. If we could get you away from the rez, that's what Mida calls it, not me, if we could get you up there, you would help run it. We would pay you a salary and you could help Mida set up a museum and cultural center for the study of Native American traditions and lifestyles. Mida says you are a writer so you could write all the literature on it and maybe even a book or magazine article. I know it's not traditional Apache country, but if you get a good place set up, I have another check ready to write to help you set up a similar one down in Mescalero."

Denzee gasped as she looked at Mida, then back at Boyd. Mida bounced over to her on the couch and hugged her. "Mom, it's perfect. It's what we always discussed, but only as a dream. Now it's a dream come true."

Denzee started to shake her head and say that this just wasn't right, but Boyd cut her off. "I know this is a lot for all of you to think about. But I made up my mind. It's what I want to do and I don't expect it to make any money. But you convinced me earlier today"—he knelt down next to Mida and her mother and laid his hand on each one's arm—"that there are things other than money. I was born into a situation where money came easy to me and I made a lot of money through no skill or creativity of my own. I took something that rightfully belonged to people who were run off the land long ago. I want to give something back. I have patience and if I don't live to see this working the way I want it, then I know it will get there eventually. I may not have the patience you have, but you can teach me."

Marybeth stood up in exasperation and chided Boyd. "Boyd, why do you insist on degrading yourself. You have worked hard all your life. You kept your business going when others all around you were going bankrupt. No creativity? I won't let you say that. I want everyone here to know that you have created a business of making and selling wind-powered electric generators. That in itself will buy a dozen Orion Retreats or whatever you call this desert hideaway. And that doesn't even include the patent you got on the contraptions that turn the waste gas that used to just burn at the wells into electric generating machines. You think the Sierra Club gives that conservation award you got for some scoundrel who just rakes in money from the poor and oppressed? Sometimes you make me so mad," she sputtered as she threw up her hands and walked into the kitchen.

Mida got up and followed Marybeth into the kitchen. She turned and pointed her finger at Boyd. "You better listen to this woman. I know some of your secrets, too. If you are going to be the brains behind this endeavor, you shape up and claim what you have earned. Geronimo would have put red ants on your tongue every time you put yourself down like that."

Ev laughed as he envisioned Boyd being tied down on an anthill in some desolate desert canyon. He slapped Boyd on the back and said, "Damned if you do and damned if you don't. Brag about being a big shot and no one likes you. Don't brag and you get hammered. I'll go get you another beer."

Boyd looked at Denzee, who just grinned at him. He patted her arm as he got up and walked over to the small card table by the woodstove. "Come sit with me, if you will be this close to a big shot. This stove feels good. Better than being outside in the snow. Or in that cold chill that my wife left me in. Let's get a game of mah-jongg going. You need to teach me all your secrets of how to play this game."

Ev rifled through the refrigerator to get a couple more beers. When he shut the refrigerator door, he looked into the living room and smiled. He looked at his mom and motioned to the other room. He sent his mom out of the kitchen to watch over Boyd and Denzee. "Mom, I think your husband has fallen head over heels with Denzee. You better go chaperon them. Besides, I imagine Denzee is teaching Boyd how to cheat at mah-jongg."

Marybeth just smiled and pinched Ev on the cheek. "You don't worry about your old mother. She still has a few tricks left herself. You think I landed Boyd by accident?" She winked at Mida as she went into the living room.

Ev turned to Mida with his stern look that always preceded a lecture to her. Mida stood on her tiptoes and got right in Ev's face. "Listen, Rock Boy. Don't give me that look. Whatever you are going to say, just stuff it. Boyd wanted to do this and he asked for my help. This is perfect for both of us. This ranch thing is his idea and we can use it for a cover." She lowered her voice and said very quietly, "we may not be there long, or, for the rest of our lives. Which may not be very long either." She added the last as an afterthought as she squinted her eyes and frowned. "I kept it secret from you because he asked me to. And it's not in our name. I just suggested Orion, which he didn't have a clue what it meant. He has already ordered a big double-wide modular home." Anticipating Ev's widened eyes, she added, "And paid for it."

"Well, you busy little *gad,* you certainly did a good job," Ev tried to get in what was left of a failed lecture to Mida when she burst out laughing.

"You ninny. *Gad* is a cedar tree. 'Gah' is rabbit if that was what you were trying to say. Or 'chaa' is beaver. I appreciate your trying to learn my language, but sometimes you really are funny." She started laughing again as Ev turned red.

"Don't you dare!" she spat at him as he reached for the bowl of whipped cream. As her hand shot out to prevent him from grabbing the spatula, he hit the bowl on the edge and flipped the spatula up in his face, showering him with whipped cream. Mida almost fell over laughing, unable to push Ev away, as he grabbed her and kissed her. Marybeth came into the kitchen just at that point. She quickly turned and hurried back into the living room.

Ev and Mida heard her say to Boyd and Denzee "You don't want to know" as they resumed a frothy kiss.

When Mida went back into the living room, Boyd motioned her to sit down next to him. He leaned over to her and said quietly, "You need to explain to me what this game is. The tiles are mahjongg, but the game your mother is teaching me is not the mahjongg I know."

"I didn't think you knew how to play," Mida said as she looked quizzically at him.

"I don't, but I have seen others play it before and this bears no resemblance to that."

"I guess you deserve an explanation, then. It is a special Norwegian version."

Boyd burst out laughing and sat back in his chair. "Now that's a new one on me. I always thought it was Chinese. Now there is a Norwegian twist to an old Chinese tradition? Played by Apaches?"

Mida smiled at Boyd and looked at her mother as she started to explain. "Mom, you should explain but I don't trust your version." Turning to Boyd, she began. "When my dad was little, there was a Chinese restaurant in a town near where he grew up. Remember, this was in a very Scandinavian part of Minnesota. Not a lot of Chinese influence there back then. Well, they would go to this restaurant a couple times a month and every time they went in, the father of the owners would be sitting in the back playing mah-jongg with his grandkids or anyone he could get to play. He was very traditional Chinese, with scraggly white beard and all. Spoke very little English, but he would always see my dad watching and motion him over and say, 'You wanna prway? I teechee.' The owners would shake their heads no at my dad and say, 'You better be careful. He cheat all time. He cheat you, then laugh rest of day.'"

My dad would sit for a few minutes with the old man before the food came. He learned how to play, but it was not the traditional rules. Of course, he changed the rules on his own by the time he taught it to Mom. They would play it on the rez during long winter nights. It is best played by four, but we almost always play it with two or three, rarely four. I'm sure we have so bastardized the rules, a real Chinese or mah-jongg aficionado would not even recognize it. So that's what you are playing and don't trust Mom not to cheat. That is also part of the family tradition."

Ev looked at Denzee and said, "Mida never told me that story. You mean you ladies have been taking advantage of me all along?"

Denzee just smiled at Ev, patted him on the cheek, and said softly, "More than you know."

Boyd, Mida, and Ev spent the rest of the weekend planning the details of the Orion Wingate as Ev started calling it. Mida suggested calling it "Itsa Ranch" since in Apache, *itsa* meant "eagle." Boyd took a full five seconds with a blank look on his face before he burst out laughing at the pun.

Denzee and Marybeth spent hours in Mida's office where Denzee was showing Marybeth the quilt patches she had brought with her. Denzee was an accomplished quilter, making traditional Apache designs to sell at the Center back at Mescalero. Marybeth was amazed at the detail that was worked into the quilted pieces. She said they should be in a museum or at a major art gallery. Denzee said they sold well on the rez, even though quilting was not a tradition of her people. Marybeth was surprised that Denzee didn't want to join the discussions about the cultural center. Denzee just said that Mida would take care of all that. She really got into that type thing and she trusted her. When and if Mida needed her advice, she would ask.

By the time their guests left on Sunday morning, Ev and Mida were exhausted. They became so involved in planning for the Orion Wingate, they almost forgot their primary mission in Utah. Boyd insisted on taking Denzee to the airport so Mida said her goodbyes at the house. When everyone had gone, Ev and Mida just plopped on the couch and looked at each other. "A few things happened this weekend," Ev said casually.

Mida smiled as she looked at him. "Rock Boy, you have a marvelous ability to understate the obvious. How are we going to stay focused on anything here for the next month or so?"

"One day at a time, honeybuns. One day at a time. And you know how I can stay focused on some things." He leaned over and kissed Mida. Neither seemed to realize they rolled off the couch and landed on the floor.

Later that evening, Denzee called to say she got in okay and Mida's brother met her at the airport. As Mida hung up the phone, she turned off the lights and sat next to Ev in front of the woodstove. She knew what he was thinking. She was thinking the same thing. Their lives, already on a roller coaster, had just turned another corner. Just as they were starting to settle into a routine, that old nemesis of her thoughts—the question asking "What is normal?"—returned. Would there ever be anything normal again in her life?

Some things on that cold November night were normal. The deer wandered in the yard as a rabbit scurried through the snow of the front lawn. The moon slowly took over the night sky and passing tatters of clouds drifted over the Milky Way. Blue lights flickered against red cliffs far off in the Utah desert as an owl echoed her lonely call through canyons of rock and juniper.

November 30

This idea of the Orion Wingate exploded and is still expanding like a super nova, to use a phrase that Ev used. I see it as ironically symbolic. Boyd sees it completely differently than Ev or I. Mom doesn't know what to think of it. We talked a little about it, but she is really clueless, bless her heart. This weekend was so different for her. It did her good and she surprised me by the way she took to both Boyd and Marybeth. She didn't know how to take Boyd, but Boyd has a way of running you over like a rambunctious puppy.

When Boyd first came to me about helping Ev, I was very hesitant. Most of this was his idea, based on just a few passing comments I made. He is very perceptive. Even though Ev has been very cool—hell, he has been ice-cold—to Boyd, Boyd knows more about Ev than anyone guessed. Marybeth is so proud of her only son, but Ev's treatment of her and Boyd up until now almost broke her heart. I feel better about their reconciliation than anything else that has happened.

I remember the first time we visited Torrey. We thought it a quaint backwater area full of hicks. But then, what is my background? I come from a backwater area full of a different kind of hick. Makes me want to forget all about Orion and set up this cultural center. Like Boyd says, who cares if it makes money? It is an opportunity that rarely comes to anyone. Talk about feeling like Cinderella! Ev is still more focused on the fact I "snuck around behind his back" than he is about the potential this thing has. I just hope it doesn't distract us. My life has been one big distraction for several months now. What else can happen?

ELEVEN

A New Conspirator

*If we once start thinking, no one can
guarantee where we shall come out,
except that many objects, ends,
and institutions are doomed.
Every thinker puts some portion of an
apparently unstable world in peril
and no one can wholly predict
what will emerge in its place.*

—*John Dewey*

*Have we fallen into a mesmerized state that
makes us accept as inevitable that which is
inferior or detrimental, as having lost the will
or vision to demand that which is good?*

—*Rachel Carson*

THE MONTH OF December passed as quickly as the storms blowing in from the California coast. Days alternated between blustery snow squalls and sun-filled days of slush and melting snow. Ev barely managed to keep his concentration as his lectures often turned into freewheeling philosophical interchanges with his students. To add to the delight of his students, he was overly generous with easy exams as well as high grades. His nightly dreams were becoming colorful although disturbing. He saw clear visions of glaciers and mastodons and ocean waves lapping on sandy shores. These places felt very familiar to Ev, as if he had been there before. He didn't mention them to Mida, fearing she would say she was having the same dreams. Ev never before had experienced ESP or premonitions like Mida, but every once in a while, he would get a shiver as he accurately guessed what another person was going to say before they said it.

Mida made a couple trips to Torrey, accompanied by Boyd. At the last moment, Boyd arranged to put the new house over a basement. This delayed delivery of the home by two weeks. The double-wide modular was finally delivered and set on the foundation. Boyd complicated the construction when he decided to make the entrance to the basement from the outside rather than cut a hole in the floor of the manufactured home. Awkward as it was, it added considerably to the usable space. They got it hooked up to electricity and propane. Although Boyd fussed that the water system was not very good, he tied into the water line that served the old house. He kept saying this was the weak link in the whole setup. A week before Christmas, the house was finished. Both Mida and Boyd were pleasantly surprised how spacious and well-built it was. Boyd arranged for a pilot to fly Mida back to Durango while he stayed at the house. He wanted Ev and Mida to come over for Christmas to join him and Marybeth, but Mida begged off, saying she had already arranged to go to Mescalero to visit her mom and brothers.

Ev's last day of teaching was uneventful. His department threw a surprise party for him, with help from Mida, of course. They gave him a soapstone sculpture of an eagle, made by one of the art professors. Ev choked up when the department head read a petition signed by a few dozen of Ev's current and former students demanding the college lock up Ev in a classroom and not let him resign. Someone went to the trouble of contacting former summer field course students to get them to add their names to the letter. Ev suspected Mida but only made a silent accusation with his eyes.

Looking at her during the reading of the letter, he saw her eyes glisten with pride, but he also noticed she had a faint blue aura about her.

He realized the color blue was taking on a special significance. He could now see occasional auras around some trees and natural objects, but the colors varied. He read about energy fields and other possible reasons for this, but gave up trying to understand why some things glowed and some didn't. Except for Mida, he did not notice auras around people. Blue was always the color around Mida. When he talked to an art professor about colors, he was swamped by references to the color blue. He even learned that blue was the official color of Christmas, although he wondered who was authorized to make that decision. Blue was the color of the ocean, ice in glaciers, the sky, and a myriad of other significant things. "Why blue?" he kept asking.

Ev and Mida drove to Mescalero after his last day at the college. Mida timed the trip so she could stop in Albuquerque to attend graduation ceremonies where she received her doctorate. By this time, Mida had all but discounted her degree and did not give the ceremony the importance Ev thought it deserved. But she did fondle the piece of paper as they continued the drive south. She was deep in thought. Ev was too, but his thoughts were of mastodons and saber-toothed tigers.

They had a very relaxing and quiet stay with Denzee. They spent a lot of time discussing the Orion Wingate and how Denzee could help. Skeptical of the idea at first, she was now starting to look forward to it. Thinking of things she could do, she went back to ideas from her college days before she even met Mida's father. She didn't want to leave her house of nearly three decades, but she started to get philosophical after Ev quizzed her about her ancestors being nomadic. They traveled about the southwest after their journeys five hundred years ago when they migrated here from parts unknown. She admitted she was being cowardly by staying in place where it was comfortable. And, she added, Mescalero itself was not the traditional home of her ancestors. People should stretch their comfort level and it was time to stretch hers. By the time Ev and Mida left, Denzee was pacing like a caged tiger, ready to leave. The fire she had known during her war-protesting days of the Sixties was returning. This was a side of her that Mida had not known. Mida liked it, even envied it, yet was still surprised by it.

Mida convinced Denzee to wait until they had things a little more organized in a couple weeks before she came to Utah. Mida's brother Alden agreed to drive his mother to Torrey in late January. Since her heart attack, Denzee was becoming hesitant to drive long distances. She hadn't decided yet whether to keep her car with her or send it back to the rez with Alden. When Mida asked how Alden would get back if she kept the car in Torrey, Denzee smiled and said her son was very resourceful.

Ev and Mida drove back to Durango, reaching Bloomfield, east of Farmington, as it started to snow. A major winter storm was breaking over the Four Corners area. They drove the last ten miles to Durango in a blizzard, with Mida actually leaning out the window at times to help Ev see enough to stay on the road. Their trip ended in a three-foot-deep snowdrift in the driveway to their house. They waded through snowdrifts the last one hundred feet. By the time they got ready for bed, the power went out, so they lay their mattress in front of the woodstove. Ev dreamed of following a giant white bison through a snowstorm to find a cave in a sandstone cliff. Mida dreamed of showing children how to decorate moccasins with porcupine quills.

The power came back on at 4:00 a.m. Ev had forgotten to turn off the lights. Mida grumpily reminded him of this as the sudden brightness shocked them both awake at the same time. Ev told Mida that she had better get used to living without all these conveniences. She mumbled something, then rolled over after telling Ev to throw another chunk of wood in the stove.

For the second time in six months, Ev and Mida spent several days packing and cleaning a house they were moving out of. Though they didn't have a long stay full of memories, Mida stood in the empty front room, thinking of Thanksgiving Day, her thesis, and the walks and bicycle rides from this old house nestled in the pine forest. She liked the house and wished she could stay longer.

On a sunny but cold January morning, Ev and Mida loaded their belongings, including endless boxes of books, in a big yellow rental truck and headed west across the southern Utah desert. Bluebell, Mida's friend from the Jicarilla Reservation, along with her cousin Betsy, came up to drive Mida's car to Torrey. From Torrey, the pair would continue to the Ute Reservation in northern Utah for a meeting with several alternative health care professionals from Utah and Colorado.

The armada of vehicles arrived in Torrey after dark. This was Ev's first time at the place, and he complained about not being able to see it. The clouds hid the quarter moon and Ev could barely make out the cliffs surrounding the house. Mida, Bluebell, and Betsy sat around the kitchen table discussing herbal medicines and strange concoctions. At least strange to Ev. He tried to stay with them in their discussion, but they kept slipping into Apache words and phrases. He enjoyed being around Bluebell but gave up and went to bed after midnight when they wanted to use him to practice a form of acupuncture using barbless porcupine quills. He drifted off to sleep as he heard the three laughing in the kitchen.

Mida and Bluebell sat up late into the night while Betsy snuggled into her sleeping bag on the sofa. Bluebell expressed her concern that Mida was falling into the trap of modern lifestyles. She called it the hurry sickness, those diseases caused by seeing time flowing as a one-way stream. She believed to heal another was to heal oneself. "We cannot separate nature from humankind," she liked to say. Healing requires the sense of reverence, oneness and unity that allows the power of healing to flower. Mida believed this, too, but she admired that Bluebell was able to fully live her philosophy. Mida realized she was in fact getting caught up in this hurry-up lifestyle, but she knew that Bluebell always was able to take a deep breath and accept whatever came along. Mida had never seen Bluebell sick and she always seemed to feel better after she visited with her.

The first full day at their new home dawned bright and cold. A light dusting of snow covered the red rocks and red soil. Ev gasped as he opened the drapes and looked out the large living room windows. He went from room to room and found equally stunning views from every direction. Wingate cliffs loomed to the north. Smaller outcroppings surrounded the house. Ev couldn't look at such a view like most people would. He looked from a geologist's perspective. They were actually on a major fault, which meant the rock formations on the south side of the valley were a thousand feet lower than those to the north. Boulder Mountain loomed to the south, with its top of lakes and meadows. And on its eastern flank, only a few miles as the raven flies, stood cliffs of orange red Wingate Sandstone, hiding in one isolated spot, a chunk of metal. Whenever he saw the rock of the Wingate formation, he wondered if he could have seen the starship sitting on the sand of the expansive desert from that spot two hundred million years ago. Closer to the house, sagebrush, pinyon, and juniper trees dotted the valley, extending up into draws and cracks in the rock cliffs. Ev thought how peaceful his new setting was.

How peaceful, yet how unbelievably insignificant in the march of earth's history. He tried, as he usually did, to visualize what this valley looked like a few dozen million years before. There was no valley. There was only an endless expanse of sand or sea, depending on just what day or millennia one looked. At any rate, it was not always a place of hospitality, such as he saw this cold January day. The hospitality resulted only from the ingenuity and technology of the human species.

Betsy was nowhere to be seen. Ev found a note on the kitchen table from her. She had driven to the nearby National Park headquarters to visit an archaeologist she knew. She would be back by noon. Mida and Bluebell were still asleep and he didn't want to disturb them. And he didn't want to go outside, at least yet.

Since Boyd had already installed a satellite TV connection, Ev turned on the tube and muted the sound. He surfed the channels in an absentminded attempt to pass the time. He longed to explore his new domain, but he wanted to sit in his warm house and think about it for a while. The sun streaming in the south window highlighted Ev asleep in a big easy chair in front of the TV.

Mida was up before the sun reached the summit of Boulder Top. Bluebell soon joined her in the kitchen. Ev knew it was best to avoid these two scheming curanderas when they were talking medicine, but he wanted to learn more about Bluebell. He sat in observation of the two women, injecting a question or two every once in a while so they knew he was paying attention, but mostly he just listened. He was fascinated by the knowledge she had of not only plants but spirituality and psychology of the human species. He mentioned that she should write a book but quickly received glares from both Bluebell and Mida.

Bluebell and Betsy left after lunch, leaving Ev and Mida to start the process of choosing and bringing into their schemes their new accomplice. Mida had already narrowed her search down to two possibilities. One was located in northern Idaho and had recently retired from McDonnell Douglas as a research physicist. He was very innovative and won several awards in his career. Divorced but with three grandkids, he hunted and collected guns. Mida was a little unsure about that last part but was otherwise impressed with his scientific credentials.

The other possibility was a retired astrophysicist from NASA. He worked in the early days of the *Apollo* program and spent the last decade on Mars research. He was living now in Tucson, although he had spent most of his time in Houston the past thirty years. His hobbies were reading science fiction, astronomy, and bowling. Ev smiled at the idea of a bowler aiming his spaceship shaped ball at pins shaped like nebulae.

Both expressed a willingness to help with the novel Mida was supposedly writing. They provided all the information Mida dared ask without seeming overly nosy for something as simple as scientific advice. Ev said the only way to choose one was to interview them. Hung up on secrecy, they didn't want to bring either one to Torrey so they decided to drive first to northern Idaho, then to Tucson. They figured they could use a genuine vacation, although northern Idaho did not seem to be a logical choice in January. Tucson would be perfect.

When Mida called the Idaho candidate, he replied he was leaving in a week to attend a big gun show in Las Vegas. He was going to stay there with friends for a couple weeks and would not be back in Idaho until February. Mida said she would arrange a time and place to visit in Las Vegas. From Las Vegas, they would head south to Tucson for their second interview. In between, they could stop at several Reservations in Arizona to visit some of Mida's friends and relatives.

A couple weeks later, Denzee arrived at Orion Wingate as the sun was setting below the western horizon of Utah. Alden pulled into their driveway with Denzee packed in the car along with what seemed like half the possessions she owned. Mida laughed as she made a comparison with Alden and Denzee packed in the car like bags of potato chips packed in a grocery bag. The first thing Alden asked was if there was an auto parts store nearby. He loved this place and was already thinking of moving up here. Ev said that if they were going to get into the bicycle rental business as part of the overall scheme of Orion Wingate, he needed someone to run it, including a repair shop. Alden raised his eyebrows in serious thought. Mida cautioned both to just cool it for now. There would be plenty of time to plan their future. Mida knew that Alden was compulsive, and it had taken years to get him to settle down in his successful business in Alamogordo. Even a suggestion like this would unsettle him again.

The first thing Denzee did was to walk around the outside of the house, pausing in each direction with her arms outstretched and eyes closed. Then she came into the house, lit a bundle of sweet grass she had brought with her and walked into each room. Mida said she already blessed the house, but Denzee just shrugged and mumbled something about doing it right this time. Mida turned to Alden and asked if Denzee had blessed that shoebox they drove up in. Alden grinned and whispered something about that being one of the longest days he ever spent. They left Mescalero at 5:00 a.m. and had stopped only three times, once to get a speeding ticket south of Mexican Water as he hit ninety miles per hour coming down a long downhill stretch.

The next day they all explored the property, with Ev and Alden scrambling up and down cliffs and hoodoos. Mida and Denzee quickly returned inside to sit at the kitchen table, discussing what they wanted to do with their cultural center. Denzee insisted on talking to the nearest Paiute elder before she made any decisions. Mida said that would be Denzee's task while Ev and Mida were gone for a couple weeks. Denzee would have Mida's car to use after Alden left in a few days to return home. Alden convinced his mom to let him take the car back since he noticed it running badly on the drive up. He wanted to do some work on it. Mida mentioned she thought there was a Paiute colony near Richfield but she didn't know if it was a formal reservation or just a group. She said the Paiute fared even worse than the Apache in being kicked around and ignored. Denzee said she would try and get the whole story since this was their land.

The next morning, Ev and Mida said their goodbyes to Denzee and Alden, then drove west toward Las Vegas. The weather was threatening, but it didn't snow except for a few miles near Cedar City. The sun was shining as they pulled into Mesquite for gas. Another hour and they checked into a Days Inn in Vegas. Ev said he wanted nothing to do with the big casinos. Mida was relieved since she didn't either. She even refused to meet their physicist in the casino where his gun show was being held. She arranged to use a meeting room on the campus of UNLV.

The next morning, at their appointed hour of 10:00 a.m., Ev and Mida sat in a small conference room in the Life Sciences building. A large man walked in and said, "Now who wants to time travel?"

Ev and Mida both stood up to shake hands with the red faced man with a shaved head. Wearing old army camouflage fatigues, he had a tattoo on his neck that disappeared under his shirt. What was visible was an American flag with the word 'White Pow" disappearing under his shirt. He had what looked like a can of chewing tobacco in his shirt pocket.

"Mr. Franklin, I am Mida Peterson and this is Ev Collins. We are glad you took the time to meet with us."

The man stood there for a second, looking confused. "You are Miss Peterson? I'm sorry, I didn't expect an Indian." He put out his hand to Ev to shake, then reluctantly to Mida as she extended hers.

Mida was taken aback and just stared at him a second. "Is that a problem for you? If it is, then we will just say thanks now and not take any more of your time."

"I'm sorry," Mr. Franklin said. "I can deal with Indians. We have lots up where I live. Many of them are good people. Now what can I do for you? Sounds like you are in over your heads on a book about time travel. I spent years thinking about that and don't have a clue how to do it. If I did, I'd be outta here in a flash. I'd go back a few hundred years to when men were men and life didn't come easy like it does today. No government rules like they keep putting on us about guns and taxes and all these bleeding-heart-be-nice-to-each-other rules."

Mida looked at Ev and both knew what each other was thinking. They hated to think they had wasted their time in coming all this way. They had to continue the interview, but they knew this partnership could not work. Mida was looking at this man's arm to see if she could see a swastika tattooed on it. She did notice a faint Confederate flag tattoo peeking from underneath his rolled up shirtsleeve.

Ev knew he should do the talking. He did not trust Mida to be very civil. Mida was not a bigot, but she had very strong views on Indian rights and the rights of other minorities. Although some people hearing her philosophical tirades on Indian rights might call her racist, Ev knew Mida was completely open-minded. With no tolerance for the views she considered stupid or hypocritical, she often cut people short as they made insensitive remarks. By his quick glance at her, Ev realized she had already branded this man she had only know for a few seconds as blatantly stupid. Probably a hypocrite as well.

Hayden Lake, Idaho, had a bad reputation for survivalists. Looking at this man with his shaven head and military clothes, Ev could only think of all the stereotypes he had heard about these paramilitary types. He wondered how this man could have spent all those years in such a structured discipline as defense aerospace research.

"Mr. Franklin, we are writing a very complicated book that requires someone to help with our research. We are doing the work on an Indian reservation in New Mexico and need someone to be there to help us. We are spending a lot of time hiking in some pretty remote areas and are using this to tie in with the physics. It is difficult to choose our research assistant by reading a resume so that's why we are visiting with prospective candidates. This is hard to explain, but it just isn't a case of sitting here asking questions. I've done a lot of reading about quantum physics and time travel. You must understand there is a lot that just doesn't make sense to a rock hound like me. We are complicating it by having our main characters a clan of Pueblo Indians. We will be spending a lot of time in some of the pueblos getting to know this clan and their traditions. Actually, some of their beliefs have a lot in common with some of the quantum mechanics weirdness. Stuff about perceptions and reality and all that. The use of mind-altering drugs, such as peyote, that they claim takes them back in time. We won't be able to pay very much but we can at least cover basic expenses as well as a little extra."

Mida barely kept a straight face as Ev made up this marvelous story. A story that would scare the red off any redneck's face. As Ev continued, Mida silently pleaded with him to stop. He kept making the situation worse and worse. She was almost embarrassed for this man, wondering what he must be thinking. Having to spend time with Indians and other inferior forms of life! How was he going to turn them down?

Finally, this huge man cleared his throat and shifted in his chair. "Miss Peterson, when you first wrote me, I got kinda excited about your book. I love to read science fiction, especially time travel. But I thought we could just sit here and talk about it. I retired on a medical disability. I have problems with the old ticker. The most exercise my doctor will let me do is carry my gun to the shooting range. He won't even let me go hunting anymore. Damn tough for an old redneck like me. I live in Idaho where it don't get too hot. I just can't take hot weather. So you see, I'm not sure I'm your man, at least what you just described. I'd love to sit here and talk physics and black holes and space aliens with you. I could give you some ideas. But I just can't go down there to New

Mexico and run around them deserts and canyons with you. You understand?"

"Mr. Franklin, we certainly understand," Ev said with a dejected look on his face. "We didn't know you had the health problems. Tell you what, if it's okay with you and if you have a few minutes, let's sit here for a while and you tell me what your ideas on time travel are. You just might have an idea or two that will help me. Mida, why don't you turn on the tape recorder, if that's okay with you, Mr. Franklin."

"Call me Tink. My real name is Tinsford, but no one has called me that since my mother christened me that when I was born. She and my old man must have been drunk on Kentucky moonshine to name anyone that. One guy in college called me that and he ended up stuffed in a garbage can outside the tavern."

Mida was struggling to keep from laughing by this time. Flipping on the tape recorder, she let Ev do the talking. Ev was improvising very well. She would have to reward him for this award-winning performance. She would laugh about it for years. That is if she had years ahead of her. It was funny now, but she would not want to be alone with this man called Tink in a dark alley anytime. Especially after he had a few beers in that large gut. Yet there was something about this guy that made her think a lot of it was bluff. Tink just might be more tolerant and bighearted than he let on.

They had a very enlightening conversation about quantum physics and black holes, Gödel, tachyons, Wheeler-Feynman bilking paradoxes, and assorted subjects that pushed Mida mentally off in a distant part of the universe. The parts of the conversation she did hear, Mida was impressed that Ev was knowledgeable on many of the theories. Ev perked up when Tink started expounding on his theories of time travel. The big man had given this a lot of thought, Mida realized. Tink leaned over and looked directly at Mida as he explained Einstein's theories on time.

"Most people think of the theories of relativity when they think of Einstein. And then they don't even understand the subtleties of the theories. Did you know that his warped space-time concept really translates into the fact that gravity is the effect of the weight of light? Light, or photons, has mass, although many physicists disputed that for years and mass is what we call gravity. I believe that gravity is the key to time and thus to time travel. Overcome gravity in a certain way and you can travel in time. Most people snicker when an educated physicist argues about how to time travel. Actually most educated physicists snicker when you even mention time travel. I believe it is possible. But you have to be moving at very high speeds to do it and we cannot travel that fast yet. Once you can travel that fast, then it still requires some special things to cross that time boundary. Fascinating. Absolutely fascinating."

"Tink, you are fascinating yourself," Mida stared back at him after he sat back and cracked his knuckles. "I think you could have helped us a lot to understand some of this stuff that boggles my mind. I hope that someday you get to do some time travel. In this life or another."

Tink responded matter-of-factly, "It's all one life. Just happens at different times. Now time, that is my specialty. We don't understand time. Just suppose you find a spaceship hidden in a mountain."

All of a sudden, Ev looked at Mida, who just as quickly looked at him.

"What do you mean by that?" interjected Ev.

"I mean you would first of all wonder when that ship landed. It could be yesterday or millions of years ago. But to the aliens, who might be onboard, who might have turned to dust, or who just might be your ancestors, time wouldn't exist as we know it. Time jumps around like spit on a griddle." Tink had a puzzled look as he stared at Ev.

"Did I say something wrong?" Tink asked.

Mida took a drink from her bottled water, then missed the table as she dropped the bottle on the floor. "I'm sorry. It's just that we have puzzled over this very question. About time, that is. You have given this some thought?" She looked at Ev again.

"I have spent days thinking about this," Tink answered as he pulled out a bandana and wiped his forehead, which had beaded with a thin line of perspiration. "Hell, I have even thought about how to get inside that spaceship. Just think about that. If you found a space shuttle or the starship *Enterprise* sitting in the middle of the desert, do you think you could get into it? Does it take some special incantation or spell? Is there a key sitting in front of the door? Does it have a door? I love puzzling over these problems."

"But get back to time and that starship," Mida said.

"What I meant was that thing could have been sitting there for a million years of our time, but to the people, or things, on that ship, those millions of our years might have been yesterday to them. I think we bounce around in time. Here yesterday, there tomorrow, who knows where next week. Stuff like that." Tink flexed his arms, raising them over his head. He looked out the window, wondering what these two strangers were thinking. "Don't you agree?"

Ev knew he might get in trouble, but he said what he was thinking. "Tink, you may not be able to come down to help us, but would you be available by phone if we called you for more of your thoughts?" He looked at Mida, who stared at him with a blank look.

"You seem like good people. Sure, I'd love to help if I could. Not too many people think about these things like I do. I always got in trouble with my boss over these questions."

Mida had softened to this big guy but still had serious doubts. She hoped Ev was just talking to be talking with his last statement. She still felt she didn't ever want to see, or hear him again.

After they said goodbye to Tink and wished him well back in cool Idaho, Ev and Mida wandered around campus, then drove down the Strip. It was a warm night, at least warm for January after they were used to snow and blizzards the past couple months. Neither were interested in going in any of the large casinos. Mida had some pretty strong feelings about casinos, especially since most reservations relied on them now for a substantial income and source of jobs. Low-paying jobs that relied on rich Anglos. She considered it a form of cultural prostitution. Ev would only comment that if he wanted to throw money away, he would just go stand on a bridge over the Colorado River and throw quarters into the water.

Ev stared at the surrealistic atmosphere of buildings they were driving past. "You know, I've never been here before, but it doesn't seem what I remember from pictures and movies. This place has changed. They seem to keep reaching new heights of ridiculous. Now this is a family place. Where are the good old days with gangsters and the Sinatra Rat Pack? Makes me think of our Nazi friend, Tink. I wonder if that was short for Tinkerbelle. Call him Tinkerbelle and see where you end up. Tink doesn't even fit in here. I kept waiting for him to call you squaw or something like that. He was probably praying you didn't have a knife hidden on you somewhere. You just might have scalped him."

Mida shook her head. "How did we end up with that after all my screening? I checked out his credentials. He is a brilliant scientist. How can you tell what someone is really like? He gave me the creeps at first. I feel sorry for him and people like him. So much hatred inside him."

"Yeah, but I noticed something brighten in him when he got talking about Einstein. I think something terrible happened in his life to turn him into what we both saw at first. I was starting to have second thoughts. I think he is salvageable. Mida, I am not so sure we should just dismiss him out of hand. He could help us."

"He wouldn't work and you know it. Don't try and save him. You, though. You were marvelous! You played him perfectly. 'We will be spending a lot of time in pueblos.'" Mida burst out laughing. "You probably made him wet himself thinking of having to hike into remote places with those bloodthirsty savages touching him and casting spells on him."

Ev grimaced as they drove past Circus Circus and the Stratosphere Tower. "No matter how big a creep, I just can't be mean and nasty to someone. I really think he was disappointed that he didn't get to work with us. Or at least with me. He wouldn't have been able to sleep nights if he thought a descendant of Geronimo was near him." Ev looked at Mida and caught a grin as she looked at the old Las Vegas Mormon Fort Historic Park as they drove past. "Did you notice the look in his eyes when he started talking about life on other planets? He really got into that. I think he really knows what we need to know."

"Yeah," Mida sighed. "Whenever our species starts to make real progress, guys like this come along. Or good people are influenced by the bad ones and turned into bad ones. He really was on his good behavior, but it was obvious I made him uncomfortable. At least at first. I think he was almost ready to accept me by the end. Did you pick up what he said about aliens and advanced races? White supremacy at its best. Or worst."

Ev almost pulled into a Burger King but kept driving. "You hungry? I think I need something but I don't know what."

Mida thought for a few seconds, then said, "There was a small Vietnamese restaurant near the motel. It looked pretty authentic. I think I'd like to go nonwhite after today."

"Sounds good to me. Maybe they cook up a nice dog steak."

Mida rolled her eyes. "Yes, Tinkerbelle."

Even after trashing Tink, Mida wondered. Maybe he really wasn't that bad. He wasn't used to someone like her being so forward, so into the things that interested him. Her intuition was conflicting her. His remarks disgusted her, especially what was inferred but not said. Yet her inner voice was telling her to be cautious. First impressions are not always that reliable. Even to her, with her increasing abilities. She didn't know what to think.

They left the next morning for Arizona. Ev was still saying that Tink might be worth looking into more, but Mida gave him one of her looks and said, "No."

This was Ev's first trip in western Arizona. He was interested in the geology of this heat-baked country between Kingman and Phoenix. Before leaving Las Vegas, they stopped to buy fixings for sandwiches. Northwest of Wickenburg, they stopped at a roadside rest area to eat lunch. As Mida made lunch on the broken old picnic table, Ev wandered off looking at rocks. When he returned, he just shook his head and said, "Desolate country. I love it. Wonder if any spaceships ever stopped here."

The next day, Ev and Mida drove on to Tucson and called Ivan Sanderson to confirm a time for their appointment. Sanderson invited them to his house, which he described as being between the planes that fly and those that don't. This meant between the airport and Davis Montham Air Force Base, where literally hundreds of planes of all sizes and shapes sat mothballed. Driving by the air base on the interstate, Ev was amazed at the planes that were sitting in rows upon rows. It reminded him of Carquinez Strait on the east end of San Francisco Bay, where all the World War II ships were mothballed. Millions of dollars just sitting there rusting and falling apart, he said.

They pulled into Sanderson's driveway, where he was sitting under a huge saguaro cactus in a yard of colored gravel. Sanderson was a small man with a shock of white hair but not that old. He greeted Mida with a tentative hug and Ev with a hearty handshake. He said he didn't know why they had singled him out, but he was honored to be asked his opinions. He invited them inside to where he had a big pitcher of lemonade and freshly baked peanut butter cookies waiting. Mida thought he seemed lonely and really glad to have someone to talk to.

He explained he was called Sandy but his real name was Ivan, after a Russian immigrant his father befriended during the Depression. Ev asked how he could work in top secret government work during the Cold War with a name like Ivan. Sandy leaned back and started a tale that he had told many times in his life.

His namesake was a Russian who spoke broken English. He escaped from a Gulag in Siberia during the early days of Stalin's reign of terror. Sandy's dad met him riding the rails from Chicago to Los Angeles. Ivan was homeless, like most of the men they were with at the time, and looking for any type of work. He told Sandy's father his story of being taken in the middle of the night from his family and sent east from his homeland near Moscow. He never saw his wife and small child again. Many of his fellow prisoners died at their camp during the first long winter when temperatures hit fifty below zero. Ivan made it to China and was imprisoned there. He finally was able to get to Nepal where he found refuge in a Buddhist monastery. A year later, he was in New York. Ivan was the gentlest, kindest man Sandy's father had ever met. One night, in the rail yards of Omaha, there was a fight. Ivan was protecting a small boy from being hurt when a knife bounced off a railcar and hit Ivan in the throat. It severed his artery and he bled to death in Sandy's father's arms. A few years later, when Sandy was born, his father wanted to honor the courage and memory of the first Ivan by naming his son after him.

Mida was touched as Sandy finished the story with a tear in his eye. She thought he must have told this story a hundred times, and he still got choked up over it. She liked Sandy immediately.

Sandy gave a resume of his education, career, and hobbies. He had been part of the *Apollo* moon program with NASA. He knew most of the astronauts, still corresponding with John Glenn. He pointed to a small flag hanging in his window. Alan Shepard carried it to the moon and gave it to Sandy. Unknown to his former bosses, he also had a small vial full of genuine moon dust. He treasured it as if it were gold, although it was obviously many times more valuable than gold. He told of his work with decontamination of moon material, including astronauts, and his research into possible life-forms on Mars. He was frustrated with the direction NASA had taken after the *Apollo* program ended. He stayed interested in his research but got so frustrated with the higher-ups and the politics of the whole space program, he retired and came here to work part-time with one of the large defense contractors. He had several offers which would probably have made him a millionaire by now, but he was happy helping out on his own terms as he put it. Even this part-time work made him more in one year than he made in three years at NASA. But after his wife died, he lost interest. He was in the process now of building an adobe house in the hills east of town, in a "quaint little subdivision," as he termed it, where he could "just sit and listen to the birds and watch the cactus grow."

Mida didn't let Ev say anything before she spoke up. "Sandy, I like you. I have an intuition about you and Ev will tell you that you better pay attention to my intuitions." Ev raised his eyebrows and nodded with an expression that said 'you better believe it!'

"Would you like to join us in a project that will change your life and could change the world?" Ev looked at her with a frown and puckered lips, but she kept going. "We have found something that we need help with. It involves something millions of years old. And we want to enter it and go back in time."

Sandy just stared at Mida, then looked at Ev. "I thought you were writing a book of science fiction."

"That was our cover. We are living what seems like science fiction, but I guarantee you it is nonfiction at its most exciting."

Sandy smiled at Mida. "You know, if you had come to me a year ago and said what you just said, I would have laughed, stood up, and escorted you to your car. Do you realize how preposterous what you just said is? It is ridiculous. You realize that."

"Yes, Sandy, it is. But you didn't escort us out of here. And you are still smiling."

"I knew you were coming. And I knew what you were going to say."

"How?"

"My wife told me."

Ev looked at Mida, then back at Sandy. "I thought your wife was—"

"Dead. Yes. She is. But I talk to her every day. More importantly, she talks to me. Tells me things I can't explain. At first I thought I had lost my mind. Then I realized it didn't make sense, but it made me think about death. Have you really thought what death means? Of course you have. You both lost your fathers."

Mida started to ask how he knew but he stopped her before she got the word 'how' out of her mouth.

"I'm not as young as you. You sure you want a white haired old geezer getting in your way? Especially one that is crazy and talks to ghosts?"

Ev looked questioningly at Mida, then asked Sandy, "Are you crazy?"

Mida reached out before he could say anything more and held his hand. "You never mentioned kids. Who do you have now to care about you?"

Sandy looked at his glass of lemonade and traced patterns in its condensation with his fingers. "You can tell I have given up on life can't you? You are right. I don't really have anyone except my bowling buddies. Let's say I'm between lady friends at this time." He chuckled at that last remark. "I just see so much potential out there and we are squandering the little intelligence we have as a species. I was part of one of the most exciting adventures mankind has ever taken. We were reaching out to the stars. We had grabbed onto one and then we just let go and it drifted away. Yes, some people may think I am crazy. But I am careful who sees me doing my crazy things. I don't embarrass or hurt anyone."

"Sandy, I have come to the conclusion we must be crazy ourselves to be sitting here right now. You can't be any crazier than we are. Maybe you already know this, but we have a star at our disposal. We cannot tell you the details just yet, but trust us on this one," Ev joined in. "We want to go to that star but we don't know how to open the door. We want you to help us."

Mida looked at Ev, then turned back to Sandy. "You are physically fit it looks like. You like to hike?"

"I could keep up with you two better than any other sixty-year-old around here. Probably better than most forty-year-olds I see nowadays." He didn't tell them that he walked almost five miles a day and swam every other day at a local pool.

"What we have to offer you is absolutely top secret. No one else on this earth knows about it except us two." Ev looked at Mida and put his arm around her. "Or maybe three, if your wife knows about it already. You would have to agree to not tell a soul about any of this. Not a living soul. You want to check us out to make sure we are not goofed up on something, I can give you plenty of references. We are both PhDs. I teach, or did teach, at Ft. Lewis College in Durango. Mida just got her doctorate from New Mexico." Ev continued to give more of their background and the story of the Orion Wingate. He did not go into any detail of Orion itself.

Sandy again ran his finger around the sweat on his glass of lemonade, which he just refilled. He looked at Mida, then at Ev.

Mida could almost see the wheels turning in his head. He was thinking and he was smiling. He rubbed his chin slowly, a habit he was to demonstrate time and again. Finally, Sandy looked deeply into Mida's brown eyes and said, "One thing I would like to know. Just out of curiosity. I assume Apache, but which tribe? And it's not pureblood is it? I have a tiny bit of Cherokee in me, so I recognize it."

Mida laughed and reached over and put her arm on Sandy's shoulder. "Chiricahua and Norwegian. What a mix, huh?"

"You are *denzhone*. Pretty. Did I pronounce it right?"

Mida smiled. "You speak Apache?"

"Only a few words. A lady I met a year ago was Apache, White Mountain. She taught me a few words she wanted to hear. She called me *hastine* and laughed. Never told me what it meant."

Mida laughed. "She called you *old man*. She was pulling your chain. Next time you see her, call her a *tulgaye*, a donkey."

"I hate to break up this party," said Ev, "but I didn't hear an answer." He didn't hear the actual word *yes*, but he knew what the answer was. They had found a well-qualified partner in their search for the unknown.

He continued, "We don't need one now. You probably want to think it over. It will take you away from your new home for a while. For how long, we have no idea. Maybe forever. It could even be dangerous. You have any questions?"

"You said you had a strong intuition, Mida. I believe it. I have a little ESP myself. I can feel and see something about you. Almost like a blue aura. Really weird, but I could feel it as soon as I saw you. I've never felt so positive about anything in my life. I don't need time to think about it. I want to buy in. It sounds crazy. Sure. But I lost a spark and I think you just relit it for me. At my age, I need to do something out of the ordinary. This sounds about as unordinary as it gets. I just need a little time to tie up a few loose ends here."

Ev smiled and ran his hand through his hair. "We have to wait till spring anyway, but there is plenty of research and planning to do. We want to take a few more days to visit some people down here in this part of the world. Then we need to get organized in our new home. Would April be okay with you?"

"I was thinking more like March. Doesn't matter to me, whatever fits your schedule."

Ev got up and shook hands with Sandy. Mida stood up and hugged him. She said, "We have a partner in our little conspiracy. We will plan on seeing you show up on our doorstep on March 21. The first day of spring. Right now, I would like to celebrate. I know a fantastic Mexican restaurant that serves a few great Apache dishes. Our treat. And it's right next to a microbrewery that I have heard great things about."

Ev and Mida left Sandy the next day after Mida showed him a short video she had taken of Orion. She made him promise not to say anything when he saw the video. It was a little hard to make out some of the details, but the impact on him was visible. Ev told Mida as they drove out of town that that was a dirty trick to give him a teaser like that. She just smiled and said it was a preview of coming attractions to whet his appetite.

They discussed Sandy for at least a hundred miles of parched Arizona desert. Ev said he was beginning to have doubts, but Mida told him not to worry. Sandy was odd and they would find out he was stranger than they realized, but he belonged with them. Maybe the father figure they both were lacking. Ev suggested more like a crazy uncle.

January 29, 1999

Sandy was a breath of fresh air compared to Tink. Ev kept apologizing for Tink all the way through Arizona. The more he thought about it, he felt Tink would have added something. He seriously has considered asking Tink to come down and help us. Just admit we made up the Pueblo story. I said, "Yeah, he would have added thirty years to my time in prison after I strangled him." I sensed something positive in Tink as well, but it was buried so deep underneath his hatred, it couldn't surface. Or at least not without some major work. Ev said that could be his helping with Orion. There are some things that affect our lives in such a powerful way, they literally change us. In Tink's case, whatever happened to him turned him bad. Maybe under other conditions, I might take on this conversion but certainly not now. We need to concentrate on Orion. I think Sandy losing his wife affected him in a similar way, but it didn't sour him on life. I think it tore out his soul and left him alone and sad but not full of hatred. He may take some of our time and energy, but I really think he will be a good addition. I certainly know how he feels. My life ended for several years when Daddy died. But when he came to me in my vision, it changed me back. I saw him so clearly and heard his voice. I don't think anyone can understand that effect who hasn't gone through a quest like that. I was hungry, I was thirsty, I was cold, then hot. Sure, I was hallucinating, but that was the purpose. Isn't it interesting that our paths can change you in such a different way than the paths of most Americans. They have some religious conversion, are born again, and say that Jesus or Mohamed or someone else now controls their lives. Wake up! Our sweat lodges, vision quests, and peyote ceremonies all awaken us to the power we hold ourselves. We don't rely on someone dead for two thousand years. Sure, Daddy or the spirit of him spoke to me, but it told me I was in control of my own life. A pretty big difference.

Back to Sandy. He was so kind and open to us. I sensed he was starting to drift, in more ways than one. I really think he was a little goofy but in a harmless way. Maybe we were the vision to him. We appeared and told him he could add meaning back to his life. Now that's a nice powerful thought. But it is a gift we gave and neither Ev nor I can take any credit or control over Sandy. Even if it was due to us, we don't claim mastery. We claim gratitude we could help someone conquer their own life. Thank you, Daddy, for letting me help someone else.

As they pulled into their newly graveled driveway at Orion Wingate, they couldn't even find a place to park. There were at least a dozen vehicles there. Ev recognized Boyd's truck as well as his mom's Lexus. He didn't know the others, but the pickup trucks looked like contractors. A couple men were laying out string, outlining a large square about a hundred yards from the double-wide.

Boyd came walking over to greet them as they got out of the truck. Ev started to say something but Boyd just put his hand on Ev's and Mida's shoulders, "Hold on before you ask what the hell is going on. I'm playing with my investment. Remember, we are in this together, but I still reserve the right to make a few decisions on how I spend my money. You need a guesthouse. You can't act like newlyweds with Denzee living in your house. I've got a crew here starting a foundation. We will have a slab poured and be ready to build the shell within a couple weeks. Contractors around here are few and far between, but I found a few hungry ones who can get humping on this thing." Boyd laughed as he rubbed his fingers together. "Money talks anywhere you go."

"A guesthouse? Boyd, aren't you rushing into—" Mida complained before Boyd put his hand on her mouth.

"Sweetcakes, if I left this big operation up to you, you wouldn't know how to spend more than $57.94. We have talked some of this over, remember? We are talking of another large building next summer, which you and I and Denzee will plan later this spring. But for now, we need a place for you to have visitors. This building is hidden from your house by these hoodoos. You will have privacy and your guests will still have this fantastic view. It will have four small apartments, plus a common kitchen. How can you have a retreat without a few bedrooms? You gonna let everyone sleep in your big king-sized bed?" With that, he let out a big belly laugh and kissed Mida on the cheek.

Marybeth came walking out of the house putting on her sweater. She came up to Mida and hugged her and welcomed her back. She gave Ev a motherly kiss and asked how his trip was. "I have had a wonderful time with Denzee. She has several Paiute ladies over this afternoon. That's why this place looks like downtown Colorado Springs with all these vehicles. And of course, Boyd is playing with his money." She laughed and put her arm around Boyd. "I gave up a long time ago trying to keep him under control. If it makes him happy, just let him do it. I don't argue with him anymore. It's useless."

Ev looked at Mida and she looked back at him, smiling and shaking her head. They both heard the door to the house open and looked up to see Denzee come out with four other ladies. They walked to their cars, obviously not seeing Ev and Mida standing there with Boyd and Marybeth. As the two cars drove off, Denzee finally noticed the group. She ran over and hugged Mida and Ev, welcoming them back with a flurry of Apache words. Mida answered back in Apache, then said, "We had a great time. We accomplished our main goal and I got to see a whole bunch of old friends."

Ev quickly countered, "Yes, the entire Native American population of Arizona are all her friends. We met every one of them. Now there are forty-five different dialects of several language groups that I cannot understand."

Denzee motioned toward the new construction. "You see what this *hastine* is doing? He says he has to build me a proper place. He thinks I will disrupt your sex life or something." She giggled as she slapped Ev on his behind. "I don't think we have to worry about that, do we Mida?"

Mida turned away in embarrassment. She said, "Let's go inside and you can tell us about your visitors. It's been a long day for all of us."

They all walked toward the house as Ev glanced around him at the red cliffs and green trees. He whispered to Mida, "You know, I could get used to this. Too bad we may never really get to enjoy it." She just looked back at him with a slight nod, yet full of understanding and agreement.

They were ready to start their journey. They knew where it began. They didn't know where it would end.

TWELVE

✳

Preparing for Entry

When old age shall this generation waste,
Thou shall remain, in the midst of other woe
Than ours, a friend to man, to whom thou say'st,
"Beauty is truth, truth beauty—that is all
Ye know on earth, and all ye need to know."

—*John Keats*

I do not know whether I was then a
man dreaming I was a butterfly
Or whether I am now a butterfly
dreaming I am a man.

—*Chuang Tzu*

Ev FINISHED WORK on the basement of their new house by adding floor-to-ceiling bookshelves for their rapidly expanding library. "It had to be down here on a concrete floor. Otherwise, the weight of the books would collapse the floor of the modular," he said with a smirk. A delivery truck brought two big recliners and a large table from a Richfield furniture store. Ev followed up the next week with two new computers and a fancy stereo system, along with a lot of new CDs. If he and Mida were going to be spending lots of time doing research, he wanted to be comfortable. Mida

243

complained about the extravagance of his den of seclusion as she called it (he referred to it as his sin of delusion).

Ev became oblivious to the noises of construction outside and of the noises of Mida and her mother inside. The noises didn't escape the local residents or local government as the small town interest and gossip ram rampant. Ev and Mida couldn't escape the talk of the town and the county.

He spent hours poring through books and articles on time travel, quantum physics, and astrophysical research. He included research on ancient geological landscapes, although he knew a lot of this information already. Or he thought he did. He learned much about ancient climates and life-forms, some of it surprising to him.

As much as he wanted to become involved in the development of the Orion Wingate, he wouldn't allow himself the time. Ev longed to seclude himself in a cozy corner of a large library, but there wasn't a library in the entire county. Soon, delivery trucks and postal carriers were delivering packages from booksellers almost on a daily basis. Orion Wingate began amassing a very complete science library as he added physics and metaphysics to his already huge geology and natural science library. Mida added her books on anthropology, Native American studies, and sociology, then started adding a new collection on creation myths and world religions. Mida not so jokingly mentioned to Boyd that the new cultural center needed a room to house a library. This could turn into their biggest contribution to the county—a real scientific and cultural reference library. Boyd said he would donate his complete collection of first editions of Louis L'Amour and Zane Gray to round out the new library. Mida smiled and mouthed the word *hastine* as she shook her head at him.

Occasionally Ev and Mida drove up Highway 12 to the side of Boulder Mountain, mostly to just sit and look out over the expanse of canyons and cliffs. When daylight lengthened February into March, they spent more time walking around their new property.

Denzee flew back to the rez in mid-February after Boyd made a sudden flight to Torrey. He had the pilot detour via southern New Mexico on his way back to Colorado Springs, carrying Denzee home. She said she wanted to see the early flowers bloom in her own desert.

As the plane taxied to the terminal in Ruidoso, she confided to Boyd that she was starting to worry about the kids. Ev and Mida needed some time alone. Boyd smiled and said they needed to be officially married, then maybe they would get serious about starting a family. Denzee shook her head as she got off the plane.

"The problem is they are becoming transparent. That's my worry. They don't need to start a family yet. The spirits have big plans for both of them. But I'm afraid they will take them away from Torrey. Maybe from us, too. Then Ev and Mida will flower and prosper. You and I may not be around to see it."

Boyd carried her suitcase into the small terminal while the pilot refueled the plane. Walking back to the plane, he yelled back at Denzee. "Are you becoming transparent too?"

Denzee turned thumbs down and smiled as she waved goodbye to him. Boyd couldn't hear her last remark as he shut the plane door. The plane turned to head down the runway as Denzee yelled in Apache that she had too much to do here; she was going to have to finish what Mida started.

Sandy called Torrey once a week to keep in touch. During the first phone call, Ev realized he had to confide all their secrets to Sandy. Sandy was getting too excited and curious to not be a full partner. He guessed correctly what the project involved and needed details. Ev described what he knew but soon realized there were not many details to share. Mida came on the extension and told about the blue light and the pulses of energy. With excitement in his voice, Sandy said something about a type of energy field and how it confirmed one of his theories on some unnamed type of cosmic particles. Mida quickly became lost in the conversation, but Ev questioned Sandy on quantum physics and some of the weirder ideas on different types of atomic particles, including the unknown dark matter and dark energy. Sandy let Ev ramble for a few minutes about mesons and gluons, then said that neither Ev nor Mida had any inkling that they were treading into a realm where few people could even dream of what they might discover. As he hung up, he said to himself that Einstein would be envious.

Every time Sandy called, he bounced new ideas off Ev. Not only was he reading scholarly articles on the subject, he was doing original research in astrophysics. He wanted to do this type thing when he was getting his doctorate years ago, but life and career got in his way. His work involved mundane things like helping get men on the moon and figuring out how to avoid bringing back unwanted life-forms from Mars. Ev joked to Mida about recruiting a latent Niels Bohr or John Wheeler for their amateur project. There was an unspoken agreement among all three conspirators that they were not just trying to enter a two-hundred-million-year-old starship. They were going on a journey in this vehicle, even if it never left the ground. They were entering a portion of this universe unseen by human eyes. Just the thought of seeing something made by nonhuman intelligent beings gave them the shivers. And Ev could not get out of his mind the comment Tink made about time. He still wondered about bringing in Tink.

With their excitement building, Ev and Mida were continually interrupted by Boyd as he got caught up in the excitement of his own project. By mid-March the snows deepened on Boulder Top and a rain and snow mix started the early flowers and greenery in the lower reaches of the nearby desert. At Orion Wingate, the guesthouse neared completion. Boyd pushed the contractors to finish, but the pace of life in Wayne County continually frustrated Boyd. He couldn't understand that high school basketball and wrestling tournaments claimed priority over his building plans. He tried to get Denzee to come back so he could involve her and Mida in plans for their cultural center. Mida pleaded with her mother to wait until May. Denzee knew something was going on with Mida and Ev but never pressed for answers. Denzee knew without asking. She simply asked Mida if it were spirits she knew. Mida said no, it was much beyond that. She told her mom she would share this with her, but she couldn't do it yet. Denzee said she would let Boyd fly her up to Torrey in May. She wanted to see the spring flowers bloom in the Utah desert and then watch them progress up the mountain.

On March 20, Sandy drove up to the growing complex at the Orion Wingate. Boyd cleaned out one room in the guesthouse for Sandy to live in, although his contractors were still working on the building. Sandy named it the Carlcabin after Carl Sagan, who consulted Sandy on one of his books. Boyd didn't understand at first who Sandy was and why he was here, but he reluctantly agreed to let him live in the Carlcabin. Soon, Boyd was so intrigued with Sandy he spent most of his time talking to him. Sandy was not able to concentrate on his work and he was not able to go visit Orion, which he wanted to do from the moment he arrived. However, since Boyd was there, Sandy rarely had any free time to spend with Ev and Mida.

Once Sandy moved in, Boyd finally got the contractors to finish the sheet rock. He hooked up the heat the day Sandy arrived and the plumbing a week later. Although Sandy was sleeping in the Carlcabin, he spent most of his time in Ev's *den of seclusion*, along with Ev, Mida, and Boyd. Mida finally had to call Marybeth in Colorado Springs and ask her to do something to get Boyd out of their hair. Marybeth laughed and asked Mida if she had any good ideas, because Boyd left Marybeth on their honeymoon to fly back to Texas to work out some details on his latest invention. When Boyd got his attention on something, she said she could parade around naked and he wouldn't even notice her. Mida laughed and said she didn't have that problem with Ev, but she didn't think she would try it with Boyd. Marybeth told Mida to have Boyd call home that night and she would try something.

Boyd left the next day, grumbling about how helpless women were. He didn't say why he was leaving and Mida never asked. Ev just said his mother could charm the skin off a snake and walked out to help Boyd arrange last-minute changes. Ev told Boyd not to worry; he would make sure the Carlcabin was finished before Denzee arrived in a few weeks.

As soon as Boyd left, Ev and Mida drove Sandy onto Boulder Mountain so they could look over the maze of mesas and cliffs hiding Orion. They couldn't see exactly where Orion was, but Sandy was overwhelmed by the ruggedness of the area. They discussed how they would get into the site as soon as possible. Once Sandy got a good look at the discovery, he would figure out what they needed to set up their entry profile as he called it. They would have to build some type of shelter against the place where they planned to enter, make it airtight, get power to it, and make or obtain a myriad of instruments. Then test the inside air, test for radiation, and test for a bunch of things that Ev never heard of, much less thought about. Mida said they needn't worry about any of that. The inside of the ship was friendly. The intelligence inside already called to her, and it wanted to share information, not hurt anyone. Sandy tried to explain that even if that were true, he still needed to set certain scientific standards. This was the most important scientific discovery of all time, and he didn't want to blow it. None of them wanted to call in any more help, so he had to do the work himself of at least a dozen experts he wished he could involve.

A few days later, Sandy chartered a small plane from Richfield. He told the pilot he was a geologist studying the cliff formations of Boulder Mountain and Capitol Reef. The plane landed in Loa and picked up all three conspirators, then flew for an hour and a half over some of the most fascinating country Sandy had ever seen. He made a special effort to fly a lot of country so as not to give away their secret location. He studied maps very carefully beforehand so he had a good idea where the ship was located. Ev and Mida gave him the high sign when they flew over the spot. It was camouflaged so well, even Ev had a hard time locating it. He could tell where the cliff location was, but he could not locate the mesa top spot, even though they had disturbed a rather large area with their excavation. Sandy was looking for access for a vehicle. He shouted into Ev's ear that there was no problem getting a four-wheeler onto the mesa top, although it would be an interesting trip. They had to get a lot of equipment in there and needed several trips pulling a trailer.

As they banked over Tantalus Flat, Ev yelled in Mida's ear that was where they met. She smiled and made a gesture in some type of sign language. Ev said to himself, "Half the time I can't understand her spoken language, now she is giving me more ways to not understand her." She shouted, "I said it was no coincidence we met there. It was meant to be."

The pilot asked if they got a good look at what they wanted. Ev looked at Mida, then at Sandy. Sandy gave the high sign. Ev gestured to head home. The pilot said over the headphones that this was sure some pretty rough country. Ev answered that it sure was and has been pretty rugged for a long time. The pilot said his great-great-grandparents came out here pulling a handcart. They left a journal and he couldn't believe what they went through. Ev said it has been rugged for millions of years before that. The pilot just grinned.

After the group landed and Sandy paid the pilot, Ev said, "Let's celebrate our little conspiracy. How about a big piece of pickle pie!"

Sandy looked at him like he had just stepped out of a spaceship. "A what?"

Mida laughed and said, "You have to try this. This little restaurant in Bicknell has been famous for years for its weird pies. They have pinto bean pie, peanut butter pie, and of course regular pies like apple and pecan. They are delicious. I'm not hot on the pickle, but I would kill for the pecan."

"A big piece of pickle pie with a slab of vanilla ice cream. If that flight made you queasy, then this is the cure," Ev said as he rubbed his stomach.

"You know," Sandy drawled in his best Texas accent, "you are both certifiable. I've been examined many times by some of the best shrinks NASA has. If they could find out what I'm doing here now, I'd go in the nearest padded cell. And to top it off, you want me to eat pickle pie!"

They stopped in Bicknell, only to find that there was no pickle pie. Clara the waitress said there was only apple and peach today. It was early in the season and the restaurant was not yet open full-time. Not a lot of locals had appetites for pickle pie in late March. Ev settled for two pieces of peach pie and ordered a whole apple pie to take home.

The trio huddled over their pie and hot chocolate and discussed what they had seen. Ev said there were two ways in, but the Oak Creek route was by far the best. Trouble was, you couldn't get off the highway for another month at best, due to snow at that elevation. You could almost get in now through the Park, but then there was that long but scenic two hour hike.

"What if we hike down from the highway?" Sandy asked. "How far through the snow is it? Maybe we could carry a bicycle if it's not very far."

Ev smiled. "Now if we had thought ahead last fall, we could have stashed a bike down there. It's not far, but it would be tough carrying one over the snow until we could use it. And we can't take one in on a snowmobile 'cause the snow is getting pretty rotten this time of year. It's just a bad transition. Not good snow, but just enough to keep us out." As he said that, a big slather of ice cream fell off his fork and landed right in his lap.

Mida groaned and said, "My god. Here we sit discussing a very complicated scientific maneuver that could determine the course of humankind and you can't even eat. Want me to get you a bib? Sandy, we just took his training wheels off his bicycle last year."

Sandy laughed as he took a sip of hot chocolate. "I suppose it's a good thing we didn't stop here first. I doubt if you could have hit your barf bag if you had to use it." His laugh turned to a choke as he spilled his drink.

Mida shook her head. "I think it's time to get out of here. I'm stuck with a couple of goofballs. Come on kids. Let's let Mida take you home for your nap." Shaking her head, she got up to leave.

Ev quickly wolfed down the last bites of his second piece of pie. "Brilliant minds have always had to put up with this type of snobbery and ridicule," he said to Sandy. He grabbed the check as Sandy reached for it also. "Our treat. You took care of the flight. Least we can do is get the pie." They both got up as Mida was already walking out the door.

Sandy didn't take long to occupy most of Carlcabin. He made a quick trip back to Tucson and came back a few days later with his van full of books, an extra computer, and assorted scientific equipment. He was also towing a small trailer with a motorcycle and four-wheeler. Ev was surprised with the assortment of toys and computer stuff that Sandy brought. He had a large graphics setup, including lots of GIS tools and programs.

As soon as Sandy was comfortable in the Carlcabin, Boyd and Marybeth drove over for a week. Boyd's excuse was he needed to furnish the guesthouse. He was driving a rental truck jammed with chairs, couches, tables, beds, and enough furniture to furnish a large house.

When Boyd first walked into the Carlcabin, he exclaimed, "My gawd, what have you done to this house?" He looked out at his truck. "There's no room for all my furniture. How can one person have this much stuff?"

"Boyd, how are we going to build and map all the trails on this expanse of desert without the equipment to do so? You have a first class set up here. Why, once word gets out to the space community, we will be booked with physicists and astronomers wanting to come here to do top secret research in a nice quiet setting. It will be the primo scientific retreat in America. We may just set up a few big dishes and this will be the top tracking station in North America."

"Sandy, you are full of bull and you know it." Boyd put his arm around him and laughed. "You got any beer in that cooler? Let's have a brew, then we can move in the refrigerator. I've got six cases of Heineken and Sam Adams in the van. Ev seems to have a preference for Adams. I have a hard time finding the German beer I love when I'm in Europe, but the big H will suit me fine. I also have a few bottles of Wild Turkey hidden somewhere in there. If we are going to furnish this house, we have to do it right." He looked over his shoulder and said, "But whatever you do, don't tell the little woman I brought this. She thinks I am corrupting her only son as it is." He winked as Sandy opened a couple bottles of a Tucson microbrewery Desert Pale he brought with him.

"You think your Texas taste for beer can handle the best Arizona has to offer? None of the big names are worth drinking, but there is this little brewery on the south side of Tucson that makes the best stuff I ever drank. I think they make it with cactus juice or peyote or something. Has a nice bite to it."

Boyd took a big drink and opened his eyes wide as he savored the after taste. "Hey, this stuff is top notch. I gotta write down the name of this." He took out a pen and notebook from his pocket and jotted down the name and address of the brewery. "I suppose I'll have to drive all the way to Tucson to buy this."

"Only place I ever saw it was the brewery itself down on Valencia Road. Next time I'm down there, I'll pick you up a couple cases."

"Sandy, you're all right. Let's go move some furniture. We need to get Ev so we have at least one strong set of arms. I've got the stomach muscles." He smiled as he patted his sizable paunch. "Now we need usable muscle." With that, he let out a big laugh and walked out the door as he took another drink of Desert Pale.

Mida and Marybeth supervised the arrangement of furniture, although they were limited by the fact Sandy had taken up two rooms of the Carlcabin with his equipment and his office. That was even after they had moved some of it to the basement of the house. They crammed chairs and dressers into one bedroom.

Mida went up to Boyd and put her arm around him. "Boyd, we know you wanted to stay here this week," she said as she looked around the cabin, winking at Marybeth so Boyd couldn't see her. "But doggone it, Sandy has got this secret moon base all set up for the next space shuttle mission, and there is no room for you. You don't mind sleeping in the back of the van, do you? Our extra bedrooms are still full of books and our junk. You know you will have to build another building for the big library, don't you? The sooner you get that built, then we can invite you to stay with us next time you are here."

Boyd put his arm around Mida and grinned at her. "Sugar plum, you better stick to what you are good at. You don't pull the leg of this Texan. I'll arm wrestle you for your own bed and then you will find that you are the one sleeping in the van. We will sleep in our very own Pecos County room down the hall. I'll just put a chamber pot in there so I don't have to wade through all the furniture if I have to get up in the night."

"Oh, Boyd," Marybeth groaned, "why are you so crude? Just put a pillow in the tub and sleep in the bathroom. I told you not to get so much furniture."

"Pecos County room?" Mida twisted her face as she looked at Boyd. "I was going to name that room the Lozen Room after Victorio's warrior sister. You know her story?"

"Oh, good grief," Ev moaned. "Who could sleep in a room named after that Amazon? I suppose you would put her picture above the bed. Good luck falling asleep with her staring down at you. I think it should be the Kayenta room and we could have Kayenta sandstone rocks on the floor instead of rugs."

Sandy perked up. "If we are going to name rooms, then I vote for the Phobos Room, named for the largest of the two moons of Mars. We could put that wallpaper on the ceiling that glows in the dark and shows planets and constellations."

"Time out!" shouted Marybeth. "I think you have all gone crazy. Is it the altitude here? Or just the overwhelming red outside? We are not naming rooms. We will sleep in the far room at the end of the hall. Then in a few days, we will leave you alone to figure out what you want to name things. You can name each chair and towel if you want. Just leave me out of it. It's bad enough I have to sleep in something called the Carlcabin. You should call it the Billions and Billions Bungalow."

Sandy laughed. "Hey, I like that. Why didn't I think of that?"

Boyd spent the week figuring where his furniture would go. He compromised with Sandy. He hired a local woodworker to put in floor-to-ceiling bookshelves in one room. He even made a quick trip to Provo to get a drafting table and small light table plus some other office furniture. He cajoled Ev into adding this to the house basement, which was becoming crowded from the library and furniture already down there. He was able to free up one room, enough so the furniture could go in there without seeming too crammed.

Marybeth spent a lot of time with Mida. She cooked several cakes and pies, freezing them as she finished. She said they had to fill the new freezer that they had brought for the big house. She knew Mida didn't like to cook, but she also knew that Mida would never admit it. Ev had confided to her that Mida just did not have the culinary talents she claimed she did. Since Ev survived several years as a bachelor, he had developed a passing talent for cooking. Thus, he and Mida shared cooking duties. Of course, Mida defiantly and continually denied any lack of culinary skill. By this time, Mida herself was confused about her cooking. Everyone thought she couldn't cook. She thought she was actually pretty good. But most of the time, she really preferred to be doing other things. That is why people got the idea she was no good. She finally agreed with her mom that she was not intended to be a domestic housewife, although she could cook when she had to.

Boyd and Marybeth left for the long drive back to Colorado Springs but only after a day delay. When Ev jokingly said he would fill the back of the rental van with red Utah rocks, Boyd said that was a wonderful idea. He could use them to build a rock walkway in their yard. The day before they left, Ev helped Boyd load a ton of Moenkopi stepping-stones into the van. Marybeth complained she was not going to help unload them. Boyd reassured her he would get a couple neighbor kids to help.

After Boyd and Marybeth drove out the driveway, Ev looked at Sandy and said it was time to go visit Orion. Sandy said that's what he had been waiting for. They all started packing for a week's stay. Since they decided to go in via the Park, they needed backpacks and their small tents. Sandy wanted to take some of his scientific equipment but decided to wait until they could drive in via Oak Creek in a few more weeks. While they were getting things organized, Mida quietly asked either of the two if they had bothered to check any weather forecasts. Both looked at each other, then at Mida. They shook their heads like a couple of four-year-olds. Mida told them to look out the window. Gray clouds painted the sky and it was starting to snow. Sandy got on the internet and discovered a major winter storm was slamming into Utah. They finished packing, then sat inside for two days while over a foot of wet snow built up around the buildings. Most of the storm was rain and not snow down in the Park, but it made the road impassable until it dried out. They had to wait another four days before they could get through on the jeep road. Sandy learned to play mahjongg during the delay.

When they finally were able to start their expedition, they drove through Torrey and down the hill into the Park. They left civilization when they turned off the Scenic Drive at Capitol Gorge and headed up the dirt road toward the old Sleeping Rainbow Ranch.

Pleasant Creek ran high and muddy from the recent rains and snowmelt. Sandy put his SUV in four-wheel drive and they cautiously plunged across the creek. Sandy did not have a lot of experience on this type road, so he eased along in granny gear for the next two miles. Ev commented that Mida had traveled this road in her car. Sandy thought Ev was kidding and said there was no way she could have gotten through. Mida laughed at both of them and called them a couple weak hearts.

Ev said, "I want to point out that one particular weak heart saved Mida's bacon when he found her broken down on the road. You may have gotten through but at a cost of trashing your vehicle."

"My car is four-wheel drive and in case you did not notice, it has a high clearance. My brother worked on it to raise it. I wasn't born into wealth so I can't afford to go out and buy a forty-thousand-dollar SUV. I get by with a little help from my friends."

Sandy laughed. "I should have gotten a picture of that. Mida driving a low rider. Does it bounce up and down?" Ev found that particularly funny. Sandy starting laughing at Ev and soon had to stop the vehicle.

Mida got out and slammed the door. "All right, you think it is so funny, you just follow me. I can walk faster than you are driving. And when you get scared of the narrow spot up ahead that is probably half washed off the cliff, you let me drive then."

Mida started walking, and as she said, she soon left them behind as Sandy crawled his SUV up the rutted, rocky path. Ev said that sometimes you can tease Mida and sometimes you better not. Evidently, he frowned, you do not tease her about her driving ability. He also cautioned Sandy not to tease her about her cooking either.

"As a matter of fact, there are a lot of things I don't tease her about. She is a pretty talented and classy lady who has been fighting in a man's world and a prejudiced one at that, all her life. Did you know she received a total of seven separate scholarships and grants to get through almost eight years of college? She hardly spent a dollar of her own, which is good since she has never had much more than a dollar.

"She sure the hell changed my life," continued Ev. "Men dream all their lives about someone like her. Sometimes I think she appeared on this road when she did last May for a purpose. She was meant to be involved with Orion. Does that sound weird?"

"This whole thing is weird to me, but let me withhold judgment until tomorrow when I actually see this thing." He pointed up ahead. "There is Mida sitting by the edge of the road way up there. She must have run. Sometimes I can imagine her riding with someone like Geronimo or Cochise. She moves like the wind."

They picked up Mida and continued on slowly up the road and over the hill. As they came to the edge of Tantalus Flat, Ev directed Sandy off the road to the secret camping spot he discovered a year ago. He explained in detail what happened at this spot and up the canyon. He gave his sermon on geology and summarized what he learned from Mida about rock art and the cultures of the area. Mida busied herself setting up her tent and fixing supper. She had been quiet since her walk in front of the vehicle earlier in the day. Ev assumed she was still angry so he didn't say anything to her.

Mida didn't want to upset the other two over her encounter, so she avoided talking to them. While she had walked ahead of them earlier, she started hearing strange noises. It sounded like the wind in the trees, but there was no wind. She felt warmth around her as if there was some presence. She noticed her hands flashed a blue aura about them for a few seconds, then they turned their normal color. An eagle appeared above her and swooped down to land on a gnarled old pinyon to her left. It chattered for a few seconds, almost like a crow, then lifted off and disappeared over the cliffs ahead of her. She sat down on a rock next to the road. The vehicle was below her slowly grinding up the road, still a few minutes off. She closed her eyes and saw a clear vision. Seagulls circled and screamed over a seashore that stretched to both horizons. The waves lapped rhythmically on the white sand. Offshore a few miles sat an island with tall arches and towers. They were made of white stone. Bells pealed a haunting melody. She listened for what seemed like hours, captivated by the sounds of both the bells and the birds. When she opened her eyes to the desert cliffs around her, the eagle swooped down and dropped a small white stone. It landed by her feet. She picked it up. It was spherical and smooth as glass and had an iridescent white color. It was cold and made her think it was a piece of ice. She held it and it turned a pale blue. As she brought it to her face, she heard the same melody of ringing bells. She quickly put it in her pocket just as Sandy and Ev drove up and stopped the vehicle. She stood up and got in, not saying anything.

All evening, as Ev and Sandy sat by the campfire talking about gas chromatographs, mass spectrometers, and ionized whatchamacallits, Mida sat and stared into the dancing flames. When their conversation wound down, she started telling them a story. It was one of many she learned as a child around campfires on the rez. She spoke of the white grizzly and the dancing wolf and the trickster coyote. The animals had stopped time when they first saw man. All animals lived in harmony, but they sensed something strange with this new creature. They went to man and tried to look in his eyes, but could see only stars. They talked to the man, but he only stared at them. They started time again and the man walked away, continually looking back over his shoulder. They called to him, but he couldn't understand their language.

At first Ev didn't understand why she was telling this story, but she was so skillful at weaving the imagery he just sat back and enjoyed it. He knew Mida saw something earlier. She shared with Ev her strange visions more frequently of late, especially after their trip to Arizona. He guessed that their nearness to Orion was having something to do with her behavior that night. Ev enjoyed Mida's storytelling because he lost track of time whenever she brought him into the world of her stories.

Mida told that story since she did have a vision that made her think about meanings and creation and the beginning of time. She said the word aborigine was derived from the words "ab origine," or the beginning of time. She always referred to her people and all native cultures as aborigine. Her people were from the beginning of time. They knew how to stop time. This was done through meditation, trances, and in Mida's experience, vision quests. Ev and Sandy had been talking of time and time travel. It made Mida think about her vision and how time seemed to stop during her vision. This always happened, and her visions were occurring more frequently. The visions didn't bother her anymore, but sometimes she could not figure out what they were supposed to mean. She knew the meanings would come to her in time.

They let the fire die down, sitting in silence for a while. They all filed off to their own tents as an owl hooted in the distance. Mida looked toward the North Star just as a few wisps of the northern lights flickered on the horizon. At least she assumed they were the northern lights. She started to say something to Ev but decided not to—just in case they were not the northern lights.

There was a light frost on the tents the next morning, so they laid them in the sun to dry before they packed their backpacks. By ten o'clock, they were on their way. They walked by way of the old mining road that hugged the base of the Wingate cliff to their west. This route took them through the Chinle Formation with its colored muds and petrified wood. They got to Sheets Draw before noon and walked up it until it narrowed. Ev noticed Sandy was a little out of shape and slowing down as they walked along the sandy red soil next to the creek. They stopped to eat lunch under a huge towering old ponderosa pine. Ev loved this stretch of creek because there was a small forest of these yellow-barked giants. No logger had ever set foot anywhere near these trees. Ev marveled that a tree could be so stately and magnificent. Mida replied she could feel the energy of these ancient trees. Sandy commented he had never seen anything so powerful other than the sequoia in California.

Ev told Sandy the going got rough from here on up so Sandy needed to set the pace. There wasn't far to go as the crow flew, but it took another hour to climb out of the canyon and over the top. Sandy led the way, slowly but steadily. Mida returned to her normal self, chatting away about the petroglyphs and ancient campsites they passed along the way. They could see a small granary on a ledge on one small side canyon. She filled him in on the history and cultures that occupied this remote corner of the world, much as she did Ev a year before. And of course, Ev intermingled his lectures on geology whenever Mida took a breath. Sandy was reeling with information by the time they climbed out of the canyon and on top of the mesa.

After walking a little ways, Ev stopped and took off his backpack. Mida did the same. Sandy said he was fine. He didn't need a rest. He was gaining his second wind. Mida told him he didn't need a second wind. This was the place.

"X marks the spot," Ev said with an air of accomplishment. "This is Baby Orion, just under this pile of dirt."

Sandy looked around. "What pile of dirt? This whole area is one big pile of dirt. How can you tell anything?" He stood with a perplexed look on his face as he slowly unfastened his backpack.

Ev walked over to a small dead cedar. He picked it up and Sandy saw that it had been cut off. Dead needles still clung to the branches. Ev tossed aside a few small red rocks and suddenly Sandy gasped. There was the metal periscope sticking up out of the ground, just as Ev had discovered it a year ago. Sandy walked over and knelt on the ground. He gently felt the object, running his hands up and down the tube. He muttered something neither Ev nor Mida could understand.

Sandy stood up and brushed the red dirt off his knees. Taking off his hat, he undid the blue bandanna wrapped around his forehead. He reached down into his pack and pulled out another water bottle since the one hanging from his pack was empty. All the time, no one said a word. Ev and Mida looked at each other, then

Sandy, then back to each other. Sandy took a drink, then wiped his mouth. He looked at Ev, then at Mida, then sat down.

The low whistle of the wind was the only sound for many seconds. Finally, Sandy broke the silence. "What the hell does a person say at a time like this? This is two hundred million years old?"

"Well," Ev drawled, "the rock it is embedded in is two hundred million years old, give or take a few million. I don't know any other conclusion we could come to."

Sandy rubbed his chin, then looked at the periscope. "This is no practical joke? This isn't some high school prank?"

Ev and Mida both shook their heads slowly as they silently mouthed the word *no*.

"You are fascinated with time travel. What are the odds this is something made by good old *Homo sapiens* in, say, the year 2200, and it went back in time. This might not be extraterrestrial at all. It may contain our great-great-grandchildren."

Mida slowly took her water bottle out and took a long drink. "We've thought of that. It could be. But even if it was, it still went back two hundred million years in order to be here. How is that for time travel? From the year 2200 back to 200 million BCE, then to now. But I don't think so. There is some form of energy in there that is not of this world. I have a feeling it is from out *there* somewhere." She looked up at the sky and waved her hands from horizon to horizon as she emphasized the word *there*.

"I don't question Mida's intuitions lately," Ev said seriously as he sat beside the pipe. "Let me ask you a question. Does this look like any kind of metal you have ever seen? Feel it, scratch it with this pick." He handed Sandy his rock pick.

"Boy, are you privileged," Mida said sarcastically. "I don't think Rock Boy has ever let me even touch his precious Esting. That thing is sacred. Be honored."

"That is *Estwing*, the best brand you can buy," Ev corrected as he handed the rock pick to Sandy. "And maybe it's a guy thing."

Sandy examined the weathered and scratched tool, then leaned down to look at the metal in the ground. He lightly tapped it, then tried to scratch it. He could not make a mark of any kind. He poured water on it, rubbed sand on it, held a match to it, did about everything he could think of. He finally handed the pick back to Ev and said, "Well, looking at the scratches on your pick, this metal in the ground is much harder. It is not stainless steel. It's not even magnetic according to this little magnet on my keychain. It has to be some alloy. I've seen all the variations we have used in our NASA fleet. It doesn't look like any of them. And we have used some pretty exotic metals. It reminds me a little of the ceramic we used in the tiles on the shuttle. But it has that odd sound when you tap it. If I had the right tools, I could tell you in a few minutes if it is radioactive.

After a few minutes of staring at it and rubbing his chin almost nonstop, he finally said, "To be honest, it is starting to give me the creeps. It has to be made of the basic elements. Anything and everything in this universe can only be made of the elements we know about. It's physically impossible to be made of any element we don't know of. And there aren't any elements we don't know of. At least any that are stable. That is basic chemistry and physics. According to the laws of our universe, if this came from our universe . . ." Sandy was talking to himself as he trailed off, then looked at Ev.

Ev stood up. "Well, we can't solve all the problems now so let's set up camp and get settled in. This evening we can dig out what we uncovered last year. You will want to go below and see the lower window. That's what we saw first and that's what zapped Mida. Then tomorrow we can get started on whatever you want to do. If we put our three tents like this"—he pointed and gestured—"we can stretch the tarp as a roof. I think this may be the best location to go in since it is easier to hide from view. But we can talk about that later."

Mida looked up when she finished unpacking and saw that both men were lying on the ground asleep. She turned her back on them as she slowly ate an apple, gazing at the back of Capitol Reef. When she finished, she looked back at them, still lying on the ground. Shaking her head, she wandered off into the miniature forest that formed the edge of the canyon below.

As she sat on a red slab of sandstone, she felt like she was being watched. There was nothing but small trees and red rocks. She heard the strange wind-like sound that she heard the day before. Then she remembered the small stone the eagle had dropped. She reached into her pants pocket and pulled it out. It was a smooth, glassy blue. It reminded her of a small cat-eye marble her brothers had played with when she was little. She started to put it back in her pocket but hesitated, rubbing it between her fingers. She looked at the rock, then held it up to her face. That same sound was coming from the rock. Holding it to her ear, it sounded like waves lapping on a seashore. Seabirds called. She looked closely at the rock. As she stared at it, she noticed the color changing. The rock was turning into what could only be described as a small crystal ball. Waves lapped on a sandy beach, with palm trees waving in a breeze. Birds came into view, skimming the water. The ocean turned to land, water draining off rocks as the land rose. The rocks were bright red, much redder than those at her feet. Then quickly as it appeared, the picture disappeared and the stone was blue once again.

Mida didn't gasp for breath. She didn't say anything. She slowly put the rock back in her pocket, stood up, and calmly walked back to where Ev and Sandy were setting up their tents. When Ev looked at her, he could tell she had another vision. Sandy even commented that she looked different.

Mida took a deep breath and said, "Let's get digging. Someone is trying to communicate with me and I want to find out what they are saying." She smiled at Ev, then turned to pick up her tent. An eagle called to them as it soared in the sky above them, then disappeared below the cliffs to the north. Mida looked up and silently said the words "Be patient, I am coming."

April 26, 1999

I am of this earth, but I am also of the skies. I don't belong here anymore. I am a visitor to my own world. I may be a goddess or I may be one of the spirits I used to hear about as a little girl. I don't even want to think about it. There is something I am supposed to do and I am waiting for someone to tell me what. This is the ultimate of all visions. *I am living a vision. I know by experience not all visions make a lot of sense at first. They all do in time.*

Time. Time is becoming more important but also more mysterious. Am I going back in time or am I going forward? Or is this the same time I am now in but in another place? Another universe or at least another world somewhere? But it is connected here. Somehow. Oh my god, so many questions. What has happened to that life I had prepared for so long?

I have never seen the ocean, so why does it feel so comfortable, like I have lived by it forever? I am a desert creature. Maybe it's a world of opposites. I want to just lie down and sleep for a month. But there is no time. Time, again. But whatever has possessed me doesn't want me to sleep since my dreams are all the same type visions. Sometimes I wonder if I have gone crazy. Is this what that is like?

Sandy was impressed but I feel there is still something strange about him. He wants to do so many things that will just take more time. I just want to go in this thing. Now.

THIRTEEN

The Pause Before the Leap

Since you are like no other being ever
created since the beginning of time,
You are incomparable.

—*Brenda Ueland*

No one regards what is before his
feet. We all gaze at the stars.

—*Quintus Ennius*

S PRINGTIME IN THE Utah desert can be frustrating as well as enjoyable. After the frustration of the rainy delay, the first full day in the desert around Orion was perfect for the explorers. The temperature rose into the 70s and passing clouds tamed the intensity of the sunshine. The conspirators stretched a tarp between the three tents as a roof and began the process of digging the trench. Ev had dug this hole once already so digging was easier this time. Sandy asked Mida to do the recording and photography. She complained about how meticulous he was, but he kept reminding her that this was nothing compared to what they would do later. Ev was puzzled by her behavior since he knew Mida to be pretty demanding herself when it came to the recent work she did to finish her doctorate.

He assumed it had to do with her anxiety to get inside the ship and find what or who was calling to her.

While Ev rested after his initial flurry of removing fill, he said they needed to go below so Sandy could see the lower window at the base of the cliff. Eager to take a break, they scrambled down the south canyon slope to visit the original Orion discovery. Ev carefully removed the rock camouflage. Sandy uttered a few exclamations to himself when he saw the window but said nothing to the other two. Mida cautioned him to be careful. There was an immense amount of energy there and it depended on the receptivity of the person whether it was overpowering or not. She had been overpowered; Ev had not. Sandy kept his distance as he puzzled again over the material the object was made of. He tried to scratch the metal or whatever it was but had no luck.

After studying it for several minutes, Sandy said they should cover the window until they were ready to spend time at this site. He wanted to examine the upper site in detail, then decide which one would be best to enter. Sometime before they left to return to Orion Wingate, he would come down here at night and look inside.

Ev walked over past the creek and showed him the four-wheel-drive road that came down from the highway and along Oak Creek. Sandy was pleased they could drive right to the cliff if they wanted. He asked where you could leave that road and drive onto the mesa top. Ev told him it was a mile or more back, but he had checked it out and it would be easy, with only a few minor gullies to negotiate. With a four-wheeler, it would be a breeze. They agreed to check that out in a few weeks when the snowmelt allowed access.

Mida had already walked back up top and was relaxing with her journal when Ev and Sandy wandered back into camp. Even though Sandy was anxious to finish the excavation of the top site, he was satisfied to just sit around camp and enjoy the view. Ev was not anxious to finish digging out the hole, fill it back in, then come back in a few weeks and dig it out again. He and Sandy talked about schedules and when they would be ready to stay here until the end as Mida termed it.

After dinner, Mida started telling stories. She didn't end until Sandy started snoring. He fell asleep after she started the tale of the Spider Woman and the story of creation. Ev had not heard several of the stories mainly because Mida recently made them up. It was past ten o'clock when she realized she had been weaving tales for over three hours.

The next day as he rested during his excavation, Ev thought about the moral of the stories Mida told. She made a skillful arrangement of these tales. He knew she was relaying a point, but he struggled to tie them all together. They dealt with creation, beginnings, how things came to be as they were. He came back to the present moment when Sandy nudged him, none too gently.

"Ev, are you with us or has the blue light kidnapped you? You have been staring off into space for about ten minutes now. Mida has told me all the secrets about you."

"Oh, Sandy, he will be all right. I think he is suffering post-traumatic pick syndrome from that dramatic act of loaning out his pick yesterday. He did the equivalent of selling his soul by that unselfish act. You and he are stronger than blood brothers now." Mida smiled as she stared at Ev, who still seemed lost in thought.

Ev finally responded rather sheepishly. "Sorry, I just was thinking of Coyote and the White Buffalo Woman. I dreamed about white buffalo again last night. He came down from the sky and landed in the middle of the prairie. Then lightning started flashing and the prairie turned to a tropical ocean. Mida, whatever spirits are haunting you are starting to come after me. At least I'm not seeing flashing lights. Yet."

"You just give it time, Rock Boy. My blue light people and I will corrupt your mind sooner than you think." Mida sat down as she picked up a small red rock and held it up in the air and pointed it at him.

"Okay," Sandy interrupted as he stepped out of the hole. "You are starting to give me the creeps with that talk. How much further till we hit the metal?"

"We can't be much more than a few inches from it," replied Ev. "I didn't really measure it before, but I think it was about belt buckle high on me."

"Yeah, that's about right," Mida said as she stood in the hole. "We are about there. I suppose I have to start documenting every grain of sand now?"

"Yeah, I'm just doing this to keep you from harassing Ev. It's either that or tie you up." Sandy laughed as he reached over to hold Mida's hand. "You stay right there, Sugar. I just need some basic measurements. When we get it uncovered, then we need to know about everything there is to know. I have to know how big to build this air chamber. We will have to make it airtight since I need to create a vacuum in it. Remember we haul in every little thing we need and we have to do it as secretly as possible. I am making this up as I go since there aren't really too many precedents for this." He scratched his white hair and licked his lips in the dry air. "I don't look forward to being out here in August when it's 150 degrees in the shade."

"This isn't Tucson or Houston. It might get hot, but usually we have nice afternoon thundershowers to cool things off. Mida got caught in one last year and almost got hit by lightning." As he waited for a reply, he heard his old friend the canyon wren. It warbled its descending scale far off in the canyon below.

"I got caught in a May thunderstorm and sometimes I wonder if I did actually get hit. That was after the blue energy zapped me. May lightning is gentle. The August bolts are the killers. Those are sent by the giant blue buffalo, not the white buffalo." Mida hugged herself and shivered in mock fright as she stepped back out of the hole.

"All right, all right. Let's get serious. Ev, I'm going to let you dig until you hit the metal," Sandy said as he stepped out of the hole after Mida.

"What the hell? I've been doing all the digging already. What is this? Bring Ev along as the human shovel and everyone else stand around and make fun of him? This is tedious work. Someone get down here and help me. This stuff is already loose, we just need to remove it from the hole," Ev growled as he got down on his hands and knees and starting carefully scraping with the trowel. He swatted at a fly that was buzzing his face.

Just as Mida started to get in the hole, Ev shouted, "Here it is! I've hit metal." He dropped his trowel and started pushing dirt with his hand.

"Okay, careful now," Sandy cautioned as he looked at his watch and recorded the time. "Is it metal or the window?"

"It's the window," said Ev as he brushed sand away with his glove. "I'm right on the edge. It goes toward you for about two feet if I remember right."

Sandy looked at Mida and said, "Mida, go in my tent and get the blanket on my sleeping bag. I don't want to let daylight in unless we have to." He measured the spot and marked it on his grid map of the site. "We are at the right level, now let's try and get to that level in the entire area of the trench. Scrape off everything from the metal, but let's leave a coat of dust on the window for now and I will cover it as well. We will see if that gives us enough room."

Ev carefully dug out all but a thin coat of dirt and outlined the window. He then took the blanket from Mida and spread it over the area.

Sandy looked up at Mida and then at the huge pile of dirt and rocks. "Mida, what I'd like for you to do is to just sit down and play in this pile of dirt. Don't frown like that. It's the easy job. Since we need to fill this back in one more time and remove it again, let's make it easier next time. Pick out all the rocks bigger than a pea and scatter them away from here. Then we will make another pile of sand and dirt to make up the difference. When we fill the hole in, it will be using just dirt and not rock. Does that make sense?"

"Sure it makes sense. I just don't look forward to doing it. I suppose you want me to count the rocks and map them where they fall?" Mida scowled as she sat down on the ground. "I guess if we are going to get dirty, we might as well do it first class." She started tossing rocks out of the pile.

Ev laughed as he looked up from his scraping. "No bubble bath for you tonight. I think this red will combine well with your blue aura and make a nice, what would that be, mauve?"

Mida's aim was very good as a small pebble bounced off Ev's hat.

The morning turned into afternoon as Ev scraped dirt, Sandy threw dirt out of the hole, and Mida picked rocks out of the pile. Before Sandy finished telling stories of the moon missions, they had emptied the hole. It measured three feet and ten inches deep, five feet and eight inches wide, and eight feet and seven inches long.

They had exposed the two windows and the door. Sandy figured that was enough space to get inside, but he thought they might need to enlarge the hole a little more in order to get the entry structure over it. Ev and Mida both grumbled when he said this, but they trusted his judgment. Ev simply said, "How much?"

"Tell you what," Sandy mumbled as he stroked his beard. "Before we go to that much trouble, I want to spend a little more time down below. I think this is the better entry point, but I want to uncover all the exposed ship down there." He climbed up out of the hole and walked over to the nearest tree. He bent over and picked up a dead branch lying on the ground, then pulled a pocketknife out of his pocket. He sat down and started to whittle absentmindedly.

Ev and Mida both stood there a minute, waiting for Sandy to say something more. Realizing he was deep in thought, they looked at each other, shrugged, and sat down in the shade of the tarp.

Ev looked over at Sandy as he continued to shave off the old brown wood, exposing clean, white, and reddish wood that looked brand-new. "And you didn't want to do that until dark?"

"Right. That gives us a few hours to just sit back and relax. I need to savor the moment. What a gorgeous day." He looked up at the sky, cloudless and the brightest blue he had ever seen.

Mida looked at Ev and whispered, "Wanna go down to the creek and clean up a little. I am really dirty and you are no Mr. Clean yourself."

"Hey, Sandy, we are going down to the creek to wash up a little. Mida wants her bubble bath after all. I have to stand there and throw rocks in the water to create bubbles."

"Oh, go bubble yourself," Mida swatted the fly that was buzzing Ev's face again. Now you are uninvited."

"Wait a minute. I'll let you hold my rock pick," Ev trailed off as Mida went into her tent and came out with a towel and her overnight bag.

Mida headed down the cliff slope with Ev trailing behind. Sandy watched them walk off. He continued to whittle, smiling to himself as he thought about this whole crazy situation. He soon noticed he was carving his stick into what appeared like a large crystal. He stared in amazement at the near perfection and evenness of the facets. He was not a good whittler and had not done any carving for several years. He set the knife and stick down on the ground, folded his hands on his lap, and shut his eyes. He wondered if the excitement was getting to him.

When Sandy opened his eyes again, he noticed the sun was lower in the sky. He looked around for Ev and Mida but didn't see them anywhere. He walked over to the edge of the cliff and looked down below him. Mida was walking back from the creek, but he didn't see Ev. Sandy hollered down to Mida who had already looked up at him. She said Ev was having a little problem. His clothes seemed to have floated downstream while he was bathing and he was looking for them. Mida had a big smirk on her face as she said this, but she seemed content to continue on up to camp and let Ev fend for himself.

Sandy shook his head and figured he had better not ask any more details. He asked Mida if she would uncover the lower window on the cliff. He decided he wanted to look inside both windows tonight and it would save time later if the window was cleared now. Mida smiled and agreed. She said Ev probably would be in no mood to do it himself.

Mida came up a few minutes later, still without Ev. She sat down in the shade of the tarp and laid down a perfect projectile point at Sandy's feet. It was in the creek where she sat down to bathe. It obviously had not traveled far in the creek itself since it was not rounded or worn. Sandy picked it up and looked closely at it from all angles. He handed it back to Mida and asked if she could tell a story about it. She just stared intently at it and said whoever made it was good. They lived here at one time. As a matter of fact, there was probably a sizable community within shouting distance of this area. She asked Sandy what he would need to survive if he were plopped down in a strange place.

He stared blankly at her for a minute, then said, "I guess water, a shelter of some kind, and food of some kind. Those are the basics. A companion or two would be nice. Of course clothes. Other than that, everything else is a luxury."

"Now look around you here. You have water, there are plenty of ways to make shelter in this country, and there is food if you know how to find it. The food around here will provide you with clothes, but for eight months a year, you really don't need them. Only if you are shy. Pretty soon, you will be the color I am. So this was a very good place to live. Are you ready to try it?"

"I think I've gotten too used to the luxuries of life. I suppose if I had to, I could, but not if I had a choice. At least for longer than a couple weeks. You going to stay here and turn into the hermit of the mountain? Or is that hermitess?"

"It would be the goddess Mida," she said playfully. She then turned serious. "Sandy, maybe you haven't been affected yet by this thing, but let me tell your future. You look in that window tonight, you will feel compelled to come back later and enter this thing. You go inside, you won't come out, at least not here in the last stages of the twentieth century. I don't know exactly what is going to happen, but something rather significant is. If you are with us, fine. If you can't live with that significant a change, then don't look in that window. It's as simple as that." Mida reached over and held Sandy's hand. She looked him in the eye and didn't say another word.

"Are you one of them, whoever them is?" asked Sandy rather hesitatingly.

"Sandy, we are all one of them. Them is us. Them is a collection of electrons and energy fields. What else is there? You of all people should understand that. You have told us as much. We have before us"—she nodded toward the blanket spread out on the floor of the hole—"the answers to every question we have ever asked. We just have to interpret the answers. They aren't written in plain English. I don't understand them, but I know someone or something is helping me to read their language, so to speak. That's what this is all about. Some other form of life. Maybe very primitive, maybe very advanced. That is why you need to look at this projectile point and look around you and be comfortable with it. Be at ease with yourself and your ability to adapt and to learn."

Mida looked out at the expanse of cliffs and trees and brushed back her still wet hair. Sandy looked at the same view. He rubbed his eyes and held his hands on the sides of his face. A lizard scurried by outside the tent as he looked into Mida's dark brown eyes.

"You put things so simply. You are much closer to this way of life than most of us. You."

"Sandy," Mida cut in, "it isn't a matter of how recently my ancestors lived off the land versus your ancestors. It's your attitude. It's your values. It's your view of what this is all about. I know you have asked questions like 'What is god?' 'Where and how did we get here?' and 'What's the meaning of all this?' That is your nature to seek, to explore, to question. Of course, I look for answers. Most people do."

"Some people do, but most of those don't really want to hear the answers. The answers will scare them." Sandy picked up the arrowhead that Mida had laid back down by her feet. He looked at it carefully. "You think you know the answers?"

"No, and I said I don't. But we are about to find out. And it doesn't scare me. It fills me with wonder and awe, and anticipation."

"You are really sure about this, aren't you?"

"Yes, Sandy, yes." Mida reached over and took the arrowhead he still held in his hands. She looked at the shaped piece of rock, then looked up at Sandy. "You hang around here after tonight and you will be too. Can't you sense something about to happen?"

"Mida, from the moment I met you, I had a sense about you. Ev, too. You could be my daughter. I think you are one of the most special people I have ever met. Yes, I sense something. And it scares the hell out of me. I'm pretty comfortable now, but you have already guessed something is missing. I think I have a body without a soul. Sometimes lately, I wonder about my mind as well."

"Don't say that, Sandy. Your soul just lost your soul mate and it's lonely. You are just temporarily lost. You are like a magnet ready to attract a lot of things. Before we interviewed you, we met with another candidate in Las Vegas. A redneck skinhead military type. A brilliant mind but a very lost soul. We have a lot of lost souls wandering around this world. It is a tragic loss of potential. Something has gone astray somewhere along the line. I think the whole concept of life has so much more to offer. We are such a small island afloat in such a huge cosmos."

Sandy looked past Mida and said, "Speaking of being afloat, I think you set Ev's clothes asail on a huge creek. Look what you did to that poor man."

Mida looked around and squealed in mock horror. She put her hands to her face and stood up. Ev was wandering in wearing only his boots, hat, and his T-shirt wrapped around his waist.

"You are going to pay for this," Ev sputtered as he crawled into his tent. "You better glue your clothes onto your clean little body. If I have sunburned certain parts, oh, you will pay."

Mida raised her eyebrows as she tried to suppress a laugh. "I told you to quit staring at me and throwing rocks. I said I didn't want an audience. You just wouldn't quit."

"Yeah, so you entice me in with you and quietly throw my clothes away as you divert my attention."

"You didn't seem to object at the time. Did you look for your shorts? There is not that much water in the creek. They couldn't have gone far. At least you found your shirt." Mida was clearly having guilt pangs that her prank went further than she intended.

"Ev, I need a little exercise," Sandy said as he stood up and stretched. "Mida and I were having a serious conversation about spirits and souls. I think I will walk down and have a leisurely stroll along the creek a ways. Mida, why don't you come with me? Maybe a wave of energy will enlighten us on several fronts. Meanwhile

Ev, you go in and put some lotion on your front and wherever else needs it. We will be back before you turn red." Mida stifled a laugh as she followed Sandy away from the tents and down the slope. They walked down the creek a half mile but never found the rest of Ev's clothes.

Later that night, as the sky Orion hugged the western horizon, Mida said a prayer and did a short dance, stopping at each direction and saying a few words. Then Sandy stepped into the hole, pulled back the blanket and brushed the thin covering of dirt and sand off the windows. He shined his flashlight into the darkness, with his face up against the cracked window. He pressed a small tape recorder next to his lips. He was talking as he surveyed the scene. Neither Ev nor Mida could totally hear all he said, but they did catch words like seat, control panel, navigator, sensor, and a few others sprinkled in. After a while, he asked Ev to hand him the big yellow flashlight lying on the ground next to his tent. Ev wondered what this was but didn't ask Sandy to elaborate as he handed it to him. Sandy lay back down, face against the window and held this new light against the window. It made a humming sound but Ev couldn't see any visible light.

Sandy let out a "Holy catfish!" as he dropped the light at one point. Mida thought she saw a blue light flicker inside but she did not want to get too close. She did ask Sandy if he was okay. He was still holding the yellow flashlight, moving it slowly back and forth, still muttering into his tape recorder. He said he was fine, but he could feel something. He was learning a lot and was almost done.

In another minute, he got up, pulled the blanket back across the windows, and came up out of the hole. "You were right," he said. "This is definitely a type of shuttle vehicle. It is tilted against the main ship. It is against the door, which is partly open. Looks like something happened here in a hurry. Either that, or a major power failure of some kind. Seems a little strange. A lot of this looks familiar. Of course, I can't tell what the instruments are, but I see a lot of similarity with what I am used to. I guess space travel is the same all across the universe."

Sandy paused, then looked at Mida. "Mida, did you see what I saw over there in the corner?"

"My journal?" Mida said with a little note of anxiety in her voice.

"Yes. I thought I recognized it. It is the one I've seen you write in. I bet you didn't notice something of mine."

Mida looked at him with a question in her eyes.

"You probably didn't see what I whittled today. I was working on it while you two were playing in the creek this afternoon. I whittled what looks like a long crystal. It is lying on the floor over past your notebook. And, Ev, I doubt if you saw your pick. It is underneath Mida's journal. This little yellow flashlight is a pretty high-tech thing I made myself. I won't go into all the details, but it did some interesting things. It showed me the outline of the pick. It is hidden but it is there plain as day."

Ev had been very quiet but finally spoke up. "Mida was pretty upset last year when she was convinced she was in that shuttle. Now you are saying we all were in it. We all are in it still? How can all those things be here with us now yet they are in there and have been for two hundred million years? Explain that to me."

"I can't explain anything," Sandy said. "I will need a few years to think this one over. We are all treading totally new ground here. But before I make any earth-shattering conclusions, I want to go look in the other window. You coming with me?"

"Count me in," Ev said rather sarcastically. "I can't exactly sit by the campfire. You ever had a sunburned butt?

Mida snorted a laugh as she leaned over to symbolically kiss Ev's bottom. "I'm sorry you got your tush fried. I do hope you tied your shirt around you as you were walking back facing the sun. And yes, Sandy, I'm coming with you. I want to see what happens down there. I didn't find it as interesting as this up here, but that is where I first met Ms. Blue Light. I think that room inside the window down there was closer to some power or energy center.

Ev picked up the yellow instrument. "What is this thing, Sandy? I assumed it was just a flashlight. Obviously it's not."

"Well, let's say it uses magnetic imaging and lasers and mass density analysis. It has a viewing screen right here. Kind of like a space-age x-ray gun. I put it together myself. Suppose I should get a patent on it and make my fortune. It does things like image the pick which is otherwise hidden from view. Does a few other things, too. But that gets into national security secrets." Sandy smiled as he added the last remark.

"National security my sunburned ass," Ev said as he looked at the instrument. "Is this a new invention or is it your version of something else out there. I never heard of such a thing. What other 'Scotty, beam me up' type toys do you have in your tool bag?"

Sandy and Mida started walking toward the lower window. Ev hurriedly tagged along, showing a slight limp.

"Did you sunburn your big toe as well?" Mida giggled as she looked back at Ev.

"Oh, you are just getting the biggest kick out of this aren't you?" mimicked Ev as he caught up with them.

"Settle down, kids." Sandy grumbled as he started down the rocky slope. "I've just had the shock of my life looking in the shuttle. I don't know what to expect down here, but it sounds like I'm in for an even bigger shock. Blue at that." Sandy slipped as he maneuvered the small cliff portion of the slope. He fell on his rear end, yelling that he was thankful his butt wasn't sunburned, but now it might be as sore as Ev's.

They reached the bottom and walked over to the now uncovered window. The scene reminded Mida of a year ago when she first looked in the window. She shuddered as she thought of all that had happened since then. She told Sandy and Ev to close their eyes and think good thoughts. She didn't want any hint of negative energy. The energy inside was friendly, and she wanted everyone to know that only friendly intentions were involved. Her own silent thoughts wished for the blue energy to help them understand how to make contact and get inside.

Sandy climbed up to the window and put his face against it like before. He peered inside, then flicked on his flashlight. Mida sat down on the ground, swaying back and forth humming a chant to herself. Ev stood next to Sandy, looking over his shoulder into the ship. Cautiously, he put his hand on Sandy's shoulder.

Everyone was perfectly quiet for a minute or two. The silence was broken as a coyote howled across the canyon. Ev jumped and Sandy dropped his flashlight. Mida looked up from her meditation and said "Boo!"

"Sorry about that," Ev said as he stepped back down and sat down next to Mida. He put his arm around her. She whispered to him, "Way to go, Rock Boy."

Sandy spent a few more minutes looking around. He tried his yellow flashlight for a few minutes but didn't see much. Finally, he stepped down and said they should cover it back up for now. He wanted to come back tomorrow in daylight, but he didn't really see much of interest in here for now.

The group made their way up the hill and back to camp. The campfire had died down to embers and no one felt like building it up. They all slowly filed back to their tents without much conversation.

Ev fell asleep easily while Mida stayed up for a while writing in her journal. Sandy lay awake for hours, his mind racing full speed. He thought about Ev's question about an item belonging to each of them being in that shuttle for the past two hundred million years. How could they be in both places? The laws of physics that guided him for the past forty-five years in school and work had been turned on their head. Maybe it somehow was an illusion. What would happen if he went out and threw his wood crystal in the fire? Would the item in the ship disappear? Or maybe he would not be able to throw it in the fire. One place had to guide both places. In a way, this was a form of fortune-telling. Why hadn't he been touched by the blue light? He knew he was totally left-brained. Maybe since Mida was obviously right-brained, she was more susceptible to this form of energy. He tossed and turned, unzipped the sleeping bag and lay on top of it. He finally got up and walked around outside.

He had read much of the popular literature dealing with quantum physics. David Bohm discussed the concept of a holographic universe. Each part of the universe contains the entire universe. This was the principle of a hologram, that three-dimensional image on most credit cards. Our DNA stores information like a bit in a holographic image stored the entire image. Our DNA is part of our body, and our body is a part of the larger universe. Thus, every atom of our body carries not only information about our entire body but the entire universe. We are the universe. Sandy, more of a traditional physicist, had trouble with that theory, although it had some philosophical appeal.

He fingered his wooden crystal and surveyed more of the literature he had read. Ilya Prigogine expanded some of Bohm's ideas into biological systems and basic chemistry. Rupert Sheldrake talked about morphic resonance and other groundbreaking ideas. Many strange theories were tossing traditional physics on its head. Sandy had always wrestled with these concepts, but they kept running through his mind this night as he was thinking of Orion and its implications.

As he stood outside his tent, he looked up at the star-filled sky. Somewhere up there, someone long ago wondered why their friends and relatives never returned from a long star voyage. Or back to his original idea, some future human wondered what happened in some flash of a time warp. Whatever happened, he was trying to discover a few answers. What was his motivation other than pure scientific discovery? Could he go back and live a life anew as Mida thought was going to happen? Was he fit to be a father of a new civilization? Mida and Ev were cut out for that. Why was he here? Would he somehow discover his late wife? Would she become a part of this? Maybe he was meant to join her wherever she was.

Sandy wandered over to the edge of the canyon and looked down in the darkness. He knew life was active down there, but at what level of intelligence? Were we really unique or did the plants and animals have a form of intelligence we just didn't understand? Sandy's mind was wandering across the entire universe. He had been uptight before most of the moon shots but never like this. His whole purpose and meaning in life was in question this night. He sat down and stared up into the sky. Of all people who should know the stars, he didn't. He was looking at Cassiopeia low in the northern sky and knew her W shape, but he didn't recognize Vega, the location of his friend Carl Sagan's fiction adventure with extraterrestrial life. Nor did he know the story of Cygnus the Swan. No matter what season, Draco the Dragon wound itself around the Big and Little Bears, with their dippers. He thought about his life's work of trying to get ourselves up there somewhere, yet he did not know the details or myths surrounding many constellations.

He had thought about life but not the kind of thought where he really expected any answers. It was all a scientific pursuit. It was a challenge to his ability to make things work. Now he sat here in the middle of the night, scared as a teenager on his first date. He felt a tingling in his hand and looked down and gasped. His hand was glowing blue. It was clenched in a fist and he was holding his wooden crystal. He forgot he had it in his hand. The crystal was blue and became transparent as he held it. It started vibrating and it turned brilliant white. He held it up into the air, pointing it toward Vega. He saw a shooting star come flashing out of the eastern sky, heading straight across to the western horizon. He then saw a faint stream of light, like from a laser, head out from the crystal and go straight up into the sky. He dropped the crystal and started choking for breath. He wiped his eyes, finding his hand damp as he removed it from his face. He looked down in the canyon and saw things as clear as day. He knew it was night, but he could see trees and rocks and objects as if the sun was shining on them. He felt the blood pulsing through every vein and artery in his body. He heard Ev and Mida breathing back in the tents.

Sandy fell on the ground and closed his eyes. He was traveling at the speed of light, passing by entire galaxies. He saw stardust coalesce and form stars and planets. He saw and heard supernovas explode into massive bursts of brilliant light. He felt himself being pulled into a blackness that covered his field of view. It was a black hole, coming closer and closer. His arm was being pulled first.

He opened his eyes and Mida was kneeling over him shaking him. She was smiling at him and calling his name. "Sandy, it's time to get up and plan on how we can go visit our friends. You were visited by them last night, weren't you?"

Sandy just blinked and rubbed his eyes. His hands were their normal color. The wooden crystal was lying by his side. The sun was up, the sky was blue, and the birds were singing. Mida sat down beside him. She put her arm around him and softly said, "Sandy, it scared me to death when it first happened to me. I guess I have accepted it now. I don't know what is happening, but I will find out. We will all find out. It is amazing, isn't it? I thought I was pretty smart, but this power or whatever it is makes me feel like a young innocent child being led through a field of flowers on a spring day." She smiled at him and he suddenly felt totally at peace.

He stood up and brushed the dust off his clothes. He was wearing his sweat pants and shirt he slept in. Or tried to sleep in. Mida stood up and walked with him over to the tents.

"Ev is in a much better mood this morning. He is cooking eggs and who knows what else. Let's eat, then I think it would be nice for us all to go for a short walk. Then whatever you want me to do, I will help you take notes or write down measurements or whatever."

"Yeah. Welcome back to Earth. I need to do something where I know what I am doing." They walked back over, said good morning to Ev. Sandy said nothing about his vision of the night before.

After breakfast and their walk, they all went back down to the lower site and Sandy took a few measurements. They covered the window one last time and decided not to use this site for the entry. They spent the afternoon enlarging the upper hole. By evening, they had it as large as Sandy wanted. The next day, they filled in the hole with sand and dirt, then broke camp, erasing all signs of their stay. Sandy put his crystal in his pack, treating it like gold. Mida clutched her small stone in her hands as she left the site. Ev played with his rock pick as he tightened the belt on his pack. He would not put it in his belt or let go of it at all. The three conspirators cut short their planned week-long trip and headed back to the truck. The weather was warm, the sky was blue, and canyon wrens were singing loudly in several canyons. Mida started singing, "We're off to see the wizard, the wonderful wizard of Oz." They made that their hiking song as the scrambled down into Sheets Draw. They stopped and ate a late lunch in a different grove of old pines, then explored a couple side canyons. Sandy explained the chemistry of the air, the rocks, the plants, and even their bodies. They felt like their old selves, simply on a desert hike.

As they came up the rise to find their vehicle parked where they left it, Mida said, "Isn't it nice to be smart enough to know you aren't smart at all? We all have a little piece of the puzzle. We now know the puzzle is as big as the sky. Let's go home and pack for a long, long trip to explore that sky."

Sandy shivered. He looked up at the sky, then continued behind Ev and Mida.

April 30, 1999

I have mixed feelings about Sandy. I really like him and think he is providing the expertise we need, but sometimes I wonder about him. He has a brilliant mind, but I heard once that there is a fine line between genius and insanity. Sometimes Sandy acts like he isn't all there. He runs hot and cold. He has been fine on this trip, but a couple weeks ago, he was really moody and withdrawn. He really impressed me the first time we met him. I felt sorry for him. I could tell he was very lonely. He talked a lot about his late wife and I know he missed her greatly. When he lost her, he lost a part of himself. I think Marybeth had a similar experience. I was too young and too involved in grief myself to feel what Mom went through when Daddy died. Mom had her children to try and corral and believe me, we were a handful. I must have been terrible. I was thinking too much of myself to think about her loss. Sandy didn't have any family or even much of an extended family. It was just him and Margie, his wife of something over thirty years.

I walked in on him a couple times and found him not only talking to himself but arguing with himself. I've seen Ev do the same thing, but Sandy is different. He seems more incoherent. Most times he is very polite to strangers, such as the workmen at the compound. But I have seen him lose his temper and blow up over what seems to me to be a very small matter. Landra down at the restaurant said he got really mad the other day when he wanted a piece of banana pie and they were out. Guess he had his mindset on banana and wouldn't settle for any of the other dozen types they had. He stormed out, almost pushing another customer out of his way. Strange behavior.

I keep thinking about Tink. Maybe Ev was right. Tink might have been all bluff and bluster. Maybe I was sent to help him, but I stormed out in my own way. Too late to change any of that. Is it something about our society and culture that does this to people, or is it purely human nature? I wish I knew how to research that. Why are some cultures peaceful and some destructive? Take the early Americans. Several tribes were known as warlike. The Blackfeet, Pawnee, Comanche, and yes, the Apache were known as always at war, always killing. Then the Nez Perce, the Pueblo, Mandan, and most of the West Coast tribes were peaceful. Why? This has to be cultural—learned. Maybe the more advanced we get, we get tensed up, protective of our intelligence, our achievements, ready to kill to protect our advantage.

What about the inhabitants of Orion? They have to be extremely advanced. The ultimate. So were they peace-loving or warlike? Did they come ready to kill intruders or new civilizations? Or were they so advanced, they had nothing to fear, thus peace-loving? Will I ever find out any of the answers to these questions?

Meanwhile, I guess it is just human nature to have a mix of all. We just have to ensure the peaceful side stays in control. Good versus evil. Probably the first cavemen asked these same questions.

FOURTEEN

—✳—

Final Preparations

*I do not know what I may appear to the world,
but to myself I seem to have been only a boy
playing on the sea shore, and diverting myself
in now and then finding a smoother pebble
or a prettier shell than ordinary,
whilst the great ocean of truth
lay all undiscovered before me.*

—*Sir Isaac Newton*

*We never know how high we are
Till we are called to rise
And then, if we are true to plan
Our statues touch the skies.*

—*Emily Dickinson*

IN MID-MAY, BOYD landed on the dirt airstrip of the Orion Wingate with Denzee as a passenger. Mida greeted her mother when she got off the plane, whispering in Apache that this was the last time she would greet her as a visitor. This was Denzee's home now. Mida was preparing for her journey, whatever that may be—mental or physical—and would be gone within a year. Denzee accepted that something significant was happening, but understood that her daughter would tell her when she was ready and not before.

As they walked from the landing strip the two hundred yards to the Carlcabin, leaving Boyd to secure the plane and unload the bags, Mida told Denzee it was time for the two of them to start planning the cultural center. Mida told Denzee, "Mom, you will be in charge, but I want to share my ideas with you. Let's design the center around cultures and beliefs."

Mida went into detail about her conviction that her heritage hid the secrets of how to survive into the future and they needed to help keep alive the ideas and traditions that were disappearing. Mida continued, "The materialistic European, Judeo-Christian culture is rapidly destroying a way of life that understood and honored a lot of sacred values. The high-tech revolution offers a lot of conveniences, but it also destroys human relationships with all other forms of life."

Denzee listened patiently to this surprisingly strong harangue. She didn't disagree with what Mida said. As a matter of fact, she had been thinking a lot of the same things the past few years. But her emphasis was to try and teach those who would listen to what she considered to be a better way of life. She wanted to get past the stereotypes and the tendency of some of her people to latch onto those things that the whites liked or contributed to economically. She didn't like the way her own reservation was playing to the gambling crowd and exploiting the sacred trees that grew on the rez. The tribe was doing fine economically, but she believed they were turning into economic prostitutes.

Mida and Denzee had engaged in this same conversation many times before. This was a debate that divided native and non-native alike. Unfortunately, it was not a debate that was seriously carried on where it was needed—in Interior, in Congress, or in tribal councils. And Denzee saw that it was not a debate that seemed important to most people under forty years old.

Denzee turned and looked Mida in the eye and said, "Mida, you know I agree with a lot of what you say, but I think you are losing touch with reality. You and I live in a realistic world, not the idealistic utopia you are talking about. Sure, my people got screwed.

A lot of people got screwed along the way. You think blacks don't have a gripe? Mexicans? Japanese Americans during World War II?"

"So, what, we just forget about it? We—"

Denzee continued walking, but wouldn't let Mida continue. "You seem to forget that you are half-Anglo. Look back to Minnesota to how your Norwegian ancestors lived. They were hardworking people, dependent on family and community, just as much if not more so than Apache. Did they get a raw deal at times? Look at the reputation their ancestors had as Vikings. Bloodthirsty savages only interested in the good life they got by raping and pillaging. Was that a fair statement? You can't find any people who don't have a little bloodlust in them as well as noble virtues. You think all Apache were saints? I love that you consider yourself Apache, but remember that half your blood is European. You are as much Norwegian as Apache. I don't want you to forget what your father gave you."

"Mom, how can you accept all this unfairness and act like nothing is wrong? I don't care if your grandparents or Dad's got the shaft. Fact is, they did."

"There is a lot wrong and we do what we can to correct it. No one person can change it—"

"Yeah? Remember Margaret Mead's comment about the only way change has occurred is by a small group of people working to change something?"

"Change occurs a small step at a time."

"Mom, that's what I am talking about! You and I starting with small steps walking toward a bigger leap. And don't preach to me about being twice blessed as a half-breed. I had to suffer that extra discrimination. You sure didn't. Apache see me as an outsider and who knows what my Minnesota relations think of this brown-skinned, dark-haired foreigner? And if I emphasize Apache over Norwegian, well, go look in a mirror. You raised me after Dad was gone and I don't remember a lot of Scandinavian philosophy from you. My point is we identify what is not right and try to change beliefs and behavior. Ignorance only breeds more ignorance and intolerance."

"You think you are the first to discover this dirty little secret of life on this earth?" Denzee threw up her hands and looked up at the mare's tails cloud formations beyond the red cliffs.

"No, but I'm one of a select few who are given an opportunity to do more than a small part to try and right the wrongs."

"Well, don't count on me to lead your crusade. I paid my dues thirty years ago. I carried banners, I protested, I crossed this country trying to right a wrong that was killing half a generation. My own father's generation lost a big portion of their young men fighting to right a wrong. I will help you, but don't anoint yourself as saint and martyr just yet."

They stood outside the building, emotions reaching a boiling point, and stared at each other, thinking what to say next. Boyd broke the tenseness as he approached with two of Denzee's bags. He ignored their arm waving and strained expressions. Standing there panting, he said next trip over from Colorado Springs he was going to bring a four-wheeler.

Mida looked at her mother and said "We will continue this later," and turned to Boyd and told him to buy locally and just go into Bicknell or Richfield today and get one. He muttered "great idea" as he walked into the Carlcabin. He set the bags in Denzee's room at the far end of the building and disappeared at the end of the hall, grumbling about having to do all the unloading himself.

While Boyd was in the back, Sandy came into the building. Sandy hugged Denzee and welcomed her in Apache. Ev had taught him a few more words, so he was able to do a fairly good job of saying, "It is good to see you. I hope we will have a happy time sharing this house." Mida giggled as she corrected him on one small mistake. He mixed up the word for house and blanket. Denzee put her arm around him and said if he wanted to share her blanket, she didn't want him propositioning her in front of her daughter. Sandy blushed four shades of red as he sat down and asked Denzee to sit and tell him about her trip.

Mida had already put most of Denzee's things from the house into her new room. Denzee said she liked the interior decorator, knowing by the reflection on a water pitcher on the table that Boyd had walked back into the room behind her. Boyd loudly took all the credit for decorating the place. He would have brought over a few paintings and wall hangings, he complained, but he didn't have room in the plane for them.

Mida scolded him, "If you bring over another truck full of things, I will have the Highway Patrol stop you at the state line."

Boyd walked over and kissed Mida on the cheek. "Sugar, would you object to some good Navajo blankets on the wall? And I know where I can get a fantastic Apache quilt to put on my bed." He looked at Denzee and grinned.

Denzee laughed and said, "What is with all this talk of blankets and quilts? Am I safe staying in this house with these men?"

Mida smiled and looked first at Sandy, then at Boyd. "I will take these men outside and tell them of the Apache curse women use on men. Then I think they won't have any more thoughts about messing around with Apache women who know how to wield the curse." Glancing at her mom, she added, "And I know a few Norwegian tricks as well."

"I'm not sure what I walked into, but I take back anything I said," Boyd said as he walked down the hall into his room and shut the door behind him.

Sandy got up and went to the refrigerator. "All I wanted to do was welcome my cabin mate. Just a simple welcome in her own language. Try and accommodate someone nicely and you get beat up on." He took out a hunk of cheese and started to walk out the door. Denzee walked over to him and hugged him and whispered in his ear. Sandy laughed and walked outside.

"What did you tell him?" Mida asked her mother.

"None of your business. It's a secret between two old-timers. You're too young to understand."

"Oh, good grief Mom." Mida shrugged as she started to walk out the door. "I'm going to the house. When you are ready, come on over and let's continue our discussion. We can figure out some details without getting into big philosophical concepts. And bring Boyd with you if you want. He won't stay out here by himself long anyway and we might as well make him feel useful."

Over the next week, the plans for the cultural center started to take shape. Boyd was mostly interested in what type building to plan. He took an interest in the displays and exhibits, but more from the standpoint of what type of shelves, cases, wall space and structural requirements would be needed.

Mida wanted her traveling exhibit to be the centerpiece of the displays. Or, at least a similar type display since the original was already committed. The emphasis of the display would explain how her ancestors communicated their beliefs and what those beliefs were. She also wanted to have a big section on how her people fit in with the environment and were shaped by it. Plants and animals contributing to how all aboriginal people lived and shaped their lives and beliefs. She wanted to grow a lot of these plants around the center. Animals also formed the basis of their religions and basic values. She found it interesting that the earliest European cultures, as they abandoned animal totems, featured goddesses and matriarchal societies. These goddesses were replaced by gods as male-dominated civilizations arose. But many of the aboriginal peoples around the world still tended to use animals as the centers of their religions. They were tied to nature and the environment.

Mida believed the way she formed the displays and presented this information would help her subtly change opinions and start reforming values. As she said, she was not interested in just throwing out some facts and information. She wanted to change people. She felt civilization was losing the important tie to its life-sustaining environment. Her mom agreed with her about that.

Denzee often threw up her hands and chided Mida for being manipulative. Mida would smile and continue on with her ideas. Ev wandered in once in a while and put in his plug for including geology and how that influenced cultures. Mida agreed, enough to make Ev think he was being part of the process, then continued on with what she wanted. That included a small auditorium, centered around a stone fire pit, for storytelling. Stories were to her ancestors what books were to European cultures. She wanted to bring in people who could tell stories in an effective manner. She knew the fine line she was treading since many native people did not like to take their stories out of the historical context of being told to their children around campfires. The stories changed depending on the situation and who was telling it. Mida agreed with this but still felt they could be used to achieve what she wanted. She kept saying that nothing was written in stone except the stone itself. Her people were used to adapting and their adaption now was to survive.

Mida and Denzee shared with Boyd only what he needed to construct the building. His present to them was the building, their present to him was unending thanks for letting them plan their dream.

A few days after Boyd flew in with Denzee, he flew back to Colorado for a week. Then he drove back over with Marybeth. True to his word, he brought back two dozen beautiful Navajo rugs. He had spent several days visiting trading posts in Arizona and Utah, buying thousands of dollars worth of rugs.

Mida had to laugh at Boyd when he started unloading the rugs. She recognized rugs from weavers she knew, one from Two Grey Hills and one from Teec Nos Pos. She asked if Boyd knew the difference in his rugs.

"Listen, sugar, I'm not just your run-of-the-mill tourista who stopped at the first road side stand he saw and paid four times what something was worth. This here Two Grey Hills is one of the finest blankets you will see. Two Grey Hills is the Cadillac, or I guess nowadays I should saw the BMW, of Navajo rugs. It was woven by Nellie Two Horse and embodies the essence of the art of weaving and design. It does not have your traditional design but symbolizes what Nellie learned in a vision when she was twenty years old. It has healing powers. No doubt you know Nellie and you could tell me what each thread in this means." He looked at Mida and smiled.

"And this little beauty is from the Teec Nos Pos area, which by the way means circle of cottonwood trees. You didn't think I would know that did you? It was made twenty years ago by Edith Begaya, who died about five years ago. It was in a storeroom of the Hubbell Trading Post outside of Ganado. Actually, it was underneath a trunk full of old records and the manager didn't know it was there. I wasn't satisfied with what I saw out front and wanted to see his collection. I had to tell him about the water design and it's meaning of connecting the underworld to the sunlight. On just these two beauties, I shelled out fifteen grand. You want to know about some of the others?"

"Why do I ever doubt you, Boyd? Why? You never cease to amaze me. Yes, I know Nellie. She and I have spent many weekends together. She taught me much about healing and some of the traditions of her people. I knew Edith, too. She had a son that I dated once. He was killed one Friday night when some drunk ran him off the road outside of Gallup. I sat up with her all night at the wake. She was a very talented woman. She was weaving one April morning when she just fell over dead.

"You made some very good choices. Now I suppose you are going to fly up to Alaska and bring back a totem pole. Then how about a good Ojibway birch bark canoe. And—"

Boyd glared at her and said, "Remember what I said about which sugar daddy is funding this thing. You want something, I will get if for you. If you don't like what I get, I will find it a new home. You just remember the Apache words for 'Thank you, Boyd, you are a wonderful person.'"

Mida laughed and went over to Boyd. She hugged him tightly as she whispered in his ear, "Boyd, we love you. You know that. And I can never repay you for what you are doing. From this goddess, you have *shijii*, my heart, *dahaazhi*, forever. But our lives would be empty if we couldn't tease you a little. Now let's go see where we can put your beautiful rugs."

May 24, 1999

I love Boyd. He is such a big puppy dog. I can't ever see him getting mad at anyone or doing something to hurt anyone. But maybe I haven't met the other half of him. He has had to crack down on some people since he has created and run several large companies. Puppy dogs can't do that. You have to be ruthless. Maybe his puppy-like behavior is the flip side, his way of counteracting what he has to do at work. But then I have been around him enough to know his basic personality. I don't think you can fake that. As Mom says, he has a good heart. A good heart overrides all else.

Mom really made him blush today. He was bragging about his knowledge of Navajo rugs. He was explaining a design to Mom. She pretended she didn't know some of what he was saying. She knows more about rug designs that Boyd will ever know. I do too, for that matter. But he has obviously studied some and he is more knowledgeable than most. Mom looked at me with that impish look that told me she was about to spring some little surprise on Boyd. She can devastate people sometimes and not even realize it.

She winked at me when Boyd looked down at the rug, then asked Boyd if he knew why there were no red yarns in that particular rug. He said it was all earth tones and red would symbolize something or other. She leaned over to him, put on her very serious face, and whispered, "It meant you were safe to have sex on the rug. If there was red, it would cause damage to your pecker if you did it on a rug with red yarn. Red indicated the burning of the sun, and have you ever sunburned your privates?" It didn't help when Mom laughed and said the red of his face was about the same color if you sunburn it.

Ev kept busy reading and researching an expanding range of subjects. He still found books on time travel but more for curiosity now than for any meaningful clues. He admitted time travel was a dead subject, at least from a pure scientific basis. It was a wonderful idea and he still thought it possible, but fit for science fiction novels and not for scientific research. He was fascinated by quantum physics, but he realized Sandy was the expert in that. Though he already considered himself an expert on survival, he read everything he could get his hands on about skills such as making clothes out of animal skins, making tools out of bone and rock, and reading stars and weather signs. He sliced open his hand and fingers more times than he wanted to remember while practicing making projectile points. He even had to go to the doctor in Bicknell once to have five stitches on his hand where he sliced it with a spear point. He joked that if some archaeologist ever found his bones, he would be

292 ✳ SANDS OF TIME

convinced that the person had been cannibalized and meat sliced off his bones.

Ev conferred daily with Sandy about the plans for the entrance module. Sandy was designing and drawing constantly, figuring air pressure and rubber seals and vacuum devices. He was listing so many scientific instruments they needed that Ev started calling him the 'ometer' man.

The day after Denzee arrived, Sandy was busy at his computer and drafting table in his office in the Carlcabin. Ev walked in and saw the latest list Sandy had posted on his white board. He exclaimed, "My gosh, Sandy, are you inventing some of these instruments? You have listed three different spectrometers, astatic, magnetometer, x-ray diffractometer, spin magnetometer, polarity reversal detector, low level amplifier with flux force heads, and biologic carbon pulsometer. Where are the laser Star Trekometer and the 'Scotty, beam me up' phasometer? I've never heard of half these things. We can't set up a permanent lab on this thing. We just need to get inside. How about an acetylene torch and a Sawzall? Oh yeah, a generator."

"This is my Christmas wish list. I've got enough stuff listed to supply a ten-million-dollar lab. I know I can't get it all. I'm just listing what any good researcher would need to do a professional job on this thing." He reached up and erased one of the laser things that Ev couldn't even pronounce.

"That's still highly classified," Sandy said with a smile. "No way I could get that. Remember, Orion is the discovery of all time. Don't you think I should try and do a top rate job of finding out about it before we go inside. We could fall over dead from something as simple as toxic gas or as complicated as magnetic force fields or neutron laser vibrations that turn our bones to jelly and make our brains dribble out our noses. We could unleash some life-form such as viruses or who knows what form of quantum plasmoid that would take over the planet after they took over us.

"You think it is easy to do basic research with stuff that has to be hauled in surreptitiously in the dark of night via a four-wheeler? Powered by a small generator that must be hidden and noiseless, while we work in a cramped tent and an air lock made of whatever can be hauled in by mule? Can you see my article in *Science* that is entitled, 'The Investigation of 200-Million-Year-Old Alien Spacecraft on a $500 Budget' or 'How to Make the World Shattering Discovery of All Time Using Only Toothpicks and Epoxy.'

"Ev, let's get real on this. You are a scientist. You know the value of research. You can list a thousand questions you would want to have answered on this. None of them can be answered in a day or with what you can carry in a backpack. I want to get inside as much as you and Mida. I have been touched by this force or whatever is in there. I am as excited as a boy looking at his first *Playboy Magazine* and as scared as when my mother discovered the magazine hidden under my pillow. But I first need to ask questions, then figure out what I can answer as quickly as possible. And by myself. I am good, but no one is that good. I may be dealing with some type of life-form that has survived two hundred million years and is about that many light-years ahead of all of us combined in intelligence. This is an intelligence and power so great that most people would bow down and build temples to."

Ev rolled his eyes and sighed. "I know, Sandy. I've got deep pockets but not as deep as you need. I wish we could get some multimillion-dollar grant and the elite of the scientific community. But you know as well as I that this would disappear from view as surely as the Ark of the Covenant if we let anyone else know about it. We have discussed this before and you agree with me."

"Yes, I agree." Sandy rolled back his chair and put his hands behind his head as he put his feet up on the table. "I am planning on asking a few old colleagues for some help. I know I can get some financial help as well as some instruments. I can do it without letting our secret out. I've got a list of names I will give to whomever we entrust with the secret if we don't come out of it alive. These people can be first on the scene and finish whatever I didn't. They can do a lot of science in a short time. This is after we go in. If we come back out okay, then we will set up a big operation and we won't worry about being discovered. We will publicize the hell out of it and no one will stop us. We will have the best and most famous minds in the world out here. If we don't come out, then they will do it without us."

Sandy looked at his list on the board. "I did a lot of this type work and thinking when I was working on the Mars Reentry Program. The moon program as well, but I was younger then. We had to think about what to do with the *Apollo* capsule and the Mars vehicles that returned to Earth. Remember, we quarantined the moon walkers. We thought a lot about what could have come back to earth with these folks. Same with the planned Mars missions. We haven't gone to Mars yet and we may not. But this thing is in a different league with something like a Mars probe. This thing is proof positive of an advanced life-form. Terrestrial or extraterrestrial. This is not speculation." Sandy leaned forward and looked Ev in the eyes.

"Ev, we have out there in front of us, something that may be the combination of a life-form with the basic energy force whose mystery has plagued the likes of Bohr, Einstein, Wheeler, Feynman, and everyone who has followed in their shoes. We are talking about the most elemental of atomic structure, an energy force that is the basis of all life. Quantum physics and biological life. The common thread. What is life but energy? And if basic energy is life, then we have knocked on the door of god and he or she has answered. What else is there?" He leaned back and stared again at Ev.

Ev bit his lip and ran his hands through his hair. "You know, Sandy, I have been having weird dreams. I dreamed again last night of sitting in the front room having a beer with Einstein. He was barefoot and had on a sweater that had a picture of Linus, you know, from Charlie Brown? He looked at me and said in his thick German accent, 'Everett, we have given you the key. Be careful what you try and unlock. This key fits some things very well. Others, it opens the gates of hell itself.' What does that mean?"

"It means don't screw it up. And that is what I am trying not to do. That is why we will probably sit here the rest of the summer and maybe winter as well before we go down there and stay until we get answers. Or someone gets the answers while they look for us. It means if you are like me, you are developing some sensory awareness you never had before. You see, hear, and feel things that are supernormal by anyone's standards. I sure am and I know Mida is as well."

"You got that right," Ev said as he corrected a misspelled word on Sandy's white board on the wall. "I feel like I am growing a new brain. I actually talked to a raven yesterday. I understood what it was saying. I understood what a stupid bird was thinking! It told me an eagle was coming over the cliff and I looked up and sure enough, the eagle soared by. And I thought that the raven should come on down since there was a dead mouse we caught in a trap. And it came down to where I had thrown it over in the sagebrush. Now is that weird or am I totally losing it?"

Sandy laughed out loud as he reached over and as he took a bite out of a Snickers. "I would be careful who I told that to, but I understand. We are changing and it is not due to this high altitude air or the Mormon beliefs here in rural Utah. I think Mida understands more than either of us, but she is not like you and me. I don't think she really cares the how or why of it. She accepts it for what it is. She is the key somehow. I think your dream Einstein was referring to her."

"Well, keep up with what you are doing. Just let me know when you see the light at the end of the tunnel. I'm going to take a break now. I told Boyd I would show him the first trail I flagged on our property. Want to come?"

"Sure, I need a break too. You walking or riding?"

"Walking. I have to get Boyd off that new toy of his. He has been four-wheeling everywhere and I don't want those tracks all over the property. My next challenge, after I discover the secrets of the universe, is to get Boyd on a bicycle."

The two walked outside where they found Boyd coming from the main house. He was hurrying in front of Marybeth who was waving a wooden spoon at him. She was scolding him about eating raw cookie dough. After the words *salmonella* and *raw eggs*, Boyd put his hands over his ears. He was glad to join them for a walk. When Ev invited her for a walk, Marybeth said she couldn't come since she had to finish making cookies—that is, if Boyd left any cookie dough.

Spring passed into summer in the high altitude Rabbit Valley and the Fremont River. Ev marked a dozen bike trails on his property, some linking with adjacent roads and trails on surrounding public lands. He drafted a brochure that lauded the virtues of Orion Wingate's mountain bike paradise. He did a little rock removal and some minor tread work, but mostly it was just a matter of marking trails with cairns or flagging. He rated them as easy, moderate, or skilled.

Mida and Denzee finalized their cultural center, even drafting a decent architectural rendering, good enough for Boyd to take to a contractor. They drew lines in the dirt as they outlined the building. Boyd convinced them to think big, saying that doubling the size of a building does not double the price. As a matter of fact, he said, it cost only a little more to add another room, a basement, or even an observation tower. They skipped the tower but did plan on a basement for storage. Boyd laughed that they might need it for housing if they kept bringing in more people to live here. Mida teased him that he and Marybeth could have a cave apartment there, but Boyd said his plans included a nice cozy log cabin for his old age. Mida accidentally saw blueprints later of that cabin—all five thousand square feet of it, and nestled up against the cliffs on the edge of the property.

Unable to get a local builder who could start soon enough, Boyd found a contractor from Colorado Springs who was able to get started immediately. Within a week, a six-person crew arrived complete with their own housing, backhoe, and office trailer.

Sandy continued to plan his entry strategy, listing most of the instruments and tools he felt he absolutely had to have. He conscripted three of his former NASA partners, one a dot.com multimillionaire of a thriving high-tech company, getting a pledge of over half million dollars to pay for the expense of the research. All Sandy had to agree to was exclusive rights for further research into his top-secret but world-class project. Ev and Mida had given Sandy permission for this scientific 'ownership' of the project.

Sandy was well known and well respected among his colleagues and had no trouble convincing others of the value of what he was doing. It was difficult keeping secret exactly what he was involved in, but simply said it would be the highlight of their lives and to just wait a few more months. Two of them wanted to come help him immediately, but he said it just couldn't be done right now. They gave him some very useful ideas, which saved him a lot of time. By his questions and their answers, he knew that at least two of them had a pretty good idea what he was up to. They just lacked the details. One of them, Sumner, showed up at Orion Wingate anyway and Sandy talked long into the night with him. Although Sandy never actually gave away any of the secret, Sumner guessed vaguely what had happened. The hardest thing Sandy had to do was to force Sumner to agree not to come back and help until he was notified later.

Afterward, Sandy conferred with both Ev and Mida. Sumner knew what they were up to and could be trusted. Sandy had not disclosed any details to Sumner, but he didn't have to. One of the top *Apollo* scientists and a PhD from Cal Tech who had studied under Richard Feynman, his pal Sumner could help with the actual entry. He was having second thoughts about not bringing him in immediately. Sumner would not enter the vehicle at first, but he could help with the testing and would be there after they entered to assist with whatever needed done. Whether that would be showing the other scientists and media the site where the three discoverers disappeared, or evaluating the results with Sandy. Either way, Sandy thought it would be a great help to let Sumner stay.

"Sandy, if you recommend him, that says a lot, but we don't know this person. Remember, we agreed no new people."

"This isn't just any new person. Sumner is one of my oldest and closest friends and I would trust my life to him. I need help in organizing and calibrating instruments. I'm not sure I can do all this myself.

"He is retired now. He drove me crazy right after he retired for about the third or fourth time. He left the university, then went into consulting. He quit that to write a book. Then he helped with a *Nova* series on cosmological research. He went to Russia and spent almost six months traveling in Siberia with old colleagues, but had to return after he got frostbite on his feet. Long story on that one. He is restless, but he is very reliable."

"You are pretty open-minded about what we have discovered. Would he be?"

"Are you kidding? Years ago, while he was a young professor at MIT, he wrote an article about the feasibility of life on earth being created by a higher form of life somewhere else in the universe. Without Sumner's help, I may not get all this to work like I want it."

Sandy looked at Ev, then Mida. Ev nodded and looked at Mida. She didn't say anything, but her look told Ev that she agreed. Sumner guessed something significant was happening, but did he understand the need for secrecy? Sandy said Sumner not only understood, he didn't think they should publicize it even after they entered. He was certain the knowledge of this would alter world history and cause unprecedented upheaval.

Within a week, Sumner returned to the growing Orion Wingate compound, parking his thirty-foot travel trailer outside the Carlcabin. Boyd had previously installed several trailer hookups along the back of the cabin, thinking ahead to the time when they would have paying guests. Ev told Boyd that Sumner was a famous scientist who was here studying astrophysics with Sandy. They would both be here about six months, and if all went well, this retreat would get more paying business in the future from this type research. Mida told Boyd that Sumner had a National Science Foundation grant, and he was leaving most of his scientific instruments as a donation to the Orion Wingate.

It didn't take Sumner long to realize that something had happened to Sandy. His old friend was acting strangely. In talking scientific matters, he was coherent, but a lot of his small talk was hard to understand. After several days, Sumner cornered Ev one afternoon and asked about Sandy. Ev agreed that Sandy was different than when they first met him, but he never knew Sandy very well before his encounter at Orion. He didn't mention any specifics to Sumner other than to say everyone who came into contact with the object was changing, himself included. Sumner started having doubts about the whole project. Not knowing Ev or Mida, he was wondering if Sandy had come into contact with a couple loonies. However, the more time he spent with Mida, the better he felt. Sandy still bothered him, but he gave him the benefit of the doubt. For now.

The first of September arrived, just as the contractor was getting the roof on the massive structure that Mida and Denzee designed. Boyd wanted originally to use log construction for the building, but it would have taken longer. He decided on sandstone slab facing on the front, with huge log supports for the large front porch. Mida could not keep Boyd's enthusiasm in check. Boyd already brought two of the Salt Lake television stations down to do a story on this great contribution to Utah. The Orion Wingate was becoming famous. They were getting letters and requests for information on the retreat. County officials were becoming nervous about this new addition to the little county. This was a tight-knit community that wanted to keep outside influence at a low key. This meant keeping control of new business as well as new ideas. As with many rural areas in the West, growth was a controversial word. The tourist town of Torrey had boomed a few years earlier, adding the first fast-food restaurant to the entire county. There were no stoplights yet, but residents were buzzing about what this Orion Wingate thing was all about. It was obviously not sanctioned by the church and the church still controlled much of Utah. Gossip sparked through the community, with a lot of raised eyebrows.

Mida and Ev finally sat down with Boyd and told him he needed to wait a few more months before opening the floodgates to Orion Wingate. They just weren't ready. Mida did not want to be distracted from getting the cultural center operational and that could take a year. Ev did not have his trails and educational programs ready. And they wanted to let Sandy and Sumner finish their research project. It was just possible, Mida said, that there could be foundation money available to build a first rate lab for scientific research. It all depended on the paper Sandy was writing on geophysics of red-bed sandstones. She was making this one up, but Boyd bought it completely. This even increased his excitement. They had to make him promise not to get NPR or PBS or anyone else involved. Not yet, Mida said, with a hint of future compromise in that position.

The aspen were turning color on the side of Boulder Mountain as the first light dusting of snow sprinkled the highest elevations with a hint of white. Elk were starting to bugle and the turkeys stirred in the pine forests. One crisp morning, Sandy and Sumner, with Ev as a guide, drove down the long rocky road that left the highway at the Oak Creek Campground. Mida stayed to supervise the building of cabinets and display cases of her cultural center. She said she didn't need to visit Orion now. She was ready and eager to enter it soon for her journey, so she would wait until then.

Sumner spent most of his life in California and, except for visits to scientific conferences and a few long stays at the NASA facilities in Houston, had not seen much of the United States. He was impressed with the scenery around Torrey and his one-day trip to Capitol Reef. Now he was blown away by the view from the Boulder Mountain Highway. Snapping pictures on his digital camera, he was like a foreign tourist. As they came off the last slope of the dirt road and hit the flats of Oak Creek, they stopped to let a flock of ten turkeys cross the road. When Sumner got out to take another picture, the slamming of the door spooked five big bucks that darted into the thick oakbrush.

"Welcome to Utah and the wild west, Sumner." Ev smiled as he opened the door to let Sumner back in the truck. "What are you going to do if you get stranded down here by yourself after we disappear into Orion?"

"I'll probably just stay down here and let the vultures pick my bones clean. That is if the bears and wolves don't eat every last shred of me."

"Well, you're in luck since there aren't any wolves here. But bears, yeah, they and the coyotes will have a feast. While you are waiting to be eaten, I suggest bring plenty of water and a good pair of boots. We can point out some places to go and visit so you can have a glimpse of heaven before you go visit it for real."

"Don't pay any attention to him, Sumner," Sandy kidded. "Ev has rocks for bones and pine sap for blood, so he doesn't understand those of us who had to sit behind a desk and work all our lives. He has spent his life in this and is quite frankly bored by what you see out there. Aren't you, Ev?"

"Not on your life, old man. I still get goose bumps when I see this country. And speaking of goose bumps, get ready for some of your own. Pull off over there, Sandy. We are looking on the cliffs of Orion."

They got out of the truck and walked over to the cliff. Sandy recognized it but only when he was actually standing in front of the pile of rocks at the cliff base.

"You mean you can drive right to it?" Sumner exclaimed. "I don't see anything."

"Well, we don't want to advertise it to the world," Ev groaned as he put his hand on Sumner's shoulder. "Look at this." He walked up and pulled off a half dozen rocks, exposing a small piece of metal.

Sumner's eyes widened as he looked at the shining gleam of metal in the rock. He cautiously walked up to the rock and slowly reached out and touched the metal. He backed off and his knees slowly buckled. He stared at the rock, then looked at Ev and Sandy. He did not say a word. Neither did the other two. Ev winked at Sandy and motioned him away from Sumner.

Ev whispered to Sandy, "That is a pretty decent road isn't it? I'd say we have another month, maybe six weeks to get in here. Then it's either wait till April or we start bringing stuff down here now. Are you ready?"

"I want to walk up top with Sumner. He will be over his shock in a couple more minutes. I need to discuss my ideas of how we can set up the entrance module. After we look at it, we will probably talk about it all night. Up to now, we have just talked theory. Now we can talk the real thing. This is probably the world expert in what we need to do. What a stroke of luck getting him involved in this."

Sandy pulled out his handkerchief and wiped his forehead. He laughed as he stared at Sumner for a few seconds. "I think back on my first reaction to this. I would love to just stand here and watch people as they see this for the first time. Now that would be a great research project." He reached down and picked up a small rock and threw it at the cliff. "Let's plan on getting together tomorrow noon with Mida. We will give the go-no-go sign then. My bet is we are ready."

They walked back over to Sumner who stood up and was feeling the metal and the window material. He tried to scratch it with a knife, but was having no luck.

"I need a piece of this to figure out what it is. I can't even begin to scratch it. What is it made of?"

"Well, gee, Einstein, you figure that out and I will give you a million bucks right here on the spot," Sandy looked at him with wonder. "We have been pondering that for months."

"What's the hardest substance you know?" Sumner asked as he looked at Sandy.

"Well, on Earth, it is diamond. We made some alloys that rival diamond in hardness, but as a pure substance, you can't beat it."

"And what is diamond made of? Just plain old carbon. My guess is we are looking at something as simple as a form of carbon that is transferred by some technology unknown to us. Or probably not so simple. I think we see a technology that has figured out how to transform something simple into something amazing. My bet is there is also silicon and maybe another element or two. A form of ceramic. I can find out easily once I get some instruments out here. Sure wish I could get a piece of this to take back with us." Sumner continued to run his hand over the surface of the object.

"Well, we don't have a tool here strong enough to take a chunk of this home. But we will have to get something out here to cut into it if we want to get inside," Sandy said as he picked up another piece of sandstone and threw it at a small lizard scrambling up the rocks.

"Don't be surprised if Mida just walked up to it and said some Apache prayer and the door upstairs just opened on its own. Her powers are starting to scare me." Ev looked at Sandy and waved his hands in a hocus pocus gesture.

"You want a vote on that, I think I'd vote that you aren't that far behind her. I mean you do talk to ravens you know. You probably called in those turkey and deer just to impress Sumner."

Ev smiled at Sandy and glanced at Sumner. "By the way, in case you haven't had a chance to observe any of this yet, we are all getting strange because of this. You have touched it now. I didn't notice you turning blue yet, but don't be surprised if you wake up tonight having screaming blue light fits and seeing mountains floating by in a sea of pink dinosaurs or something weird like that."

Sumner started to laugh but noticed that Sandy was not laughing. As a matter of fact, Sandy was looking extremely serious. Almost worried. Sumner realized this really was not funny. All three of the conspirators were saying and doing things that only a short while ago, he would have walked away from them all shaking his head.

"Let's climb up top and see where we plan to enter," Sandy said as he put his arm around Sumner and started walking up the slope.

Ev walked over and started to pile the rocks back up against the cliff. He looked up at Sandy and shouted, "Don't take too long, guys. I have arranged to have a bear wander out of the woods in precisely one hour, so we need to be back up the road by then."

The next day, five minutes after noon, Sandy and Sumner walked into the cultural center, where Mida and Denzee were sitting by a sheet of wafer board set up on sawhorses as a tabletop. Ev was standing in the corner looking at the walls with Boyd. Marybeth was putting on her hat, getting ready to go for a walk.

Ev looked at Denzee and said, "Denzee, I promised Boyd I would show him the pictographs in that little side canyon over by the creek bed. How about if you take him and Marybeth and interpret the rock for him. When you get back, we will have a big lunch ready."

"Sure. Mida told me you were going to talk physics, and we would be bored to tears if we had to listen to it. Mida, you coming with us?"

"No, Mom, I want to go in and lie down a few minutes. I am getting a headache. You are a good guide. Give Boyd and Marybeth a first class tour. And go easy on the tall tales and mumbo jumbo Apache stories."

As the three walked toward the cliffs to the north, Ev pulled up more old metal folding chairs and sat down with Mida and the two scientists. "Well, doctors, what is the verdict?"

Sandy put his hands on the table and cleared his throat. "It is almost October. Either we go in next week or we wait until spring. I don't want to be doing all this work with these delicate instruments in freezing weather. I figure it will take us up to a week to get the module built. Then several days to do what we need. Maybe as much as two weeks at the most, but I have no doubt we could step into that thing well before October 15. Sumner wants to start tomorrow, but once we start, we all need to be there and ready to do our thing. We have the momentum now. I vote to pack up and head down there."

"I am ready now," Mida said as she looked around her new building. "I don't really want to leave this wonderful creation, but Mom is ready to take it over. And I have been mentally preparing all summer. I won't need to pack much. I've been thinking for months about what to take and it can all fit into my backpack and daypack." She looked at Ev.

"I'm ready now, too." Ev raised his eyebrows as he rested his chin in his hands. He sighed, saying, "I don't think I could stand the suspense of waiting six months. One thing we need to be aware of. Hunting season is already open and rifle season will be in full force by then. We could face intruders down there. We just need to be on the lookout for people."

"Actually that could work in our favor," Mida said as she sat back in her chair. "We won't be out of place with an ATV and some tents sitting on the mesa top. And we will have the entrance well camouflaged anyway won't we?"

"People don't walk more than five feet from a road anymore, so all we would have to worry about is someone following our ATV tracks. We will leave the ATV for Sumner to get out. We can have Denzee drive out the truck."

"You really are going to leave me down there, aren't you?" whined Sumner.

"We need you to stay for a day or two in case we don't come out right away. Chances are, we will walk in, look around, and come back out in a few hours. Mida doesn't think so, but I'm not so sure." Ev waited for Mida to respond.

"Think what you want, Rock Boy. I don't think. I know. We aren't coming out."

"Thanks, Boris, for that cheerful note." Sandy got up and walked around the table.

"Well, that's three votes for, none against. Looks like we head out. When?" Ev looked around the table.

Sandy looked at Ev, then pushed back his chair. "I think I am the weak link in this race. I need a day or two to pack up the instruments. It will take us probably a half dozen trips to get everything down there. Today is Friday. Let's plan on starting the exodus Monday morning. Are you going to say anything to Boyd or the others?"

Mida said, "I plan to tell Mom everything. We need her to help us follow up after we are gone. Ev and I will do that this afternoon. We won't tell Boyd or Marybeth. Denzee will do that later. For now, they will all think we have gone on a camping trip, a backpack trip. Otherwise, Boyd would want to go."

"Boyd will be suspicious of us taking all these instruments on a pack trip," Ev said as he looked at Mida.

Mida looked back at Ev. He caught her off guard and he knew it. She hadn't thought of that little detail. Boyd was into everything around the Orion Wingate and there were few secrets he didn't know about.

Mida thought for a minute and realized everyone was looking at her. "What am I, the queen bee who has to think of everything?" she moaned. "I feel like the head conspirator in some massive plot that is ready to roll with machine guns blazing. All right. I will have Denzee tell Boyd she wants to go down to the Pine Mountain Trading Post near the Arizona border on Monday and get some more rugs. She knows the manager and wants to have Boyd meet him. She will say that she and I need more trinkets for the displays but want Boyd to be the one to help make decisions. Once there, she will want to head south into Arizona for another trading post. If that won't work, then we will just tie and gag Boyd and throw him in the trunk and tell Marybeth to get him back to Colorado Springs before he passes out from lack of air."

Ev let out a whoop and slapped his thighs. "Mida, you would be a great queen conspirator. I think we should take you out for a big banana split or something."

Mida looked out the window toward the cliffs. "Remember, Mom will be returning with Boyd and Marybeth in a while and we said lunch would be ready."

"I'll go order a pizza or better yet, a big bunch of Navajo tacos from the Wickiup on the edge of town. They make great tacos."

"Okay. We are set. It all comes down to this. Do we all need to do a blood oath or something significant like that?" Sandy said as he looked at Mida.

"You do what you want. I think we all just say our prayers to whoever we want to say them to, go look at the stars tonight and tomorrow night, and pass silently into the breeze." Mida got up and walked out of the building. She stood there, looking at the building, then looked up on the cliff tops, made a small gesture with her right hand, and walked to the house.

Ev got up to follow her. "I think we each need to spend some time alone. It's either the end of something or the beginning of something even bigger. Write your memoirs if you want. Just don't be very wordy." Ev started to go toward the house but veered off to his truck. He almost forgot his assignment to drive into town and get the food.

Sandy looked at Sumner. "Well, buddy, we have work to do. You will be the most famous scientist on Earth in a couple weeks. Your place in history is assured."

Sumner was still sitting at the table. He looked up at Sandy, then looked at his fingernails. "You realize I envy the hell out of you. I don't want to be in your shoes, but I envy you. I feel like Queen Isabelle waving goodbye to Columbus. What do I say after you disappear over the horizon? Or what will I say to you when you walk back out after an hour or two?"

"Time will tell. The consensus among us three is we don't walk back out. Don't ask me why I think that. That thing has spoken to all of us. We don't have hunches anymore. We have knowledge of future events. I don't understand it. Part of me says we disappear and part of me says we look at an old wreck and find nothing." Sandy shrugged and walked back to the Carlcabin as Sumner watched him disappear.

"Say hi to Einstein for me, then," Sumner said to himself as he continued to stare off into the vast expanse of red cliffs and green trees. He watched an eagle soar overhead and disappear over the red Wingate cliffs. Was he getting as crazy as the rest of them?

As Ev started the truck, he saw a car with California plates pull into the driveway. He stared vacantly until he finally recognized the driver. It was Mida's old roommate, Sarah. Although he never met her, he knew her from photographs. His mouth opened with astonishment and surprise.

"Sarah!" he said to himself. "This will ruin everything! What the hell is she doing here?"

He slowly turned off the key and got out of the truck. Sarah pulled up next to him and parked. As she got out, she accidentally hit the horn. Jumping at the unexpected noise, she dropped her keys in the red soil. She looked at Ev with a grimace that expressed her thoughts at this time—what else can go wrong?

"Hi, Everett." She reached out to hug him as he stood there staring.

He finally stepped up to her and put his arms around her. "I'm sorry, Sarah. Forgive me. I am just shocked to see you. I mean we didn't expect you. Or at least Mida didn't say anything. Welcome to Orion Wingate. You look very nice."

"And you are so polite. I am a mess and you know it." She ran her hand through her windblown hair. "I'm sorry for just showing up, but . . ." She choked with emotion. "Oh god. I practiced this while driving over half of Utah and now I can't say it."

"Mida!" Ev yelled at the top of his voice. When she didn't come out of the house right away, he opened the door of his truck and laid on the horn. After several seconds, she stuck her head out the door and started to say something, then froze.

"Sarah? Is that you? Sarah!" Mida ran out and threw her arms around her old friend. Sarah burst out crying. Mida tried to calm her but soon found tears running down her own cheeks.

Ev tried to say that she drove up just as he was leaving, but he realized no one was listening. He quietly got in his truck and drove off on his previous mission for food. He thought about what Sarah's arrival would do to their plans. Never mind that Mida loved her old roommate. They could not change their plan now. They just couldn't.

✴

FIFTEEN

The Door Opens

*I believe no man can summon all his
strengths, all his will, all his energy
for the last desperate move, till he is convinced
the last bridge is down behind him
and there is nowhere to go but on.*

—*Henrich Harrer*

*The fairest thing we can experience
is the mysterious.
It is the fundamental emotion which stands
at the cradle of true art and science.*

—*Albert Einstein*

Ev RETURNED IN an hour with a passenger seat full of takeout boxes of food. He also cradled in his lap a speeding ticket. Ev was furious. He did run a Stop sign and pull onto the highway. He got away with that minor indiscretion, as did dozens of people every day in this sleepy little village. What he didn't get away with was passing an RV pulling a huge boat. The long vehicle assemblage, with New York plates was driving about five miles per hour, the driver gawking at everything in the town. It had its right turn signal on, but would not turn off the road. Ev was already worrying about the sudden appearance of Sarah. His mind racing with distractions, Ev finally had enough and whipped into the other lane to pass. In his frustration, he was up to forty miles per hour before he knew it. The speed limit was twenty-five. Of course, the county sheriff happened to be sitting at Brinks Burgers, sharing local gossip with the bishop, his cousin. The ticket cost Ev only fifty dollars or thereabouts, but it was the principle of the thing. It was always the principle of the thing, Ev thought. This jerk of a gawking tourist should have his license pulled, as well as his boat and RV confiscated, but that never happened. Ev longed to just disappear into the bowels of Orion and become part of the red rock cliff.

When Ev pulled into his driveway and parked, it seemed everyone in the compound descended on him for the food. It didn't help that he miscounted and was one dinner short. He thought he added one meal for Sarah, but her presence meant he was two short. He was not hungry at this point anyway. Mida could read Ev like a book and she pulled him aside and started massaging his back.

"Just let it go, Everett," she whispered in his ear in her sexiest voice. Whenever she called him Everett, he knew he had her full attention and her full powers. "Let's eat, then I told Mom we wanted to talk to her after lunch. It's time to bring her into the conspiracy, although she knows all but the littlest details already."

Ev stared at Mida asking a question with his eyes. What about Sarah?

"In case you are wondering about Sarah—"

"Well, kind of! What is the deal with her? This could ruin everything." His frustration accented every word.

"Just calm down. Sarah is nearly hysterical. I can't deal with two crazy people now. She left her husband. She came home early four days ago and caught him in bed with another woman. Age-old story, huh? Evidently he had been away a lot recently and she just thought his recent disinterest was newlywed adjusting."

"I wouldn't call them newlyweds anymore."

"Yeah. Looks like newly nonweds. I don't think this is repairable. Pretty hard on her. She is definitely not the type to put up with that behavior. They are done. I feel so bad for her. I never met him except at the wedding. He seemed a little arrogant, but I trusted her judgment. 'Big city lawyer' type in my opinion. Not like a good old country boy rock hound." She rubbed his back more, then gave him a kiss.

"She is sleeping in the guest room. I gave her an herbal mixture that will help her sleep. She drove straight through from the City."

Ev still had a questioning look. "What does she do to our plans?"

"Let's worry about that later. We will figure it out."

Ev and Mida went behind the house carrying one large Navajo taco plate. The rest of the group sprawled throughout the unfinished new building.

Their problem with what to do with Boyd was solved when he received a frantic call after lunch from one of his business partners in their wind generation business. This required Boyd and Marybeth to quickly pack up and head back to Colorado Springs. They apologized profusely, but Ev said to take their time and make sure to make the world safe for wind generation. Ev would spend more time with him when he got back. He gave his mother a tighter hug than usual when he said goodbye. He was relieved he didn't choke up. As she drove off, he brushed away the tears rolling down his cheeks.

Later that afternoon, Mida and Ev sat on the couch in the living room, with Denzee propped on several big pillows on the floor and Sandy sprawled on the recliner. Sumner was outside packing instruments. Ev peeked in on Sarah, sound asleep in the spare bedroom.

With the tape recorder and video camera rolling, Ev recounted every detail concerning Orion from the minute the air force jets knocked the rock off the cliff until his speeding ticket that morning. Mida was constantly interrupting, adding details Ev didn't even know she knew. She told for the first time about her trip into the Park the day before she met Ev. She spent the entire day high-centered and stuck on the four-wheel-drive road. She finally was rescued by a Park Service employee on her day off who happened to come riding her bicycle up the road. For some reason, this made Ev mad. He was getting overly protective of her, even though she had survived quite well in more remote places than where she got stuck a year ago.

As the story continued, Sumner walked in, unnoticed by all except Mida. Ev began to get restless as he tried to sit back and listen as Mida starting planning for their activities starting the next day. She went into detail about how Denzee was to lead the rest of the world to Orion.

Denzee made little reaction to the full story. She already guessed much and she had some psychic powers similar to but much less than Mida. She was not surprised when her daughter told her that she would probably never see her again after she entered this mysterious vehicle. Mida tried to prepare her mother for the public reaction once it became known.

Mida looked at Denzee and said, "You know the story Dad used to tell of the Norwegians in Minnesota. That is a good example of what will probably happen when something like Orion is made public." Denzee nodded and smiled. Mida took a drink from her large glass of lemonade and slowly set the glass down on the table.

"Well, I'm sure you are going to enlighten the rest of us who have no idea what you are talking about," Ev said as he waited for enlightenment, opening a new bag of corn chips. "Now is a very good time while the tension is high."

"Just let me finish. I was composing my thoughts." Mida frowned at Ev, then looked at Denzee. "It should be no secret that Norwegians were the first Europeans we know of that visited North America. They either landed or at least saw the shores of New England as far back as AD 800 or 900. Personally, I think people were traveling all over the world and had visited each other millennia before that. I mean, look at the temples and pyramids of South America and the theories of Thor Hyerdahl. Not to mention the underwater sites off Alexandria, India, and the Caribbean."

"But you digress from this interesting tale of your ancestors," Ev interrupted.

"Yes, sweetheart, I digress. Thank you for pointing that out. May I continue?" Mida smiled that cold smile that Ev likened to a cobra ready to strike.

Ev frowned as he opened a bottle of Sam Adams.

"The Norwegians were my ancestors as much as the Apache. Either way, I can trace lineage here on this continent long before most people. Well, after the Norse settled Iceland and then Greenland, they visited the Cape Cod area and we think actually settled near Providence. There is a stone tower there that more than likely was built seven hundred years ago. Around the mid-1300s, a mission was sent to Hudson's Bay and then inland. There have been artifacts discovered, including the famous Kensington Stone found in Minnesota. The men were never seen again but did leave a message on this stone. It was controversial, of course, and many so-called scholars did all they could to discredit the authenticity of this stone. You may also have heard of stories of early American explorers being surprised to find some Mandan Indians in North Dakota that were blond and blue-eyed. The missing men could well have wound up in North Dakota and mixed with the Mandan."

Ev fidgeted and said, "You are not digressing again, are you? I'm sure this is leading up to something important. And relevant?"

"I'm enjoying it," Sandy interrupted as he reached over to Ev for the bag of chips.

"Well, it is very interesting," Mida said as she glared at Ev. She looked at Sandy and smiled. "Thank you. The point I am making is this. A plain Swedish or Norwegian farmer who settled that part of Minnesota—which by the way is near where my father was from—soon after the whites pushed out the Lakota or Ojibway or whoever else was there first, was clearing his land and pushed over an aspen tree. Wrapped up in the roots was this stone which had very weathered and obviously old runic writing on it."

"Roonic writing? What is that?" Ev muttered.

"Runes. You don't know what runes are? They were an old form of alphabet. How can you not know what runes are?"

"Children, will you please stop squabbling and Mida will you please get on with this story, which I'm sure will be much more

314 ✳ SANDS OF TIME

interesting if we can ever hear it!" exclaimed Sandy. Usually Sandy enjoyed this verbal jousting between Ev and Mida, but he was tiring of it at this particular moment.

"This farmer found this stone and tried to get authorities to help him understand what it was. To make a long story short, he was made fun of, discredited, accused of forging the writing, all kinds of ridiculous things. Just because he found something unusual and something that disproved a lot of conventional thinking about so-called facts of history. People just wouldn't believe the implications of what he found. He found obvious evidence of European presence in Minnesota in 1300. And because he found it, he was accused of forging the stone and making it all up. People don't want to be hit between the eyes with new and history-altering facts. What do you think people will try to do to whoever announces the discovery of something like Orion? Orion is a little bit more history-altering than the fact that a few Norse explorers got lost in Minnesota a hundred and fifty years before Columbus blundered into Cuba. Don't you think?" Mida looked around the room.

"I thought the Minnesota thing was proved a hoax," Sandy said with hesitation.

"Proves my point. People go to a lot of trouble to discredit something at odds with traditional belief." Mida looked at Ev for support.

Ev picked up his cue. "Well, I didn't know that, whether it's true or not. It's not surprising. And by the way, Columbus didn't make it to Cuba." Ev looked at Mida with a blank stare. "Blond Indians in North Dakota, huh. You would be foxy with blond hair."

"Ev, will you get serious?" Denzee chastised him. "I don't plan to be the one to announce anything. You are not going to set me up for this. I would be hounded and you are right. I would be ridiculed and accused and have my fifteen minutes of fame, which I really don't care to have, thank you."

Sandy chimed in, "We will be the ones to enter Orion and if Mida's hunches are correct, and I have to admit, my hunches agree with hers, we will not come out, at least here and now. Or in our present form. That means we will have left something that will be easily discovered. It's only a matter of time, but it will be found. We need to think about who will find it and how. I don't think we should just wait for someone to stumble on it. And I don't want to put the burden solely on Denzee or Sumner, either. That's why I have plan B, with my silent colleagues and benefactors."

Ev grabbed another handful of chips as he talked. "Plan B in just a minute. I had this problem since the minute I first watched the rocks fall off the cliff and expose the metal. Who can we tell? Pardon me if I claim a little ownership of this whole thing. Ask Mida about how I agonized over who to share this with. I felt I was taking a chance bringing her in that day I met her. She was a perfect stranger to me. We have maintained strict secrecy, bringing in Sandy, then Sumner, now Denzee. The only ones who really know the full story are here in this room. The burden falls at least partly on you, Denzee, whether you like it or not. Sumner, you are now in on this up to your eyeballs as well. We didn't have any choice and now you don't either."

Denzee shifted on her pillows. "You set me up to live here. You think I will be able to maintain any life at all living here within miles of this type of discovery? And being part of the secret investigation of it! Not by myself."

"Mom has a point. She needs more than Sumner, who probably doesn't want the responsibility either. Sandy, what is plan B? I assume this involves your friends that helped contribute money and equipment. Are they trustworthy?"

"Oh, they are trustworthy. And very well connected scientifically. One is even in politics. Not all of them are retired, and they have excellent reputations. I don't think they would knowingly want to be part of this, but we could bring them up here to discover it. The world doesn't know that Denzee or Sumner knew ahead of time. She could lead them to it, on instructions from Ev and Mida. Something like, 'If we don't return by a certain date, come looking for us here as indicated on this map.' I can send them invitations in advance, set to arrive when we know it would be safe."

"I want Boyd to be part of it. He brought me up here and he is pretty well connected too," Denzee said as she shifted on the pillows again.

"Okay, this all sounds like a plan," Ev said as he set down his bottle of Sam Adams.

Sumner had been sitting quietly on the floor by the front door. He raised his arm, like a third grader asking to go to the bathroom. When no one noticed him, he spoke up. Like a comedian setting up a punch line, he said very slowly, "Maybe you might want my opinion. About your plan you think is ready to implement."

"You haven't even talked this over with Sumner?" asked Denzee as she leaned over almost in Mida's face.

Mida looked at Ev, then back at her mother. "Well, we're making this up as we go! You think there is some script for this? Ev?"

Ev sat up. "Sandy, surely you and Sumner have discussed this. What the hell have you two been talking about for days on end?"

Sandy shifted in his chair as the spotlight suddenly turned on him. "We talked scientific stuff. How to get inside the thing. What to test and how. What dangers there were to all of us. You sure are damn right about no precedent for this. I haven't even thought about what happens after the door opens. Or shuts."

"Listen, folks." Sumner stood up. "I love Sandy like a brother. If he told me to walk into a burning building, I would do it. I trust him. He and I are scientists. We ask questions, then we try to answer them. Our life's purpose is to solve challenges. In a rational, logical manner. To make the world conform to our theories. Or change our theories if the world gets more complicated. Well my world just got more complicated. I'm in this thing, whether or not I think some of you are as loony as a duck. And quite honestly, I am beginning to wonder. I like all of you, but I'm not into this mystical metaphysical stuff that seems to be happening. I do not know why Mida turns blue, why Ev talks to ravens, why I have started waking up in the middle of the night hearing some kind of bells or carillons ringing out beyond a crashing surf."

"You sure it's not the wind chimes I put out—"

"No, Denzee, it is not the damn wind chimes. And never mind what I hear or see. That's not the point. I will do whatever you want. It's just that I'm here and I like to be involved in whatever may kill me or eat me."

Ev stared at Sumner as he slowly sat back down on the floor. "A year ago, or actually year and a half ago, if I had viewed the tape of this discussion, I would have said it was a pretty stupid sci-fi grade C movie. Goofier than the looniest duck I ever met—"

"Don't look at me when you say looniest, sweetie pie." Mida looked at Sumner, then said, "Sumner, I apologize if we left you out. You are key to this thing happening. We are all fumbling along with this one."

"I know." Sumner smiled as he looked at Sandy, then raised his left eyebrow. Sandy smiled back.

Ev took a swig of beer, then continued with his original thought as if nothing had interrupted him.

"As I was saying, we leave sealed instructions for our attorney, Texas State Senator Franklin, and maybe others in addition to Denzee and Boyd. On a certain date, well, after we know for sure whether we are safely back here, safely dead from some extraterrestrial creepy crawly, or safely somewhere out there in never-never land, everyone is to open their letter. In that letter, we explain what we have done. We can include the tapes we are making now. A short history of our discovery and our research. This will all be based on our not coming back. If we come back, then we obviously retrieve the letters without disclosing what was in them. Instructions will tell people to meet here at the Orion Wingate on a certain date. If it is not next week, then it will have to wait until next May. Either that or Boyd rents a helicopter to get in to the place."

"You include a tape of this meeting, then that proves Sumner and I knew in advance," Denzee objected.

"You and Sumner edit out any proof that you were here. The camera is pointing at Mida and me, not you. It would only take a little editing to delete conversations with you. Fair enough?"

Mida leaned forward and continued, "The group will include Boyd, Mom, Sumner, Sandy's other friends and the people we send instructions to. No one will know what is going on. They will discover the ship and will see where we went in. What happens after that will be up to the group. I don't see how it could be kept secret after that. Do we want some media there, such as PBS or National Geographic photographers or something like that?"

Sandy perked up and added, "You know, we are assuming the thing will still be there. There is a chance that our entering it will do something to space-time and the ship could even disappear. With us in it of course. This is bordering on time travel and no one that I know of ever disappeared in time. Who knows what will happen? I think we will need to leave this video and all our pictures as evidence just in case everyone gets there and there is nothing to see. What a story that would be! Three missing people and absolutely no evidence except our vehicle and tents. If somehow we go back or even forward in time, do all our earthly possessions and evidence of them disappear as well? That's a time travel unknown. If we disappear, then maybe we never really existed. Or a parallel universe takes over and we never existed in that universe."

"This is getting too weird for me." Denzee threw up her hands and stood up. "Are you here or are you some figment of my imagination. I certainly know Mida was no figment with all the pain she caused me when she took forever to be born."

"Mom, they don't all need to hear that story again." Mida sighed as she blushed. "We don't know what is going to happen, but we all need to be prepared for all kinds of possibilities."

Sumner stood up and stretched. "I don't want to think about disappearing spaceships or even people. If you and it disappear, then the whole thing is off. I'm not risking what is left of my reputation relating a cock-and-bull story with absolutely no evidence to support it. I still don't understand why you are all so convinced we will never see you again. I believe you will walk into that thing, find some interesting things, and come out and tell us all about it. Then we will call in the rest of the world and deal with whatever happens. Sandy, I am surprised you are buying into this disappearing thing."

"We will find out soon enough," Mida said as she got up.

"Well, I suggest we all take the rest of the day to pack, prepare ourselves for all of these possibilities, and just get some rest." Sandy got up and reached again into Ev's bag of chips. "And maybe enjoy a few of life's small pleasures before we lose them." He glanced at Denzee after his last remark.

Sandy put his arm around Sumner and walked out the door.

Mida and Ev disappeared into their room, to go through their backpacks for one last time. They had packed not knowing where or when they were going. They did not expect to have any of the comforts of life as they were used to once they got into the ship or to their destination, if there was a destination.

Early that evening, Ev and Mida plopped on the sofa in the living room. They had finished packing and didn't feel like doing anything else. Everyone else had disappeared into their own spaces, trying to make sense of what was happening. Sarah wandered into the room, surprising the two.

"Sarah! I forgot all about you," Mida almost yelled.

"Damn it all to hell! You scared the bejesus out of me!" Ev stood up quickly, not knowing what else to do.

Sarah smiled as she grimaced. "I'm sorry to frighten you. I've been lying in bed awake for hours. You aren't the only ones scared. I'm frightened to death."

"Oh, Sarah, I feel so bad about you. I hope it was good while it lasted. Your marriage," she added quickly as Sarah looked puzzled.

"I'm not talking about my marriage. I overheard your meeting earlier this afternoon. I heard everything. The spaceship. Your leaving. You believe you are going to die. I can't—"

Mida sat upright and looked at Ev, then stood up and walked to Sarah, putting her hands on Sarah's shoulders.

"You were awake then? You waited until now before you said anything?"

Sarah nodded.

Mida hugged Sarah, then held her by her shoulders. She said softly and soothingly, "We are not going to die. We don't know for sure what will happen, but I believe something significant is going to happen to Ev and me. Sandy, too. Maybe everyone. Oh, Sarah."

Ev rubbed his chin, then cleared his throat. He had to think quickly. He knew Mida would get too emotionally involved to make logical decisions about this. "Sarah, we have three choices. You stay here and help Denzee take care of Orion Wingate but like all of us, you are bound to absolute secrecy for now. Later, get involved with the publicity or not get involved. Your choice. But Denzee will need help and support. Or you come with us and help us down at the cliff. You will be exposed to this thing and who knows what effects it will have on you. Then you will be bound to help Sumner and Denzee." He stared at both Sarah and Mida who were looking intently at him.

"That's two. What's the third?"

"We tie a concrete block on your feet and take you into the middle of Lake Powell."

"Ev, that's not funny." Mida gave Ev a glare that he had seen only once or twice before. He realized his joke was a mistake.

"All right. What else do you expect me to say? We don't have any other choices. Sarah, you stumbled into the middle of something and now you can't just walk out. You are in this as deeply as the rest of us. Do you understand why we have to keep this totally secret?"

"Not really. It sounds so sinister. Why are you doing this? Why not someone like government scientists. You shouldn't be involved in this."

"Sarah, you and I need to go sit in the kitchen, like old times, and talk about this. You are tired. You are confused and not exactly clear headed right now. Ev, go for a walk or something. Sarah and I need to be alone." Mida led Sarah into the kitchen while Ev walked out into the cool night air.

As he shut the door and looked up at the stars, he muttered to himself, "We don't need this. We just don't need anything to get in our way right now."

At eight o'clock Monday morning, a small caravan of vehicles left the Orion Wingate. Most were crammed with scientific equipment, building materials, backpacks, tents, and other assorted baggage. Ev and Mida, with Sarah's help, carried in the packs, tents, and food from the Oak Creek road. They drove to the base of the cliff, not worrying about anyone seeing them. Sandy and Sumner hauled equipment with the ATV and its trailer by way of the overland route along the plateau top. They didn't worry about anyone seeing them either. If they were seen, they were hunters setting up their camp. They made four trips to town and back to Baby Orion, finishing the last one just as the sun set behind the mass of Boulder Mountain. They made three more trips on Tuesday, finally finishing moving all their supplies to the cliff.

Ev and Mida set up six tents, three by the upper site and three hidden in the trees nearby. Two large wall tents by the site housed Sandy's lab. Sandy's sleeping tent was by his lab; Ev, Mida, and Sarah were in the trees. They stretched a large tarp between the tents, hiding the makeshift building they were constructing over the entryway. Then they laid a large camouflage netting over the whole thing. When they finished with the camouflage, Ev stepped back and laughed. "Right out of *Indiana Jones*," he muttered as he put his arm around Mida and admired the effect. No one would be able to tell there was anything there unless they stumbled on it. And in this location, no one was likely to stumble in for years. Or so he thought.

Sumner, Denzee, and Sarah made several trips back to town on Tuesday, gradually taking the vehicles back. They left the ATV at the Orion location but parked Ev's pickup back up the road near where the ATV route started. Sumner was indecisive. He wanted to stay and help Sandy with the building and the equipment, but he didn't like the idea of being there after they entered. After long conferences, they all decided he would stay and help, along with Sarah, then go back to town with her and wait there with Denzee. He would sleep in one of the equipment tents.

Mida said a very tearful goodbye to her mother. This surprised Ev, since Mida had shown such rock solid stoicism and lack of emotion up until now. Denzee and Mida had been having long talks for weeks, covering everything under the sun and even beyond. Mida believed she would never see her mother again and Denzee accepted that also. Ev knew he would choke up and made no effort to hide it. He asked Denzee, with his voice cracking, to take care of Boyd and Marybeth. Then he just lost it. Denzee held him tightly, then turned and got in Sandy's van and drove back up the road. By nightfall of that first day, the conspirators were unpacked and alone in the red-rock desert.

They were now an expedition of five. Three who would enter this mysterious visitor from somewhere out there, from somewhere far in the past. Maybe from far in the future. Two, who were even more scared than the three, not knowing what they would do if the three did in fact disappear. They sat around a small campfire, exhausted from the two days of moving and unloading. Even though they were only a few miles from the highway and a few more miles from their home, they might as well have been on another planet. For all they knew, they soon would be.

"It's been a year and a half since I found this thing," Ev mused as he watched the flickers of the campfire. "I feel like I was here to watch the beginning of life. A few rocks fell while I stood here watching, and now we are on the verge of opening the secrets of this egg."

"Nice choice of words, Rock Boy." Mida smiled as she held his hand. "Do you get the feeling this was meant to be? You being there at that time, me coming by the next day?"

"And us finding someone of Sandy's caliber," Ev quickly added, looking at Sandy. "Sumner, you might be bravest of all," he added as he looked at Mida.

Mida caught her cue. "Sarah, you are the innocent victim. You stumbled into this and are now caught like a moth in a web."

"Yeah. One pitiful life ends and a new one begins. I might as well go with you." She trailed off into an awkward silence. Everyone looked at her but no one knew what to say.

Sandy looked up at the sky, now glowing with the brilliance of the Milky Way. "Whether it was meant or not, it happened. Something has been changing the three of us for weeks." Looking at Ev and Mida, he added "I've only known you for a period of months, but I have noticed a change in both of you. Me too. I am different in a way I find hard to explain. Something weird is going on, but I am not scared. Anxious, yes. Full of suspense, yes." He paused as he put a small chunk of pinyon on the fire. "Well, actually I am terrified, but not in a way that means I am scared for my life. I am terrified I will not be able to do what I am supposed to do. And I don't have a clue what I am supposed to do."

Sumner looked at Sandy and said, "I guess that's why I am here. To give you moral support and technical assistance. But don't expect a lot. This is new ground for everyone."

Mida laughed. "That's for sure. It is all ad lib from here on. We prepared our whole life for this. Like the warrior going into battle or the shaman dealing with a new spirit demon. You do what comes naturally. You react, using all the training and knowledge you have in your bones. You will be guided by your spirits. Isn't that what life is all about anyway?"

"Well, the suspense is killing me," said Ev. "You can only stand so long on the cliff waiting to jump into the water. I'm ready to jump. Somehow, I am determined I will actually fall asleep tonight, and tomorrow night, and however many nights we are camped here. Then, we will hold hands and all jump off the cliff. If I ever sleep again after that, who knows. Right now, I don't care. I just want to jump."

Mida got up, pulling Ev with her. "This is getting too serious. I suggest we all go to our tents and try and sleep. *Iskaa*, tomorrow, will be busy digging and building."

Ev and Mida walked Sarah back to her tent, but Ev left as the two stood outside talking for several minutes. Finally, after a long hug with Sarah, Mida went to her tent and tried to write in her journal. Words would not come. She couldn't concentrate. She still had her original journal, or at least the one that went back for more than a year. Her collection of five other notebooks covering the past ten years were safely stored back at the house. She had taken the precaution of making copies of this journal and left them with the others. Since she had seen it in the shuttle, she often wondered what happened to it. And to her. Whatever the outcome, whether her bones were lying in the mother ship or whether she simply left the notebook in the shuttle and she went another direction, she wanted to keep her thoughts so someone would be able to read them. She stared at the page, unable to write anything, for several minutes, then set the book aside and crawled in her sleeping bag.

Eight hours later, the sun rose over the red cliffs to greet Ev, who was sitting outside his tent. He had slept well, but awoke an hour before sunrise and could not go back to sleep. So he got up, dressed, and sat down on the ground outside his tent, awaiting this bright old friend whom he wasn't sure how many more times he would see. He could hear Mida softly chanting in her tent. He knew it was an Apache prayer. She had been doing that more often recently.

Wednesday started as a beautiful autumn day. Many of the birds had already left for their journey south. The hummingbirds were gone. He hadn't seen a bluebird in a few weeks, nor had he heard the buzzing of a nighthawk. He smiled as he heard an elk bugle up on the mountain above him. Some critters stayed the course. They showed a courage he admired.

Mida rolled up her deerskin dress that she had worn when troubled during her life in difficult situations most of her life. She shared many joys and sorrows with that soft tan-white reminder of her long dead father. Unable to sleep, she had put it on and chanted for a few minutes. Then, through with the ritual, she opened the tent flap to see the red of the cliffs glowing with light of the morning sun.

Sandy was walking back to the tents from a short morning stroll. He checked the tents that housed his makeshift lab and all his equipment. He chuckled when he thought of the value of what sat in those tents. And what would happen to all of it in a couple days? He was glad Sumner was here now to help him.

Sarah lay awake most of the night, reliving her marriage in her mind. She vowed today she would put her past behind her. She would not think of him or the disgusting things he was doing with that bimbo in their bed. You think you know somebody, she thought. What had she gotten into here? Mida was her closest friend and was the natural one to come to for help. Now Mida needed help and Sarah was in no position to help her. She got up, brushed her hair, tried to put in her contacts, but could not open her eyes. She put on her thick glasses and walked outside to start a new day.

Sumner could not sleep as he lay awake with worry and anxiety. He arose early and took a long walk along the cliffs. He watched the sun rise over a red landscape that took his breath away. He knew they all had a couple days before the unknown, but he was as nervous as he had ever been.

At the same time that Mida and the group gathered around the still warm ashes of the campfire, Denzee was finishing her breakfast by herself. She got up early and fixed biscuits and gravy, ham, and her special herb tea. She had not been alone much lately and enjoyed the peace and quiet.

Denzee put the instruction letters in the envelopes that Ev and Mida addressed earlier and drove Boyd's four-wheeler into town to mail them. She wanted to walk but her muscles were sore from all the moving of the past couple days. There were six letters in all. One package addressed to State Senator Franklin in Austin, Texas, contained a videotape. Denzee was singing to herself as she drove back to the compound. The die was cast, she thought. She was ready to continue with her new life. She was confident in the future.

Ev and Mida quickly dug out the hole that exposed Baby Orion. Throwing dirt into a wheelbarrow that Sarah dumped a few feet away, they made fast work of clearing the door to their future. When they had swept the floor clean of the last grain of sand, Sumner and Sandy went to work building the entrance chamber. With no good way to get an airtight seal over the ship surface, they asked Ev to dig into the surrounding dirt so they could tightly bury the edges of the molded Plexiglas bubble. This was to be the vacuum chamber in which the instruments were placed. Most had wires or tubes coming through predrilled holes that Sandy previously tested to make sure would hold a vacuum. Then, late in the day, all the explorers started work on the makeshift wafer board shack that was extra protection from the elements. There were still thousands of dollars' worth of instruments that did not go in the bubble. Sandy did not want to take a chance of losing any of the equipment, even though he expected he would never see it again. Since Sumner expected to be held accountable for the equipment, he mothered over it like a goose over her young.

The next day they finished the shack, then put together the mostly prebuilt shed to house two gasoline-powered electric generators. It took them about four hours to get it put together. It was built right next to the tents, but had so much insulation, that it made very little noise. Mida couldn't believe they made it so quiet. She asked why motorcycles and ATVs couldn't be made so quiet. Sandy laughed as he said no one would buy them, for one. Secondly, most people didn't notice the noise anyway, he said, since we were all gradually destroying our ear nerve cells through loud music and traffic noise.

By the end of the day, they were almost ready. They needed a couple more hours to finish the shack, then to move in the equipment. Sarah was excited at the final result. She was most impressed with the way Sandy planned to get inside the ship. Since they still didn't know what the thing was made of, Sandy had obtained the most high-tech laser cutting saw, still classified as top secret. Sandy said this was guaranteed to cut through anything. In addition, there were instruments designed to cut a small diameter hole precisely to fit the inserting probe tip.

The airtight bubble covered the entire door. This left little room for Sandy and Sumner both to sit outside the bubble but inside the wood structure. Sandy was glad it was almost October and not July. He might worry about freezing his instruments, but he wouldn't have to worry about cooking himself in a windowless room in the process.

For the fourth night, the five sat around a campfire, anxiously awaiting the next day. Sandy estimated that by midmorning, they would be ready to start the process of testing. Ev said it would be the day they jumped. Sandy cautioned him to be prepared to spend another day or two. He didn't know how long it was going to take him to do his studies, then try and open the door. He was assuming everything was going to work as planned. It might not, he said. Besides, they were still ahead of schedule.

October 1, 1999

It seems to be coming together. Clearer than ever before. Ev always talks about that seagull in the book. Now it makes sense. We strive for perfection. Each of us has perfection of something. Artists, writers, musicians, thinkers. What am I striving for? Will I know perfection? The perfection of the earth must surely be this slickrock country. The rocks, spires, canyons, cliffs, colors. Perfection of life is the redwoods, the gnarly junipers, the hummingbird, the antelope running across the plains. When we hit perfection, do we pass onto the next plane? Is that what extinction means? Did the saber-toothed tiger reach perfection, then go on to his next world? Is that where we go next? Is that Orion? Is this the door to the next world? Have I reached perfection, or can I not go in until I do? This thing haunts me. The blue lights—are they the stop light, the green light to enter? If I can go in, can Ev and Sandy as well? I feel like I am being stretched. Like a light beam expanding to the heavens. I am there yet I am still here. I cannot go back to the way it was. What if I cannot enter my new world, but now I don't belong to this one anymore. Too many questions. No answers? Yet.

The next morning started cloudy, with Sumner fretting about rain, but within a couple hours, it cleared up. They quickly finished screwing on the panels for the sides of the shack. Ev even cut a couple holes for windows so he could see in while Sandy worked. By ten o'clock, Ev busied himself putting away all the tools, while Sandy donned a white lab coat and sat down at his control panel. Mida started pacing around the tents trailed by Sarah. Sumner whistled as he started unpacking equipment. He called to Mida to say a few words. She said five words in Apache, looked at Sandy, and impatiently said, "Begin your operation, Doctor."

With little to do for the time being, Ev and Mida took Sarah on short tours of the area. Walking along the creek, Sarah shouted when she saw a pair of undershorts wrapped around a rock. Ev glared at Mida and told her to not say a word.

Sumner carefully and meticulously set up the instruments while Sandy hooked up wires and plugged in power cords. After several hours, he finally said it was time to turn on his toys. It was past lunchtime, but no one even thought of breaking to eat.

The first thing Sandy did was insert a drill-probe into the ship's exterior a millimeter or two. He finally found out what the material was made of. It was heavy to silicates, including some aluminum and boron, carbon, oxygen, hydrogen, and other trace elements. As Sumner first suggested, there was very little metal other than those in the silicates. It was a form of ceramic or something else that was beyond our technology. Sandy asked Sarah to take notes and transcribe his data readout from the computer, just in case something happened to the hard drive.

Then he tried to get readings from the spectrometer through the window, but something shielded the readings. He guessed some type of force field, but it could have been some type of shielding from the material itself. Sandy muttered 'how can you test for something that you don't have the knowledge or technology to do the testing.' He looked up at Sumner and said it was like a Neanderthal examining a computer.

He carefully inserted small analyzer probes into the ceramic body. He tried the accelerated meson fluxometer to test for subatomic particle populations, the Weber bar to test for gravitational waves showing anomalies in the gravitation fields, and all the other "ometers" he had in his tool kit. He was getting pages of computer printouts. He told Sarah to not bother keeping notes at this point. Just collect the printouts and put them in the waterproof pages in the briefcase. Lights and oscilloscopes were flashing and beeping, reminding Ev of a science fiction movie where a monster would soon rise off the table. The camouflage netting and bare wafer board walls added to the eerie atmosphere.

About midafternoon, Ev finally wandered off. He was getting bored with the endless testing, but he was also getting hungry. He asked the others if he could get them anything to eat but both said they were too busy. Ev made a quick sandwich, then wandered off.

In about an hour, Ev came back from his wanderings with his pick in his hand. He had a small gash on his forearm which was smeared with dried blood. Sandy looked up and asked Ev if he could get him a Snickers bar. Mida chimed in that she could use a sandwich. Then she added, "Don't get any blood on my sandwich please." She knew not to bother asking how he cut himself. He was like a little kid playing with his toys. The rocks were his toys.

After a hurried lunch, mostly eating while they worked, Sandy said it was time to insert a couple of the larger probes inside the ship. They needed to test the air for breathability as well as radioactivity or any other toxicity. He warned there was a slight chance that anything breaking through the ship might cause some reaction, so be prepared. Motioning to the generators, he asked Ev to make sure they were full of gas. He didn't want their electricity to fail at this point. The power was not enough to do what he wanted, but he said it should work well enough. He and Sumner adjusted the voltage or wattage or something or other to meet the supply they would get out of two generators. Ev just nodded since he had trouble knowing what watt lightbulb to put in things. Electricity was not one of his strengths when it came to understanding technology.

Sarah watched as Sandy maneuvered the metal probe up to the window. He adjusted dials and noticed the protective cuffs on the bubble inflate. The pressure gauge hovered at zero, which meant the chamber had a good vacuum. If whatever was in the ship escaped, it would not get out of the bubble. Unless it dissolved the bubble. Sarah grimaced as she thought that if it dissolved the bubble, it would dissolve them as well, so who cared? There was a whirring noise as the probe cut through the window. It formed a tight seal as the probe sensor slowly advanced into the glass.

"It works!" shouted Sandy as he fidgeted with the controls. "The probe is in and we did not lose pressure or the seal. What an invention. Now for the test. Let's look at the air."

He watched the computer screen intently as he typed furiously. Mida held her breath. She also held onto Ev's hand, squeezing it tightly. Sweat was pouring down Sandy's forehead.

"I'll be damned. Look at that. It is strictly oxygen, a little higher than what we are breathing here, and nitrogen, with a few other elements. Basically it is Earth atmosphere, pretty close to what we are breathing. No radioactivity. Some strange ionization, but nothing harmful."

Ev commented that the mixture sounded like what the Earth's atmosphere was millions of years ago when suddenly the probe lit up like a Christmas tree. Sparks flew and the computer went dark.

"What the hell?" Sandy yelled as he flew off his chair. He landed against the wall of the shack. Mida screamed as she fell backward. A blue light flashed across the outside surface of the ship like a bolt of lightning.

"Damn, I wish I had watched a few more *Star Trek* episodes." Ev muttered as he ran up to where Sandy was blinking like an owl. "Sandy, did we disturb a force field or antimatter shield or something like that?"

"We sure disturbed something. I don't know what happened but something is pretty protective of itself in there. I have a strong surge protector on all the equipment just in case. I just hope I didn't fry things too bad. Wow! Look at where the voltage meter froze." He tapped the dial. It had frozen off the scale. "That's enough power to light up the entire state of Utah. How can this type of energy be stored for two hundred million years and still be holding tight? What is in this thing?"

"Look inside," Mida exclaimed as she had her face up against the bubble. Blue sparks and flashes were crawling and shimmering inside as far as they could see.

Sumner rubbed his head where he had knocked it against the wall. "Whatever it is, I think it is some kind of protective device or maybe a warning system. I don't think it is any kind of contamination from us. We had a real good seal. Of course, the probe itself touched the interior. Let's see if we can get the computer up again."

The light show inside the ship was easing, although there were still occasional flickers of light. Sandy put a stethoscope against the outside of the ship. He listened for a minute and said he could hear some noise inside but it sounded echoed and very far off.

Within a few minutes, Sumner had the computer back up. "We lucked out on that. Don't think anything was damaged. Look at the biological readout. All zeros. Nothing in there of a life-form that we know of. I think the initial flurry is over. I'm going to try the next probe. Hold your breath."

"I haven't breathed in five minutes anyway," whispered Mida as she still held onto Ev. Ev didn't say anything. His hand was numb from Mida's grasp.

Sandy was amazed that his equipment still worked. "This had to be electrical but that kind of jolt should have fried everything within sight of this ship. Us included. I really don't understand it, but I think we have just been introduced to some type of energy totally unknown to us. Ev, this is your 'Star Trekometer' as you call it that we are reading now. It will tell us some things about gravitational fields and subatomic goings-on. Too technical to explain, but it will come in handy for Sumner when he studies this data later. It might give us a clue as to how far this came and what types of gravitational fields and other deep space anomalies it went through."

"I just want to know if we made someone mad," Ev stated as he finally pried Mida's fingers off his wrist.

"No, we didn't," Mida said slowly as she looked in Ev's eyes. "Something just communicated with me."

Ev looked at Mida with a confused look on his face. "Did that surge of power fry your brain?"

"It touched my brain and said 'come on in. We would like to visit with you.'"

"Oh yeah, and did it give you a combination to the lock?" Ev looked worried.

Mida started writing on her pad of paper. It was a series of numbers. She gave it to Sandy and said to reprogram his thingamagidget.

Sandy looked at her with a more confused look than Ev. He looked at the numbers, then looked at his computer screen. He let out a gasp as he saw those same numbers scrolled across the screen. His readout on the biological data had disappeared. The probe had pulled back into its tube.

"Oh man, this is getting too weird for me," Sumner groaned as he looked at his control panel. "It threw out our probe. If we get a smiley face come up on the screen, I'm going home."

"Just plug in those numbers. It will open the door." Mida tapped on the computer screen.

"Mida, I love you dearly, but sometimes you scare the hell out of me," Sandy said as he started typing in the numbers. "Are you Mida or are you taken over by some alien life-form?"

Mida said something in Apache which made Ev grin.

Ev smiled at Mida and replied, "Just don't say that in English. Yes, Sandy, it is Mida. No alien would know that. I think Mida is just a step or two ahead of us in being transformed by whatever is in there."

A raven flew overhead as Ev looked up. "I think it's me you need to worry about. That raven just said goodbye to me," Ev said as he took off his hat and rubbed his hair. He noticed that the sun had gone behind Boulder Mountain. They had all been so busy, they didn't notice it was getting late.

"I'm not sure what those numbers mean. I put them in the computer but nothing happened. I don't know how to use them. They don't seem to be a radio frequency. They may not be our number system. They are not binary, but notice they are all below 5. A base 5 system? That doesn't make sense. Mida ask your source what I do with the numbers."

"Don't expect me to know what it means. I just know someone gave them to me. You have to figure out what to do with them," Mida said as she looked from one scientist to another.

They all stared at the screen. The numbers were there in bold type. Sandy wrote them down on a piece of paper. He rearranged them. He wrote them out longhand in English. He asked Mida to write them in Apache.

By this time, it was getting dark, enough for them to have trouble seeing what they were doing. "We've got some lights if you want to keep working," Ev said hesitatingly. He wanted to keep working, but knew everyone was getting tired.

"I hate to end a good party." Sandy gritted his teeth as he talked. "But I think we need to stop for the night. I'm not sure any of us will get any rest, but I think we need to try and sleep on this problem we have. If nothing works tomorrow morning, then we start up the super saw and cut our way through. I just don't know what to do with these numbers. Mida, you seem to have that extra sense. You need to put your power to work and come up with the answer."

"Listen," Mida said, "we are tired and we still have a ways to go. I really know these numbers will open the door, but I agree we will think better if we get some rest. I am tired and quite honestly, my mind is getting numb from all we have done today. If the numbers do not open the door we will have to cut through the door and that could take hours. After that, we go in and I don't want to stumble in dog-tired."

The group made a quick supper, then went to bed. They did not even make a campfire. Surprisingly all slept well that night. Sarah was not even wakened by a coyote howling from the adjacent canyon.

The next morning, the group was up at sunrise, sitting back at their positions where they left off the evening before. Sandy asked Mida if she had any revelations. She said no.

On a long shot, Sandy had earlier prepared several remote control gadgets that he pointed at the window. There was a good chance that the door was designed to open from the outside by electronic signals. What kind of signals was a mystery to Sandy and most likely beyond his knowledge of wave lengths, frequencies, or any type of electronics. Even though he knew they had the secret in Mida's numbers, they all drew a blank at how to use them. He said he would try a few other things first. Sumner said he was just stalling. Sandy nodded yes.

His first attempt used the universal homing beacon of the cosmos as he called it. It was the radio frequency of 1,420 million cycles per second, which he explained as the frequency of precession of the spin of an electron as it circles the nucleus of hydrogen. Mida laughed and asked him to speak English. He said it was the most prominent radio frequency in the universe. It didn't work. He tried the other devices, with no luck. He even had what he called a Mida (modal interference digital analyzer) that he hooked up to his computer and scanned through several thousand combinations, including Mida's numbers. Nothing worked. The door did not open, lights did not flash, sirens did not sound. Mida even put her headphones from her CD player on the side of the ship and played a selection from Peter Paul and Mary. She said if there were any universal sounds of peace, then this was it. Sumner looked at her with a scowl but didn't say anything. That didn't work either.

Sandy said there just had to be a clue about how to use the numbers Mida gave them. All looked at Mida but no one spoke. With human minds deep in thought, a chorus of bird chatter broke the stillness. A flock of pinyon jays flew in a long stretched out formation overhead.

Ev cleared his throat and spoke. "This has to be universal. Something that applies across the cosmos. What would stay the same anywhere you went?"

Sandy scratched his chin and looked at Mida. "Obviously certain mathematical concepts, such as pi or wavelengths of atomic elements. Atomic structure, such as oxygen and nitrogen having a set number of electrons or atomic weight."

"Bingo!" exclaimed Sumner. "You may have it. Atomic weights. But we need to know what number system is being used. We can assume this system is a base 5 system or else it is base 10 and just by coincidence there are no numbers above 6. What are the odds in a string of seventeen numbers, there would be no 6s, 7s, 8s, or 9s?"

"We could sit here for days trying to figure this out," Sandy said as he started tapping his pencil. "I will convert this to a base 10 system, but also use it as base 5 to start with. That will give us two sets of numbers." He mumbled to himself, "Now how the hell do you convert this?"

Sarah had been sitting on a nearby rock. She stood up. "I have no idea what a base 5 or base 10 is. I thought numbers were numbers. This suspense is driving me crazy. Why don't you just cut through the door?"

Sumner looked at her and smiled. "Sarah dear, I wish I had your innocence. I've always believed that knowledge only begets ignorance. The more we know, the more we know we don't know. The less we know, the happier we are."

"Did you just call me stupid?"

"No, Sarah," Mida cut in. "In his muddled up scientific way, he said he envied you. Take it as a compliment."

She leaned close to Sarah's ear and whispered, "Take it from me, you are smarter than him in a lot of things that count."

Sandy continued Sumner's thought, "Trust us, we will cut through if we have to. But we are so close. We have been handed a code. Now what to do with it. We need to be smart enough to figure it out. We are obviously dealing with an advanced intelligence that is light-years ahead of us. They wouldn't want some Neanderthal entering who just happened to wander by and throw a rock in their window."

Sarah sat back down. "Pardon my dumb analogy, but maybe it is like in Tolkien, when the group was standing at the gates of Moria and trying to read the runes?" Sarah and Mida had spent long hours discussing the Lord of the Rings Trilogy.

Mida brightened. "They thought it was a code and they tried to think of all the incantations and spells they knew. The runes said 'speak, friend, and enter." They interpreted that to be 'speak *comma* friend *comma* and enter.' They needed to speak some magical phrase. Then Gandalf, after emptying his brain thinking of all the incantations he knew had a flash of insight. It wasn't 'speak, friend.' It was 'say *friend* and enter.' They just needed to say the word *friend*. Once he said the word for *friend*, the doors opened right up wide as could be. There is a big difference to a seemingly minor variation of words. It was simple once you realized it. Do we need to insert a comma or leave one out?"

"Okay, okay." Sandy waved his hands. "Let's think this through. We are not dealing with any language other than math as a universal symbol. This set of numbers is a key to open the door. It is nothing physical or material. What else does that leave? Sound waves or light waves. Light waves can be radio waves or some frequency of atomic emissions. Thinking universal, if these are atomic weights, how does that open the door? The numbers themselves don't do it."

"Are atomic weights universal? I mean will those be the same across the universe?" Mida asked.

"Since I haven't been across the universe, I can't say for sure. But everything we know points to that. It has to be. Our spectrographic analysis shows that far off galaxies are made up only of the elements we know. The way atoms are structured, there cannot be anything different. Only at the discontinuity at the site of a black hole do all laws of physics disappear. And since everything is ripped apart in a black hole, then it doesn't matter what happens in a black hole. So the answer is yes, this is universal." Sandy leaned back and looked at the ship. "I just hope we are as smart as someone in there hopes we are."

"Now, to test my knowledge of chemistry," said Sandy as he started scribbling.

"Oxygen is 16, boron is 11. I am going to have to assume commas since I don't think there is a 161. I know gold is 197. I learned that long ago when I was shopping for a gold engagement ring for a girlfriend who dumped me in college. I vowed to drink 197 bottles of beer to drown my sorrows. I think 195 is platinum."

Sumner continued, "There is another 19 later, which is fluorine, so I am guessing 195 goes together and it is not 19, followed by 51, which I don't know what it is."

"I think 51 is either chromium or vanadium," Ev said quietly. He looked up at Mida and said, "There are some things I remember from basic chemistry. Geology is chemistry, just like everything else."

Sandy ignored Ev's explanation. "There could be some different versions here since we don't have the commas I would like to have. So then 1 would be hydrogen, krypton is 84, fluorine is 19, and magnesium is 24. I need an atomic chart and I'm guessing on magnesium. I can't remember for sure if it is 23 or 24. If it's not magnesium, it is silicon. I guess if one doesn't work, we try the other."

"Magnesium is 24." Everyone suddenly looked at Sarah, whose soft voice uttered those words.

"I don't even know what atomic weights are. My husband, my former husband, had a legal case just last month that he had to know chemistry. He brought this big chart home and hung it on the wall. I happened to be sick at the time and asked him to buy me a bottle of milk of magnesia. When he gave it to me, he said something like good old atomic weight 24 will take care of your tummy. I didn't know what it meant, but he said magnesium was number 24. I remember that well. I want to forget about everything else about that scumbag." She looked up at the sky and turned around so they wouldn't see her tears.

Mida broke the awkward silence that followed. "You have all those memorized?" she asked Sandy with a look of awe. "Some of those elements I've never even heard of."

"Believe it or not, I had the chart memorized for many years. I can still see it in my mind. If you had trouble with these simple elements, what would you have done with astatine, cerium, gallium, lanthanum, ytterbium, and samarium?"

"You are pulling my leg, aren't you." Mida grinned as she looked at Ev for some confirmation.

"Trust the man, my dear. He speaketh the truth. And much to your chagrin, your cute little body is made up of all of those weird combinations of circling electrons. You are just a bundle of energy that comes in different packages we put labels on. It is all the same stuff. Just like broccoli is the same stuff as cabbage, perish the thought." Ev grimaced as he envisioned tiny brussels sprouts dancing with cabbage.

"Yeah, but what does it still mean? We have to get pieces of gold and platinum and the others and hold them against the window?" Mida looked around. "I don't think we have them sitting here in our chemistry lab. And I thought krypton was made up for Superman."

"No, krypton is real. But remember what we said. It has to do with light or sound waves. Frequencies. I do have a chart here that should list the spectrometer numbers for each of these." Sandy jumped up and started shuffling through file folders at his feet. After a minute he held up a chart.

"Right here, folks. Let me program the transmitter real quick and Mida, do your magical powers thing you do so well. And, Ev, you hold your breath. You may even want to talk to your raven and ask his help, too."

"Here goes nothing," he said as he finished entering the last number. He pushed the button. All three looked intently at the window. All they could hear was a faint hum. You could hear the grains of sand expanding in the heat. You could not hear anyone's heart beating since all had momentarily stopped.

After about ten seconds, they heard a beeping. The window turned blue. There were no flashing lights or streaks of lightning.

"Look!" Sandy shouted as the crack outlining the door became visible. A louder sound came from inside the ship. It was a type of whirring, hissing noise that reminded Ev of a giant sucking sound. They all jumped back as the door started opening.

Ev shouted, "We hit the jackpot on the first try. The gates of Moria are opening. You are a true genius, Sandy. You too, Sumner. And Sarah."

The instruments fell as their floor rose. The bubble came loose with a sucking sound of its own. Sparks flew once again as wires were pulled loose from instruments.

"Holy mother of Geronimo," Ev shouted as he grabbed Mida.

"I wish you would not use that term, dear," Mida chastised him as she pulled herself up out of the hole. "The egg is cracking and we are ready to do a reverse hatch."

Ev jumped out and stood outside the shack. He looked at Mida, then looked at Sandy as he crawled out himself.

"I don't think we will get an engraved invitation. I suppose it is time isn't it?" Ev said as he stared open mouthed.

Instruments had fallen off the table, wires were still sparking, the computer screen went dark. Some of the instruments fell into the widening hole. The door was fully open.

"Sumner, please go turn off the generators," Sandy calmly said. He started gathering file folders, putting them in his briefcase. Mida and Ev walked up carrying their backpacks. Sandy's was sitting next to the open door.

"Gentlemen," Mida said very slowly and deliberately as she reached down and picked up her journal she had left lying on the ground, "we have unlocked the door to the secrets to the entire universe. Your hero Einstein would be proud."

"Ladies first," Ev said as he swooped with a bow. Mida dropped into the opening, followed by Sandy and Ev. Sarah leaned over to say goodbye to Mida. As she reached down to touch Mida's outstretched arm, Ev stumbled. As he reached out, he accidentally grabbed Sarah's hand, pulling her into the void. As she grabbed for something to stop her fall, she grabbed the door and pulled it shut as she fell in. The last thing they heard was an explosion and sudden scream from Sumner standing outside, then complete silence. The door was closed and they were inside.

SIXTEEN

✳

Inside Orion

Any sufficiently advanced technology
is indistinguishable from magic.
One man's magic is another man's
engineering. After all, what are miracles
but phenomena which on account of
our ignorance, we cannot explain.

—*Arthur Clark*

Now my suspicion is that the universe
is not only queerer than we suppose,
but queerer than we can suppose.

—*J. B. S. Haldane*

THEY ALL STOOD motionless getting used to the darkness. There was some light coming in from the window, but only enough to tell they were standing in a small space. Ev got out his flashlight and shined it around. They were, as they suspected, in something like a cockpit of a small plane that was tilted partly on its side. There was red dust coating everything. They could tell little more than what they had been able to see from the outside. The other side of this small cramped vehicle did have another door that was halfway open. It was not directly attached to the main vehicle but was up against it. The door or opening to the bigger ship was open so they could go from one to the other. There were stalactites and stalagmites in the opening, which indicated the two had not had a tight seal. Over the millennia, water had seeped between them, leaving stains and deposits that partially blocked the opening.

Ev pushed against the door in which they entered, but it was now locked. He pounded on it; he looked for buttons or levers to open it. He couldn't remember the sequence of numbers, but that didn't matter since he wouldn't know what to push even if he did. Nothing moved. The window was deeply tinted, which kept them from seeing anything clearly. He thought Sumner might try and look in, but there was no sign of him.

"Let's move into the mother ship," Ev said as he struggled to climb over debris that covered the floor, or wall, or whatever it was they were standing on. "We can come back to this, but right now, this little space is kind of creepy. I don't know what Sumner's scream meant, but whatever it was, he is on his own now."

"So are we," Sarah moaned as she rubbed her shoulder.

Mida took off her pack and set it on a flat object that was against the wall. She quickly put her journal in it, when Ev stumbled as he started to climb into the opening. He fell on top of her, knocking his head on the wall and knocking Mida down on the floor.

"You guys are really getting started out right," Sandy said as he reached down and picked up the flashlight that Ev dropped. Just about the time Ev and Mida stood upright again, the entire mother ship began glowing with a yellow then green light. The door to the larger space made a grinding sound as it strained to close.

"Quick, let's get in there before it shuts," Ev shouted as he pushed Mida toward the opening. He grabbed his pack and helped Mida with hers. They literally fell into the opening, with Sandy pushing Sarah against them from behind. The door made several metallic noises, then stopped moving. It would not shut, although it had closed about half the space. Rock and debris prevented it from closing all the way.

"I can just see us getting stuck in the shuttle pod and not being able to get back out," Sandy said to himself as he brushed red dirt off his shirt. "Is everyone okay? I know Ev has been falling all over the place. Sarah, you hurt your shoulder when you fell?"

"I guess it's okay. It hurts like hell, but I think I probably just strained it or pulled a muscle."

"Where don't I hurt?" said Ev as he noticed he had cut his hand in the melee. Wiping the blood off his finger, he added, "I couldn't get a footing. That place was cockeyed with no place to stand. Sarah, you really are in it now. I'm sorry I pulled you in. You aren't supposed to be here."

"Yeah, thanks for the one-way ticket. It would be nice if you could go open the door and let me out."

"That door won't budge. I didn't hear it make a click, but I didn't hear any clicks when it opened either. It didn't seem to weigh anything, but it was on some hydraulic lift or something. It seemed very solid."

"How are we going to get out?" Sarah whined.

"We worry about that later. I don't think that will be a problem," Mida said as she hugged Sarah.

"Rock Boy, you better be careful or you are going to bleed to death before you get to see anything in here today," Mida said as she reached over and wiped blood off Ev's forehead. He had obviously banged it hard when he fell. She then noticed that she had a gash on her arm as well.

"Ouch," he said as Mida dabbed his head with the bandanna she had tied around her neck. "I don't remember hitting anything but that is sore," he exclaimed as he felt it. There was a growing knot on his head.

"I noticed some of the crusting of the rock was really sharp in the door opening," said Sandy as he took off his pack. "Looks like both of you found that out the hard way. Well, we are inside and something triggered the lights. You didn't hit a light switch when you fell did you?"

"I can't even tell where the light is coming from," Mida said as she looked around. "It seems to just glow from everything. It's really weird."

Mida noticed Sarah holding her arm close to her. "Sarah, all this meticulous planning we all did and here you are with nothing. No pack, no clothes. I hope you don't feel unwanted. I'm sorry you fell in, but I'm really glad you are with us. Let's see if we have something to act as a sling for your arm."

As Mida rummaged through her pack, Sandy undid the belt to his pants and used that to hold Sarah's arm to her chest.

"That feels better. It only hurts when I move it."

They stood and looked around them. They were standing in a large room, with ceilings about ten feet high. There was another shuttle sitting in front of a door about twenty feet to their left. Some storage tanks lined one wall and there were banks of control panels along another wall. The room seemed to be the size of a large garage. There were three doors to the outside of the main vehicle, with the one they came in the only one open.

"Looks like somebody went out for a spin and didn't come back," Sandy said as he looked at the one door with no shuttle parked in front of it.

"And somebody came back here but didn't make it inside," Mida added as she looked back at their door.

"I still can't believe that there is some power source that still works after all this time. Maybe it isn't that old after all. Or," Sandy hesitated and rubbed his chin, "that periscope thing has been sticking up in the sun for a few hundred years. Maybe it activated something by solar energy. Or maybe just the fact we exposed parts of the ship to the sun for the past year, that was enough to energize something."

"Whatever it is, there is energy here and pretty powerful at that. Who knows what else was activated or energized." Ev walked to a doorway opposite them that went into the main vehicle. "I vote that we start exploring. If there is something intelligent in here, it knows we are here. We might as well go looking for it with our hands extended in friendship."

They hefted their packs and walked through an open doorway from the bay to the main vehicle. There was a long corridor that curved ahead of them, lined with doors along its length. The walls appeared to be the same material as the outside of the ship. It seemed metallic but was slick and shiny like glass or plastic. The floor had the same pattern as what they saw in the lower window the year before. It seemed to have a faint glow as they walked over it. There were small circular openings in the ceiling every ten feet. Mida guessed they were either ventilation or speakers. There were no obvious light sources although the entire area was illuminated with the greenish white glow.

As they walked, Sandy commented he felt he was being watched. But they saw nothing that gave any clues as to what form of life lived here.

"You know, this seems strange to me," Ev commented as he walked. "This is essentially a cave, where you would expect the temperature to be cool and the air damp. That's not the case here. It seems the perfect temperature and humidity. I don't even notice it."

"You're right," said Sarah as she held her arm. "I've got goose bumps but not from cool air."

"Oh, thanks," Sandy said, looking behind him down the corridor. "Now you've given me an idea. This is some climate-controlled atmosphere to sustain life in some form of suspended animation. Something could be hibernating here, with this mystery energy source keeping things heated and dried at just the right setting. Now we have probably set it off and these things will be waking up."

Mida answered, "No, I don't get that feeling. You keep saying I have this supernatural power. Well, it says we are safe and we are also alone. There is nothing here, at least right now. Let's keep walking and see what we can find." She tugged Ev along, who had stopped to retie his shoelace.

They came to the first door, which was open. They looked in the room cautiously, then walked in. It was a large room, with six-foot-tall ceilings, slightly shorter than the main corridor. It was lined with cabinets and bins. They were full of crystals and glass-like disks. They reminded Ev of music CDs but without the center hole. There was a row of windows along one wall. One was ceiling-to-floor. They obviously faced the outside of the ship since red sandstone was up against the outside of the window.

Along another wall was a large control panel with buttons and switches and display screens. A large panel looked like it was made of small colored blocks that Sandy guessed were lighted controls of some kind, but without being lit, he couldn't tell for sure.

"Sandy, look at that over in the corner. It reminds me of a huge version of a kid's gyroscope." Ev walked over to it and started to touch it. His hand bounced back as it hit an invisible barrier that prevented him from reaching it.

"Don't touch it," Sandy warned. "It has some kind of protection, but I don't see any glass or physical structure. It is some type of navigation device. And I will lay odds that this wall display is some form of celestial navigation analyzer. I think we are in a main control room. But there are no chairs. That is an interesting clue about what these things were like."

"I don't like calling them things. They are beings that are much more intelligent than we are." Mida walked over to the outside windows. "We have no idea what they looked like, but let's not start speculating about some monster or alien beings based on some science fiction we watched as kids. This is the real thing."

Sandy motioned back to the corridor. "Come on, let's keep exploring. I'd like to find the crew quarters and engine room."

They walked back into the corridor. They followed it for a ways, but it soon came to a dead end. There was no door and no stairs. It just ended. The four stood there puzzled as Mida ran her hands along the wall. As she touched it, the wall started moving. She jumped back as a door appeared and then disappeared. It didn't slide into the wall, it just faded away leaving an opening. They walked into a small room and soon found themselves vibrating. After a few seconds, another door opened behind them and they walked into another room, with a ceiling of almost ten feet.

"That is the strangest elevator I've ever been on. Look, this is obviously the engine room with the power source for the whole ship," Sandy exclaimed as he walked up to a large clear-walled cylinder in the center of the room. There were tanks and smaller cylinders lining one wall. The other wall was lined with more crystals of all colors. Some were as big as a person.

"This reminds me of the computer Hal in the movie *2001*. Remember, the crystals floated in and out of their little holders while Hal itself was singing Daisy." Sarah reached out to touch one.

"No," Sandy almost jumped to grab her. "We don't dare touch any of these things. We have no idea what they might do. This is the main power source, and obviously it is turned on. This ship is powered up somehow. Touch that and we could all vaporize or end up who knows where."

Sandy walked over to the main clear cylinder in the center of the room. It started glowing a pale blue.

"Is this the source of our blue light?" asked Ev. As he walked over, the blue started moving, like a translucent curtain. It circulated in the cylinder. "Wow, like a blue aurora borealis."

"I don't know about you," Sandy said softly, "but I need to stop for a few minutes and rest. I didn't get much sleep last night and right now, I couldn't even tell you whether we have been in here five minutes or five hours. I am completely disoriented."

Sandy took off his backpack and sat on the floor. Ev and Mida did the same as they stretched and rubbed their shoulders. Sarah sat down next to Sandy. He reached over and adjusted her sling. None expected to have to carry their packs very far, but they all had utilized every cubic inch of space in them. The packs were stuffed full and quite heavy. They sat on the floor and looked about them. For several minutes, no one said a word.

The four seemed to withdraw into their own world and thoughts. Sandy pulled a small tape recorder out of his pack and started talking into it. Mida found her notebook, almost ready to fall out a side pocket of her pack, and started writing. Sarah sat with her eyes closed. Ev dug around in his pack and found a small first aid kit. He dabbed something on his head and arm, wincing as he did it. He then got up and wandered over to the window and carefully inspected the rock on the outside of the window. Sandy cautioned him again not to touch anything. After a few minutes, Ev wandered back to the center of the room and lay down against his pack. He asked Sandy what he was thinking.

Sandy tried to explain to Ev what he thought the cylinder contained and how it produced the energy. As Ev started looking at the ceiling, Sandy realized he had lost him in a flurry of technical jargon. Ev and Sandy didn't notice Mida walk over to an alcove along another wall. She stood there for a few seconds watching a panel in the wall. It started to glow blue.

With Sarah apparently asleep, Ev and Sandy were sitting on the floor talking when they heard a thud. They looked over and saw Mida sprawled on the floor. She lay without moving. All of a sudden, while Ev jumped up and started to run over to pick her up, she just disappeared. One second she was there, the next she was gone. Sarah, awakened by Ev's movements, opened her eyes in time to see Mida disappear. She let out a scream and grabbed Sandy's arm.

Ev felt the floor and immediately jumped back. An eerie glow of bluish light hovered where Mida had been.

"I got a shock," he said weakly as he looked back at Sandy. "She just disappeared. She's gone. They took her." He knelt on the floor looking back and forth between Sandy, now holding Sarah tightly, and where Mida disappeared. He almost whimpered like a lost child not knowing what to do.

Sandy stood, with Sarah still clinging to him, dumbfounded for a few seconds, then walked over to Ev and touched him on the shoulder. "Let's be careful for a minute, Ev. It has something to do with this alcove here. I think Mida was standing in there and probably touched something. We have no idea what their technology is capable of. They may have taken her to another room. She may show up here in a few minutes with a fantastic tale to tell."

Ev slowly stood up with a blank look in his eyes. He started to walk into the alcove, but Sandy held him back. "I have to find her," he stammered to Sandy. "We have to do this together."

"Why did I come here?" blurted Sarah as she sat down and started to cry. "Now Mida is dead. We are all going to die."

"No, Sarah. Here, let me get you a drink of water." Ev pulled out a water bottle from his pack, but Sarah waved him off and said, "bloody savages, don't even have any chairs for us. I'd say let's sit down for a minute, but there is nothing to sit on. I guess the floor will do."

Sandy pulled Ev down as they sat on the floor, their backs against one wall.

"Wait." Sandy whispered the word again. "Wait."

"Wait for what?" Ev looked at Sandy, then touched his head very gingerly where he had cut himself earlier. He winced at the pain.

"I don't know. I just heard the word *wait* in my head. Something put a thought into my head that just said 'Wait.'"

"Someone talked to you? I didn't hear a thing."

"Not really talked. I didn't hear a voice. It was more of a thought. Strange."

"Was it Mida's voice?" Ev looked really confused.

"It was not a voice, Mida's or anyone else's," Sandy said impatiently. "I just thought the word *wait*. What else can I say? Something made me think *wait* and I will wait. We don't have anything else to do. At least I don't."

"Well, maybe if I go stand where Mida stood I can follow her."

Sandy actually leaned over and thumped Ev on the side of his head, being careful not to hit his sore spot. "Ev, will you get yourself together. We knew strange things would happen and now they are happening. We are all in this together and I'm sure we will stay together if we want to. Trust Mida on this. She said these beings are friendly and invited us in here. We have to do this their way. We sit here and wait. Eat a snack or something."

Ev started to look in his pack when he said, "My pick is gone. I put my pick in this pocket and it's not there. Did you see it?"

"Ev, I didn't see your rock pick. It probably fell out somewhere. I think that's the least of your worries right now. Oh, good grief, Ev, it's right there." He reached over and pulled Ev's pick out of a back pocket on the backpack.

"That's my good luck—" Ev started to say but was halted in midsentence as sparks started to fly where Mida had fallen. A sparkling sound like static became evident, then a blue aurora started to flicker in the alcove.

Suddenly, as quickly as she disappeared, Mida appeared. She was wide-eyed but had a big grin on her face. She reached out to Ev, but her eyes rolled back in her head and she collapsed on the floor.

Sarah screamed again. Sandy reached over and grabbed Sarah, shaking her hard. "Get hold of yourself, Sarah. You may not want to be here, but you are here. You have to expect anything. I'm not going to put up with you screaming every time we see a blue light. We've been living with this for months. Strange things are going to happen. Get used to it."

"I think she just fainted," said Ev as he cradled Mida in his arms. "Hand me that water bottle."

Sandy picked up the bottle that Sarah refused and handed it to Ev. Kneeling on the floor beside Mida, he started to put the bottle to her lips.

Sarah jumped toward him and knocked the bottle to the floor. "Don't give an unconscious person water. She could choke on it. Remember, I am the nurse here. Just be careful. Here, put some water on this bandana and squeeze it on her tongue. That will be safer."

All of a sudden, the lights went out. Sarah stifled another scream as she dropped the bandana. There was darkness in the room, although a faint glow did come from somewhere down the corridor. Both Ev and Sandy started to say something, but then the lights quickly came back on. Ev looked down at Mida who was still unconscious while Sandy looked around the room.

Sandy tapped Ev on the shoulder and said, "Here we go, Ev. Meet our friends."

Ev looked up and saw a ball of intense white light about ten feet away. At that moment, Mida woke up, looked at the light, and smiled. She said, "Thank you," then stood up, almost knocking Ev over in the process.

Ev started to say something, but Mida put her hand to his lips. She laughed, then looked at the light and said, "These are my companions. This is Ev, this is Sandy, and this wonderful but confused lady is Sarah. She wasn't supposed to be with us. We have prepared ourselves to meet you but she hasn't. I think they are a little surprised and probably worried about me."

Ev was watching Mida and not the light. Ev looked at Sandy, who looked back at him with a look of total confusion. Sarah sat with her eyes wide and mouth open. Mida spoke to them but her lips did not move. They heard her thoughts in their minds. Mida noticed their expressions and laughed again.

They heard her say-think, "I'm sorry, but the looks on your faces . . ." She looked at the light and smiled. "This is so new to them. To us. I had my shock earlier and now I'm used to this communication. We have to give them a little time to get used to it. Maybe you'd better explain."

The light approached closer, and touched both Ev and Sandy, and enveloped Sarah in a blue glow. They had a feeling of warmth and pleasantness. Sarah sighed and smiled broadly. Their initial fear and confusion left them. Ev noticed the throbbing in his head stopped. They looked at Mida and she smiled back at them. The light entered their minds.

"Welcome. You are in our vessel we named *Renaissance* in your language. I am called Vandara. I am an avarnan, just as you are humans. We communicate by brain waves. Obviously, I don't speak your language nor you mine. We overcome that barrier by a way I doubt you will understand now. Let's just say we are automatically translating each other's thoughts. And don't worry about communicating this way. You only communicate to me what you want to. You may still think to yourselves and keep that secret. I am not privy to your innermost thoughts."

Mida thought, "Vandara took me on a short voyage. I spent what seems like hours visiting with her or him. She took me back in time and then brought me back here to just after I left. I hope I wasn't gone very long. I'm sure you missed me." She kissed Ev on the forehead and put her hand on Sarah's shoulder.

"You scared the hell out of us," Ev said, noticing a strange look on Mida's face.

"This is so weird," Mida thought to the others. "When you speak aloud, I hear a sort of echo. We need to stop using our vocal chords."

Sandy thought, "I heard it too. It may be a little hard to break a million-year-old habit."

"You will all do fine. Mida had a hard time getting used to it. Actually, I visited with Mida for about a full day of your time. Don't look so surprised, Mida. As you say, time flies when you are having fun." Vandara's laugh sounded like a smooth purring.

"I thank you for coming to see me. For reasons I will explain later, I had to wait for you to contact me. I could not come forward into the future to contact you, although we know you have been visiting outside *Renaissance* for a short time. I came here to take you back with me. I took Mida earlier since she was standing in our transporter. She triggered the call button. I would have brought all of you if I knew you others were here. If you are ready, I will do it right this time." She purred again.

Ev and Sandy looked at each other, then looked at Mida. Neither said anything or thought anything. Mida stood by Sarah holding her hand.

Mida walked over to the light. She touched it and thought to Vandara, "We will come but I want to visit with my companions first. I want to share with them my experience. Once they know what I went through, they will be enthusiastic to come too. I think they were really worried when I disappeared. We have waited for this moment for so long."

Vandara explained that it was difficult to keep coming and going in time; thus, she would wait here for them to talk. When she finished with that thought, she faded to a small point of light and settled in one of the crystals.

Mida walked back over to Ev and hugged him. "This is so fantastic! Let's sit down. I want to fill you in. Vandara is so wonderful. I don't know if it's a he or a she. I get the feeling there is a blurring of that distinction. Just think of that." She giggled.

"What would we do if testosterone and estrogen evolved into some mixture that simply did away with gender?"

"As long as it lets us have some kind of fun the old-fashioned way," Ev commented as he looked at Mida and smiled.

"Oh, Ev, we are at such a higher level of intelligence here. We are ready to go soaring into the clouds and you still want to stay on Earth and ride a tricycle."

Sandy interrupted this conversation which he saw rapidly degenerating. "Well, Mida, I am anxiously awaiting your report. You were only gone less than a minute. You just disappeared. When Ev touched the floor where you were lying, he got a shock."

Mida looked at Sandy, then Ev, then Sarah, and thought to them, "I am still getting this echo when you talk out loud. I think Vandara said we could do one or the other, but he or she, I'm going to call her a she, doesn't talk out loud. I'm not sure they have vocal chords. I have a feeling she is ageless. I think they have progressed to a point where they basically live forever."

She went on to describe her experience. Someone or something had called to her from the alcove, so she walked over and saw a light on the screen. Touching it, she heard it say, "Thank you for calling me. Step back and I will bring you to me." Mida stepped back and the next thing she knew, she was flying through the air. It was the strangest sensation—she went back in time. She hadn't gone anywhere, because she returned to them, but a moment later in Earth time.

The others were mesmerized by Mida's story. They watched her and listened to her thoughts. At first the thoughts were a little jumbled and incoherent. They tended to race around more than if she was actually talking. After a little while, they became more concise and orderly.

When she had landed in the past, she noticed the room was the same as the one they were now sitting in, but sunlight was coming in the windows. There was a lot of activity, with people milling around. These people had a more distinct shape than the ball of light that was Vandara when she appeared before all four of them just now. The figures were still mostly light, but did have a more defined form and face. They were shorter than her and seemed more hunched over, but they made her think of humans. They didn't notice her at once, but when one looked over and *shouted,* they all stopped what they were doing and stared at her. She looked around and noticed one figure was standing behind her, purring like a cat. It touched her on the shoulder and she immediately felt at ease. She had a wonderful feeling of peace and pleasure.

She heard everyone conversing, but they weren't talking. They were thinking thoughts that she could understand. The figure next to her introduced herself as Vandara. She held her hand on Mida's head for several minutes. Mida felt a tingling in her head, but just stood perfectly still. Her thoughts were racing and she sensed that her entire brain contents were being massaged.

Vandara thanked Mida for allowing her to get caught up on who Mida was and where she was from. Vandara said Mida had a lot of knowledge but wished for Mida to let her know exactly how she got here and where she was from. When Vandara had pulled Mida back in the past, she didn't realize Mida wasn't alone. She apologized for bringing Mida back alone. She would return Mida to her friends, then bring them all together.

Mida told Vandara how they found the ship and that it was encased in rock that was two hundred million years old. She was intrigued by this, although it took a while to explain what a year was and how it related to Vandara's time frame. Vandara asked all about the geology and what type rock it was. Mida smiled at Ev and said she really needed him there on that, and she assured him he would be able to fill the avarnans in on all the details.

Mida then told Vandara about the blue light and the increase in psychic powers that she and Ev and Sandy were getting. By this time, Mida had gathered quite a crowd of avarnans. Several introduced themselves to her and touched her with their hands. On each one, she got the nicest sensation. She tried telling them about her time. The year 1999 meant nothing to them, so she had to describe the sun and how long it takes to complete a revolution for a year. They seemed to understand that. Vandara mentioned several times that time was a concept that Mida didn't really understand. She said there were so many things Mida didn't understand and they would try and be patient with her.

"Oh, Ev, it is the most wonderful feeling being with these people. They are from another star system and are so advanced. Yet they are so interested in us and want to know the most intricate details of everything. One was fascinated with my clothes. It even lifted up my shirt and looked underneath."

"Yeah, I do that and I get slapped," Ev interrupted.

"Your motivation is just a little different, I'm sure," Mida said as she continued to explain her encounter. After a few minutes, or what seemed like minutes, she had been left alone as all the others, including Vandara, gathered in a corner of the room. She knew they were communicating, but this time she could not hear them. They had the ability to exclude whomever they didn't want to hear them.

"From what I gathered during the conversation with me, the planet they were from was nearing extinction. Their sun was in its death throes and was expanding to become a red giant or something like that. They had to go out and explore other planets. Previously they had pinpointed ours as the nearest one that was likely to have life on it. They were here to plant the seeds of intelligence was the way Vandara phrased it. I told her we had intelligence, although sometimes I wondered if we were on a path of self-destruction. She said all intelligent life goes through that phase. If we get through it, then we are on a path to self-enlightenment. These were Vandara's words."

"Sounds good so far," Ev commented as he looked at Sandy. "But I wonder what the hitch is."

"There is none, Ev. And if you remain skeptical like that, you may cause a hitch. These beings are genuinely peaceful and full of good. Now here is the interesting part. We had a little trouble with placing dates with events, but it sounds like when they landed right here, they had made an error in their calculations and they landed two hundred million years ago, but they were actually here one million years ago. Is that weird or what? When I went up in the air with Vandara, we traveled forward to one million years ago."

"Now you really confused me," Ev said as he looked at the small spark of light over in the corner. "These people are from one million years ago, but they goofed and landed two hundred million years ago? So what we are in is what, one million years old or two hundred million? Or are we still here in 1999?"

"Ev, you always wanted to time travel," Sandy smiled at him. "Here is the ultimate. You go from 1999 to 200 million BCE, then to one million, then who knows where? I've always wanted to believe in time travel, but the physics of it is beyond me or anyone else. And I really am looking forward to learning how they travel faster than light. It just cannot be done in my limited worldview."

Ev was rifling through his pack looking for what, he didn't know. Rather absentmindedly, Ev continued in obvious confusion as he repeated himself, "So if we are sitting here in this two-hundred-million-year-old ship that is really only one million years old, are we still in 1999 or have we gone back in time?"

"Ev, I really wonder if you hit your head harder than we realized," Sandy frowned at him. "Mida just went back in time, but you and I have been sitting here in good old 1999. We haven't done anything yet. That spark of light over there is calmly waiting for us to brace ourselves to take this big quantum jump that Mida already took. I wonder if you need to get a good night's sleep before you go."

"No, I'm all right. There is just so much happening so fast. And yes, Mida really scared me when she disappeared. I just got upset thinking we had lost her."

Mida reached over and kissed Ev. "What a sweet thing to say. I would miss you if you disappeared, but we are on a journey that we are committed to and who knows if we will all stay together. This isn't a weekend camping trip. We each have to be ready to go it alone if we have to."

"Thanks for that vote of love and affection," scowled Ev as he tore open a bag of peanuts.

"You know what I mean, Ev. My heart would be rendered asunder"—she grabbed her chest—"but I would have to go on. I would not sit here and mourn myself into oblivion. We all have to be ready to do that."

Mida looked at Sarah and smiled, but Sarah shrugged and said, "Don't expect me to understand any of this. I am just along for the ride."

"Mida is right," Sandy said. "As much as I have grown to love both of you, I would go on, too. This is the ultimate adventure anyone in history has ever taken. I will lay odds that within a week or less, we will have done and seen so much, we won't even remember anything of our past lives. Sarah, even though we have barely met, please feel at home with all of us. The three of us spent a lot of time together planning this, not knowing what in the world to expect. You are one of us now. Think of me as a long lost uncle."

As Sandy hugged Sarah, Ev said quietly, "Maybe I did hit my head pretty hard. And it seems like I've been bleeding from one wound or another all day. But I will not be able to lay down here and sleep. Do you think I could fall asleep for one second while waiting to go back however many million years? They will have to give me a shot of something to put me out."

"Rock Boy, you think I have been perfecting my healing skills? You should see what they have the power to do. One touch from Vandara or any of them, and you will be in perfect health. To be honest, I sprained my ankle earlier today when you fell on me and it was hurting like hell. It doesn't hurt at all now. And that little cut I had from the fall is completely healed. Not a scratch!" She held out her arm for Ev and Sandy to see.

The four sat nibbling snacks but more out of nervousness than hunger. Sandy chuckled as he thought about the scene: four dirty, tired humans sitting on the floor of this super high-tech space ship from the past, with a sleeping avarnan, whatever that was, curled up in a tight pinpoint of light over in the corner. One of them had already traveled back into time with this space alien, and one had banged his head and was a little woozy. Another was a jilted newlywed, nearly hysterical a week ago and here only by accident. The fourth was a prominent astrophysicist who is now told that he can travel with beings who had vacated their soon-to-be-melted planet, traveling faster than light, misjudge time and land 199 million years off course.

"Mida, lovely princess of the past"—Sandy loved to dramatize things at times—"I think we all need some good rest. But we are also anxious to get going with Vandara. Do you think you can call her over and start this journey, but relay to her we need to rest. Maybe she can give us some energy potion and restore our sanity. I for one am ready to go, but I think the excitement will overwhelm me sooner than later. By the way, do you know how to wake her up?"

"I am awake." The words came into Sandy's head, as it obviously did to the others as well since they jumped in unison. The light was full size again and hovering next to them.

"What the—" Ev exclaimed. "We thought you were asleep. Did you listen to all we said?"

"No, I did not hear your conversation, and no, I was not asleep. I was in a resting state, but it is too hard to fully explain to you right now. I knew when you were ready to call me. I can tell you all need rest. If you all step over into this spot," she said pointing a ray of light to the alcove in the wall where Mida earlier stood, "I will start your journey. You see, I am not actually here. I am really back in time, but my thoughts are here. That is why I don't look like I did when Mida came back to me earlier. There is so much that you cannot understand, but I will try to explain it to you the best I can. As we travel, you will be asleep. You will arrive fully rested, although the trip itself is usually quite tiring. I have healing powers and I will use them on you. Are you ready? Put your things together and we will go as a tight group."

The four stood there and looked at one another. Mida picked up her pack and the two others did the same. As they hefted on their packs, Mida pulled the others to her in a big group hug. She motioned to Vandara to join them. As they stood there, aglow in the light of this advanced being, Mida said a few words in Apache. Vandara made a purring sound and led them to the alcove. They stepped in it and immediately disappeared in a burst of bright light.

SEVENTEEN

✳

Meanwhile, Back at the Ranch

Time goes, you say? Ah no!
Alas, Time stays, we go.

—*Henry Austin Dobson*

As far as the laws of mathematics refer
to reality, they are not certain.
So far as they are certain, they
do not refer to reality.

—*Albert Einstein*

IT HAD BEEN seven days since Denzee left the cliffs of Oak Creek for the last time, leaving the explorers on the doorstep of their quest. According to the schedule that Ev and Sandy prepared, it should have taken them up to four days to build the structures and another two days to do the testing. That meant they entered on the seventh day if not sooner. Sumner and Sarah were to drive back to Torrey as soon as the others entered the rock. Maybe earlier. They only had enough food for six days, if they stretched it. If the explorers had not returned to Orion Wingate by the eighth day,

Sumner was supposed to drive back down and do a quick check to see if they were still inside the ship.

Ev and Sumner knew it probably wouldn't take that long. The instructions in the letters sent to the other scientists were for them to open the sealed packet inside the envelopes on and not before October 9.

Their instructions were to meet in Torrey on October 12, Columbus Day. Or as Mida called it, the Day of Infamy. This didn't give them much time, but everyone had been forewarned that they should plan on meeting in Torrey "about mid-October" anyway, regardless of what happened with the entry attempt. Even if nothing happened and the trio walked in and immediately walked back out of Orion, they still wanted to show the ship to the others. The only difference was if nothing had been heard of from Sandy by the ninth, they would read the description of the secret in their letter and know that the explorers had disappeared. Otherwise, they would have heard from Sandy or Sumner and would have been invited to come up and see the thing for themselves and discuss the entry with the disappointed conspirators.

Denzee had told the conspirators that it all seemed complicated and out of some spy novel, but this would be the way all three wanted it. The hardest thing for Denzee was to tell Boyd and Marybeth about it when they returned. She did that on day seven, when they returned to Orion Wingate.

Late in the afternoon, Boyd drove up in a new Ford Explorer, with Marybeth following in their car. Honking the horn as he parked in front of the new cultural center, he yelled for Ev and Mida to come out. Quickly, Denzee walked out to meet them, ready to tell them what had happened. Boyd didn't even give her a chance. He pointed to the decal on the side of the new white SUV and exclaimed proudly that this was the official car for the center. Denzee just stared at the blue letters framed around the red cliffs: "The Orion Wingate Center."

"What do you think? I know you two haven't come up with the formal name yet, but this will have to make do until you decide." He handed Denzee a small package wrapped in white tissue paper.

"This is for you and I have another just like it for Mida. I got them in New York where I had to spend the last couple days. Boy, is it good to be back here. Where are the kids, anyway?"

"What's the matter, Denzee?" Marybeth asked as she noticed the worried look on Denzee's face. "Is everything all right?" she asked with a mother's intuition that something was wrong.

After a few seconds, Denzee said, "Ev and Mida aren't here right now. They are with Sandy. I think you need to come in and sit down. We need to talk about a few things that involve them."

"Denzee, you are scaring me. Are they all right?" Marybeth asked as she grabbed Boyd's hand.

"They were okay the last I saw them, which was a week ago. You probably need to go freshen up for a few minutes, then come on into the house. I have some tea heating up and I made a fresh apple pie this morning."

"We stopped at the Visitor Center down in the Park," Boyd said, as if proud he did not have to go freshen up. "Let's go in now and talk and sample some of that pie. I don't suppose you have ice cream to go with it?"

"Good lord, Boyd, doesn't anything phase you? It sounds like Ev and Mida are in trouble and you only think of eating?"

"Now, pumpkin, the lady said they were all right. Just sounds like a little off schedule is all. Both of those kids can take care of themselves. They've been many places I wouldn't think of going."

The three of them settled into the living room of the main house after Denzee prepared the herbal tea and gave Boyd a double slice of pie with vanilla ice cream. Marybeth was too worried to eat anything.

"I really don't know how to begin this," Denzee started as Marybeth tensed up, holding Boyd's hand tight enough to cause him to drop his fork from his other hand. "I guess I start from the beginning."

Denzee spent the next thirty minutes recounting the entire story. Boyd was so intense in his listening that he did not eat his pie. The ice cream melted and ran over the plate onto the coffee table. No one noticed. When Denzee got to the scientific studies, she said that Sumner and Sarah should have returned by now. She mumbled, "Days ago." She was very worried that something had gone wrong, but she was waiting as the instructions said. She then handed Boyd one of the envelopes with the instructions, personalized by Ev. Marybeth read the note and burst into tears. She asked what day this was. Denzee replied calmly that this was day seven and tomorrow she intended to go to the site and check it out. She was scared to go, but that was what the schedule said. Boyd replied calmly that he was accompanying her and nothing was going to stop him.

Denzee finished by saying quietly she knew Ev, Mida, and Sandy were fine. It was Sumner and Sarah she was worried about. They should have returned by now. They were all involved in something no one else in the history of mankind had done and were doing what they had prepared for all their lives. "I know in my heart I will never see them again, but I cannot feel sad for this. We must go on."

With that, Marybeth again burst into tears. Sobbing, she asked why Ev hadn't told her anything. His own mother. He never said a word to her.

Marybeth's actions were upsetting Boyd more than the story Denzee just told. "Listen, sugarcakes, we don't know that. That is only Denzee's opinion. She could be wrong. They may still be down there coming out of this spaceship after spending a day or two finding all kinds of fascinating things. Oh, I can't wait to find out what wonderful scientific discoveries they have made. Just think of the implications of this."

"I really think that if things had not gone the way they expected, they would be back by now. We will find out for sure tomorrow, hopefully. I have been listening to the weather and it sounds like a storm is coming this way, but may not be here until late."

"Well, then let's go right now," Boyd started to get up out of his chair.

"No, we have done it according to plan so far. We wait one more day. We will leave at daybreak tomorrow. Who is going to go?" she asked looking at Marybeth.

"Well, of course I am," bellowed Boyd. "You will want to see this thing, Pumpkin."

"Oh, Boyd, how can I possibly go see that thing? My baby disappeared in it."

"Well, your baby will be one of the most famous people in history because of it. You heard what Denzee said. We will be inundated by reporters and scientists. We will want to know firsthand what this thing looks like."

Denzee cautioned them that the time was not yet right for that. "This does not go public yet. Those are specific instructions from all three of them. We wait another week. We just go down tomorrow to make sure they are either still there or gone." She looked apologetically at Marybeth when she realized what she said.

Denzee looked at Boyd and continued, "When this goes public, Sumner, assuming he is okay, and you will be the lead on it. There will be several other people here to go down officially and make it public. These are all very high-level people, well respected and well known. One is a senator from Texas."

"Oh, is it Kay? I know Kay well. Or even Phil Graham. I don't know him but I have met with his aides many times."

"I don't remember the name. I know the letter was addressed to Austin.

"Oh, a state senator? Get me the name. I know quite a few of those folks, too."

At daybreak the next morning, Boyd pulled onto Highway 12 south out of Torrey, with two nervous passengers in his new Boydmobile, as Denzee called it. Two of them were thinking of their children and whether they would ever see them again. One was thinking of the scientific impact this discovery would have on the world. If it made it that far. He knew the secrecy of the government, especially the military, dealing with any so-called extraterrestrial events and was actually scared of what could happen. On the other hand, Boyd was more concerned with his wife than with the fate of his step-son. He was envious of Ev, and he was also thinking of the economic implications of the new scientific discoveries from the advanced technology he was about to see for himself. Boyd did not need any more money, but he simply wanted to create businesses and satisfy consumers. There was not a greedy bone in his body, but there were a lot of curiosity bones.

The sky was its typical brilliant blue, but there were a few high mare's tails clouds and a southwesterly breeze, which Boyd knew meant a weather system was on its way. This was October and a storm meant snow in the high country certainly. It might mean snow in the lower country. They needed to get down to Orion and back out again quickly.

As they drove along the highway, they were slowed down by a herd of cattle on the road. Several cowboys were riding along pushing them south. The cowboys had on blaze orange vests and their horses were decorated with orange ribbons. It was the end of the year for these cattle on the mountain. Boyd thought it was good they were coming off. He wouldn't want to get caught up on top with a storm coming in.

The aspen were mostly bare, with a few straggling leaves dropping and twirling as the breeze started to gust. When he rolled down the window to say something to the two cowboys following behind the cattle, he felt a definite nip in the air. He made a comment to the closest rider about the change in the weather. The young man smiled and said that these old girls, referring to the cows, knew when to come home. They were smarter than some people, he laughed. The other rider spoke up. Boyd suddenly noticed it was a girl. She said that females always knew better than the men when it was time to do anything. Cows or people, she laughed, it didn't make any difference. The young man looked at Boyd and muttered something about letting them think that, then he spurred his horse and galloped off the road to push back two calves that had headed off across a meadow.

A few minutes later, after navigating through the cattle on the highway, Boyd turned off onto the dirt Oak Creek road. As he started down the hill, three cow elk ran across the road in front of them. This was hunting season and the mountain was astir with animals and people with guns stalking them. Denzee said something in Apache. Marybeth looked at her and asked if she could share that with them. Boyd looked around and asked if she wanted to stop. Denzee put her hand on Marybeth's arm and said quietly, "I just asked Ussen to run with the elk. He provides for every living thing. Each of us has a purpose and I want the elk to serve their purpose."

Boyd was complaining about the rocky road and whether it would ever end. He put it in four-wheel drive when he hit the first rocky grade. Denzee reassured him they were almost there when they came out onto the sagebrush flats. She guided him across the sagebrush and past the wheel tracks that led off to a couple hunter camps that weren't there a week ago. When they came to the trail that the conspirators used to haul in equipment with the ATV, they found Ev's pickup sitting behind a juniper where they had left it a week ago. Denzee suggested they follow the ATV route. The several trips with the ATV had smoothed out most of the steep draws and gullies it crossed. She didn't know if either Boyd or Marybeth could climb out of the canyon from Oak Creek itself. It wasn't a long climb, but it was steep and rocky.

It was after ten o'clock when they parked next to the tents. Marybeth gasped at the elaborate setup. Everything was as the explorers left it. The camouflage tarp was still in place, as were all the tents and the generator building. Obviously, no one had wandered onto the site. And just as obvious, no one was there. There were no signs of Sumner or Sarah. Boyd walked under the tarp and saw the door to the ship closed. He knew the door had opened since all the instruments had been upset. Wires were dangling, with one loose wire disappearing into the door. The Plexiglas bubble had been upended.

"Wow, what a setup. This looks like something out of the movies." Boyd reached down, still talking to himself, and picked up the top-secret laser saw. "What in the world is this?"

Marybeth and Denzee were already looking through the sleeping tents. They found Ev and Mida and Sandy's empty sleeping bags but no packs or other personal things. Both Sumner's and Sarah's things were there, undisturbed as if they had just been used, but the red dust on the sleeping bags indicated they hadn't for several days. Denzee was explaining to Marybeth how they had brought all this in a week ago. She looked up when she heard a noise overhead. An eagle was circling. She watched it for a minute, then said something in Apache. Marybeth didn't ask her what she said this time. She felt she knew already. Marybeth whispered goodbye to Ev.

Boyd wandered into the instrument tent. There were several boxes of instruments next to the computer hard drives. "Let's get as much of the equipment into the truck as we can. This may tell us what happened. Besides, this stuff is worth more than I want to imagine. I guess we are lucky it didn't rain or snow in the last week," Boyd said as he picked up the hard drives and carried them over to the back of the Explorer. "I hope we can get all this in here."

Marybeth was in the shack, down on her knees looking into the ship's window, feeling the surface absentmindedly with her left hand as she peered into the window. She jumped back with a cry and called for Boyd. "Oh, Boyd, they are in there."

"You see them?" Boyd yelled as he stumbled into the shack.

"No, but I see Mida's hat. I know that's what it is. Look, Denzee. It's over there on the floor."

Denzee lay down on the window looking in. "It's so dark in there. I can't quite make it out. Does anyone have a flashlight?"

"I do. I put one under the driver's seat." Boyd ran over to the Explorer and opened the door. He reached under the seat and pulled out a large Mag light. As he slammed the door, he heard a voice yell from down below. He walked over to the edge of the cliff and looked down. There were two men on horseback down by the creek. They were obviously hunters as they were covered with blaze orange, as were their horses.

"Any luck up there?" yelled one of the men as he looked up at Boyd.

"Not at all," yelled Boyd. "I think we picked a bad spot to camp up here. Haven't seen anything. I think the elk are all still too high up the mountain. This is damn tough country down here. Where you camped?"

"We are up at Oak Creek but thought we would try some of this country down here."

"Say, a couple of our folks are overdue. Have you seen anyone?"

"Not a soul. Did ride by a couple camps up the road a ways, but no one around."

"You are going to have a tough time with those horses. Most of these canyons are cliffy. I wouldn't want to get a horse in here. Just lizards and pack rats down here. We may leave our tents here, but I think we will go back up into the aspen for a day or two. Sounds like a storm may be moving in. That may drive the animals down here in a few days. I'd head back up if I were you. We will be driving out in a few minutes."

"Thanks. This is our first time down here. Does look like tough country." He took out a cigarette and lit it. "Hope you don't get snowed in down here."

"That happened to me about five years ago. We were stuck down here for a week. This time of year is still early enough that we won't get stuck all winter. I wouldn't say that a few weeks from now."

The hunters waved and wished Boyd luck in getting his big bull. They yelled to tell Boyd if he needed a horse to pack out anything, just look them up. They were going to be camped up by the highway for another week. Then they rode off the way they had ridden in.

"Whew, that was close." Boyd dabbed his forehead with a large red bandanna as he handed Denzee the flashlight. "I was afraid they were going to either come up here or else tell me they were the game warden and were going to arrest me for being up here."

"Yeah, they might arrest you for hunting without a rifle," said Denzee. "You are a pretty good storyteller. I think some of Mida rubbed off on you. She is one of the best I know." Denzee leaned back down on the window and shined the flashlight into the ship.

She shifted around and tried to shade the window. Boyd took off his sweatshirt and draped it over her head to keep out the sunlight.

"Thank you," she said as she stood up. "It is really hard to see in there very well. The window is heavily tinted, but I could see the hat. It is Mida's. She is in there. Or was."

"Oh, Boyd, can't we help them?" cried Marybeth as her eyes started to tear up again. She sat down on the edge of the ship where it disappeared into the rock with her back up against the wall of the shack.

"I think they are beyond help from us. Besides, we don't know how to open this door. Hopefully they left a record of how they got it open. Maybe if we start pounding on the door, we could get their attention. I'm sure they are still in there."

Marybeth picked up wires as she tidied up the mess. She started to unplug the extension cords when she noticed the small hole in the window and looked for the probe that went in it. She found it and absentmindedly put the probe back in the hole.

Suddenly they were all knocked to the ground as an explosive flash of light enveloped them. There were no sounds but their screams as they hit the ground. Denzee fell on the exposed part of the ship, but when she recovered from the shock of the flash, she screamed again. There was no ship. It was solid rock—red rock, just like the surrounding rock.

"My god. It disappeared. The ship is gone!" Boyd stood up and dusted himself off. He held his right hand, which hung limp. It had a bluish color to it. He just stared at the ground.

Marybeth lay on the ground and started screaming. Boyd ran over to her and tried to cradle her in his arms but cried out, too, as pain shot through his right arm.

"Are you hurt?" he said as he shook her.

"They are gone. They disappeared. They were in there and now it is gone. Oh my god, Boyd, they were in there!"

Denzee climbed out of the hole in the rock. She didn't tell anyone that her left ear was numb where it had touched the ship when she fell. She also couldn't see that it was light blue.

Boyd said quietly, "I think we just watched our explorers make contact with whoever they made contact with. Either they or we just entered a parallel universe. I think it was them."

Marybeth slumped to the ground as she fainted. Boyd dropped to the ground with her. He looked at Denzee and fought back dizziness himself. He looked at the rock and muttered, "Ev, old boy, someday you will have to very carefully explain all this to me. I sure the hell don't understand it now. Denzee, please help me with Marybeth. Let's get out of here"

Denzee leaned down and whispered something in Marybeth's ear. She then pulled something out of her jacket pocket and put it in Marybeth's mouth. Suddenly Marybeth opened her eyes and looked around. She stood up, brushed herself off, and limped back to the vehicle. She wiped her eyes and said, "Let's go home." When she sat down in the back seat and took off her boot and sock to look at her foot, she stifled a scream when she noticed two of her toes were simply missing, with a faint blue scar covering where they used to join her foot. She quickly put her boot back on and sat back in the seat and closed her eyes.

Boyd looked back at the tents as he started the vehicle. "I have to believe that for some reason, Sarah and Sumner went in the ship with the others. It doesn't sound like they planned to. Maybe one of the three called to them once they were in and when they went inside, the door shut and they couldn't get it open. Maybe Sandy and Sumner's friends can help solve this mystery when they get here." He looked at Denzee and said, "Did we get all the computers out of that tent?"

Since they did not go down below, no one saw the cougar and coyote tracks in the wet sand by the creek. Wind during the past week had erased any tracks in the sand next to the tents or at the base of the cliff. There was no trace of Sumner. When the door had opened and after the four had fallen into the ship, a flash and explosion followed. The blast blew Sumner backward, disorienting him. As he flew backward, he tried to stand up and run, but he ran right over the edge of the cliff, falling dozens of feet to the pile of rocks below. The fall didn't kill him, but the broken neck paralyzed him. He only lay there a couple hours before the cougar smelled her prey. Sumner felt no pain.

When the group reached Ev's pickup, Denzee told Boyd to stop. She would drive it back to town. By the time the two vehicles reached the highway, the sun disappeared behind a wall of clouds coming in from the west. As they drove into Torrey, it started to snow. It snowed for two days, leaving a blanket of white a foot deep in Torrey.

Boyd and Denzee discussed long into the night the merits of bringing in the media to join the group of scientists who would be arriving soon. Boyd wanted the publicity, but Denzee argued that without the ship as physical evidence, they were opening themselves up to ridicule. There was no evidence of this fantastic tale. Boyd said there were four eyewitnesses plus tapes. Denzee said that was not enough. And besides, tapes could be manipulated and were not good solid evidence. Boyd said there was all the computer data. Denzee said this would not prove anything.

"Boyd, I know Ev, Mida, and the others want this story told. But stop and think about it. We will tell the world we found a spaceship, which isn't there. We have five people who disappeared, and we will say that they entered this spaceship, which doesn't exist, and disappeared along with the ship. There is no evidence. Nothing there. You and I and Marybeth don't understand what happened and we were there. What would you believe if you saw this story on TV?"

"But think of the implications of this? Think of what it means to us as a species. Our history. The future of space exploration."

"You think I haven't thought of all that? Mida and Ev lived with this for over a year. It changed them. They gave it a lot more thought than you or I. That thing could reappear as well as it disappeared. Mida could come out of the sky on a beam of light, looking like a white buffalo, and proclaim the planet as hers. But in the meantime, we will look like fools. We are the big losers in this. We know this happened but we can't tell anyone."

Boyd fidgeted in his chair. "It just isn't right. We have to do something."

"Let's wait until the others get here. We can discuss it with them. They are supposed to be some of the brightest minds in this country. We will take them out to Orion, or where Orion used to be. That is if we can even get there a few days from now. With this snow, we may not be able to. We will examine the computer records and the notes we found and we will videotape everything we do. These scientists can do some more testing. Surely, with all those instruments, they can test for anything."

"But that's what we need to have on film. Our investigation of the site. The tents still set up. The wires and generator and all that. What if I get a camera crew and reporter to follow us, but wait before we make anything public. I can get our PR people from my company. I can guarantee their secrecy. If we decide not to go public, then we don't. I just don't want to miss that opportunity."

"You may have a point with that. You sure you could guarantee their silence if that's what we decide? And it will have to be a group decision."

"I didn't build several companies worth over twelve billion dollars without dependable and trustworthy partners and employees. And I will arrange to have a helicopter here to take us down there and to help bring out all the equipment. You can't beat that kind of offer now can you?"

"Okay, Boyd, you win. Have your media people here with our team of scientists. Now it's time for bed."

Boyd could not stay out of the planning for the scientists' arrival, and he realized that Torrey was not the easiest place to get to. The nearest commercial airports were Salt Lake City or Cedar City, neither of which was convenient to Torrey. He made a phone call to one of his business partners and arranged to use the company Lear jet to fly all over the country and pick up the scientists.

The phone calls began on the evening of October 9. Boyd took the calls, saying Sumner and Sandy were both gone. That's why he needed someone here to help him. He did not go into detail about his experience with the disappearing ship. He just told the callers they needed to gather in Torrey in three days.

While Boyd, Marybeth and Denzee waited for the scientists, they slowly realized that they had been injured in the disappearance. Boyd did not have full use of his hand. Denzee's ear kept its blue color and soon her hearing started to get worse. Marybeth was scared to death of her missing toes and wouldn't even let Boyd know until three days later. Marybeth didn't want to see a doctor. Boyd didn't know what to do since there didn't appear to be any infection.

The three kept to themselves and didn't leave the compound for several days. They were anxiously awaiting the arrival of the experts. Boyd was starting to have headaches. He was not getting much sleep since he kept waking up from strange dreams of saber-toothed tigers, mastodons, and huge bison. The dreams were vivid, more so than he ever had before in his life. He didn't explain them to anyone, not even Marybeth.

Finally the twelfth arrived. Boyd and Denzee drove to Loa to meet the jet. The Loa runway was not certified for the jet, but the pilot landed without any trouble. Boyd greeted his new friends, who were full of questions. Since they had to ride in two vehicles, Boyd avoided telling any of them anything until he got back to the compound. The film crew was taking video and pictures of everything that was going on, including the plane departing in an explosion of noise on this patched little runway.

Marybeth had cleared the main bedroom of Ev and Mida's things, putting hers and Boyd's in their place. Denzee already moved her things into one of the spare bedrooms in the main house. She also cleared Sandy's room, stacking his things in a corner. That left the cabin for the newcomers. The film crew would sleep on cots in the unfinished basement of the Center.

After the group returned from the airport, they were shown to their rooms and told to reassemble in the living room of the main house at 3:00 p.m.

The group was a who's who from the aerospace community. Boyd recognized most of the names, but Denzee and Marybeth had not heard of most of them. They had been prodding Boyd for information since they arrived, but got only silence or small talk. Even though Boyd prided himself on his knowledge of science, he was unable to answer any of the questions. He was unable to understand many of them.

After brief introductions and a round of refreshments, Boyd stood up and walked over to the VCR. He said he wanted to show the group this summary of Orion. Denzee turned off the lights in the darkened room as Boyd hit the Play button. The group watched in rapt attention, with only a cough or muttered exclamation breaking the taped narrative.

When the tape was finished, Boyd opened the drapes and turned off the TV. He stood by the fireplace and slowly drawled, "Gentlemen, you all know why you are here. We wanted you here to go with us to the ship and confirm that our explorers had indeed entered the thing. We have before us the scientific discovery of all time. The three of us"—he nodded at the ladies—"have been there. We saw it. We touched it. We were the last to see the five of them." He avoided adding the word 'alive.'

"But—I sense a very huge *but* coming on, don't I?" said Dr. Larry Andrews, former astronaut and current researcher into the possibilities of life in other worlds.

Boyd stared at Andrews, then shifted on his feet. "Yes. There is a huge *but*." He hesitated again, looking around at the group. "We went out there a few days ago to make sure the explorers were not still there either waiting to get in or dazed from some strange experience. This was according to their previous instructions to us.

"Something had not gone according to plan. I expected Sumner to be here doing what I am doing now. He was not to go with them. Nor was Sarah, who was not part of a genuine plan. She is the genuine innocent bystander. They should have helped the three get inside, then they were to come back here and help you. They were nowhere to be seen. We can only guess they entered along with Ev, Mida, and Sandy. There is no other evidence of them. We found evidence that someone had in fact entered the ship's door. We found their data and some notes about how they had opened the door. Very interesting. But no one was around."

He looked at the table full of equipment and data that was at the side of the room. "Then all of a sudden, while we were standing there, the ship just disappeared. As if it had never been there. Not a trace. It was there one minute, then gone in an explosion of light.

All of us are suffering some effects of it. I still don't have complete use of my hand and Denzee has been losing her hearing. Look at her ear."

The group looked at Denzee as she pulled her hair back and exposed her bluish earlobe. Marybeth looked at Boyd, then pulled off her slipper and sock, exposing her missing toes. Several in the group gasped as she said very quietly, "I lost these at the same time. They just disappeared. Blue seems to be a very becoming color."

"Boyd, you know we all respect and trust Sumner and Sandy. If you had called us without their involvement, we wouldn't have given you the decency of an answer. We don't know you. But what you are telling us stretches the imagination." Dr. Billy Joe Stanton drug out the last sentence in his Georgia drawl. He then stood up and walked over to look at Marybeth's still uncovered foot. Billy Joe was a famous author, medical doctor, and leading authority on the power of prayer and thought on medical science. His last book made the link between quantum physics and medicine. He was definitely on the leading edge of medicine, often hanging over that edge. He carefully inspected Marybeth's foot, then looked at Denzee's ear.

"Well, we obviously need to go out to the site and look at what is left." Dr. R. D. Bentham was the leading quantum physicist at Cal Poly and author of over a dozen books on space-time, quantum physics, and time travel. "Even if you say nothing is left, I want to take a look at it. I assume it is easily accessible?"

"I've got a helicopter landing here at 0900 tomorrow morning," Boyd proudly announced. "It will be about a ten-minute flight from here. We had a little snow the other day and this will be the easiest way to get us down there and back out. We still need to bring out the equipment. I understand you helped loan us this small fortune in instruments."

"May not be a small fortune anymore if it's been sitting out in the snow." Bentham snorted as he frowned at Boyd.

"Don't worry, Ardy, we brought back the most expensive and the rest is well wrapped up and covered. We have the hard drives here with us and I want you to look at the data we have." Boyd

374 ❋ SANDS OF TIME

walked over to the corner of the room and pulled off a tablecloth that was covering some of the instruments. "I am counting on you to reconstruct what they did. Mida took some pretty good notes for a while and we can follow a lot of what they did."

The group gathered at the table to spend the next three hours in rapt attention as they carefully reviewed all the data they had. Boyd motioned for Denzee and Marybeth to adjourn with him to the kitchen. "These are the best minds in the world and I think they may leave us in the dust pretty quickly. I will wait for them to come to some conclusions, then I will rejoin their world."

The next morning, the helicopter landed right on schedule in the parking lot of the center. Boyd joined the camera crew in the first flight out to the site. After the helicopter left them and flew back to Torrey to pick up the others, the crew started filming the site from all angles. A few minutes later, the ship returned to Oak Creek with the rest of the group. The camera crew filmed the group as they landed and slowly made their search of the empty hole. They took the remaining instruments out of the tent, walked around the site, took plenty of pictures themselves, did more tests with several new instruments they brought with them, then stood around the hole and discussed what they were seeing.

The group reassembled that afternoon at the cultural center at the Orion Wingate. Denzee and Marybeth had made a huge pot of chili and several pans of special Mescalero cornbread. Knowing the Utah liquor laws and the lack of any decent liquor store within a hundred miles, Boyd had previously arranged for the helicopter to bring in a good supply of wine, beer, and a variety of liquor. The group enjoyed the makeshift feast and made good use of the large fireplace in the great hall of the center. The day had been chilly but productive.

As Marybeth was clearing the plates from the tables, Ardy set up a large white board and a flip chart easel. He cleared this throat, looked at the assembled crowd, and said simply, "Now what?"

Thomas Wayne French, known among his peers as Jugs, even though he had PhDs in physics and molecular biology, and several top awards including a recognition from the US Congress as well as the president of the United States, stood up and walked up to the flip chart. He drew a big question mark on the paper, then sat down.

"Anyone else and I'd be suing you for wasting my time. Sumner and Sandy both are well respected. I believe them. And I believe they left us for an adventure each and every one of us would give his reputation for. You ask what do we do now. I don't see that we have much choice to do anything. We have no evidence. I for one am fascinated by the data you have shown us. There are some things there that don't make sense. We have a spectrographic printout that can't be. We have data indicating a substance that doesn't exist—the material that made up the spacecraft. We haven't invented that yet, at least on this planet."

"Yes," Ardy interrupted. "We have data that tells us some unbelievable things. But these are just printouts. A third grader could make this up and print it on a piece of paper. A high school computer nerd could fabricate the video."

Jugs continued, "You hit it on the head, Ardy. This means a lot to us. But we can't dance with it. I want to stay here and do more looking at what Sumner found. But I can't see any of us going anywhere with it. We'd be laughed out of Houston and Pasadena if we even mentioned this to anyone. I don't care what reputations are sitting here in this room. We are helpless."

Billy Joe looked over his half-glasses and caught Ardy's attention. He had seen that look many times before. "Billy Joe, something is nibbling at you like a gator nibbling on a frog as you like to say."

"Folks, I agree sum total, but something still is eating at me. We have to take this somewhere. We may have a possibility. Denzee come over here." He motioned for Denzee to join them. She had been standing by the door looking out the window. She slowly walked over to where Billy Joe stood to meet her.

"Denzee, I don't pretend to know your language, but I do remember that Denzee is close to the word in Apache for beautiful maiden or something like that. Is that right?"

She muttered yes, it meant pretty one. She was obviously embarrassed.

"I don't mean to embarrass you, but your name is very appropriate. And it may help us with a breakthrough. Can I look at your ear?"

Denzee pulled back her black, gray-streaked hair. Billy Joe looked at the ear very carefully. Then he pinched the ear and asked if she could feel that. She shook her head no. He pulled out a pocketknife and pierced the ear slightly. A spark jumped from her ear to his knife blade. The ear did not bleed when he cut it. She again said she couldn't feel it. He then asked Marybeth to come forward. He went through a similar inspection of her foot. He repeated the process once more with Boyd's hand.

"Ladies and gentlemen," Billy Joe drawled as he walked up to the white board, "we may have our opening. I want to do some tests on these folks. I want to take them back to Houston and have a couple more folks look at them. I think we have evidence of our unearthly visitors. We are seeing something here that cannot be explained by any medical or biological theories on this earth. I'm not going to try and explain it here until I am a little more certain. But if this proves to be what I think it is and if it progresses the way I think it will, I think we can go public. But"—he looked at Denzee and Marybeth—"you have to be willing to do this. You will be tested and prodded and poked and violated like you never thought possible. I don't want you to answer right now. Think about it and ask me more questions tomorrow. We have plenty of time. But you are holding the dance card."

The group continued their discussion well into the night. Boyd, Denzee, and Marybeth left soon after Billy Joe's announcement. They were joined later in the big house by the film crew and the helicopter pilot. Boyd agreed to have the helicopter and film crew leave the next day. He didn't know if any of the others would be ready to fly out yet, but he wanted to get the helicopter and the media folks back to their regular jobs as soon as possible. Besides, he was footing their costs.

The group of scientists filled the board with equations and symbols for hours. They argued and theorized and shared philosophies. Billy Joe thought later that it was too bad the cameras were not still rolling since this discussion could enthrall seminars and classrooms for years. The group adjourned at midnight and reassembled at eight the next morning. They developed a plan for further study and assigned tasks for each of them. Two wanted to stay and decipher more of the test results of the entry into the ship. The rest had to return to conferences, seminars, and legislative appearances.

As the group was breaking up for the last time, ready to head to the airport to fly out, Boyd said, "I want to thank you for giving us the support we needed. We have just become part of history-altering events. More than anything else any of you have ever done. And every one of us has been a significant part of scientific history up to now. I don't know where this will lead, but I want every one of you to think about those who are not here. You all knew Sandy and Sumner. You didn't know Ev and Mida. That is your loss. I have no idea what happened to them. They may show up again or they may never see this earth, or at least this earth in the twentieth century again." His voice cracked at the last remark. "We may have a tough road ahead of us. We may be challenged and ridiculed. But we have a plan and I respect everyone here. We will stick together and we will solve this mystery. Let's keep in touch and be safe."

EIGHTEEN

Vandara

One does not meet oneself until
one catches the reflection
from an eye other than human.

—Loren Eiseley

We have it in our power to
begin the world again.

—Thomas Paine

Ev, Mida, and Sandy opened their eyes at the same time. Sarah slowly opened hers to see the others staring at her. She smiled at them, then rubbed her eyes. They felt totally relaxed and refreshed. Ev gently touched his head and found no trace of any cut or bruise. Sandy rubbed his chin and said he felt like a fifteen-year-old again. Mida reached over and kissed both Ev and Sandy and gave Sarah a big hug. Mida laughed as she asked Sarah if this was better than San Francisco.

They were standing exactly where they were when they disappeared earlier in a flash of light. Or when they left 1999. They hadn't moved from the spot they were standing, but were now in a time distant from their own by nearly two hundred million years. They would not have known anything had happened except now they saw out the windows along the walls. There was sunlight streaming in, illuminating them as well as several bright spots of light milling around the room. As Mida experienced earlier, they were the center of attention of the beings that inhabited this vehicle.

Suddenly Vandara thought-spoke to them. They turned around and saw her standing behind them. She had a much different appearance. It was more of a human-like form, like the others in the room, yet the form seemed indistinct, bathed in the bright glow of a white light with a very slight blue tinge. She said they were now back at the time she first learned they had been at the ship in the far distant future.

Ev looked at Sandy and shrugged. "I'm sorry, Vandara, but you are going to have to be very patient with us. Or at least me. I didn't understand a word of what you just said. Can we start from the beginning? I am a geologist. I study rocks and the earth. I deal with vast spans of time and know when the rock that this ship is encased in was just sand. I need you to give me some chronology of what has happened and where or when we are."

Mida giggled as she put her hand on Ev's arm. "She knows all that, sweetie. She knows everything about each of us."

"She is right," Vandara purred. "Let us come over to what you call a lounge and let's be comfortable while I discuss our situation."

They walked through a door that suddenly appeared out of a solid wall and entered a very comfortable but dimly lit room. Vandara continued, "We, that is those of us who live here, are not all of the same development. Some of us are more advanced as a state of energy, with a loss of many of our physical forms. Others are more like you, in a less-advanced energy state. I will explain all this to you in due time. Anyway, I do not rest or sit like you, but some of us need physical support, so we have this furniture. Make yourself comfortable."

They sat in the plush chairs, nearly disappearing in the velvety softness.

Vandara continued her thought discussion. She explained they had a very leisurely trip back in time. During the trip, she studied each of the four very carefully. She read their brains and cells, she told them. She had the ability to interpret each of their memories, experiences, and all their past that was stored in their cells. Mostly their brains, but all cells in their bodies have memories. She had made that survey of Mida when she came back earlier. She didn't tell them that she felt Mida was more advanced than any of the others.

Vandara had not visited the Earth-time in which they lived, the late twentieth century they called it, but she knew as much now about it as they did. She gave a few examples to prove that she understood their time, history, and culture. It was as if she shadowed their lives and read the books they read, and talked to the people they talked to during their lives. Even though there were many things they had forgotten over the years, the information was still stored in their neurons and chemical and electrical makeup. The human species had not yet unlocked the mystery of memory, but she was able to tap into it. They would soon find that there was such a large gap between their level of intelligence and hers that she would have a hard time explaining a lot of things.

"I understand you have advanced a great deal and humans are relatively intelligent compared to other forms of life on this planet. Those of you sitting before me are among the top level of intelligence of your species, but as a whole, you humans have a long, long way to come. You are at a stage where there is a great disparity. Your technology is exploding, but you are widening a gap between the most intelligent and the average people. This is a very dangerous stage. You are actually creating a new species. You have been living for a short time, roughly fifty of your years, with the ability to destroy your species and the rest of life around you. It takes time for your society as a whole to catch up with your science. I can't foresee the future, but your civilization is entering a critical phase now.

"Mida, I know you are interested in healing and social aspects of life. You are a bringer and sustainer of life. Ev, you are a scientist who studies the very earth at your feet. You are fascinated by time and I have some wonderful surprises for you. Sandy, you are also a scientist but interested in the makeup of the universe itself. You will be amazed at the physics and engineering of our vessel. And you, Sarah—"

Sarah quickly responded, "Yes, I am the odd one out. I don't belong here. These three were supposed to be here, but I got here by accident. Don't try and analyze me. I'm just an ordinary person with no special ability."

"Oh no. Don't think that. You are a very special person. You are a healer but in a more physical sense. Mida works with the spirit. You work with the body. You are a nurse and a midwife. I have learned a great deal from you. I will explain more later, but I am very pleased with how you add to this group. I will tailor this visit with all your interests."

"What amazes me," Ev said as he looked around the room, "is that you can communicate with us as you do. Not the thought waves but just the language. I'm sure you don't call this planet Earth and you don't have words like *social* and *physics*."

"Remember what I said about reading your minds and your histories. Of course, we call this something other than *Earth*. But I have the power to translate. You have an advanced intelligence, although still quite primitive to me. Any lower form of life and I would read mostly emotions such as fear or hunger."

"Well, I guess we take that as a compliment of sorts," muttered Sandy.

"It is not meant as a compliment or a put down. We have to deal with what we each are. You have nothing to fear from me or any of us. We have come on a peaceful mission, but we came knowing there was not any form of advanced intelligence on this planet. Remember we came here a million years before you existed. Right now, we have a little problem and are stuck about 199 million of your years earlier than we intended."

"You are stuck? That doesn't sound reassuring. What does that mean for us?" Sandy looked worried all of a sudden. "And I am dismayed that such an advanced life-form made a mistake."

"Let me get to that in a minute," Vandara said.

Her voice, or her thoughts, did not carry emotion, so the four had a hard time attaching emotion to what she was saying.

She took several minutes to bring them up to date on the facts of her mission. Her planet was dying. The avarnan sun was in its final stage of life, like Earth's sun would be in the far distant future. Avarnans had millions of years to evolve. Their species had advanced to a stage where they were nearly pure energy. However, they were losing the physical forms and functions their bodies had earlier. Avarnans had what humans would call supernatural powers. It was simply an eventual outcome of any life-form. Avarnans were evolving into pure energy but were not quite there yet. The pure state of life in its final energy phase would be what humans would call God. Vandara purred and said she didn't consider avarnans to be gods. Or goddesses, she added as she reached out and touched Mida. She added as an afterthought that they were aiming toward a state of perfection.

"Like that seagull, you know, the one in the book," mused Ev as he shifted to keep from disappearing in the plush chair.

"Oh, Ev, don't trivialize what she is saying," Mida frowned at him.

"No, Ev is not too far off," Vandara quickly replied. "That book dealt with serious issues of who you are as a species. It used seagulls as the metaphor, but it basically asked what you are about. You come to life to achieve perfection. This is not an easy task. You get lost in living, in surviving. As your species evolves, you master one chore, then move on to the next. Each time, you, or what some call your soul, advances toward that state which is ultimate in its design and achievement. But in doing this, you leave behind most of your kind. Look at the difficulty the seagull had in getting others in his flock to follow him. He was ridiculed. He was an outcast. He couldn't convince others, so he went on alone. My species went through that for millions of years. We didn't annihilate ourselves in the process, although I don't understand how we didn't. Anyway, you are early in your process of soul advancement if I can call it that. But you are headed in the right direction."

"Unfortunately, there are a lot of birds left back in the flock, circling in utter confusion and ignorance," Sandy said. "I remember the book and I'll admit, I envied him and in some ways, identified with him. That sounds a little egotistical, but it just seemed like so many of us just didn't get it. Or care to get it."

"Exactly my point. Evolution is a very slow process. Your species is struggling with it. The four of you are understandably impatient, but you still have a great deal to learn."

Vandara said that avarnans made it that far and left behind the strife, turmoil, hatred, and ignorance. Humans did have that positive thing to look forward to. But, she said, they had a long way to go; that brought her back to why she came to earth. The avarnans were doomed on their planet. They had the ability to travel and pass on to other life-forms what they as a species learned over the span of their existence. Their earlier expeditions of exploration discovered the planet Earth had the spark of life. It had the essential ingredients. But remember, she said, she was looking into the future just by talking to the four of them now.

When this ship that Mida and the others were calling Orion came here a short time ago, by Vandara's measure, before the four came onboard, intelligent life on Earth had not advanced very far. Vandara stopped and was silent a minute. Then she explained she had to be very careful in imposing her values because all life is precious. The life that was created here on Earth only a few million years ago, of their time measure, was complex, complicated, and interrelated. There really has been no life-form that was not part of this wonderful creation. All have a very significant part in the process, and life itself is a process. It is not about one species being able to talk and communicate and write poetry and build bridges and discover the secrets of the atom. Usually one species does break through and achieves this, but any species that gets that far and expects to go further does not do it by overpowering and destroying other life-forms. All are part of a web and we all must use each other's strengths. "Just because an eagle or a blue green algae does not possess advanced intelligence by human standards does not mean it is not intelligent. It just plays a different role in the web of life," Vandara added.

Mida held Ev's hand and whispered in his ear, "This is what my ancestors have been saying for years."

"And some of your ancestors are different from Ev's and Sandy's and Sarah's, but we will get to that later. Actually, go far enough back and you all have the same ancestors," Vandara continued. "We came to this planet to plant the seed of advanced intelligence, which was slowly being formed already. We cannot create life on other planets when some form of life already exists, but we can do some playing around the edges." With that statement, she purred, which was her form of laughing.

"So we came to your Earth about one million years before your time. We have the ability to go back and forth in time, but it isn't that easy. When we first got here, we went back ten million Earth years and did a little tinkering with some DNA. That put the spark of intelligence on track, which involved the evolution of two-legged creatures. We meant to come back to our original time and see if things were still on track, but we made an error in the time phaser. We arrived here two hundred million years before your time. We didn't know that until we landed in this huge sand pile. That is when I noticed in one of our instruments that you were nosing around our ship far in the future. I did a little tinkering and was basically playing with you. I did not come forward in time as my entire being since that is much more difficult than going back. But when you penetrated this ship, that changed things. I had to come forward and bring you back.

"You see, you are from a time when I don't exist anymore. My planet is long ago destroyed by the time of your year 1999. You are in my future. And the fact that you found this ship encased in solid rock"—she looked out the small window and pointed at the red sands—"means we didn't leave here, where we now sit."

"Man, I always wanted to time travel, but this is so weird. I am getting lost in this journey," Ev said. "You can go back but not forward in time. Or at least not forward from your real time. You came here, then went back in time, started life, then went even further back because someone pushed the wrong button."

"We did not start life. It was already started. I cannot explain the process that creates life. Even we do not fully understand that yet. We hurried up the process but actually got caught in a time warp in our travels. Travel in time is not easy and not always controllable. And, Sandy, I know you are wondering how to do that. I will get to that eventually."

"I guess right now, I could say I have all the time in the world. Or in the universe. I will wait for you to get around to it." Sandy laughed. Then he abruptly changed the subject. "Wait a minute, I want to get back to this problem of being stuck. What is going on with this ship and us in it?"

"It is very simple," said Vandara slowly. "The fact you are here means we never leave this place, at least in this dimension. We landed here by mistake. When Mida came back earlier, I took her up in the shuttle. I wanted to give her a head start and she could help me explain things to the rest of you. When it landed, it hit something in the landing bay. We had to back it out and it caught the power relay. To make a long story short, we lost power. To make matters worse, whatever we did affected our system and now it seems the chemical makeup of this sand we are sitting in is preventing us from fixing the problem. Right now, we cannot move the ship. And it is obvious that we stay here since you found the ship trapped in rock. We stay here." Her repeat of that phrase emphasized its seriousness. She seemed to be thinking about her statement as she said it.

"But you are sounding quite calm about it. That means we are trapped here, too." Sandy was getting nervous.

"Wait a second," Ev interrupted. "We came in here and you took Mida up in a shuttle and it was because of us that the ship got stuck. This can't be. We weren't here originally, two hundred million years ago. Or what was supposed to be ten million. Or maybe even one million. My god, this is so confusing. When you were here, you got stuck without us since we were not involved at all. You were sitting here for two hundred million years before we came along. Now you say you got stuck here because of us, which caused you to be embedded in rock for us to find. We come back in time and cause you to get stuck before we ever existed."

Mida burst out laughing. "Do you have any idea of what you just said? I hope you understand it because it made absolutely no sense to me at all."

"I'm afraid to say this," offered Sarah, "but I think I understand what he is asking. How could we cause this when we weren't around?"

"I understood you, Ev. You have a good point, from your perspective. You are just now being introduced to that wonderful dimension of time. Ev, you have expressed a very strong interest in time and time travel. It is new to you. And you don't even begin to understand all the implications of it. To you, it all seems quite impossible. Take my word on it. It is very complicated for your intelligence level. But you must realize you found only this ship in the future. You didn't find us did you? It has to do with time. I guess I'd better explain a little about time."

Ev interrupted, "You mean you can change the future? Or the past?"

"We can't change it, but time isn't as simple as you think. It is time for a lesson in time. You call time the fourth dimension. You are right in a very simple fashion. Time is a dimension, just like width, depth, and height. There is another dimension, too, which I cannot even begin to explain to you. And I won't even try now. As for time, it is difficult for you to really understand the full dimensions of time. We are not locked into the results of the past, present or future."

Sandy interrupted, "I have tried to understand time in my work. I work with space and our travel in it. Einstein called it space-time and I'm not sure he really understood it. He unlocked a door into the understanding of the universe, but I don't think he knew what he unlocked." Sandy took off his watch and looked at it. "By now, you know what we know about time. Are we right about what we are thinking?"

"One of you remembers a story about flatlanders. In it, you puzzle over the problem of how to explain the third dimension to a two-dimensional creature. There are beings called flatlanders who live in only two dimensions. They are visited by three-dimensional creatures. As the three-dimensional being reaches down and intersects the plane of the flatlanders' world, the flatlanders see only a hand or actually a flat line suddenly appear in their world. It moves about and appears and disappears. They can't comprehend it and call it magic."

"Yes," Sandy answered. "I have used that story many times. It makes you think about things you cannot understand due to mental limitations. To many animals, we perform magic because they just cannot comprehend things. It also reminds me of a story of people who lived somewhere near the southern tip of South America. When they first saw Europeans, they didn't recognize the huge ships as being worthy of even paying attention to. They were used to canoes or something like that and a huge ship was beyond their world. It just didn't register. When the explorers came ashore in their small boats, the natives got all excited. Those little boats were something they recognized and they saw these people as dangerous intruders and fought them off."

"I'd say that quantum physicists live in a magic world of their own. I don't understand most of what they talk about. Maybe they are in touch with two or three additional dimensions." Ev commented.

"Look at the powers shamans have. A lot of mystics and people are in tune with supernatural powers. They are ridiculed and laughed at. Are they seeing some dimensions the rest of us don't?" Mida asked. "I have been fascinated by the powers that a lot of the aboriginal cultures have."

"Mida, you are wonderfully perceptive. This talk about dimensions is very important. You are on the right track about time as another dimension, but it is not as simple as you make it out to be. I'm afraid I may not be able to fully explain all the ramifications of time. I am proof that we can move in time. I am here conversing with you and we are of totally different time periods of existence. Time is everywhere at once. Time is not a one-way street. Sandy, your scientists call it the arrow of time, meaning everything is sequential and once a second is gone it is gone forever, so you only move forward incrementally. That is not true. You are your past, present, and future, all at once."

Vandara noticed the expressions on all four faces and purred as she glowed brighter. "I have totally confused you, haven't I?" She moved to the other side of the room. "Let me try something. I'm sorry if I shock you."

Suddenly the light that was Vandara vanished, and a man walked over toward the four sitting on the couch. Mida screamed and jumped up. "Daddy!" she cried and ran to throw her arms around the young man standing there smiling.

"Hello, princess. You are a beautiful woman. I missed a lot, didn't I? I'm sorry I left you the way I did. It must be years in your time, but it is only a few minutes for me. This is a fantastic journey you are now on. I envy you. You have a task ahead of you that will make your mother and me very proud of you. Maybe someday we can talk about it. Right now, I can tell you just don't understand." He pushed Mida away from him and held her hand. She felt a warm glow from it, then he just disappeared. Where he had stood, Vandara suddenly appeared again.

"That was my father!" Mida exclaimed as tears ran down her face. "I felt him. It wasn't just an illusion. What did you do?"

"I cannot explain it. You cannot understand it right now. Just enjoy the moment." With that, the light of Vandara disappeared again and another man appeared.

"Oh my god," Ev stammered as his eyes opened wide and his mouth dropped open. "It is my father!" He jumped out of his seat as his father walked to him and hugged him tightly.

"Son, I can only be here for a few seconds. We will meet again and then we can catch up. For now, Vandara has asked me to reassure you that you will be okay. Remember the long talks we used to have about your obsession with time travel? We both had it wrong. I want to thank you for helping your mother after I left. I'm so glad she is happy again. Goodbye, Everett."

Ev tried to hold onto him, but he faded away as Vandara appeared again.

Ev stumbled as he tried to remain standing. Mida stood up and grabbed him, holding him tightly. They just looked at each other.

Before Vandara could say anything, Sandy quickly said, "Please don't bring back anyone for me. I don't think I could handle it right now. Please."

"Yes. That is enough for now. I know that was a shock and I am truly sorry if I caused pain. I wanted to demonstrate what is possible when you are fully in control of the dimension of time. You see, it is not one-directional. What is past is not gone. What is to come is not unknowable. The entire universe is energy. You and I are energy. What is energy? Sandy, you know more than anyone else here, but you really don't understand it either."

Sandy just stared at Vandara, not saying a word. His expression was a combination of total confusion and amazement.

"I'm beginning to think this is just a big dream. This cannot be happening," Ev said as he sat down, still holding tightly to Mida.

Vandara purred again as she reached out and touched Ev. He smiled as her glow enveloped him. He said, "Thank you. That helped me understand. Your touch is so reassuring."

"But our talk about time and the predicament we are in now." Sandy pressed Vandara to get back to the subject they had avoided for a few minutes.

"I tried to tell you," Vandara said slowly. "In many ways, time is an illusion. In the vacuum of space, where there is no matter, time does not exist. We have to be careful about putting a sequence on time. What you think may happen may not. You thought you saw some people from your past. Was it really your past? Or was it my ability to reconstruct from your own memory, something from your past? Or were they from your future? Remember the story of the flatlanders. Did you just see a hand reaching down from your fourth dimension, but you couldn't really understand it since you cannot yet comprehend the dimension of time?

"I told you there is yet another dimension. And it is not a theoretical dimension only used by mathematicians. Sandy, you guessed it somewhat when you think of parallel universes. That is a very simple interpretation of the fifth dimension. But I have to keep it very simple. I cannot explain it to you otherwise because you would not be able to comprehend it. There are other tracks we take, again all at once, through time. You call it a parallel universe where you continue on with a different decision or action, running through life but on a different course. There is much more to it than that, but you get the idea. For now, let's just say that we are engaged in several versions of this ship and this sand desert we are sitting in. I want to leave it there for now since you are not yet ready to get more involved." Vandara stopped and moved back and forth like she was pacing the floor.

"This has been nice for me since I love to share learning and help others understand. You are not ready to join me at my level. You have to learn to fly first and you are just taking small steps. But all in good time. Just imagine that you found a small boy from centuries before your time. How could you explain to him such simple things as shoes, televisions, computers, automobiles, and toilet paper. I want to stop here and let you digest some of what you have been told. We have a gift of time to spend together and you have a lot to try and comprehend."

Before any of them could say anything in reply, Vandara disappeared. The glow brightened, then faded away. There was nothing there. A thought appeared in their minds that said "Rest now."

Ev looked at Sandy, then Mida. Sarah started to say something, but her words faded before they came out her mouth. They sat in total silence for several seconds. Sandy was the first to speak. He said, "Look out the window. It is dark outside. We have been sitting here all day. Whatever that may mean. Who knows anymore what time is. At least by old-fashioned Earth time, it is night time now."

Mida laughed. "I just had a vision. I could see Boyd and Denzee sitting in front of the fire at Wingate Orion. Do you think I could appear in front of them?"

Ev laughed. "Why appear as yourself? Come back as Lozen or Geronimo and really scare the hell out of them. Would you come back in the past, present or future?"

Sandy looked at Mida and said, "Mida, I think you have already come back. Or gone back. I didn't say anything, but I saw you in a dream I had before we left. You were floating and had a light around you."

Suddenly, another light entered the room where they had come in through the door earlier with Vandara. It spoke to them. "Vandara asked me to come in and see to it that you were comfortable. My name is Lona. I am having some food brought in to you. This is rather difficult for us since we do not eat like you do. But we do have the ability to make some things that you do eat and will give you nourishment and renew your energy. After that, we have a room where you can lie down and sleep. Vandara said you would all be too excited to sleep, so we have something to relax your energy."

Sandy laughed as he stretched his neck muscles from side to side. "If you have the capability to relax my neurons, how about doing a little hard wiring and advance their intelligence by a few millions years? I think I am going to need it."

Lona purred, but it actually sounded more like a laugh than Vandara's. "You are having a hard time adjusting to a few new ideas? Let me give you a piece of advice. At some point, ask Vandara about something very simple. You need to remember we are beyond your experience and there are some things we have probably forgotten. Vandara is beyond a lot of the rest of us. She is very intelligent, but sometimes gets wrapped up in her knowledge. She has forgotten how to do some very simple things. Knowing how and when to adjust to simpler life-forms is part of intelligence. I don't know you and I don't have any idea of what your experience and knowledge is. But you have curiosity and a desire to learn. I can tell that by just listening to your vibrations."

Mida perked up. "Listening to our vibrations? What does that mean? Are you telling us you can read our minds, too? Vandara said she could read our brain waves and learn all the stored information we have in our minds. Is there something more? Can you hear what we are thinking?"

"Oh no," exclaimed Lona. "We cannot interfere with your ongoing thoughts. But you give off vibrations of energy that describe your state of mind. All your thoughts are personal. What we can read is experiences, facts, and bits of knowledge you have heard, said, or saw. Your thoughts to yourself are just that. Oh my, I don't know if I can explain that any better. Now I have said enough. I don't want to excite you any more than I already have. You need rest and nourishment. We know what some of your favorite foods are. We are trying to make those now. You may have to bear with us since we have to invent some of them."

"Invent our food? Now that's a new one on me," Ev smiled. "How do you invent a French fry? This should be good."

Mida suddenly said, "Oh, you know what? We had food in our packs. I wonder if they are using that. I can just see Ev's plate. A steak-sized Snickers bar!"

All four burst out laughing, while Lona expressed a confusion that she held to herself.

As their laughter died down, another light came in through a door on the far side of the room with a platter of food. Ev gasped in surprise as he looked at the heaped plates of vegetables, breads, and fruits. There was a large pitcher of a light golden liquid, which he first thought was beer, but it turned out to be more like water with a faint taste of some kind of fruit. All four of them ate like they had not eaten in days. In fact, they had not eaten in over forty-eight hours. They had no way of knowing that much time had passed in this strange new world.

"Wait a minute, Lona," Sarah perked up as she reached toward the light form. "You are different from Vandara. You say she is more advanced. Are you from the same planet, what was it, Avarra?"

"Avarna. Our star system had two planets with life. I am from the twin of Avarna. Of course, we share the same fate. There are several species on this vehicle. We are similar, but different in many ways. You might not notice the difference. Think of the advances you have made in a short two or three million years of your time. Think of what we have gone through in several hundred million years. You will learn more of this in due time. Now you eat, then rest."

Lona left the room while they ate, but after they finished, she came back and led them into an adjacent room, where each had a small but comfortable alcove with a bed and a soft music playing. They discovered a unique but effective way of relieving themselves, then they all fell into their beds and slept for over twenty-four hours. Whatever the method of relaxing their neurons, it worked very well. None of them dreamed nor even turned over in their sleep.

They were awakened by a pulsing beam of light that cast the whole area in a green glow. The four were dwarfed by a large screen filled with a picture of the Earth. It was a picture they had become familiar with as children—the Earth as seen from space. But there was something strange about this picture. The continents were not shaped as they should have been. The clouds were swirling over the globe and the oceans were blue, but the familiar shapes of North and South America, Africa, and the other continents were not there.

Ev started to say something about continental drift and Pangaea and Gondwanaland, when the scene shifted. The camera, or whatever it was, came closer and focused in on the area where they were. They zoomed down like an airplane and circled a vast expanse of desert. Red sand dunes were everywhere. Then they were sitting on the sand looking at a huge silver spaceship. Bright glows of light were moving everywhere around the ship.

Suddenly the hidden door opened and Vandara entered their room. With her was another glow but with much more distinct features. Vandara said, "I want you to meet Delsan. He is our chief engineer. He is in charge of the ship itself. Sandy, you will spend time with him. He is our master of physics, of time travel, of our energy systems."

In another few seconds, another form entered the room and Vandara motioned for Sarah to come to her. "Sarah, I want you to meet Mellon, our healer, or doctor in your language. She would like to spend some time with you." Sarah followed Mellon out the door after the doctor touched the others in a strange form of hello.

Then Delsan spoke to the remaining three. "I welcome all of you to our vehicle. We have not had many visitors. I am proud of our vessel and love to show it off. But this is not the best time to be here. We seem to have a little problem. We are working on it and hope to have it fixed soon."

Sandy stood up and extended his hand. "I don't know your customs, but we shake hands when meeting new people. I am honored to meet you."

Delsan extended his arm and a glow enveloped Sandy. Sandy fell back as a big smile erupted on his face. Sandy laughed as he widened his eyes in pleasure. "Wow. I think friendship would gain a new meaning if we had that kind of feeling when we touched another person."

Vandara purred as she said, "Let's just say it's the feeling of pure energy. It is the essence and meaning of life itself. That is what you humans have to look forward to."

Ev and Mida both extended their hands and received the same experience. Ev asked, "It was nice, Vandara, when you touched me, but the experience was not quite the same. What is the difference? And what are your reactions when we touch you?"

"Meeting any other creature is enjoyable," said Vandara. "Delsan is what we call selenar. He is actually a different species from us avarnans, but also from our planet system. I say he because his species has not yet evolved like avarnas. I don't have what you call a gender. You call me a she, meaning the female half of the species. We don't have male and female as you are used to. I am using your language and will say he or she, but it is not that simple. I will refer to Delsan as he, but I will let you call me a she, even though that is not correct. Mida, you look confused."

Mida laughed as she said, "Vandara, I have spent much of my education studying the difference between male and female and their role through history and culture. We have very distinct differences in the way male and female behave. Now you say there isn't even any difference in your race. This kind of throws me for a loop. And I won't even ask the obvious question of how you reproduce." She looked at Ev and added, "Although I'm sure it is on your mind."

"I'm on good behavior here," Ev quickly replied as he grinned at Vandara.

"We don't reproduce because we don't die like you do."

Sandy interrupted, "I don't want to get into that detail right now. I want to spend time with Delsan and get some answers that have been eating at me since I walked into this ship. I want to know what kind of power you use, what this ship is made of, how you time travel, how you go faster than light—"

"Whoa, all in good time," Delsan laughed. His laugh was more familiar. It was actually a boom as his whole form vibrated. "Vandara told me about you and your work. I want to know as much about you as you do about me. I might even learn a few things from you. You were a pioneer in early travels and primitive physics. I want to talk to you just like you would want to study an early life-form from your world. You might help us get out of this problem we are in right now."

Ev interrupted, "I hate to break this to you Delsan, but I don't think you get out. You are stuck here forever. We found your ship encased in rock this sand turned into over time. You don't get out." Ev looked at Delsan, then turned to Vandara. Both were purring.

"Ev, you haven't grasped yet what I have been trying to tell you," Vandara calmly said as she touched him. "Remember what I said about time. The past, present, and future are all intertwined. What you experienced may yet change. You discovered one of what you would call a parallel universe. You can discover another. With Sandy to help Delsan, and with both of you to fill us in on your lives and world, we may travel another path."

Sandy laughed as he rubbed his chin. "Don't expect too much from me. I had trouble understanding the physics of my time. I imagine the physics of millions of years in the future may just leave me more than a little confused."

"Well, let me take you on a tour of my vessel and we will see just how much you know already. I know you are an expert among your people." Looking at Mida, he asked, "Can I borrow your companion?"

"By all means," said Mida. She touched Sandy and whispered something in his ear that made him laugh. Then she said out loud,

"Just think of your friends sitting back at Orion Wingate wondering what is inside this bit of metal or plastic or whatever it is."

Ev watched as Sandy and Delsan left the room. He looked at Vandara and waited for her to say something. Finally, he said, "What is in store for the rest of us? You can probably guess what my wish is."

"I gave you a little travelogue this morning when you first woke. One of our shuttles came in and you got to see their view. Did that whet your appetite?"

"I thought I was dreaming. That was a live view? It came in so fast."

"You were seeing what our pilot was seeing. I told you we can go faster than light. You all seem to think that is impossible, but you will discover a lot of things that you thought could not happen in this universe. I'm sure Sandy is reeling already at what he is discovering."

Vandara looked at Mida. She said to her, "Mida, I want you and Sarah to spend time visiting with our crew, to learn more about our society and our healing systems. Sarah already has a start. Ev, I want you to explore our surroundings and find out what you can about what is out there. I will grant you your wish, but I will wait awhile before doing that.

Mida put her hand on Ev's shoulder and looked at Vandara. "I feel like we have found the magic lamp and you are the genie granting us our wishes. You obviously know mine is to learn about your culture. I have lived Ev's dream of time travel for so long, I feel like it is my dream, too. I'm not into geology like he is, but the quick trip you gave me the other day made me curious about what has happened out there." She nodded out the window as the sun shone brightly over the red sand desert.

Vandara said, "Our evolution has brought us closer to the ultimate. Everything in the universe is energy. What is energy? That gets a little hard to explain, but it is the same energy that your species has recently discovered. It is formed to make atoms, which make things, which make you and everything around us. But the pure energy. . ." Vandara paused and her glow flickered. "The pure energy is still a mystery even to us. But it is the final state we all are heading toward. When we get there, then maybe we all go to that next level. You call it heaven, I call it something else. It is a state, a phase, a something that is that great mystery."

Ev started to ask a question, but Mida gave him a look that made him close his mouth. They both knew that Vandara smiled, but neither could actually see it.

"Mida, you are a storyteller and you have thought of stories dealing with creation. You both just saw the Earth in its early form, although the creation was old and forgotten even at the time you just witnessed. Just remember it is all about evolving and learning and building on what will come naturally. You humans are very early and still quite primitive in many ways. Early on, you competed for food. You killed, pillaged, plundered, and fought quite barbarically. You still do in many ways. But you are getting past that. You still compete. Now you are competing for space, for things, possessions, religion and nationality. You will get beyond that, but you will always compete. We compete for energy. You do too but not in ways you might think."

Vandara moved and adjusted position. Ev asked, "You don't have a form quite like us. Can I ask if you get uncomfortable?"

Mida spit out a laugh. "My god, Ev, why don't we degrade a little and get personal?"

"Now, Mida," Vandara purred. "Ev has a legitimate question. I am actually like you but simply more evolved. Think of yourself compared to this Lucy that your anthropologists have dug up. Think how you are just like her yet how different as well. My physical form has shifted to be seen more as the energy it really is. You are made of the same energy, but it hasn't reached the point where it overpowers the physical form it comes in."

Ev forgot his earlier question but found another to ask. "How do you compete for energy? That is different than food. To us, food brings energy."

"Good question. No, it is much different. You have noticed my energy when I touch you."

"I feel your energy without you even touching me. It seems to just, well, just be there," Mida said as she looked down to avoid Vandara's power. Mida was beginning to feel the avarnan-like energy, as well as that of Ev, Sandy, and Sarah, but was hesitant to say it out loud.

"Yes, one of you said it was like a cloud. Do you know what an atom is made of? The components of the atom, which was formerly described as electrons orbiting a nucleus full of protons and neutrons, is simply a cloud. Of energy. It is a force that is there. We compete for that force of life. Life is a collection of energy that has that spark of life, which no one can really explain. Certainly, I can't explain it to you. It mystifies me, although I have a better feel for it than you do."

"But what do you mean 'compete for it,'" asked Ev.

"I am getting there. You are impatient, Ev."

"Just let her get to the point, Rock Boy," Mida chided.

"And you can be a little on the domineering side, Mida," Vandara said quietly.

"Ha! She has you figured out," Ev blurted out smiling at Mida.

"May I continue?" Vandara said as both Ev and Mida blushed and looked at each other.

"We compete by trying to steal the energy from each other. We do this by our personalities, by the way we use our own energy. Don't you both feel, how shall I say this, inferior right now? Don't I intimidate you, Mida?"

"Well . . ." Mida paused. "Yeah, but you should. You are much more advanced, almost like a god compared to us."

"There you go again. I am more advanced, but I am not a god. I have power over you and, if I was so inclined, could do harm to you. But we are not inclined that way. We are much more sophisticated in how we compete, but we do not use violence. We grow by using our energy to steal yours. We dominate by lessening your energy so you feel beholden to us. But even that way, we don't harm each other. We just joust for energy. More playful than anything else. I think you compete for it as well but don't even know you do it. Think about your relationships with each other or with others."

Mida almost jumped up. "What comes immediately to my mind was the power Sarah's husband had over her. I do think they loved each other but he did control her. She let him. I think he thrived on that power. Would he be draining her power to feed his, on purpose?"

"I don't know your kind well enough to say. But probably more subconsciously than on purpose. It is more like instinct."

"I've known several professors who used their knowledge to totally intimidate their students. They knew facts the kids didn't, and they used that to feel powerful. They fed on that just as if it were food."

Mida looked at Ev. "I hope you weren't one of those."

"Of course not. I never saw myself as smarter than my students. I just had a few years head start. I learned as much from my students as they learned from me."

"And that's why I love you, Mr. Humble Pie." Mida leaned over to kiss his ear.

"I think we all need to recharge our own energy. I have much to think about." Vandara's glow flickered, then she left the room.

What Vandara did not mention was what she was thinking about their future. She had been outwardly very calm and matter-of-fact about their situation with the power supply. In fact, she was very worried about what to do with her new guests. She and the avarnans could use their so-called fifth dimension to escape. But her visitors could not use this dimension. They in fact were stuck along with the ship. Or were they?

Weeks passed as Ev explored the sand dunes around the ship while Sandy spent long days with Delsan. Mida spent time with several different avarnans. Sarah spent a lot of time with Vandara and Lona. The four travelers rarely saw each other except briefly at night in their sleeping room. Ev talked geology, astronomy, and life-forms with the scientists on the crew. Mida and Sarah talked medicine and healing, sociology and mythology with the crew doctors. Sandy talked engineering, physics, and technology with Delsan and his engineers. The avarnans learned a great deal about humans and the planet earth.

Little progress was made on solving the problem of the ship's energy, but great progress was made on the understanding between these vastly different species.

Early one morning after Sandy left with Delsan, Vandara came into their room and looked out the window. Sarah had already gone off with the ship's doctor, whom she had been spending more time with. Vandara followed Mida's gaze out the window at the bright blue sky over the red sands. She glowed brightly, then said, "It is now time to take you and Ev on a time journey. You have a marvelous planet that is teeming with life. I think my home was like this once. Let's walk down to the shuttle area. I want to take you for a ride."

Ev and Mida followed Vandara through the ship. They entered the shuttle bay, which looked vastly different from the scene that greeted them when they first entered the deserted ship. The doors of all three bays were open and the sun was streaming in, reflecting red on the shiny walls. Ev squinted as he walked over to the open door and stepped outside. He shaded his eyes as he looked around him at the view in all directions. He looked at Vandara, then Mida. He smiled, then laughed. "Let's go flightseeing," he said as he looked around him at the expanse of sand that ended only at the far distant horizons.

Unknown month, unknown day

We have been here for how many days? I haven't been writing every day and sometimes, I'm not sure what constitutes a day. If the Avarnans have a daily rhythm (what is that called—a circadian cycle; I always think of the seventeen-year cicadas—do they have cicadian circadian cycles?), I can't tell what it is. I don't get tired but Vandara makes sure we do get sleep but how often, I don't know. None of us has a watch that works and I don't always pay attention to sunshine coming in the windows. And Ev says the day was not always twenty-four hours long—it was different millions of years ago. So who knows!

Sometimes I am bursting with a desire to go back and tell people about what I am experiencing. Vandara says we can't go back, so I guess our old life is totally gone. When I think about it, it really hurts, but two of my best friends are sharing this experience with me. I wish I could talk to Mom, but somehow, I know I will be able to communicate with her someday. According to what Sandy said, maybe I have been already.

I have given a lot of thought to all my research and questions. Seems pretty irrelevant now. To be wrapped up in the study of our primitive ancestors, how they thought, what part spirituality played in their evolution, how they developed, then to be fast forwarded millions of years' worth of evolution to a culture that has to be near the ultimate in power and energy—it is more than one can deal with. I keep thinking I will burn out some of my brain circuitry. This has to be difficult on Ev and Sandy in particular. The little I see of Sandy, he seems to be in heaven. Maybe he is, literally. He is learning so much but a lot of it conflicts with what he knew before. To have your lifelong learning changed or proved wrong or at least very incomplete—that is tough. Ev is sort of in-between. I think he feels trapped. He wants to travel and explore different landforms. I guess a geologist naturally feels trapped. His subject matter deals with vast time periods and to be stuck in one period, whether it's Triassic or the current era, is frustrating. Especially now that he has been able to be in two vastly different times, and to see the rock of one era being formed by sand of a much earlier era—now that's a mind bender. What's a mind bender to me is the scale of millions of years. We live for less than one hundred years. How can anyone possibly comprehend a million years, much less two hundred of those?

Then there is poor Sarah. She is keeping busy, but she didn't have the luxury or burden of anticipating something like this for months like we did. Her life just ended one day and wham—here she is in a dream world. She has taken great comfort from Sandy. I know they are sleeping together and good for her. Talk about being vulnerable and on the rebound! This is the ultimate. Ev avoided her for a while, but he has taken a very protective interest in her, although I don't know who he is protecting her from—certainly not Sandy. From herself?

Seems we have been doing a lot of study and work on some of the scientific aspects, but I have been kept very busy by several different Avarnans on the do I dare say "human" aspects of life. They have *shared with me their daily life, as it was back on Avarna and its sister planet. They actually had a couple different species. I liken it to humans living alongside Neanderthals. There was a sharing of cultures, but one always seems to come out on top. The advanced one of course. That's why I am paying attention to how we are changing simply by our being close to this unbelievably advanced culture. I swear they don't know the meaning of the word hate or anger or greed or any of those negative things. Unfortunately, they don't have much humor either, but they appreciate our humor. They see it as pleasurable, but they sure don't get the subtleties of many of our jokes. I guess some of them do have a little cutting edge, which they might see as negative. Very interesting.*

I talk about the others changing. I honestly feel I am becoming more Avarnan, losing some human qualities. Or I am reviving human qualities I felt I always had but only marginally? I don't know why I am continuing to write here. I think all this is in the past and I am beyond a lot of this. It might be helpful later in understanding this transition. I don't know what is coming or what is next, but it is truly a new life. I am ready and excited and a little scared. Shouldn't that be normal? But then what is normal?

NINETEEN

A Flight of Fantasy

Nothing abides. Thy seas in delicate haze
Go off; these mooned sands forsake their place;
And where they are shall other seas in turn
Mow with their scythes of whiteness other bays.

—*Lucretius*

The mountains, I become part of it . . .
The herbs, the fir tree, I become part of it.
The morning mists, the clouds,
the gathering waters,
I become part of it.
The wilderness, the dew drops, the pollen . . .
I become part of it.

—*Navajo chant*

Ev STOOD OUTSIDE waiting to get in the shuttle for his trip. He spent much of the past few weeks exploring the nearby sand dunes, never tiring of the monotony. His thoughts were always on the present, investigating what was at his feet. Today was different as he thought of what he was about to see. The air he was inhaling was from a time before dinosaurs reached their dominance. It was from a time when this spot of future Utah was on the equator, when the continent of North America was not yet its familiar shape. The only pollutants were from some distant volcano. Pure air circled the globe, untainted by vehicles or factories or anything else man-made. Ev took a deep breath, anticipating his dreams and wishes. He let out a shout of joy that made Mida jump. There were no echoes. The sand absorbed his voice as it absorbed his presence.

Vandara enjoyed the glee from this species she was beginning to understand. She called to Ev to come into the shuttle.

Mida walked over and grabbed his hand, bringing it gently to her lips. "Come, little boy. It's time to go see the circus and maybe even fly to the moon. Your dreams are coming true. Enjoy them while you can. We don't know what comes next."

That strange being of light known as Vandara closed the shuttle door and touched a large green crystal on the control panel. Before he could say anything, Ev noticed the shuttle was hovering quietly above the ship, which appeared huge, but which was dwarfed by the immensity of the red sand sea around it. They slowly rose higher and higher above the ground.

"Wow, look at the view," he finally squeaked as he put his face against the window. "In all directions, it is just big red sand dunes. Wait! Look over there." He moved to the edge of the window. "A lake. Look how green the water is. Oh, wow! You can tell the direction of the prevailing winds. The sand dunes are all moving in the same direction. If Dr. Davidson could only see this. He was the sedimentology professor who tried to explain the Triassic to us."

Mida watched the monitors on the control panel that showed views in all directions. "Ev, I don't see any signs of life at all. Not even a bird out there."

"Well, for starters, birds haven't evolved yet. Just the early dinosaurs. We have to wait another fifty million years or so for the first birds to appear. Think of that. Fifty million more years. *T. rex* isn't even out there roaming around yet. And look down there. It's a continent-sized desert with nothing living in it anyway. Doesn't matter that there aren't any wrens or eagles or coyotes or woolly mammoths. They wouldn't be in this desert. It is just raw earth. Oh man, can you believe this?"

"Ev, sweetie, you are drooling on the window. Look over there. That is the ocean I saw on my first trip up here. Look at that beach! My gosh, it is brilliant red sand that stretches for miles. No roads, no buildings. No expensive resorts. We sure wouldn't see an undeveloped stretch like that on any 1999 beach." Mida quickly went silent as she realized what she said. No one else would ever see such a sight. No one. Ever. Except her and Ev.

Ev looked below in fascination as they rose higher. The shoreline did in fact extend for hundreds of miles, stopping the western reach of a brilliant blue ocean that stretched in three directions to a distant horizon. It was a shoreline that was very impermanent, advancing then retreating, but on a scale of millions of years. This part of what would later be the United States was a very fickle thing geologically. There were no rivers that ran into the ocean here. Whatever water came from the distant mountains spread out and formed vast deltas and swamps in some places. In others, it just disappeared into the red expanse of sand. The waves of the sea broke on the shore in unending lines and curves that hypnotized Ev.

"See that out there?" he pointed to the middle of the ocean. "That is about where Boulder and the Flatirons now sit. Farther out is the Colorado-Kansas border. Just think of the changes that will occur down there in the next two hundred million years. My god, I can't believe it. The fish and other creatures in that water will turn into fossils that will excite anyone who finds them in our lifetime. And they are living and breathing down there right now."

Vandara touched Ev on the shoulder and said to him, "Enjoy it. You are seeing something no other human will ever see. You are seeing a planet that is unbelievably ancient by your reckoning. It is so far distant in your small frame of reference you cannot comprehend it. Yet you are seeing the very last stages of its long existence. It is living and breathing but at a rate no one can see. There has been life down there for billions of years, but you consider it still very primitive. This is one of the miracles of the universe. Life is the ultimate goal of any planet. It is amazing even to me and I have seen more than you can imagine." She moved another crystal and the shuttle moved with a speed that caused both Ev and Mida to gasp. Suddenly they were so high, they could see the entire ball of the Earth far below them.

"I want to circle the Earth for you so you can get a total view of the land and water. I know it will change significantly over the next two hundred million years, but you still know it much better than me."

For what seemed like hours, the three sightseers flew around the globe, seeing views that astronauts and cosmonauts would see in a couple hundred million more years. They flew high, then would zoom down to near the surface to look closer at something Ev or Mida would point out. But no one would ever see the continents in the configuration that Ev and Mida saw below them. Mida just shook her head in confusion, while Ev tried to identify what would be Europe and Africa and India. Mida kept saying that it didn't look like anything she knew. Ev asked Vandara if there was any way she could put latitudes and longitudes on the map that was showing on the monitor screen. She said she could, but it would not be to any reference that he knew so it would be meaningless.

Finally, Vandara told Ev he would get his lifelong wish. They were going back to the early Earth, before there was any life larger than a microbe. She explained that they needed to be moving at very high speeds to be able to move in time. Ev looked puzzled and asked how she brought them back to the ship a few days ago. It wasn't moving nor were they. Vandara's light flickered, which was the first indication, besides her occasional purring laughter, of something other than pure thought transference. She hesitated, then said that was something different. She could not explain it very well. Bringing them back was not time travel per se. It involved the fifth dimension more than the fourth.

Ev twisted his face into an expression of confusion that made Mida laugh.

"Wait a minute," Ev said as he rubbed his eyes. "You brought us from 1999 to 200 million BCE, but that was not time travel. Because we were standing still. But now you are flying around at supersonic speeds so we *can* time travel? Something strange here. Are we or are we not here and not standing back in 1999?"

"Ev, why do you keep asking these same questions?" Mida asked as she held his hand. "We are here of course. Remember that time is beyond our comprehension anyway. Right, Vandara?"

"Remember when I said there would be many things that I just cannot explain to you? Well, this is one of them. You may never fully understand all the aspects of time. It is more than just going back or forward in a straight line and seeing what once happened or will happen. There are subtle variations. You are still stuck with the idea of time as being linear. Mida, you believe that many native peoples believed time and everything else ran in cycles. Your modern scientists spend a great deal of energy proving that time is linear and one way. But then, they start with badly misplaced assumptions."

"Are Mida and I still standing back at the ship in 1999 in one universe while we are here flying around in another universe at the same time?" Ev asked as he looked at Mida.

"Ev, you have a curiosity that is very valuable and will help you when we get back. I will just let you wonder for now. Now hang on."

Suddenly there was a flash of light and a sensation of intense pressure that knocked Ev against Mida and Mida against the wall. The scene below them suddenly changed. They were looking down on vast expanses of water, partially hidden by enormous banks of clouds, with no land in sight. As they descended to the Earth's surface, they came through layer after layer of clouds, moving between towering cumulus thunderheads that threw jagged bolts of lightning in all directions. The clouds changed colors from brilliant white to orange, pink, then to blue and purple. As they passed towers and mountains of cloud formations, Ev realized these tropical clouds must have been over sixty thousand feet high. It was almost psychedelic as they moved through changing shapes and colors, all the while seeing glimpses of blue sky and blue ocean beneath. They finally broke through the clouds as they hovered just above rolling whitecaps of a blue ocean.

Skimming over the surface for a few minutes, Vandara pulled the shuttle back up to a height of several miles above the surface. Ev recognized nothing at all. Finally, they came over land, but it was totally barren of life forms. Towering volcanoes burst up from long chains of mountains, with rivers and canyons cutting jagged valleys and gorges in the browns and tans and blacks of bare rock. There was no color green or any evidence of plants on the land. As they hovered above the mountains, they saw violent eruptions of fiery red lava bursting from the tops and sides of mountains, cascading down into boiling rivers of moving, liquid rock. Steam exploded from this bubbling mass as it tumbled down the cliffs into the ocean waters. Mida shouted when she saw a meteor explode onto a cliff to their right. It was like an artillery shell, but long before mankind had invented such a pale imitation of the explosive force of nature.

Ev stared out the window with his mouth open, unable to say anything.

Mida chuckled, then reached over to touch Vandara. She felt a jolt of energy as she made contact. She asked Vandara if they were witnessing creation itself.

"Every moment is a moment of creation," Vandara answered. "There is the wonderful force and miracle of creation constantly, but we usually don't see it or understand it. Mida, you are a storyteller. You dream of weaving the many stories of creation with the facts of what actually happened and how your species responded to it. You are also what you call a goddess in the sense of being able to channel this creative energy to influence others, but you don't realize it. You studied gods and goddesses and their myths as you attempted to understand how they fit into your stories. Now you can tell this magnificent story."

Mida looked at Vandara, then looked at Ev, still mesmerized by the view he had always dreamed of. She looked out the window and put her hand on Ev's shoulder.

Mida started speaking, almost as if in a trance. "Life didn't start down there on the Earth's surface. It always was there. The human species doesn't understand what life is. For us, on this planet, we started as a collection of stardust. Stardust and sunbeams and an explosion of life bursting forth. It was a frenzy of power and energy, pent up in lonely isolation for half of eternity. Moving billions of years across a frozen universe, from one history to another. We ponder how it began and our best scientists form theories that stretch intelligence. They guess and they calculate, but they miss the point. It is all life. The entire universe is alive. Life is energy and life is forever. It never stops and it never began. And, Vandara, you as a new observer of Earth life and a seasoned observer of life in the universe, understand it will never end. That is why you came here, to give it a gentle nudge and lead it to the form you know and love."

Mida returned the surprised look Ev gave to her, then continued. "The human species was born in fire and fury. We began in a simple form, but connected with everything. That is what we have failed to understand. Life isn't just flowers and chipmunks and hummingbirds. Life is the energy that everything shares. It is an intelligence that permeates everything made of electrons and photons and the universe that makes up each individual atom. The story on this planet earth begins with bare rock. It was nurtured with sunlight and rain. It grew in the seas and silently crawled around in the rocks. It changed and adapted to every nook and cranny that it could find. It hasn't ended with humans and humans aren't the pinnacle of the story of life. We aren't the only ones to understand it. All forms understand and communicate. We just don't have the ability to understand forms besides ourselves. And most of the time we don't understand ourselves. All life is so precious and it is all so interrelated. We look for the truth of myth, of what beings started life and control it. We are all the mind of God. Collectively, we are God, each of us a tiny piece of the grand orchestra.

"We give the life on Earth a name. We call it Gaia, after the Greek earth goddess. But it is not just those things that grow and die. Earth itself is alive. The sunshine lights and gives life to the seas and the basic forms of life. The nutrients of the rock and earth itself contribute to the breathing of the atmosphere. The seas exchange water from clouds to rain and snow, carrying the energy of life from sky to water to soil to plants to animals and back in one big cycle. Earth is indeed alive and we are such a small part of it. Humans as well as avarnans have the audacity to think they each are the apex of intelligence. How do we measure the intelligence of the plankton in the sea, of the thousand-year-old redwood tree, of the humpback whale? Every cell of every living creature, as well as the rock of Earth itself and the water in the seas and in the clouds that encircle the Earth, carries with it the intelligence of the entire universe. Just because one may not understand the language of the Inuit or the Mandarin Chinese or the cry of an eagle doesn't mean they aren't intelligent. It means one's intelligence is still far from complete. My ancestors understood more than we give them credit for. We understood the interconnectedness of life. We know that all life is a small part of the whole. Why do you think we believed the coyote to be a symbol of stealth and humor? The eagle representing strength and courage? The hummingbird a sign of joy and happiness? You were starting to talk to the raven. You instinctively knew the raven meant knowledge, a bringer of life. We are all intelligent life; it just comes in different forms."

Mida took a deep breath and smiled at Ev. He continued to just stare at her.

"Oh, silly, will you get a grip?" Mida reached over and gave Ev a kiss on the cheek. "It is still me. I am not possessed by some mysterious force. I don't know why I said all that. I suddenly had an epiphany that made everything come together. There is a big story there that I need to develop into the epic I once told you about. Do you think I can develop that into a story?"

"Yeah," Ev said wistfully. "But who are you going to tell it to?"

Vandara lit up the console as she flickered brighter, then dimmer. "You may be surprised how you will be able to teach others. You will begin the myths that will create a civilization. And I am impressed that you understood what you are seeing. You are a teacher yourself Ev. You love a quote that says to teach is to learn twice. Don't you feel the same thing, Ev?"

"Actually, I was thinking along those lines as I was watching the scenery below. But I was so awed by the sheer visual force of it,

I didn't put it together like Mida did. I do have to admit, seeing the world from this perspective is very interesting to me."

Ev then began his own story. As a geologist, he always focused on minute details of rock chemistry and structure, yet he had to step back and see landforms and continents. Smiling, he said, "I see the ultimate view of continents now, the ultimate in detachment. And perception certainly is reality as they say. We humans of the twentieth century study the Earth from a very close-up view. A microscopic scientific view."

Ev admitted he had a very narrow window of observation. "We explain history in millions of years when few among us have any concept whatsoever of a century, much less even a millennium. That is insignificant from a whole-Earth perspective."

He looked out the window again and expressed awe that he had just seen changes that occurred over a billion years. That overwhelmed any form of reality he dealt with for his short intellectual span of only a dozen or so years.

"My god, I am not prepared to analyze and comprehend any of this," he said. "And, Mida, how does this relate to civilizations and culture? Any civilization is so small compared to what is out there."

Before allowing Mida to say anything, he looked at Vandara and asked her, "And by the way, Vandara, what do you mean about teaching others and creating civilizations? The past year, we thought a lot about this, about telling others about our discovery. No one will believe us. We will be treated as madmen. Or worse. What aren't you telling us? Do you drop us off in the future, after we destroy our old civilization?"

Vandara's light flickered. "There are so many things I am not telling you, I don't know where to begin. Let's take things one step at a time. Remember I said you have to learn to walk before you can fly. You are of this earth. You need to understand what you are and how you belong to this force you call life. But you have to understand about perception. Ev, you are right about seeing things in a different light. What you are seeing is based on the senses you have. You don't see many of the things I perceive down there.

Your eyes see things differently than other beings, even on your own earth. Do you think a snake or firefly sees the same things you do? Of course not. What is it you are perceiving? It is simply the existence and movement of what you call atoms and their components.

"Ev, you have a saying 'if a tree falls in the forest and you are not there to hear it, does it make a noise?' What is your thought on that?"

"I don't know," Ev said as he looked absentmindedly out the window. "I have played both sides of that one. Of course, it creates sound waves, but without an ear to hear the vibrations, then you could say there is no noise. So the answer is both yes and no."

"Well, let me complicate your life a little. It not only does not make a noise, but if you are not there, there is no forest to begin with, much less a tree to fall. Your observation is what makes reality. Look down there below us."

Vandara turned the shuttle so the window was facing Earth. "If no one was at the creation to observe the earth or anything else, then all possible results were created side by side at the same time. There are unlimited possibilities of what can and will happen. Our observations are now determining the past. But there is no fixed past. Mida this helps answer some of your questions. There is no such thing as the absolute present. What is present to one could be the past or future for another. There is no definite future—it is determined by intelligent beings. Every observation is the start of a wave to the future and is the receiver of a wave from the past. Your brain is the device that enables you to determine the future and resonate with the past. The past and present exist side by side as well as the future. If the waves resonate or match, then that probability is the actual happening."

Mida smiled and threw up her hands. "Like you think I am going to understand any of this?" She laughed and then added, "It does remind me of a quotation from St. Augustine. It was something like this: 'If you ask me what time it is, I don't know. If you don't ask me, then I know.'"

At the mention of St. Augustine, Ev thought about something he read in his extensive research recently. This concept of time and the universe was not new. Parmenides, a Greek, thought of space and time in a metaphysical sense. St. Augustine thought about it from a theological viewpoint. And Einstein thought about it from the science of physics. All these great thinkers viewed time as an illusion. There was very little difference between past, present, and future. This concept allowed for no free will, no determinism. It caused much discomfort in religion and science, since things or events didn't happen by causality, they just were. Ev loved this philosophizing but was far from understanding what it all meant. It was certainly beyond his understanding before, and was even more confused now. As he stared at the oceans below him, he started to drift off into his confusion over space-time when Vandara brought him back to the present, whatever that was.

"Very good. You both will become visionaries. You will successfully match far distant waves. Understanding what will happen in the future is not really that difficult. Some of your people, I believe you call them shamans and seers, have been able to do this. They have been ridiculed by much of your society since the science behind it is not understood. It is simple for me, but it uses years and years of experience and learning that you don't have yet. Mida, you are a shaman and seer in training. You may know it or you may not. But you have the powers I am talking about. You need to tend them and nurture them. Ev, you have to help her."

Before either could respond to Vandara, she continued, "Getting back to your points about reality, Ev, reality is the past that agrees with your memories. The knowledge of a single happening, not tied into other events, is not knowledge at all. Knowledge without a memory of the past and an expectation of the future is not knowledge. Real knowledge is the relationship of the past to the future.

"Mida is right. Life permeates the universe. Each form of life is a universe unto itself. All life is interconnected. You break one thread and it unravels in ways we are unable to comprehend. Every atom in your brain is connected to every other atom in the entire universe. Your scientists who grasped the primitive understanding of the planet itself being a living organism were very perceptive, even if they never did fully put together all the pieces of that giant puzzle. Your species has not understood this very well. As a matter of fact, you have done your best to destroy this connection. On your planet, and mine as well in the early years, there were mass extinctions. Catastrophes that did immense damage to these interconnections. But that also is part of the story of life. The ability of life to respond to this disruption adds new twists and turns to the overall evolution."

Ev interrupted, "Well, help me understand this mess we humans are making in our twentieth-century. If there have been mass extinctions before and it was part of Earth's evolution when we weren't even around, then why is it so bad that we are creating our own mass extinction now with our lifestyle?" Ev looked at Mida as if he was proud of asking the question.

Vandara adjusted the speed of the shuttle, making it hover in one spot much higher than it had been for a while. "It is bad in the sense that one species is causing it due to short-sighted greed. But I use the word *bad* carefully. As you have heard before, nature is amoral. There is no good or bad. It is bad for your species since you are working yourselves out of a job, so to speak. Some of your activists, if I use that word correctly, think you are ruining your ecosystems. Ruining nature. Well nature cannot be ruined. Life is whatever is there and you cannot destroy it. Only nature itself can destroy it. On my planet, our star is destroying it. I should say changing it. But until your sun engulfs this planet in its death throes in the future, your species cannot destroy life. You may destroy your place in it, so it ends up being bad for you. But nature or life will adapt and do quite well, thank you. As a matter of fact, who says your species, or mine for that matter, is the ultimate highest life-form? You said this a few minutes ago, Mida. We avarnans understand and agree with what you said. We have had a long time to learn humility. We stand in awe of our planet every morning. Or we used to." She transmitted a deep sorrow—emotion that she had not communicated in her conversations until then.

"There is no guiding hand that we know of, nor is there some end objective of my life or of your planet Gaia. This has been the subject of eons of questions by all intelligent life-forms throughout the universe. We see evidence of intriguing clues there might be, but if there is, no one has come forward to claim the title of king or god. I've come to the conclusion life is one gigantic roll of the dice, regardless of your Mr. Einstein's reluctance to accept that.

"My planet is being destroyed, but in reality, it is only being rearranged. The new form won't have a memory of the past, at least that we can understand, but this universe is billions upon billions of years old and it has undergone many transformations. You are made of stardust as Mida just said. That is true. Your very form and the form of what you see down there is just recycled energy. It has the experience of being former Evs and Midas and mastodons and *T. rexes*. And avarnans. That is the magic we don't understand or most certainly don't appreciate."

Vandara slowly lifted the shuttle higher and higher, until Ev noticed Earth had shrunk to where it filled the entire window, with the black of space outlining its edges. From what he remembered of pictures of Earth from the moon, they must be halfway to the moon.

Mida gazed out the window, lost in the infinite expanse, her mind floating like the blue and white ball below. She looked at Vandara and said slowly, "Vandara, you said a while back that I was a goddess and didn't know it. What did you mean by that? Or my being a shaman. Just because I got a sudden vision and started that story?"

Ev and Mida both looked at each other as they suddenly heard a series of clicks coming from Vandara. This was a sound they had not heard before and they couldn't tell if it was coming as thoughts or as actual sounds. Vandara didn't say anything in their thoughts for several moments. Her light seemed to fade slightly, then it started to turn color to a pale green.

"Vandara, are you okay?" asked Mida as she reached out to touch the form of light.

"Yes, I am fine," she finally said. "I have been debating with myself how much to tell you. Actually, I hadn't made up my mind yet, but I think I just now did. Mida, I called you a goddess because you have the power to form opinions. You are a natural leader, a seer, a holy person. You have goodness in your heart and have spent your life learning how to heal, how to nurture and improve life. You are concerned about how people act together and help each other. You studied gods and goddesses in your journey. How do you define goddess or god?"

Mida thought a minute, then shrugged, letting out a deep breath. "I'm not sure I have really come to any conclusions although I certainly have thought about it. Yes, I talked about spirits and creation myths and those that are worshiped as creators. I guess a goddess is a creator, but one that is the original creator. We all create, at least those of us that create children by a pretty natural act." She smiled.

"But there is more to it, isn't there?" She looked at Vandara for a reaction. Getting none, she continued. "To me, a goddess should embody goodness and kindness. She should set the example for all to follow. I'm not big into hero worship, but she should take this worship she will naturally get and turn it into worship by all of all. A goddess is all-powerful but just as humble. Certainly not the jealous, egotistical, thunderbolt-wielding god that leads warriors into battles of destruction that so many religions throughout history have portrayed."

Ev added his thoughts. "I wonder if a god or goddess is the ultimate scoutmaster. You have to get others to believe in what you have created. Also to reach the end goal that you had when you created everything in the beginning. I don't know. A good leader often has to punish wrongdoers, so what happens when people don't follow god? Doesn't there have to be some mechanism for correcting incorrect behavior?"

"You as god have defined what is correct, right?" Mida looked out the window at the earth slowly spinning below. "I think you lose some of your righteousness if you want to call it that, if you resort to any form of unkind acts to alter someone else's behavior."

"The end justifies the means or doesn't it?" asked Ev as he felt a deep division coming between Mida and him. They had many philosophical debates over the past year, usually ending in an agreement to disagree.

Vandara said, "It is an interesting concept, isn't it? The reason I brought it up is that you will have a lot of time to think about it. You two are creators and will function as a god and goddess, if you so wish. I haven't told you about my dilemma because I was not sure how to resolve it. You found our ship in the rock cliff of your time. That meant we did not leave which also means you did not leave once you came to see us. But there it gets complicated. You are trapped in one universe. The one you see out that window."

All three glanced out to see Earth slowly increasing in size as they came closer.

"I and my crew have the power to leave, but you cannot come with us. I have to decide what to do with you. I have now decided."

Ev and Mida just stared at Vandara. Neither said anything. Vandara adjusted the crystals again and they went through the jolt of moving in time. The inside of the shuttle began to reflect blue as they neared the ocean surface. The shuttle skimmed over the surface so close that Ev and Mida could see the individual waves. Soon the reflection turned red as they passed over the red sand desert. Before anyone could speak again, the shuttle landed on the sand just outside Orion.

"Vandara, you should be in show business," Ev said as he bit his lip. "Your timing is exquisite. You aren't getting away with this, though. I'm not moving until you tell us what you decided."

Mida rubbed her eyes, then took a deep breath. "I'm sorry. This trip is so ridiculous. Vandara, you surely understand the absolute unbelievability of what has happened to us. We are just two ordinary people who stumbled onto something by accident over a year ago. We have gone through life-changing experiences, climaxing when we entered a space ship from another world and another time. Now you say we will become gods because you can't take us with you as you somehow leave, although you never actually left when we found you. I'd hate to have to put that into a story."

Ev cleared his throat and said rather defiantly, "I'm still not moving until you spend a little more time filling in a few details."

"What do you wish to know?" said Vandara as she started putting things away. She pushed a button which opened the door. A blast of hot air entered the shuttle as a breeze whistled through the opening.

"For a start, are you the gods that created life on this planet?" Ev blurted out.

"Oh my, no! I tried to tell you that before. We cannot create life. Life is present already throughout the universe. Weren't you listening when I talked about life?" Vandara pressed the button again and the door slowly closed. Cool air started blowing over them and all the lights went out. "Okay. Let's start from the beginning."

The red glow of the desert reflected on the inside of the shuttle. The light that was Vandara glowed an eerie red.

Vandara slowly said, "Let's start from the beginning and review the situation. Forgive me if I have assumed more than I should. I thought you were understanding what was happening."

She related the facts once again for these two frightened earth beings. Since her planet was probably uninhabitable by now, she had nowhere to return to. She and her crew left years ago on a final mission to visit other planets that they knew or suspected of abundant life.

The ship came here at a point Ev and Mida measured as one million earth years before their time. After Vandara arrived, she and her crew went back ten million years in time and tinkered with DNA to put the spark of advanced intelligence into life-forms that were the ancestors of humans. Then when they started to return to the time of their arrival, one million years ago, they had a time error. They landed two hundred million years ago by mistake and that is when Ev, Mida, Sarah, and Sandy arrived in the ship. They intended to check on the progress of their earlier tinkering but didn't make it there yet. They still intend to. Vandara admitted that is where Ev and Mida now come into the avarnan's plans.

"That is what I meant by your being a god and goddess. You will be the original humans."

Mida interrupted quickly. "Wait a minute. You misjudged somewhere along the line. There were already original humans. We are here right now, which proves that since you only just got here, we evolved without you. We can't go back and start something that was already here."

"Oh, children, you just will not be able to understand. You are not comprehending the properties of time. Remember what I said about it being past, present and future all at once?"

Ev reached down and fingered his belt buckle. Holding the buckle in his hand, he asked, "Is this metal that was made in my life time of the twentieth-century USA?"

"It has always existed, but let's not get into that," Vandara said. Both Ev and Mida sensed an irritation in the manner of Vandara's last thought. "This discussion is over for now. You go back and rest. Then think about our earlier discussion while we were circling Earth. Think about what life is and how your species fits it. I will visit with you later and describe in detail what your plans will be. And while you are at it, think about whether it was accident or design that the jets flew by right when Ev was watching the cliff, the rock fell and exposed our vessel, and Ev found Mida exactly when he did. Is all that pure chance? Think about it. I leave you with that."

"You can't leave us like this!" exclaimed Ev.

"I could leave you in a much worse shape." Vandara motioned for them to leave.

Mida climbed out of the shuttle as soon as Vandara opened the door. Ev followed, staggering a little as he shuffled through the red sand. He reached down again to pick up a handful of hot sand and let it sift through his fingers.

Ev and Mida walked to the open bay door, looking back at the shuttle sitting in the sand. A strong wind was starting to blow, moving grains of sand at their feet. They looked up and noticed dark clouds coming in from the north. There were flashes of lightning that were more intense than anything Ev had ever seen.

Ev started to complain about the way Vandara left them hanging, but Mida put her hand over his mouth. "She is in control. We are powerless right now. Regardless of being a god or goddess, we have no choice but to let her tell us in her own way and time."

Ev stared at the shuttle, lost in thought. He mumbled, "She better get that shuttle back in here soon. It could get buried in the sand in minutes when this wind really hits. As a matter of fact"—he looked at Mida—"this entire ship could be buried very easily in a night's time."

Mida nodded in agreement. "I remember my dad telling me a story of when he crossed Wyoming once in the winter. He got caught in a blizzard and the car was completely buried in a snowdrift. He pulled off the road since he couldn't see to drive. He fell asleep and woke up later with the VW encased in snow. He rolled the window down and literally swam out through the snow. It was only a few inches to the top of the drift, but he was completely buried. I guess a good strong wind can do wonders with snow or sand."

"Kind of makes me wonder if this place has ever seen snow. I think we are pretty close to the equator now. Or at least much closer than Utah is." He jumped as a lightning bolt hit close to the ship. "This is Utah, isn't it? Boy, this is so weird."

Mida put her arms around Ev as they stood there watching the storm. She wondered what a goddess would say at a time like this.

Sometime after

A lot to think over. How about an understatement of all time? I am convinced now no one will ever read these words, but I feel better writing them. Always before, writing this has helped me put things in perspective. How do I put all this in perspective? I keep thinking this is just a dream, but what a dream! This journal is left in the shuttle. I wasn't. Unless my bones dissolved to nothing. Maybe that is possible in two hundred million years. But then, what about fossils? The journal is valuable to whoever finds it, but then, who finds it? Will Sumner get the door open again and read these words? Hi, Sumner. Hi, Mom.

Vandara says we will become gods. Yeah. And I am a shaman in training, whatever that means. Explain that so I can understand it. All I wanted to be was a PhD. Then I got my ticket punched and maybe I could guide a few students studying under me. I don't plan on guiding a civilization. A goddess? Now there is an ego trip. Do I now have supernatural powers where I can throw a lightning bolt at those miserable little humans that Vandara created? If Vandara cannot explain this to Ev and me, how can we understand enough to be all powerful? And where do Sarah and Sandy fit? Are they goddess and god as well? Do we all create descendants who turn into us in a million or two hundred million years? I couldn't even talk to Ev about any of this after our trip. He seemed so stunned, I worry about his sanity. But then mine isn't in tip top shape right now either. I think back to our rather humdrum life back home. We worried about income taxes and traffic and what to cook for supper. Sarah worried about her husband who diddled his secretary. Now if she is a goddess, she can fry that weasel husband. But we must be good and set good examples. She will turn him into a snake and watch him slither away. Time to go to sleep, as if that is possible. Maybe I can dream an answer. After all, I am Mida, Mother of Mothers. Give me a break.

TWENTY

Goodbye

Let us unite, let us hold each other
tightly, let us merge our hearts,
let us create for Earth a brain and a
heart, let us give a human meaning
to the superhuman struggle.

—*Nikos Kazantzakis*

Imagine a place on Earth so awesome,
So vast, so pure,
We can hardly breathe its air.
Imagine the Earth alive with morning,
Shimmering white nights,
No end of sky
No end of sea.

—*Carole Forman*

THE AVARNANS INCREASINGLY worried over the failing power supply in the ship. Sandy, absorbed in scientific curiosity, spent the last several days with Delsan and other crew members crawling through tubes and crystals, in and out of walls, floors, ceilings, and even digging through the sand underneath the belly of Orion. Something suddenly changed for the worse after Vandara left in the shuttle that morning. Delsan didn't call her and ask her to return to the ship, but he wanted to. Sandy was still learning the details of their power system, but he partly understood why it was having problems. This vast expanse of sand was the culprit, preventing the repair of a simple accident weeks earlier.

Sandy was receiving first-hand training in laws of physics and matter that he previously thought were impossible. When he rode the shuttle with Delsan to Mars and back, he experienced how it was to travel faster than light. Actually, it wasn't physical speed that exceeded the speed of light, but travel in space-time that gave the same effect. He breathed a sigh of relief when Delsan explained this. Sandy fretted for days over how Einstein could have been wrong. It turned out Einstein was wrong on several things but not the speed of light. That was a technicality, though. Sandy still had trouble with the physics of space-time. He thought about how quantum mechanics altered greatly our view of reality. Now these new laws altered it even more. Shaking his head, he said he couldn't argue with reality, even if he didn't understand it.

As he and Delsan finished one particularly intense discussion about physics, Sandy thought about his studies long ago in classical physics. Equations didn't care about positive or negative time, he remembered one teacher saying. He asked what negative time was. Negative time was the past. The argument went something like this: if the past determined the present, then to keep things symmetrical and in balance, the future would also have to determine the present. He thought about one memorable discussion in a conference of physicists where Richard Feynman and John Wheeler, two of the most prominent physicists of the midtwentieth century, talked about point charges. These mysterious charges radiated out to distant objects, then were radiated back to before the original charge was made. It was a case of future behavior of a distant object determining a past event. The implications made Sandy's head spin, but he couldn't shake off the meaninglessness of such theoretical musings. His career dealt with the real world and real physics problems, not theory. Maybe he was in the midst of these point charges in Orion and with the avarnans. He thought about asking Delsan but decided not to. He didn't want another six hour discussion about things he would never fully grasp. Past, present, future. He now lay awake at night trying to figure out the difference in these once perfectly understood concepts.

There was another reason he lay awake nights. Sarah was usually in his bed with him. Sarah was the odd person out in this adventure. Ev and Mida were always in conference with an avarnan. Sandy was engrossed in constant conversation about engineering, physics, and power systems. All three of them planned to be here. They wanted to be trapped in this fantastic situation. Sarah was caught here by accident. Not that she wanted to be anywhere else. Her life in San Francisco had been turned upside down, destroying her comfortable career as nurse and wife. She loved nursing, and until that terrible day, she thought she loved her husband. At first, Sandy tried to console Sarah as a kindly uncle would. It quickly turned more passionate as each of them realized their lives were completely changed and whatever rules there used to be, they were now shattered.

Vandara knew of the situation with Sarah, but this advanced being was still learning about a primitive species and their strange emotions. She wanted to spend more time with Sarah, but was occupied with the power crisis of the ship. Sarah spent her days sharing medical information with several different avarnans. Not knowing what was to happen to her, though, made concentration difficult for her. It seemed natural to her in this strange situation to form an attachment with Sandy, even if he was old enough to be her father.

On this stormy day, with thunder echoing across the desert expanse outside, Sandy walked out of the main engine room and noticed Ev and Mida walking down the hall toward him. They both had a strange look on their faces.

"You look like you swallowed a mouse." He grinned at them and hugged them both. "Seems like I haven't seen you in a long time, whatever time is. What have you been doing?"

"Oh, not much," Ev smiled. "Just going on the ultimate adventure ride of all time. Vandara just took us for a little shuttle trip out to the moon and back. And we went back a billion or two years in time and saw the Earth in its infancy. Just a typical day's work for a field geologist."

"Yeah, and you are just so calm about it all, aren't you?" kidded Mida as she glanced back at Ev and grabbed Sandy's hand. "Sandy, it is more than anyone could dream of. We have traveled and seen things that I will never be able to comprehend. You will have to talk to Vandara and see if she can take you and Sarah on a trip like that."

"You forget that I took a flight to Mars the other day. But none of us will be taking any more trips for a while." Sandy looked worried but didn't go into detail then about the latest power problem. "And don't underestimate what I have seen lately. I haven't exactly been sitting at the kitchen table reading comic books myself," Sandy said as he motioned them into a large but empty room off the hallway. "Recognize this?" he asked as he looked at the small window at the end of the room.

"Is this the room we first looked into from the outside?" Mida asked as she ran her hands through her hair. "My gosh, I can't believe it. It is, isn't it? It seems like years ago." She walked over to the window and gave a yelp. "It's almost covered with sand. It's only an inch below the window. The ship is being covered up."

"Yeah, the sand is what's giving us problems. I think the silicates and iron oxide are messing up our generators. And the weird thing is this ship is made of silicates among other things. It is doing something to the magnetic pulses and ionic translators. I can't believe how simple their power system is. It took me a while to figure it out but once I made a major paradigm shift, it was very easy. Their power is from the most basic energy source. It is atomic but not nuclear in the radioactive way we think of it. But somehow the sand is plugging the system and we can't seem to unplug it. It is actually short circuiting it."

"But it's not affecting the shuttles. We were able to travel around the Earth in one."

"And I went to Mars and back. The shuttles were fine, but I think they are in trouble now, too. They need recharged from the ship's main power source and they can't be now. But even when the shuttles worked, the avarnans couldn't do anything but putt-putt around our solar system for a few trips. It's like us being able to use the golf cart to go to the store but the cart doesn't work to get us out of the county. The shuttles are probably good for another short trip to the store and then they are history if we can't get the big ship energized."

Mida slid down the edge of the wall as she sat on the floor. "But why are you even fiddling with the ship. We know it doesn't make it. We are here. That is proof that they and you never get anything fixed. If you fixed it, then you wouldn't be here because the ship wouldn't be here. Or there."

"Oh god, don't get started on that again," Ev mumbled as he followed Mida to the floor and plopped next to her. "I still don't understand why they don't have simple things like chairs," he said as he shifted against the wall.

Sandy walked over to the window just as the first grains of sand started to cover the bottom. The wind was howling outside as dark clouds showered the landscape with lightning bolts. Sandy rubbed his chin, a nervous habit that was getting more pronounced, then looked at Ev.

"Ev, why aren't you growing a beard? It's been days, maybe even weeks, since I've shaved, but no stubble. And, Mida, I don't want to get personal, but have you had a . . ."

Mida cut him off with a wave of her hand. "No and I have lost track of time anyway. I don't even want to think about it. I'm probably pregnant and this kid will actually be my great-great-to-the-ten-thousandth-generation-grandfather. Figure that one out. Sarah hasn't either. Speaking of Sarah, where is she?"

"Right here," Sarah said as she walked in the door. "I heard voices in here. And don't worry about me. I am pregnant in case anyone is interested. Congratulations, Sandy." She walked over and hugged Sandy.

"Wait a minute. Not by me. I—" Sandy stuttered as he rubbed his chin. "I was fixed years ago. Snip, snip, and I am safe to wander the streets." He looked at Ev.

"Whoa, don't look at me. Sarah, tell them it couldn't have been me."

"You are off the hook, Ev. Mida, you know I wouldn't."

Mida put her arm around Sarah. "Are you sure you're pregnant? Something strange is going on and I haven't—"

"I'm a midwife. I ought to know these things. I could tick off all the symptoms."

Sandy walked over and sat down next to Sarah, propped against the wall. He cleared his throat, then started. "It could be me, I guess. Stranger things have happened." He put his arm around Sarah. "Whatever else is going on with us there is nothing we can do. I think that same feeling of helplessness is affecting the avarnans. Even though these people are extremely advanced, they really are trapped. I've noticed Vandara is pretty tight-lipped, if she even has lips, but Delsan opens up to me a lot. He is nearly in a panic. They are essentially the last of their species. There are no rescue ships. If they are in trouble, we are too. We know they don't leave here, but I haven't seen anything resembling our own bones. What happened to us? What will happen to us?"

"You talk about helplessness. Well, we have no choice but to just wait and see what happens. Why worry about it. We die somehow. We would have died eventually anyway, so what's the difference? Would you trade this experience for another twenty years back in the year 2000?" Sarah gave Sandy a peck on the cheek.

Mida was absentmindedly tracing the faint pattern on the floor with her fingers. She said slowly, "Vandara took us back in time in the shuttle but said she had to be traveling at pretty high speed to be able to do that. I don't understand how we were brought back in time to here. Vandara wouldn't even try and explain it. Do you have a clue?"

"You need to understand a little quantum physics and a little of their mysterious fourth and fifth dimensions. Most physicists in our time think time travel is impossible, but those that keep a faint hope alive for it still say you need to be moving and somehow tag onto the energy of a black hole or something like that. No one knows. Or knew. Remember when Vandara brought back an image of your father?"

"It looked like more than just an image to me," said Ev.

"I don't know. I still think she was playing mind games with us. She conjured up a very faithful image from your memory cells or whatever stores your thoughts. In a way, that is not time travel, but it is some overriding presence of our being. That gets beyond my physics-oriented scientific mind and into metaphysics, which is not my expertise. Matter of fact, metaphysics is beyond science and lacks a lot of credibility with the crowd I ran around with all my life. We are more than just what appears in this body."

"No. I don't buy that. I never saw or met Mida's father, yet I saw him. She never met my father, but she saw and heard him. Isn't that right?"

"Good point. I didn't know them either, yet I saw and heard them, so it can't be our memory of them bringing them back to apparent life." Sandy rubbed his chin again.

"You know my beliefs in spirits and life after death," Mida said. "Our souls do come back in different forms."

Sandy replied, "Yes, and that whole subject of souls and spirits has presented massive theological, physical, and scientific problems throughout history. The whole heaven and earth and god thing. Where do souls go? And just what are souls made up of? I think we have the answers here if we can only get them to explain it to us in terms we can comprehend. None of this phantom two extra dimensions. They don't consider themselves special and maybe they are not. But they are essentially gods to us. Just like I was a god to my dog."

Ev looked up at the ceiling. "Well, I for one am ready to abandon my scientific curiosity and scientific constraints. I believe Vandara. We are intellectually unable to understand it all. Like the little kid who just likes to watch the magician and not worry about how the tricks were done. Matter of fact, when you learn how the magic is done, it sort of takes away the awe and wonder. We are here and we can't go back. Or did Vandara ever say whether or not she could beam us back. I don't know why she couldn't. Do we even want to go back?"

"I can't believe you said that, Rock Boy. You, the questioning scientist." Mida shook her head. "Do I want to go back? Sort of depends on what our options are. If it is sit here, starve to death and be buried by sand, then I guess I opt to go back."

"You have options."

All four jumped to their feet as they stared at Vandara, who just entered the room, accompanied by Delsan.

"I wondered where you disappeared to," Vandara said as she told them to sit back down. "I'm sorry we don't have better accommodations for you."

"I could go get something to make them comfortable," Delsan said.

"No, we won't be here long. I don't like being in this room." She seemed to slump a little as her light flickered. "It is where we lost four of our crew members." Vandara stopped and did not go into more detail. No one pressed her for more information.

"I said you do have options. But going back to your time when you entered this ship is not one of them. If we could take you back, you would have very big problems. You see, the ship isn't there anymore. You would go back to a tomb encased in rock."

Ev reached out to touch Vandara but was knocked back against the wall. "What did you do to me?" he shouted.

"I'm sorry, Ev, I didn't mean to hurt you. You are changing as we speak. I didn't realize how frail your bodies and energy are. You are all emitting . . ." She stopped as she was searching for a word. "I don't know the word in your language. I don't think you have a word for it yet. I will just say a certain type of pulse that worries me. If we had full power, I could solve the problem. We don't. Our shuttles have enough power for maybe one more trip. I can take care of possibly one of you with the decay you are having. I guess going so far has been bad for your systems."

"Why are you just now telling us?" Mida asked like a hurt child.

"I just now found out. We started detecting the waves from your energy field just a few minutes ago. I scanned you when I came in a minute ago and it confirmed what I had worried about since our trip earlier. On our trip to explore your planet, I didn't activate the . . ." Again she stopped. "Here is another one I don't have a word for. I will call it an antimatter shield. Although, Sandy, that is not correct either, but it is the closest we can come for now. It is another term and scientific concept you haven't discovered yet. Sandy, maybe Delsan can give you a lesson in that. It is vaguely related to antimatter but not that simple. Delsan activated his when he took Sandy up, but I didn't realize you needed it as much as you obviously did. I should have known better. Sarah is basically unaffected, and Sandy is in better shape than Ev and Mida. That is why I have the following proposal."

Ev and Mida looked at each other, then at Sandy and Sarah. All had a puzzled look on their faces.

Vandara continued. "We can treat Sandy using the ship's power we have left. Sarah doesn't need much and she will be okay. I think we can help you, Sandy. It will correct your energy field." Looking at Ev and Mida, Vandara said, "You will be healed by another method. It means a one-way trip. Delsan wants to keep Sandy here to help fix the power system." She now looked back at Sandy. "You understand some simple things we are not familiar with. But that means you stay here and work with us. We just don't know how much time we have. It may end up being the length of your normal lifespan anyway."

"So I never leave here. Does that mean when we entered the ship, whenever that was"—Sandy rolled his eyes—"we probably walked by my bones sitting in the corner of some room?"

"Not that simple. Your body decayed in a normal way, but your energy stayed here."

"But you just said the ship isn't back in 1999 anymore. Can you explain that?" Ev said, with a little irritation in his voice.

"Sandy's energy was in the ship when you discovered it. Remember the blue lights? That was Sandy. He was giving out forms of energy that were affecting all of you."

"Cool. I was the ghost that was affecting myself. Eternal life. How weird can this get?" Sandy laughed.

Vandara continued, "When we brought you back here to meet us, we knew that the ship had been discovered sometime in the future. Since you just walked in, then others could come in too. This was a discovery that we didn't want to happen. We made the ship disappear in your future world. It is still out there, but in another dimension."

Vandara apologized for what she was about to say since she knew Ev and Mida were still reeling from their earlier technical discussion. She talked directly to Sandy, essentially reviewing what he knew very well. She started talking quantum physics. Sandy knew this was as elementary to Vandara as his trying to explain to a chimpanzee why two plus two equaled four. According to the Heisenberg uncertainty principle, an observer cannot know both the location and the energy of something at the same time. The measurement of one changes the other. Electrons don't orbit a nucleus of the atom but instead exist as a cloud of possibilities, with each possibility jumping from point to point in quantum jumps. The collapse of the wave function is what is called the observer affect. When observation occurs, the many probabilities change to one certainty. In a parallel worldview, which approaches a description of that mysterious fifth dimension, the wave doesn't collapse. The observer becomes part of the wave in one universe, with many others still out there. This gives an idea of what happened to the ship after the four explorers entered it. Perception is reality as you say. The existence of matter and the perception of it are one in the same."

"Another clue, Sandy, is from your favorite physicist, Mr. Einstein. He helped coin a concept you know as the Einstein–Podolsky–Rosen effect. This is a strange concept to many humans but it helps understand a lot of what we use in our travels. Two things once connected can travel to the far ends of the universe and be separated by millions of light-years. But they are still connected and the measurement or use of one will affect the other. And remember, everything was once connected at the beginning of the universe. You call it the big bang." Vandara paused and watched as Sandy cocked his head in thought.

"I know most of all that already, but I have this strange feeling that my earlier beliefs may be a little lacking in depth," Sandy said with a shrug.

"I know Delsan has been explaining a lot of technical details to you. You stay with us and you will really understand a lot more. You will even understand how the ship disappeared."

"That still sounds like an offer I just cannot refuse." Sandy said as he looked at Sarah. "But Sarah. Can't she stay with me?"

"I am carrying his child. Or do you not understand that concept?" Sarah said with a shake of her head. She reached over and put her arms around Sandy.

"I will be very honest. I don't mean to offend anyone here. Sandy is old by your standards. He can provide a very valuable service to us here. It does condemn him, but if my guess is right, it is the choice he would make. He would probably not provide a similar service by going with the rest of you."

"That is rather brutal. And emotionless. Shouldn't he choose himself? What about me? Don't I have any say whether I stay with him or he goes with us?" Sarah was visibly upset.

"I think the obvious question," Mida said very calmly, "is what happens to us. What is this adventure he cannot help us on?"

"You will start a new civilization on this planet. I will be able to take you forward in time from now to the point when I first came here. That will be one million years before your time of 1999. I will take you wherever you like. I cannot leave you at the exact location where the ship is now, but anywhere else, you guide me there. I will leave you, with nothing much more than what you have with you. There will be a few things I can do to your bodies and your abilities. There will also be a few tools I can leave you, but not very much. You will be on your own. You will be alone. After that, it will be up to you. God and goddess."

"So that is what you wouldn't tell us earlier," said Ev.

"You are still leaving me out of this," said Sarah, becoming more irritated.

"As I was saying," interrupted Vandara, "you have skills that will aid this new life. On Earth. There is nothing magic or sacred about sending just two of you out there. Besides, the way you build a population, the more females the better. I said you would be a god and goddess. That was a manner of speech. Our objective at this point is to ensure a population of advanced beings. It is not to ensure your bliss and happiness. Three would be more secure than two. I haven't decided for sure yet, but I don't have very many choices."

"Wait a minute," interrupted Sandy. "You say the ship disappeared. In relation to when we entered the ship and you brought us back in time, when did the ship disappear? This is important."

"I don't know. In dealing with variations in time and in the dimensions we are dealing in, it is almost impossible to pinpoint something like that. Just like there is no way to compare the time of right now with the time of when you left. You are here and totally disconnected from your old time. You cannot say, 'I wonder what the folks at home are doing right now.' There is no 'right now.' It doesn't exist. Your previous life is in the future, a long way from happening. And by the same thought, your people you left behind cannot be thinking, 'I wonder what Ev and Sandy and Mida are doing right now. Again, right now doesn't exist. You don't exist. Your lives are long over with."

Mida looked puzzled. "I got the impression from what you were saying about time is that a bunch of things were occurring almost simultaneously. Like the past one on one stage, the present was taking place on the adjacent stage, and the future was happening on another. You said time is not linear or sequential."

"Mida, I can't handle that right now," Ev whimpered. "At this point, I don't even want to know. Just listen to the lady do her magic tricks and don't analyze the trick itself. Sandy, go on with your question."

"The reason I asked is that we went to great efforts to collect data and document our discovery of the ship. We wanted several of our companions to find the ship as we left it. Or entered it. In just a few days after we entered, they were to come and find it. I don't think they would have wanted to enter it."

"Of course they would," Vandara purred. "That is precisely why you disappeared and left no tracks. No one will ever have any evidence this ship was there. You had hoped for some claim to fame in your scientific circles. Sorry. Your friends will be left with nothing to prove anything. Some events of history are left best in secrecy."

"But," Ev said, slowly standing up, "this type of factual evidence could change our entire civilization. It is the most significant discovery of what actually happened in the history of our world. People need to know something like this."

"You did not listen to what I just said. People need to know something like this? Ev, this is something that is a million years off. You are second-guessing what, in your minds, is so far off in the future, a million other things could change between now and then. What happens one million years from now is of absolutely no concern to you now."

"But things have to happen just as they did or else we wouldn't be here. Right?" Mida asked.

"No. Sometimes I think you are not listening to me. The fifth dimension. The world you experienced is not there and may never be there. But assuming it will be exactly as you left it, do you really think your world could absorb a discovery like this? From what I have gathered from your thoughts, I don't think so. No offense intended, but your world has a long way to go before it could understand this story. Even though your technology and science have come a long way, your beliefs, cultures, and religions are still very primitive. Just look at the history of war and killing and hatred in your lifetimes. We have lost much of our ancient history, but we did similar things. Gaining the wisdom to accompany the technology is a very slow process."

Mida perked up. "Well, if I don't get my question answered, you don't either, Ev. Vandara, let's go back to your plans for us. I agree with Sarah. She should have a choice of where to go. I think Sandy would be a great help to us. Four would be better than three."

Sandy stood up and paced around the room. "This is very difficult for me. Let's face it. Our old lives are over. Gone for good. I would prefer to stay here. I am old but my curiosity is here, with this unbelievably advanced technology. If my choice is to stay here and learn or to go back to the cave men and run around in hides and throw spears at mastodons, that is an easy choice. I would love to be with Sarah. She has put a spark back in my life, but she is young and should help you. Kind of an old-fashioned concept, but Mida and Sarah are to mother a new race. Ev, you are the lucky one here."

Tears welled in Sarah's eyes. She tried to answer Sandy but couldn't speak. Mida hugged and held her for a minute.

Vandara touched Sarah with her light. Sarah did not jump back like Ev did earlier, but instead, she pulled away from Mida and smiled. She kissed Sandy and said, "You are right. Maybe I am meant to lose two men who meant a lot to me. You for only a short time, but my memory of you will be better than the other one."

"We don't have much time. Agreed, then? I will take you on one more shuttle trip. It will be a one-way trip for you. Maybe me too. I will take you three forward in time to a period of one million years before your former time. Life is well along and things look much like they did for you in your 1999 world."

"And you leave us. By ourselves. Oh, now that's just real nice. I don't suppose you could leave us maybe a million years later?"

"If I could, I would. But there is a reason I cannot take you back to 1999. It has to do with a basic law of the universe. I think Sandy probably knows it. It has to do with a paradox in time travel. And this time, it is plain and simple time travel, in the fourth dimension. But then, you don't understand that any more than the fifth dimension, so I won't go into that. It is the best I can do. But it also serves my purpose very well. It is something we were going to do anyway." Vandara stopped. She went out in the hall and took Delsan with her. She appeared briefly in the room again and said, "Please excuse me a minute," then she disappeared.

Sandy leaned over and whispered, "Delsan shared a little with me about what they had intended to do even before we showed up. I didn't tell you this earlier, but I have spent a lot of time documenting some basic science and background for you. I didn't know exact details, but I was very sure at least some of us would have to fend for ourselves in a lonely and otherwise humanless world. You will be pleasantly surprised. I don't think it's a case of you being dumped in the desert or the jungle. Or in front of a continental ice sheet staring down saber-toothed tigers. I think you start something like the lost continent of Atlantis."

"Oh, Sandy, get real," Ev said as he paced back and forth in the room. "There was no lost continent of Atlantis." No one spoke again for a few minutes.

Vandara came back into the room a few minutes later. She was alone. "I would like for all of you to go back to your sleeping quarters. We will prepare the most comfortable setting for you that we can. You will have a meal and I want you to spend the time visiting and sharing your thoughts and experiences. By the time your sun rises again, you will go your separate ways. We will take Sandy to the healing room right now and take care of him. Tomorrow morning I will take Ev, Mida, and Sarah with me for a short training session, then we will go on a trip. Hopefully, I will return, after leaving you in a location you will pick out for me. I want you to be thinking of where you would like to spend the rest of your life."

"We have a choice?" asked Ev as he looked at Mida.

"You have a choice. Anywhere in this world you wish to go, I will take you there. The three of you will start a new civilization."

"Oh, that's great. I didn't bring anything. I wasn't supposed to be here." Sarah puckered her lips in frustration.

Sandy laughed. "Think about it. It doesn't really matter. In a few weeks or maybe months, whatever you brought will be used up, worn-out, and useless. You will find, invent, and make whatever you need. If you don't make it, then you don't have it to use. I know we all spent hours thinking about what to bring. So what if you don't have a roll of toilet paper. A year from now, that, along with your toothpaste, aspirin, and Snickers bars will be a distant memory."

Ev looked confused as well as worried. "What is the training? How to start fire from rubbing sticks together and which plants are safe to eat?"

Mida laughed. "What I always wanted and dreamed of all my life. Being a baby factory living in the wilderness. By the way, you have a trick up your sleeve, don't you?" Mida asked as she looked at Vandara.

"I can't make you be like us, but I can give you some of our powers and a few tools. You were already starting to get these powers before you entered the ship. You will have extraordinary, by your standards, ability to communicate and to perceive things. I think you call it paranormal or extrasensory ability. That extra sense that Mida already had, only on a much smaller scale. Healing powers. Knowledge of what is to happen. Intuition. Help me out on this Mida. I'm not sure I can find the right words."

Mida continued. "Powers that my ancestors already had. I guess because I gave it to them a million years ago. We were a part of nature, able to communicate and understand the other life-forms. I think this is the secret that much of modern civilization lost somewhere in their rush to civilize things. We were part of nature and not above it. Yes, we had the ability to overcome and change nature through our technology, but we lost the ability to live within or even understand nature's limits. Ev and Sarah and I will be starting out fresh with almost a magical power to live with nature. And we will not have that lust, greed, or whatever that sent us on the destructive technological race of the past five hundred or so years."

"And tools?" asked Ev. "You will leave us some phaser gun or something other than a flint arrowhead for me to shoot saber-toothed cats with?" He looked at Vandara seriously, with no hint of humor in his question.

Sandy burst out laughing. "If I could only have a picture of that. Ev wandering around in a loincloth with his rock pick hanging from his sunburned and peeling shoulders, giving the mating call of some ferocious beast trying to get close enough to ambush it so he can drag it to feed Mida and Sarah with triplets tugging at their feet while Mida tries to catalog the edible plants of the area with a piece of charcoal on homemade papyrus." He laughed so hard, he had to lean over with his hands on his knees.

Mida said, "Rock Boy meets saber tooth. Muscle against fang." Then all four exploded in laughter at that vision also. Vandara watched in silence, trying to understand the humor. Finally, she purred, not at their vision, but at the fact these humans were obviously enjoying themselves.

Sandy burst out laughing, "Write a book of your adventures and encase it in sandstone and leave it where I can find it in my twentieth century life. Try and illustrate it while you are at it." This brought a new wave of laughter.

"You have a wonderful sense of humor," Vandara said, rather wistfully. "I'm afraid we have lost a little of that ourselves. Let me explain some of what I have in mind. Ev, you do have some excellent skills in tool making. Don't sell yourself short on that. But, yes, I will give you a solar powered weapon that stuns a victim. And the energy of your sun gives you the ability to do practically anything.

"Best of all, I am giving you a device that, using the simplest form of energy, can rearrange the very atomic structure of materials. A dream of your alchemists, you will be able to turn lead into gold. If you know the chemical makeup of things, you will be able to manufacture them in atomic form, using any material at hand. This is a powerful thing I am entrusting you with. It goes to the most basic structure of the entire universe. Everything is made of atoms, which are made of electrons and protons and neutrons, which are made of—well, you get the picture. Basic building blocks. You had not learned how to do this yet. I don't think you even had any idea it could be done." She looked at Sandy so he could confirm her guess. He shook his head no.

She explained that Sandy and other scientists had been trying to figure out what the atom was made of. "We avarnans have known that for a long time. The next step once the building blocks are known is to rearrange the atoms. Human scientists were experimenting, unfortunately, as a way to destroy things—the bomb. Once we got by that, civilization need never lack for anything again. Humans would then be able to continue their lifestyle with the comforts they were used to and would be able to construct their dream world. But it takes wisdom to go with that knowledge." Vandara gave Ev and Mida that wisdom and cautioned them to use it well.

"You are giving us a magic wand. Is there a catch?" Ev asked lowering his eyes from the brilliance of Vandara.

"Yes, of course. There is a catch to everything isn't there?" Vandara's light grew brighter then flickered. "You must demonstrate to me how you plan to use it. You must tell me your objectives for your life. What do you want to see before you spend your allotted time on this new Earth? And that time will be many times what you would have spent on your old earth."

"Ev, we are being given the keys to heaven. Vandara, how much time do we have before we either leave here or die?" Mida asked as she walked over to look out the window again. The sand was nearly covering the window.

"Time is something we are short of, so to speak. You do not know the danger you are all in right now. It has to do with the electrical and energy make-up of your bodies. You are a vastly different species than I am. I never really had the opportunity to do extensive testing. I made assumptions about how you would react to what you have been through. Your trip here and trips while you have been here have done significant damage to your bodies. That damage is not irreversible, but it needs tended to very soon or it will become irreversible.

"Sandy, I want you to follow Delsan as soon as you leave this room. We will try and take care of you right now. For Ev and Mida and Sarah, I want you to go back to your room and talk about what I have told you. Within a few hours, Sandy will rejoin you. Then you will have your parting feast. In a few hours after that, I will take you three, after you say goodbye to Sandy, with me. I will give you a very quick training session on a few things, including the equipment you will be taking. You will tell me exactly where you want to go. Our chief healing specialist will perform a few minor adjustments to you to prepare your bodies. Then you will begin your new lives. Hopefully, I will return here to continue work on this ship."

Mida smiled, then fingered her shirtsleeve. "Sort of makes studying for my doctoral exams rather trivial, doesn't it? Dr. Peterson and Dr. Collins, doctors of abnormal space-time continuum happenings." Realizing the upcoming problem of not excluding Sarah, she quickly added, "And Nurse Sarah."

"I still have one more question," Ev said as he reached over and grabbed Mida's hand to keep her from pulling a thread from her shirtsleeve. "You are fixing up Sandy right now to stop this fatal disease or whatever. You never really said you were fixing us up the same way. How do we escape the progression of our deterioration? I mean, you make it sound like our bodies are coming apart at the seams due to bombardment by gamma rays or neutrinos or space gobblies. You don't have the energy necessary to do this, but you do some operation and we are okay to send off on the yellow brick road. I missed something there."

"Appropriate question, Ev." Vandara moved about the room. "Let's see if I can answer it. It is difficult since we are talking about a technology and some basic science that you don't have yet. Remember, I said I didn't put up the so-called antimatter shield. During your travels through time, you were bombarded by a type of energy field that you have never experienced before. You might say a form of what you call dark energy. We only find it when we go back and forth in time or travel at what Sandy refers to as warp speed. You don't know what it is since you have no experience with the full dimension of time. If I can do certain maneuvers when I take you forward in time, I can reverse the effects. There has been no permanent damage yet, but there soon will be. Let's see. Ev, you like ice cream. You can leave a bowl of ice cream on the table and it will soften before you eat it, then left out long enough, it will melt. The melting is irreversible but the softening isn't. You can set the soft ice cream back in the freezer and it will be okay. Once it melts, it won't be the same. Your bodies are soft ice cream right now and another day or two, you will be melted. How is that for an explanation?"

Mida laughed once again as she reached over and poked Ev in the ribs. "Do we change that to Rock Boy the ice cream man melts as he approaches the saber-toothed cat. The cat looks confused, but then proceeds to lick up his would be foe."

"I really don't think this is that funny," Ev said as he playfully pushed back Mida. He snorted as he tried to hold back another laugh.

Sandy walked toward the door. "I don't know about you, but I am ready to continue Sandy's Big Adventure. I feel okay but I don't like to have something wrong with my atomic structure. Think I will go stand under a hot shower of fortified electrons or whatever they plan to do to me. I'll see you all later for our last supper." He kissed Sarah and whispered, "And our last dessert." He waved his left hand in a salute, then went out into the hall and followed Delsan down the long corridor.

Vandara went toward Ev and Mida, motioning Sarah to join her. Ev backed off, remembering the last time he touched the light that was Vandara. She purred, then gently enveloped both of them in a warming touch. "Last time was like a shock, Ev. Let me soothe you now. I have come to like you all very much. I would not do anything to hurt you. I am counting on you three to do wondrous things."

Ev felt like all his worries left him as a sensation of warmth coursed through his body. Mida started humming one of her father's songs. Sarah smiled as tears again ran down her cheeks. The four of them stood for several minutes in a group hug.

Finally, Vandara backed off and said very softly, "It's time for you to go back and rest. Enjoy yourselves. I will come get you in the morning." She left and disappeared down the corridor.

Ev, Mida, and Sarah stood together for another minute just holding each other. Finally, Ev ran his hands through Mida's glossy black hair, now showing a streak of gray running along the right side of her head. He stepped back and looked out the window which now showed a brilliant orange red glow of sunset in the small opening at the top of the window not covered by sand.

"Looks like our storm is over and we didn't quite get covered up. One more storm will do it."

Mida walked to the window and peered out the small opening. "Isn't it beautiful? You know, one thing I wanted to do was stand out there about where we camped originally back in our other life, and look up at the stars."

"We can still do it. She wanted us to go back and talk and think before Sandy came back. We can go get someone to open the door and we can walk outside and talk and think there instead. I'd like that too."

Ev and Mida walked down the corridor, with Sarah following behind, and found someone working in the shuttle bay. Mida asked them if they could go outside. The form, much like Delsan, gladly opened a small door for them and left it ajar for their return. They walked out into the warm evening air. The wind had died down to nothing and the stars were shining brightly. On the lee side of the ship, the sand had not drifted much, but they hit a huge drift when they walked around the front of the ship. They walked to what was the west side of the ship, where the small window was just barely visible above the sand. Half the ship was buried.

Ev looked up in the sky, but didn't recognize any stars or constellations. There was no Big Dipper, no Orion, no Cassiopeia. Ev tried to think what time of year it was. As far as he knew, it was November, but he could not judge how long they had been gone. He mentally went through all his old friends—the Northern Cross with Deneb and Cygnus, Vega, Arcturus and Boötes, Gemini with Pollux and Castor. Nothing he recognized.

He held Mida's hand and stared straight up. "My god, nothing is the same. The sky is so different. You think a few things in the universe are constant, but when the stars themselves shift into unfamiliar patterns, what is left?"

Sarah slowly walked over to Ev and Mida and put her arms around Ev. "Talk about a third wheel, this takes the cake. Mida, you think we can share this hunk? We shared so much of our lives before."

"Sarah, if this is our future, I can't think of a better way to live it. I'm sure we can gang up on him and make him our slave. Now that is a true goddess!"

"This is both heaven and hell," muttered Ev as he continued to stare at the stars. "You know, all the time we have been here, I never really looked up at the night sky. Look over there. What a perfect circle. Oh, wow, that is magnificent. Eight, nine, there must be ten stars in a perfect circle. Look how bright those three are. And up there, that looks like a huge letter H. The Big H and the Big O. I'm sure we can come up with very colorful names. Why haven't we come out here at night before now?"

"Look, a shooting star," Mida said excitedly. As they stared upward, they saw another. And another. As they watched, they started seeing more. Some were faint and hardly visible. Others were bright, with long sparkly tails. One lit up the sky almost like lightning.

"I heard about this. A meteor storm. There are dozens of shooting stars. What a fireworks display. Just think, specks of dust. Must be in our honor. If we were home, I'd say this was something like the November Leonid meteor showers. Or in August there are the Perseids. I don't suppose those were around this long ago. I think they usually come as we pass through a comet's tail. Who knows what kind of comets were around then? Or now."

Mida let out an "Oooh" as another brilliant one passed overhead. "Remember this sky is from two hundred million years ago and no one has ever seen it and no one ever will. This is our only chance."

Sarah added, "But this won't be our sky. In our sky, the H and the O will probably be gone. Maybe your old friends will be there again for us. It will only be a million years before the sky we grew up with. How quickly do the constellations change over time?"

Ev stretched his neck back and forth. "No one knows. Oh, I suppose someone could figure it out, but this is new territory for even the most brilliant astronomers. We don't know motions in the sky. We revolve around the sun and the sun revolves around a center of the Milky Way. But what does the Milky Way revolve around? And what do the galaxies in the constellations revolve around? Is there a center of the universe? Does Vandara worship a god? You know, we have spent a lot of time with Vandara but I don't feel I know her. Do you?"

"No," Mida answered as she put her arms around Ev. "She is wonderful and she is strange. I can't really see her eyes and the eyes tell you so much. I couldn't tell you what her personality was like. Maybe avarnans don't have a personality. They may have evolved away from quirks that make them human."

"Boy, you got that right. No human traits I can see."

"You know what I mean," Mida said as she squeezed Ev's fingers together.

Ev sat down on the sand and pulled both Mida and Sarah down with him. "Just listen to that. No crickets, no coyotes, no airplanes going over. Not even a wind blowing. Quiet like we have never heard."

"Well, where do we go?" Mida finally asked as she wowed another fiery streak in the sky.

"Huh?" Ev was mentally up there in the sky with this strange bunch of stars.

"Vandara wants us to pick our Garden of Eden. Where do we go?"

"Oh yeah. Boy, what a decision. I haven't thought about it. Where do you want to go?"

"I'm not a world traveler like you. My universe is mostly New Mexico. It is nice and I could live there forever, but we have to think of a few important details. Like the climate, the available food, ability to travel around—you know, things like that."

Ev looked at Sarah. She shot back, "Don't look at me. I don't have a clue. Besides, I'm just the tag along sex object."

Mida glared at Sarah. "That will be the last of that kind of talk. We all have to adjust and we are now three equals."

Ev continued as if he hadn't heard the last exchange. "This is going to be tricky. I'm not even sure what America looked like a million years ago. I mean things like glaciers and rivers and type of vegetation. And it doesn't have to be America. It could be anywhere in the world."

"Yes, but think a minute," Mida said as she lay back in the sand. "Remember what Vandara implied. And what you know about history. There were humans wandering around Africa and maybe Europe and where else?"

"Well, human or prehuman. Yes, you are right. We don't really know for sure if they had traveled to the American continents. Probably not, but I'm not sure they couldn't have been like the horse. The horse evolved here, then became extinct. We have never found evidence of human or humanoid forms over here, but that doesn't prove they weren't here. I guess we assume they weren't here. So that means we have North and South America to ourselves."

"Will we be in the ice age?"

"Hmmm," thought Ev. "That could be tricky. The ice ages stretched over a long period. There were several. I don't remember exactly when the interglacials were. And it depends on Vandara's definition of a million years. Was it a million exactly, or maybe 900,000 or maybe 1.1 million. Look at what happened in only the last 10,000 years. We went from Wisconsin being under a mile of ice to it being populated with cheeseheads. I guess we better play it safe and figure there could be continental ice sheets. So northern climates and maybe seashores could be out of bounds. I just don't know about rivers. Even though I have a good idea of mountains and lava fields, I still don't know details about rivers. I think we need to be near rivers. We need a decent climate with a good growing season and good seasonal rain."

"My ancestors did okay in the deserts."

"Did they? They built pueblos and things, but they didn't exactly thrive. They mostly disappeared after a few hundred years."

"They also moved around a lot. Nothing says we plop down somewhere and never move from that spot."

"You got a good point there. If we have wisdom that Vandara expects us to have, we adjust as need be to conditions. We don't have all the facts, so we make an educated guess, then we try it out. That is the good old scientific method isn't it? I don't plan to break a leg, so we should be able to move around. We just go domesticate a horse or camel or whatever."

The three lay in the sand for an hour debating criteria for their new home. The meteors continued as they tried to count for a while but gave up as Ev would see one in the north and Mida was looking in the south. Then Sarah would look east and Ev west. They gave up at six hundred and twenty three, give or take a few dozen as Ev said.

They discussed how they would create a new life, especially if they were producing children as fast as they could. They tried to imagine what life would be like, even with Vandara's high-tech toys. Ev talked about some of the books he had read on life after disasters. He had read several about the survivors of wars, disease and other catastrophes, and how they tried to continue civilization. Invariably they failed. Seems they all reverted to primitive lifestyles. Continuing education and learning and any form of technology seemed impossible as humans reverted to life thousands of years old.

Mida then reminded Ev that until one or two hundred years ago, her ancestors had lived that way and had done quite well. Ev said that 'well' was a relative term. He said they didn't have a language. She said they did too. Ev said not a written language. She asked if that mattered. Their debate deteriorated into philosophical parries about culture, art, government, technology, the wheel, weapons, medicine, agriculture, and a million other things. Sarah still felt left out of much of the discussion. Ev and Mida had spent thousands of hours in this type of debate; Sarah was discovering it for the first time.

After mentally exhausting themselves, Ev and Mida were frightened back to reality when someone walked up to them and spoke. It was Sandy. He said he went back to their room but couldn't find them. Someone said they were outside, so he came out and heard voices.

As Sandy put his arm around Sarah's shoulder, he looked at Ev and asked, "This is close to where we camped a long time ago, isn't it?"

"We camped here the very first time I brought Mida to see my discovery. When you were with us, we camped on the other side, up above the periscope or whatever that thing is."

"It's a radio antenna," said Sandy. "As well as a few other electronic purposes. Oh, wow, did you see that shooting star?"

Both Ev and Mida laughed. "We've been lying here watching this fantastic meteor . . . what did you call it Ev, a storm?"

"One of the most impressive meteor storms you've ever seen, Sandy. It puts the best Leonids or Perseids to shame."

"Sandy, are you cured?" Sarah asked as Ev stood up.

"As well as an old fart like me can be. Didn't feel a thing other than a funny tingle in my . . . well, let's not go there. It took more energy than they expected. Delsan is really worried that we will have to start powering some things down. I can't believe they don't have a bunch of solar panels or something simple like that. Maybe we can build some. Yeah, that's an idea."

"Let's go in and eat," blurted Ev. "I can't remember the last time we really had a meal. I don't know how long we have been here, but I swear we haven't eaten. They must be feeding us with some kind of energy. By the way, Sandy, I want you to look up in this sky. What do you see? I mean besides the meteors."

Ev and Sandy discussed the stars and astronomy and philosophies of the universe, interspersing an occasional "Wow" or "Ooh" when they saw an unusually impressive meteor.

Mida walked over to the ship and climbed the dune piled up against the window. She wiped away some sand covering the window and peered in. She had a flashback to when she first climbed up to this same window and shined a flashlight in it. What a difference she thought. That was in an entirely different world. This ship is sitting here being covered up by sand that turned out to be the solid rock that entombed the ship two hundred million years later. She stepped back and looked around her. No red sandstone cliffs, no coyotes or owls. No Big Dipper. No doctoral thesis to finish. She closed her eyes and said a prayer. She then undid the miniature squash blossom necklace Boyd brought to her from the trading post where he picked up those Navajo blankets just a short time before her world changed. She laid the silver and turquoise necklace in the sand just beneath the window and said another prayer.

Finally, Mida turned to Sarah, sitting quietly only half-listening to the two scientists discuss the sky. "We have to go in now."

Sarah poked Sandy in the ribs while she flipped Ev's earlobe. "Come on, slaves, it's time."

Ev said he wanted to take advantage of this intelligent person while he could. He was going to miss having these scientific and philosophic discussions. As soon as he said it, he knew he shouldn't have. After Mida's reply of "What am I, warm beer?" he followed behind her as she walked around the ship and into the door, apologizing the whole way. Sandy said to forget it, Ev had screwed up good on that one and only time would smooth it over.

The meal was superb, even if everything was manufactured. The four talked for several hours. While Ev and Mida argued about where to live, Sandy and Sarah slipped away to say their farewells. When they returned several hours later, Ev and Mida were still debating. The sun had risen outside.

Knowing that their time was almost up, Sandy reached into his pack and pulled out a bundle of what looked like were CDs. There were also several small crystal rods in the package. He handed these to Ev as if they were made of gold.

"Ev, don't ask questions right now, but I want you to take care of these. They are a quick summary of a lot of what we want to preserve for the future. The avarnans use the crystals, but they serve the same purpose as our CDs. I put information on both, just in case. Vandara will give you the technology to use both, but it may take a while to learn to use them properly. I feel like they need to be preserved."

"But what are they?" Ev started to question, but Sandy just said they were like encyclopedias, of both human and avarnan knowledge. He would have plenty of time to study them, so just keep them safe.

Sandy turned to Mida. He pulled her aside as Ev busied himself putting the package in his backpack and whispered to her. "Mida, I made an extra copy of some of this on CDs. I want you to see that these somehow make it back to the twentieth century. If I and a team of scientists had this information during our time, we could have done wonderful things in science, medicine, and technology. This information could change our world. I thought about leaving them on the ship, but since the ship has disappeared, it can't do anyone any good now. I know you will somehow see they make it to the future. I encased them in a watertight gold covering."

Mida looked at them carefully, then slowly put them in the pocket of her baggy sweatshirt. She stood for a minute, obviously thinking about her newest charge. As Ev rejoined the conversation, Mida slowly backed off and quickly left the room. Ev started to ask something, but Sandy just said, "some female thing I imagine."

Mida ran down the hall, rushing past Vandara who was coming toward their room. "I'll be back in just a minute, Vandara. I have to do something very quickly." Before Vandara could say anything, Mida was down the hall and out the door to the outside. She ran through the sand around the front of the ship to where she had hidden her treasure a few hours earlier. She dug into the sand and found the necklace. She buried the gold packet underneath the necklace, then covered them both with sand.

She closed her eyes and whispered a prayer, she ran back inside, just in time to see Vandara enter their room. "Someone, please look closely in the rock next to the hole where the window was in the cliff. Please. All you need to do is stand there and this will call to you to uncover it. I know it will work. I sensed there was something here. Mom or Boyd or someone, please look here."

Vandara came in and said, "Come, it is time to travel. Sandy, I will see you later."

Ev and Mida hugged and held Sandy, already holding Sarah tightly, not wanting to let go. All four had tears running down their cheeks when Vandara gently pulled them apart. Mida winked at Sandy and smiled.

"Who knows, when you all figure out the time dimension, you may meet again."

With that, Ev and Mida picked up their packs and followed Vandara out into the hall. Sarah took the pack Sandy had packed for himself. He took out a few items he said he would need but left most things, including his clothes. He sighed as his eyes said goodbye to Sarah. He walked into the engine room to find Delsan.

TWENTY-ONE

※

Alone on a Distant Shore

And on her lover's arm she leant,
And round her waist she felt it fold,
And far across the hills they went
In that new world which is the old.

—Alfred, Lord Tennyson

There is no death! The stars go down
To rise upon some other shore,
And bright in heaven's jeweled crown
They shine forever more.

—John Luckey McCreery

VANDARA LED Ev, Mida, and Sarah toward a large room located just off the shuttle bay. The three travelers plodded down the long corridor like pack-laden scouts trying to keep up with their leader. Sarah stumbled along as she adjusted straps to the pack which Sandy had previously worn. As they passed next to the shuttle bay, they all stopped to look at the crew. The large bay door was open and a crew of four avarnans was working on the shuttle. In a manner of speaking, they had the hood open and were tinkering with the engine. Several more avarnans were outside actually shoveling sand out from in front of the door. Mida had to laugh at the crumpled up piece of metal they were using as a shovel.

As Vandara entered the room, she stopped and told them to set their packs outside the door. She then told one of the crew to take the packs and set them in the shuttle. The room was different from most they had seen in Orion. It had tables, shelves, cabinets, and even chairs and large pillows. Ev commented that he finally felt at home. He walked over and plopped down on a very plush pillow, as big as a sofa. Mida told him he had better get used to not having such comforts as she sat cross-legged on the floor.

Vandara also told him not to get very comfortable. Rather impatiently, she said she wanted to know what they planned to do once she set them down at their destination. Ev looked first at Sarah, then at Mida and nodded for her to answer.

Mida started her monologue as if she had long rehearsed it for presentation in a school play. She cradled her notepad on her lap but didn't look at the pages of scribbling she had written in the past few hours. She silently fingered the wooden crystal that Sandy slipped in her hand as he left her. She said that the three of them wanted to establish a society where love and respect became the standard. They would keep alive a tradition of learning and challenging their minds. Since they would be starting from scratch, with no technology to complicate things, they would focus on basics, especially environmental matters. They would create and keep myths and stories with morals to them. They would encourage spirituality but would let religion develop as people needed it. They would never allow any discrimination or bigotry, mainly by setting examples and encouraging it through open-mindedness. She felt strongly that hatred and evil were learned; if there was no one to model it, maybe they could keep it out of future generations.

It was all pretty high-minded and philosophical, thought Ev. He began to wonder about including an objective for having fun and enjoying sunsets and waves on the shore. He finally spoke up. "For one thing, I want to create an alphabet that does not have an X or Q in it. And there will not be any words with a 'ph' or 'sch' or 'gn.' I will spell words just like they sound. And I will codify a list of original commandments, with the first one mandating people to have fun without hurting anyone else. And in the first legislative session, my first law will be to outlaw stupidity."

"Oh, good grief, Rock Boy. Vandara, those were not in our list."

"Relax, Mida. I want you to take this seriously, but Ev has a good point. It is something my species seems to have lost somewhere along the line. Yes, by all means, have fun. And do it in a way that is not at the expense of someone else. You will have a very heavy weight on your shoulders and from the time I have spent with you, I know you will set a very good example. But remember, all you can do is start things off. Others will carry them on after your time is up."

Mida and Ev continued to describe in more detail how they wanted to create a new civilization. Sarah agreed with what they were saying, but she let them do all the talking. They knew the hard part would be to assure continuance after they were gone. Mida's research and study of other cultures and civilizations would be used to mold their model. After presenting their outline, both Ev and Mida smiled and realized they pleased Vandara. Sarah silently clapped in approval. However, Vandara knew that no matter how thoughtfully these humans made a plan, the implementation of that plan would depend on so many variables. This was a gamble and all knew it. Vandara offered many suggestions, which Mida quickly wrote down as Vandara spoke. Most were quite philosophic, which Ev wanted to discuss in more detail, but they all knew time was short, so the discussion was brief.

Vandara looked up as someone else walked into the room. This avarnan was very similar to Vandara, but her light had a greenish tint to it. "I want you to meet Mallon. Sarah has already spent much time with her. She is our healer, or doctor in your language. She has studied your knowledge and memories and did some tests on you while you were asleep. She is now our expert on humans." Vandara purred while Mallon made a clicking sound as she reached out to touch Ev and Mida as they both stood up.

"I'm so glad to finally get to talk to you two. Sarah has been very helpful to me." She leaned over and embraced Sarah. "She has been the guinea pig, to use one of your phrases, but I did spend a lot of time with you two also, while you were asleep. I'm sorry I have done this in secret, but I didn't want to disturb you. I needed more data than just Sarah, but mostly it was testing what I learned from her with you. You are similar, of course, but remarkably different. You are used to more sleep and rest than you have been getting. I have kept you going and have done a little repair work on your bodies. Yes, Ev, I have fed you in a way you are not used to. I know more about you than you do now. Please sit down and let me explain what I have done and what I will do now."

Mida said, "It's nice to meet you, but I wish you had talked to us before now. I feel naked that you know so much about me but we haven't had the chance to visit more with you."

"Mida, she is fantastic. She taught me so much about healing and the biology of our bodies. I doubt if I would have learned any more if I had gone to medical school. So much we don't know about our cellular structure. You joked about Doctors Ev and Mida. Well, look on me as Doc Sarah, your medical doctor, from now on."

"Sarah has been so wonderful. It was not necessary for you to learn about me. It was necessary for me to find out more about you. Just your knowing I was studying you and probing your innermost secrets would have adversely affected my ability to do just that. Sarah may not realize, but I spent a lot of time while she was asleep also. At any rate, you know more than is obvious to you right now. A lot will surface over time. Sort of like a time-release capsule you swallow."

Ev and Mida sat back down on the couch next to Sarah, while Mallon actually sat down beside them. Vandara disappeared into the shuttle bay.

Mallon started her explanation. "By exploring your memories, I have been able to reconstruct your body's make up structurally and chemically. Your anatomy is very interesting, but quite primitive to me. I have studied your DNA and have been able to determine a lot of your evolution. Your DNA tells a lot. Your species will make progress when you learn to unlock the secrets hidden there. It really is a blueprint. It is also a history book."

Mallon looked at each of them to see if they had any comments. Ev wanted to ask so many questions but knew there just wasn't time. No one spoke. She continued. "By determining how you are meant to work and what can go wrong, I have learned what needs done to keep you working in perfect health. By doing a little modification to your energy field, I can reconstruct your DNA to avoid such things in your future as cancer, heart disease, susceptibility to viruses, and many other things. I also gave you a life span that in your time, equals about three hundred years. You will need all this in order to do the work we want you to do."

"Are you going to make us into someone more like you?" Ev asked.

"Oh no. I could not do that and I would not. We really should not interfere in a major way in creating or destroying life on another planet, but we can make sure that some things will likely happen. That is why we came."

"You don't consider this interfering?" Ev asked sarcastically.

"You would say it is borderline. But then look at it from our viewpoint. Our home planet has been destroyed. If we want to stay alive, we need to take drastic measures. We want to preserve some of the things we have learned as a species. We planned to leave some of our own to do that. But that bothered many of us. By using you to do our work for us, that solves part of our ethical problem. Since you are from the evolution of life that began on this planet, you fit in much more than we would."

"But you just said you are tinkering with our bodies and our DNA. Sounds like major interference to me." Ev continued his argument. Mida scowled at him but said nothing.

"Minor adjustments that are simply meant to assure your survival. It wouldn't do us a lot of good if you fell over dead from some human disease or malfunction three days after you start your work, would it? Most changes I am making will not be passed on to your offspring. They affect only you." Mallon clicked and purred.

"If you want us to do your work here, you have not told us what that is," said Mida. "Vandara has made us tell what our plans are, but hasn't given us directions of what she wants."

Mallon purred like Vandara. "You really don't understand yet, do you? We want to preserve intelligence and the curiosity and challenge it creates. We want you someday to follow in our footsteps and explore the universe to continue your objectives when your world is ready to disappear. Life is a cycle that flows throughout the universe. There are others out there, but this is such a big universe, and you don't often run into other civilizations."

Ev frowned and shifted on his pillow. "You just want us to be there and be ourselves? But how can we guarantee anything? We were already here. We are from the future. Life is already started on this planet a million years ago. You're right. I still don't understand."

Mallon made a strange noise and stood up and paced back and forth. "With all the time you have spent with Vandara and me and the others, I thought you understood by now. You are about out of time, but let me summarize things one last time. Life was here in a primitive humanoid form. Intelligence was here in all forms of life. But would it have advanced to our level? I don't know, but we want to ensure it. By using you humans, we will keep it in the family, so to speak. But there will be a few more things I need to do to you. I will give you a few special abilities that will make you a little more like us. I will sharpen your powers that aid understanding, perception, and ability to communicate with other species. You will understand some of the things your ancestors did not, things that were considered magical or even evil by many. But it all is part of understanding basic capabilities. Your greatest thinkers struggled for the past few hundred years to understand some basic questions: Who are you, where did you come from, what are you doing here, and what is the meaning of life?

"Your species has floated, not knowing the answers. You will have them, at least as much as we have them. You have searched to learn who God is. You will be God. Each of you is a part of God, just as Vandara and I are, at least as you have defined the concept. But keep in mind that this whole subject of God, or more aptly, religion, is what has caused a lot of problems in the journey of your people. Your belief in certain traditions and rituals has gotten in your way. Each of you has the power of God. You don't need to rely on some heroic figure. Your mind is your god. Don't let someone else hijack it."

"So you make us perfect, in your image, then place us back in our world to maintain a perfect life. Pretty heavy burden. And it does sound a little god-like to me." Mida smiled. She added, "But I still am fuzzy on this time travel aspect of it. We are from 1999 and go back. Does that change 1999 when it comes again or did our going back make the 1999 we knew possible? If so, then what did it matter? It was going to happen anyway."

Ev looked at Mida with a smile. "You are starting to sound like me."

Mallon threw up her hands and exclaimed "Vandara! Help me. These humans are so . . ." Her light actually flickered as she searched for words.

Vandara came back into the room. Mallon went over to her and conferred. Their lights dimmed, then brightened. After a few minutes, Vandara came over to the couch.

"Your curiosity is wonderful. However, I am going to try for one last time to explain this. Listen carefully. It is a very simple explanation that you will be able to comprehend. If you remember nothing else, remember these, my parting words to you. Here it is. You simply cannot understand! That's it! There is nothing more I can say. You are not capable of understanding! Not yet. You cannot compare your old world and your old time. Your 1999 doesn't exist for you anymore. You have been taken out of time and your previous existence has not happened. And it may not. You have to believe that you simply cannot understand this. I know it may not make sense to you. Just keep thinking of the flatlanders. There is nothing more I can say. There is nothing more Mallon can say. At some point, you may come to understand, but we cannot make that happen as easily as some of the other things."

She went to the far wall. "Now I am going to have Mallon take you into this chamber and you will go in. You will feel strange sensations. It will take about five minutes of your time. You will then come out and I will visit with you and show you a few tools I will give you. Are you okay with that?"

"Will we remember any of our past?" Ev asked.

"Of course. Nothing will change of your previous lives or memories. You will remember all you have learned up to now. You lived a life in your old time. That isn't taken away from you. What has been taken away is your ability to interact with all those who formed those memories. They don't exist anymore. If you didn't keep your memories, then you could not even function. Your memories make you who you are. And you are all wonderful, intelligent, curious, perceptive beings.

"All this procedure will do is correct a few abnormalities in your chemical and energy structure. You will be able to see better, hear better, feel better, and if we are lucky, maybe start a basic comprehension of the time dimension." She purred and Mallon clicked after she made the last statement.

Sarah stood up and said, "Let's do it. You have me excited about my new life. I'm ready."

"Let me ask one more question," Mida said as she slowly got up. "Remember when we first came, you brought my father to see me? Will I have a chance to go back and visit my mother or even my father again? You said it was basic time travel. You said past, present, and future were all the same, or something like that."

"When you finally leave your present form years from now, you will be able to, since all energy goes back to the same source before it is reassembled. I may be able to do something about making you appear in her dreams or something like that. But to go back, or actually forward, no. It is an energy field. After some time with your new abilities, I am hoping you may be able to do more with it but not yet."

The three of them went slowly to the chamber with Mallon leading the way. They stepped in, held hands, and Mallon shut the door as she backed out. It was totally black. They heard a buzzing, then sparks filled the chamber. They closed their eyes and held each other for several minutes. They felt a tingling all over their bodies. Even with her eyes closed, Mida could see a rainbow of colors. Ev heard the blood flowing through his body. Sarah smelled the ozone of electricity in the air. They felt a sense of energy flow into them and enter every cell.

The sparks stopped and a red light came on. Mallon's thoughts entered their minds, telling Mida and Sarah to step out for a minute so Ev could be alone. After she left, the sparks came back on. After about two minutes, Ev heard Mallon tell him to leave and Mida to come back in. Ev left, Mida entered and went through the same process. Sarah followed after that.

Unknown

It's time. I only have a few minutes since I am writing this as Ev and Sarah go in the bubble machine. I think I have finally figured it out. When we go back or forward in time, we leave the universe we are in and somehow go into what Ev terms a parallel universe. That has to be their magic fifth dimension. Vandara keeps insisting we cannot understand all this, and I will take her at her word. I surely don't understand it, but I feel this is what's happening.

She says the ship disappeared, so Mom and Boyd and Sumner can't see it anymore. It doesn't exist. I think after we leave, Sandy and the Avarnans somehow fix the problem. As they fix it, they leave and go to a parallel universe. In doing so, the old ship stayed put (and the original Avarnans stayed here or somehow escaped, but the ship stayed). But they entered a completely new universe. Sandy makes it! So maybe we will see him again. Then Vandara was somehow able to cross over to the old universe (where the ship was left and we found it) and made it disappear.

This is what is hard to figure out. I am the cause of the ship getting stuck in the first place. Vandara takes me for a shuttle ride and when we land, something goes goofy. I arrive and the problem starts. This is what doesn't make sense because the ship is there in the twentieth century for us to find, but let's forget that part. We go back in time and fix the problem. So we are the cause and the solution. I thought I understood it. Wow!

Ev and I will spend the rest of our lives trying to figure this out. But my intuition says time travel also involves parallel universes. That's why the famous grandfather paradox (why is it always a grandfather and not a father or mother or grandmother) isn't really a problem after all. A person can't go back and kill (how about kiss) their grandfather (or grandmother) because when you go back, you go back in a parallel universe. Nothing changes in the original world, but now you are back in time seeing your grandparents and the only thing different in this new universe is you!

I suppose I should quit thinking about this. It doesn't matter. We start over. We may have memories, but our lives start right now. It is up to us. The challenge is tossed down and we accept. I accept and I am capable of starting over.

Here comes Ev. We are ready. This is the final *entry in Mida's (the elder or original) journal. My next entry will be in our new world. Wish us luck! Goodbye.*

When Sarah came back out, she went over to Ev, looked at him, touched his face, then kissed him. Then she hugged Mida and held her for a moment.

"What'd you do that for?" Ev asked as he stepped back and looked at Mallon, almost expecting to be chastised.

"Just want to see if the old Ev is still there. I think this one is even better. Besides, you belong to me now as well as Mida. We are all one," she smiled and put her arm around him. Mida choked a laugh.

Mallon led them to the pillows and asked them to sit back down. "You will be nearly immune to disease and sickness. Your immune systems are what you would call supercharged. Your senses are now heightened from what they used to be. You will hear things, see things, smell and taste things you never before noticed. You will sense things happening before they happen. Don't be surprised when all this occurs. Also, don't be surprised when you keep on going when you think you should be getting old and slowing down. That will take a long time in your reference frame.

Mida lowered her eyes, then looked at Mallon. "We will have to have a lot of children to keep the race going. Are they going to be like us?"

"They will be like you in having heightened senses and extraordinary powers. They will not have the resistance to disease that I have given you. Their life span will not be as long either."

"We will have a problem that I don't know how we get around it. Our children will have to have each other's children. Isn't that bad from a genetic standpoint? Where does the diversity come from?" Sarah pondered this as she said it.

Mallon thought for a minute. "This is not something I know much about from any personal knowledge since we haven't reproduced for many years. But from your minds, I gathered a lot of information. I knew that was a problem. I was able to do something to your eggs, Mida and Sarah. And I'm not sure how successful I was with Ev, but when you have children, each will be as if they came from different parents. The genetic structure, which is your blueprint, will not be that similar between your children. I was able to alter the mitochondria as well as the regular DNA in your reproductive cells. This will give some diversity to start. That is why you need to have as many offspring as possible. After that, you need to monitor who reproduces with whom. Oh, one other thing, both of you will be very prolific with twins and even triplets."

Ev perked up. "I never really planned on much of a family. I guess I am forced to become very fatherly now. And a polygamist to boot."

"I guess we owe you a big thanks for all you have done. I don't know what else to say," Mida reached over to touch Mallon. "I'd give you a big hug, but there is nothing substantial there to hug."

"Thank you. It has given me a great pleasure to get this close to a new species. And I can feel your hugs. You were thinking it, and I felt it. Consider me hugged. I leave you now and wish you a wonderful future. You will enjoy pleasures and a life that makes me envious. You are starting a new life and your future is now up to you. Have a safe voyage." With that, Mallon enveloped the three in her glow, then quickly disappeared out the door.

Vandara, who had been standing in the corner, came over to them. "Well, we are in the last phase of your preparation. I give you your gifts now." She handed Ev a large container made out of what looked like crystal but seemed much more solid. It had two chambers, separated by what looked like an aluminum or stainless steel compartment. On the side was a keyboard and display panel.

"I had to modify this for you and your alphabet and numerical system. Delsan had his crew working on this for several days. It presented a little challenge to them, but they were able to do the translations so you could use it. We even had Sandy try it out and he was fascinated with it. He wanted his own, but of course, he doesn't need one.

"Here, I will show you how to use it. You place any object in here. I have a handful of sand from outside to demonstrate." She put the sand in one compartment. "Now I look up on the chart." She turned the box over and a periodic table was inscribed on a gold plate attached to the bottom. "If you want to turn this into silver, you enter the atomic number 47, hit this button, and wait a few seconds, and the atoms in the sand have turned into silver." Before their eyes, the sand turned into grains of silver. "Or copper, enter 29 and you have copper." The silver turned into grains of copper.

"Sandy said neither of you would know the atomic numbers, so we had this plate engraved with the elements. If you want a gas, you need to put your original material in this vial. This atomic structural converter is powered by an energy source that in your lifetime, and well beyond, you will never need to recharge. You can use it as much as you wish. The only thing is that you are limited in volume to whatever fits in the chambers. We use ones much larger, but this is the best we could do for you. And of course, you can start with a mixture of elements, but you end up with pure whatever. If you want to make stainless steel, then you have to combine the separate elements on your own. This only deals with pure elements.

"Oh yes, I would advise that if you use this very much, you should not stand too close. We don't know what it would do with your own structure. With occasional use, you shouldn't have to worry, but a lot of use—well, just be careful."

Ev started to say something, but words would not come out of his mouth. He just stared at Mida.

Mida looked at him and said, "Well, Rock Boy, you have the ultimate chemistry set. I wouldn't know what to do with it. But I'm sure you can use it well."

Vandara then showed them the stun gun, which Ev called the zapper. That would serve as his weapon if he ever needed it. She then gave him a laser-like cutting tool, somewhat like the laser saw that Sandy had used to help enter Orion. She gave Mida several crystals, which had healing powers as well as the ability to renew plant cells. Mida called the green one the ultimate refrigerator hydrator without the refrigerator, and another she called the sterilizer since it killed viruses and bacteria. She gave Sarah a small instrument with several buttons and three attachments. It was a healing laser that could repair cellular damage, including nerve damage.

"You will not have the need for power to run tools like you are used to. But I am giving you several atomic-powered and hydrogen-powered energy cells, which you may find useful someday. They provide the type of electrical energy you are used to from your power systems, including both alternating and direct current. This is so primitive to us, we had a hard time developing them for you. Sandy gave us a basic energy lecture on your systems.

"And here is something that Sandy said you would find useful." She handed Mida what looked like an ordinary laptop computer. Mida opened it and laughed. "Just what we need in the wilderness. A computer, Ev. And look, it even has the Pentium trademark. Look at this, Pentium 66. I suppose Sandy helped with this, too?"

"Yes," Vandara purred. "He told us what he wanted it to do and we easily constructed it. You can write, document, calculate, research, but not print on paper. We haven't used paper for millennia, but you will have to either make your own paper, or learn to store things here. It has a capacity of what Sandy said was ten trillion gigabytes, whatever that is. It is very small to us, but Sandy nearly fainted when our engineers developed it and told him how much room it had. It is primitive by our standards, but seemed very advanced to Sandy. It is also powered by an energy cell that will never run out. We constructed the programs to match what you used in your time. Sandy tested it and said you will enjoy it. He had our people develop these discs," Vandara held up what looked like regular but miniature CDs. "They have on them much of the scientific data we have on our onboard systems. It is mostly astronomical and navigational data, but there are some discs with some of the chemical and biological data of your planet for the time period you are going to. There are many photos and images of your planet. You can enlarge them to get resolution to about six inches by your measure. Sandy said you can spend weeks on end exploring them. He even put some games on it, whatever that means. He said to tell you that mah-jongg is in there. But he wasn't sure he got the rules right since you two seem to make up your own when you play."

Ev laughed. "Sandy never told us about these toys. He has been busy in Santa's little workshop hasn't he? You must thank him profusely for us."

"And tell him our first child will be named for him in gratitude," added Mida. "I mean it."

"Now for the last thing before your trip, I need to know exactly where you want to go. I need that since we must go straight there and I must come back immediately. We have a major problem with power in the shuttle."

Ev was gently putting the gifts into the pack Vandara provided for them as he looked up at Vandara and said, "I was hoping to circle around and explore before we decided. I don't really know what things look like and I want to pick a spot that meets my criteria."

"I'm afraid you don't have that luxury. I am chancing it even making it back here after I let you off. I have to go directly there, let you out, and rush back here. We have not been able to recharge the power units in the shuttles. And I just looked out and another storm is blowing sand again. I don't want to fly in a sandstorm, but we have no choice. Your sand seems to be our downfall here with our power source. We need to go now, and you need to tell me on this map where you want to go." Vandara showed them a screen full of photos of the Earth she had taken on the earlier voyage when they first came to Earth.

"Boy, nothing like putting pressure on. Mida, Sarah, did you have any preferences from what we talked about last night?"

"No. I told you I could go anywhere. We agreed to stay south away from any glaciers. And to avoid humid areas or extreme deserts or rain forests or areas with volcanic activity. What does that photo show?"

Ev and Mida both looked at the map. Sarah shrugged and backed off.

Ev's eyes widened. "Look at the ice sheet. Wow, that covers all the northern half of the US. And look at South America. I never thought of glaciers down there." Ev ran his fingers across the map. "I don't recognize the river systems. The Mississippi isn't where it should be, nor is the Missouri. And look at Florida. It doesn't even look like Florida. The ocean level is way off. This doesn't match with what I envisioned. Of course, we never knew that much about the exact location of the ice sheets. And this is several ice sheets earlier than our last one, which we know the most about. Look at the West Coast. Wow. Puget Sound isn't even there."

Vandara started moving toward the door. "Let's go. You can decide by the time we get in the shuttle. When we get there, you point on the map where to go. I will enlarge the spot you point to and we will get a close-up view. You point exactly where and I will enter the coordinates. We will go there and you will immediately leave. We will say our goodbyes now. I am sorry, but we have no time."

"Will we ever see you again?" Mida asked as they almost ran to the shuttle.

"Never is a strange word and has a different meaning to me. I don't plan on it anytime soon, but don't be surprised to see me or one of our crew sometime. Who knows, even Sandy could show up. It depends on what happens here."

They climbed into the shuttle as Vandara embraced each with her light as they entered. "I have enjoyed our short stay," she said to them. "May peace and love be with you. We are counting on you to keep our dreams alive. I am sorry to be in such a rush, but you really don't know the danger we are in."

As she closed the door, the large shuttle bay door opened. Sand blew in, covering everything with red. She quickly flew the shuttle out the door, which closed immediately behind her. Sand was already starting to drift heavily against the ship.

"Ev, point to the spot you wish to go."

Ev looked at Mida, then turned to Sarah. He slowly pointed his finger at the map. "I guess we go here. We can always move if we don't like the neighbors. It's far enough south to escape any effect from the ice sheets. It's not on a coastline. And even though it is a million years before our time, I think we are somewhat familiar with the general landscape and maybe even some of the flora and fauna. We can live with the climate and it should be easy to travel around."

Vandara enlarged the image to a very high resolution. "Point again and I will fix the coordinates. That is exactly where we will land. When I get close, I will open the door and you will need to jump out. I cannot actually touch down but I can hover a foot above the surface. As soon as you exit and get your packs out, I will shut the door and take off quickly. Again, be careful and, as you would say, Godspeed."

Ev looked at the map, looked again at Mida, then motioned her with his eyes to point. "It needs to be a joint decision. Use your intuition."

Mida looked at the picture for about five seconds, then quickly set her finger on what looked like a large grassy meadow next to a medium-sized stream. A large lake was nearby.

Vandara entered some numbers, then the shuttle shot high into space with lightning speed. Ev looked out and saw the earth recede below. Then they experienced the flash of light that indicated the time change. Their bodies tingled from the change that Vandara wanted. They were now completely recovered from their deterioration. The jolt from the time warp shook the shuttle. Mida's notepad and Sandy's crystal, which she had set on the seat next to her, fell silently to the floor. They landed on top of Ev's rock pick, which in his haste he had not tied securely to his backpack. All these slid under the seat, unnoticed by either Mida or Ev. Suddenly, the earth looked completely different, yet very familiar. Of course, it matched the photo now. They quickly came down to earth, above the meadow surrounded by forest, with the stream flowing by pure and clear into the lake.

The shuttle stopped six inches above the ground. Tall grasses, green and fully seeded out, waved in a light breeze. The grass was touching the bottom of the shuttle. There was no wind or downdraft from the shuttle. It just sat in midair as the door opened. Ev threw out their packs, then helped Mida and Sarah jump to the ground. He handed Sarah the pack with Vandara's gifts. She set them on the ground carefully, then helped Ev step out. They held out their hands to touch Vandara. She glowed brightly, then spoke in their minds one last time.

"Your names are appropriate now, aren't they? *Ev* and *Mida* backward are almost *Adam* and *Eve*. That is significant to some people back in your time isn't it? You are the original inhabitants of this land now. Treat it well." She waved and her light flickered brightly, then faded. The door quickly closed after the three stepped back. Mida fought back tears as she waved, staring at the sky as the shuttle disappeared.

Ev, Mida, and Sarah stood staring at the brilliant blue sky. They heard birds singing in the trees along the river. They felt the breeze as it touched their faces. They continued to stare at the sky hoping to see a glimpse of the shuttle, knowing it was probably already back at the ship. Or at least they hoped it was back. They feared for Vandara and the rest of the crew on Orion. But that was almost two hundred million years ago. The ship was by now covered by solid rock. There was nothing they could do. They looked around them, then sighed.

"Well, Rock Boy, I guess this is it. We are it. There is no one else. No one. Anywhere. Sarah, we are about as alone as it is possible to be. Ussen, what have we done? What are we to do now?" Mida wiped tears from her cheek.

Ev didn't say anything. He had a huge lump in his throat that prevented him from speaking. He was holding back tears himself. He sat down in the grass, pulling both Sarah and Mida with him. He pulled a tall grass out of its node and put the end in his mouth. He chewed on the sweet tender end as he tried to regain his composure.

Mida sniffed the air and sighed as she looked around. "It must be late spring or early summer. I smell deer or elk or whatever is here. I guess we don't go into town and find a motel, do we? Nor do we look for a restaurant." She paused as she put her arms around Ev. She then burst out crying, like she had never cried before. Sarah put her head on Mida's shoulder and joined in the crying.

The three sat on the edge of a small grassy meadow, next to a stream which emptied into a large lake in the expanse below them. Gulls and other birds swirled above them, filling the air with familiar sounds. They looked off into the distance behind them to see high snowcapped peaks on the horizon. Small white puffy clouds drifted over them, casting fleeting shadows followed by brilliant sunlight. They were sure that no other human being was within ten thousand miles of them. But far off, across a slowly widening ocean, a group of hairy, human-looking figures sat around a fire in a comfortable cave. Tomorrow was another day for them. They crawled onto their pelts and watched as the fire flickered down to embers.

For Ev and Mida, tomorrow was the beginning of an adventure they had only dreamed of the past year. For Sarah, it was a shock and surprise she had never dreamed of. Their world no longer existed and they were here to fashion a new world. They sat on the ground, looking into the night sky for something they would recognize. They fell asleep in each other's arms as a lonely meteor shot to earth, headed for distant remote canyons to their north in a place to later be called Utah.

EPILOGUE

Now we will feel no rain
For each of us will be shelter for the other.
Now we will feel no cold
For each of us will be warmth for the other.
Now there is no more loneliness
For each of us will be companion to the other.
There is only one life before us
And our seasons will be long and good.

—Adapted from Apache wedding blessing

It is necessary, therefore it is possible.

—G. A. Borghese

VANDARA AND THE shuttle approached Orion, which was quickly becoming buried by blowing red sand. As she slowed to land, her power shut off. Unable to brake as she neared the doors, half-buried in swirling sand, she hit the ground hard at an angle, up tightly against the half-open door. The crew had tried to shovel the sand from in front of the door, but could not keep up with the drifting. Vandara climbed out of the shuttle, tilted at almost a ninety-degree angle by a large drift. As she half fell out of the door into the shuttle bay, she left behind items she did not see or even know were there.

Mida's notepad lay on the floor. It carried notes and questions, perceptions and ideas she had gleaned from the past hectic year. In her precise and flowing script, it left a trail of adventure and detail of canyons and rock, flowers, and prayers. There were small drawings of plants and butterflies. There were doodles of hearts and arrows made while Ev talked on the other end of a phone line. It was a diary and it was a journal. It was also a record of dreams and expectations of a new life. And it was to lie on the floor of a vehicle never to fly again, lost under drifting sands for time beyond belief.

Under it was the rock pick that Ev carried over mountains and canyons in search of answers to questions he now had forgotten. It was a cold, yet solid friend. It had cracked open rock that had lain hidden from the sun since the earth began. It found fossils and gold veins. It was a security blanket that had crushed scorpions and broken open deer thigh bones to expose bloody and nutritious marrow. It had no script or message, yet it spoke of what it knew—power and force. Next to it was a small wooden carving, shaped like a crystal, which Sandy had given Mida as a good luck charm the last time he saw her.

Vandara entered the shuttle bay, noticing one of the other shuttles was gone. She asked what happened to it. Delsan was standing there next to Sandy. He admitted that he had taken a gamble. They needed water to try and wash the sand out of one of the pipes that was plugged. This was an idea Sandy had and it made perfect sense to Delsan. Levoran, Delsan's assistant, had taken the shuttle out to get water from the sea that was not far distant to the east. He had not returned. They lost contact with him. They now feared him lost.

Sandy wanted to go with Levoran, but Delsan insisted he stay here. He could help fashion a primitive solar panel that might get them some form of power. Sandy for the first time sensed panic in the avarnans. He wondered if they really did have an escape plan. Would he have company for his final days or hours aboard Orion? Or would they desert him to stay entombed forever in this marvelous time capsule? He asked Vandara as she rushed by him about Sarah and the other two. She touched him and he felt a glow of warmth. She continued on without saying a word. Her touch told him that his friends were now on their own. He envied them and he feared for them.

The spring after the disappearance of the time travelers—after the snows melted from a milder than normal winter—Boyd, Marybeth, and Denzee continued with the development of the Orion Wingate. The two mothers lacked the enthusiasm they had when their children were in charge of planning this retreat, but Boyd made up for any lack of energy. They spent a difficult winter undergoing a series of tests in Texas and California. Their mysterious ailments worsened, then changed, disappeared, then reappeared in amazing new forms. They were in no pain and suffered no discomforts, yet they were bothered by the strange qualities. Denzee believed it was the work of spirits playing with her.

Billy Joe Stanton called often to check on the abnormal physical conditions resulting from their injuries. Billy Joe found unique electrical readings from both Marybeth and Denzee. He kept the results secret but he was convinced he had evidence to support the unbelievable story.

None of the group of scientists that visited the site doubted what had happened. But several didn't want to do anything more due to the lack of evidence and the ridicule they, as respected scientists, would go through making such a claim without any proof. A couple of the other scientists were still intrigued by the readings from several of the instruments. They visited Orion Wingate in late April and arranged to visit the site again with Boyd and Denzee. Marybeth opted out since she did not want to visit the grave of her son as she referred to it.

On a warm and sunny spring day, the group arrived at the site. The trip down the mountain was difficult, since the road, rocky as it was, was still muddy, with an occasional snowdrift. A light snowpack and a very warm March had allowed an earlier than normal access. Larry Andrews and Jugs French accompanied Boyd to the top of the cliff while Denzee stood at the bottom looking up at the solid rock cliff. She could still see where the window had been exposed in the rock. Now there was just a small alcove in the rock wall.

As the scientists talked and argued above, Denzee quietly walked over to the cliff. She closed her eyes and listened for spirits talking to her. She heard none, although she was drawn to the edge of the cliff. She climbed to where she was eye level with the opening where the window used to be. She laid her hand on the rock and closed her eyes again. She felt something. It was a strange sensation she had never felt before. As she moved her hand over the rock, a small piece the size of a quarter broke off. She jerked back her hand as she felt a shock. She looked down and embedded in the rock was a silver sparkle. She touched it and without knowing why, cried out for Mida.

She backed down the rock pile, not taking her eyes off the cliff. She walked back to where the van was parked and looked through the toolbox Boyd kept in the back. She found a hammer, walked back to the cliff, and started tapping on the rock.

Boyd found the discussion on top of the plateau boring so he wandered to the edge of the cliff. He saw Denzee take something out of the van, so he watched her as she walked back to the cliff. He watched her hit the sandstone with a hammer and pull off a chunk of rock with silver and blue embedded in it. She carefully broke off small bits of red rock which exposed a silver and turquoise miniature squash blossom necklace. She tapped the rock gently to release the necklace and held it up to her chest, matching it with the one she wore around her neck. Boyd had given them to her and Mida shortly before Mida disappeared. Denzee fell to the ground, clutching both squash blossoms to her chest. She cried out as she heard clearly her daughter's voice, "Mother, be safe and never forget." Boyd scrambled down the cliff and raced to where Denzee was lying. As he checked to see if she was still breathing, he saw that Denzee was clutching two silver squash blossoms, and see the word "Mid" engraved on the back of the portion exposed between her right thumb and fore-finger, just where he'd had it engraved on the silver several months ago.

Boyd did not go over to the cliff. He did not tap on the rock any further. The gold-encased messages from Sandy remained hidden by one inch of red Wingate Sandstone. Guarding the ship called Orion, the gold case, holding secrets worth infinitely more than a cliff of gold itself—the secret buried by Mida two hundred million years before—remained unseen by human eyes. Boyd carried Denzee back to the vehicle.

The winds blew gently across the canyons of southern Utah as civilization greeted a new millennium. A time period as arbitrary as the name Utah or the tribes of humans called Ute and Piute. Canyon wrens continued to warble their descending aria hidden in the red and orange cliff walls. Eagles and ravens continued to soar in the thermals as they had for untold centuries. The pine and juniper sent their roots searching through cracks in the sandstone for microscopic nutrients and droplets of moisture.

At the bottom of Lake Powell lay a silver object embedded in red Wingate sandstone. Right beneath the bridge that crossed the Colorado River this spot was less than fifty miles from the red cliffs that bordered a remote stretch of Oak Creek located just west of Capitol Reef National Park. Lying about a dozen feet underneath the surface of the rock, now covered by several feet of water was the shuttle that entombed Levoran, a being from a far off planet, long ago incinerated by a now brown dwarf star past the group of stars called Pleiades. Resting in the mud right over the tomb was a small pebble of granite that only a few years ago sat in a rock pile in Rocky Mountain National Park. This small rock was thrown off the bridge by a young geologist one summer day not so long ago.

Life continued, as life had on earth since it began. In the outback of Australia, a white haired old Aborigine looked to the stars to find answers he knew were there hidden in his dreamtime. In a rock walled pueblo in New Mexico, a tribal elder held a handful of small pebbles and called to his spirits. On the windswept plains of

South Dakota, a shaman burned sweetgrass and chanted to White Buffalo Woman. In Pasadena, a PhD. in astrophysics scribbled an equation on a piece of paper and whistled for his assistant to come see what he had just deduced.

Holy men and women of dozens of religions continued to pray to their gods, asking for answers to why they were here and what they needed to do to obtain lasting salvation. Universities offered courses in mythology and philosophy, looking for similar answers of how we got to where we are and why we act as we do.

Life on earth continued on its race to wherever it was going and people still searched for the same answers that Ev and Mida asked back in 1999. A million years had passed since this same young couple plus a frightened young girl sat on the edge of a stream next to a meadow and listened to wolves howl in the distance. Alone in a new world, with the hopes of a civilization, expectant of dreams and a future unknown to them.

The End of *Sands of Time*

About the Author

JOSEPH COLWELL has worked and lived across the west for over fifty years. During his college years at the University of Idaho, he spent summers working in Idaho state parks, Mt. Rainier National Park, and Grand Canyon National Park. With his degree in wildlife management, he spent the next twenty-seven years with the US Forest Service, working on five different national forests. While on the Dixie National Forest in southern Utah, he spent much time exploring the slickrock canyons of lower Boulder Mountain and adjacent Capitol Reef National Park. Retiring from his Forest Service career, he continued work on wildland fires as a fire information officer, assisting the general public and homeowners in understanding wildfires.

He has authored two books of nature essays: *Canyon Breezes: Exploring Magical Places in Nature* and *Zephyr of Time: Meditations on Time and Nature*. Both were published by Lichen Rock Press.

Joseph and his artist wife, Katherine, now live on their forty-acre nature preserve overlooking the North Fork Gunnison River Valley of western Colorado. They created Colwell Cedars Retreat, which offers a peaceful secluded haven for guests as well as wildlife. It is also a great place for thinking about geologic time. He can be reached at ColwellCedars.com.

CPSIA information can be obtained
at www.ICGtesting.com
Printed in the USA
LVOW12s1447010418
571875LV00001B/244/P